Roan stepped past him, out into the cold, and flinched as icy snowflakes stung his face. His shoes crunched in several inches of fresh powder, all the leafless trees glowing with a mantle of white. "You said you liked the snow," Ishaan said, stepping up behind him.

Roan didn't move, not even to draw breath. Ishaan was doing it again, so close Roan could feel him though they weren't touching, just like the river, just like the changing booth, only this time, Roan wasn't going to speak or move and screw it up. He stood, trembling, waiting, as Ishaan's warm breath slid through his hair, across his cheek, under his collar. *Touch me*, he begged silently. *Don't make me wait anymore.*

Ishaan stepped past him and the breath left him in a rush, his whole body cold and shaking. What had he done this time? He turned just as Ishaan slipped on the flagstone sidewalk. Roan reached out, grabbing Ishaan's arm, but Ishaan landed on his back in the snow anyway, with Roan lying on top of him.

"Sorry," Roan gasped as he scrambled to get up. "I tried to—Are you okay?" He looked down into Ishaan's face, his cheeks pinked by the cold, his lips parted as he fought to catch his breath. It couldn't be easy, with Roan practically lying on his chest. Roan started to push himself upright, but Ishaan grabbed the front of his coat. Roan stared at him, waiting, but Ishaan made no further move. What kind of game was this? His hand red and nearly numb with cold, Roan reached up and brushed a wayward curl back out of Ishaan's eyes. Ishaan tightened his grip on Roan's coat, but did nothing to stop him.

This was a bad idea. Roan knew it. He knew that Ishaan would just pull away at the last second, shove him off, get up, and leave him in the snow. He knew it, but he couldn't help but pray that he'd be wrong. He leaned closer, hesitated, his eyes searching Ishaan's. He saw fear and uncertainty and pain, but also a deep longing, a need that mirrored his own. This was going to hurt so much. Roan closed his eyes and pressed his lips to Ishaan's.

Breach

Breach

Katica Locke

This is a work of fiction. Any resemblance to names, places, events, or persons, living or dead, is only coincidental.

Breach

Copyright © 2013 Katica Locke
All Rights Reserved
www.katicalocke.wordpress.com

ISBN-13: 978-1492731955

ISBN-10: 1492731951

Author's Note

This book contains scenes of intercourse between adult males that are of questionable consent and one scene that borders on non-consensual sex. I would not describe these scenes as rape, but sensitive readers might feel otherwise. There are also brief mentions of rape and underage sex that occurred in the past. If you are sensitive to any of these subjects, you may want to reconsider reading this book.

One

Roan rose from his seat and pulled his battered suitcase down from the overhead storage compartment as the train began to slow. Something touched his shoulder and he jerked away, nearly dropping the heavy case on the gray-haired man standing beside him wearing the neat blue jacket of an attendant.

"Sorry 'bout that," the man said, his voice thin and fluttery. "Didn't mean to startle you, but Shesade is the *next* stop. We're just pulling into Devaen to refill the boiler for the climb up the mountain." Roan's eyes darted from the old man's moist lips to the V of pale skin at his throat, to his bony hands, spotted with age and lined by bulging purple veins. Roan swallowed hard and took a step backward.

"Oh. Th-thanks, but I'm getting off in Devaen," Roan said. The man raised his wispy eyebrows, the afternoon light sparkling in his watery blue eyes.

"It's been a while since I've heard someone say that," he said. "You're—" He frowned and looked Roan over from head to toe. "You're not hoping to see Mr. Darvis, are you, because those lawyers in the fancy suits didn't have any luck, so..." Roan glanced down at himself, worn leather boots and mud spattered up the legs of his jeans, his good blue shirt missing a button on the left sleeve.

"I'm not a lawyer," Roan said. "I'm just looking for a quiet place to relax for a while."

"Devaen's quiet, for the most part," the attendant said. "Just be sure to lock your doors and windows before you go to sleep. There's a demon in that town."

Roan's fingers tightened on the handle of his suitcase.

"A demon?" he said with a forced laugh. "Surely, a man of your years doesn't believe in demons. They're myths."

"Believe it or don't, it's your choice," the man said, his tone short, "but there's a reason all the windows in the inn are nailed shut. Thank you for choosing the Trans-Eshaedra Railroad and have a nice day." Roan watched him walk away and sank into an empty seat, one hand absently combing back through his unkempt blond hair.

Demon. He hadn't heard that word since he left Prythaen, shouted at him as he scrambled into a moving freight car. It seemed like setting himself up for failure to stop in a town already disposed to believe in demons, but he really couldn't afford to make the three hour trip on up the mountain to Shesade. His hands were already shaking, and that old man had looked way too alluring for his comfort.

The train clattered and lurched and finally squealed to a stop in a long hiss of steam, like a dragon sighing from within the belly of the iron beast. No one else in the car moved to get up, or even looked out the windows for that matter, as workers filed out of the station house to fill the steam engine with fresh water. They'd need a full head of steam to make it through the pass between the jagged black peaks looming in the northwest sky.

Suitcase in hand, Roan stepped from the train to the weathered platform, red paint peeling off the window trims. He couldn't tell what color the rest of the building had been. Aside from the railway workers, the platform was deserted, and they paid him little attention as he crossed the platform and descended the steps into a wide, flat dirt road. This had to be the industrial end of town, the train station built across from a farrier and a slaughterhouse, the mingled scents of scorched metal and smoke, blood and shit almost enough to turn his stomach.

He started up the road, passing several warehouses, a tannery, a potter and brick maker, a feed store, a general store, and then a clothing shop and a dentist's office. The road grew hard with packed gravel and he got his first look at the inhabitants of Devaen.

None of them looked like demons, though they stared at him as if his horns had begun to show. He fought the urge to check and shoved his hand in his pocket instead. He smiled and nodded as he passed, but more often than not was met by wary, if not openly hostile stares. What the hell had happened to these people?

He glanced around, up and down every side street that he passed, and his heart began to creep up in his throat as he neared the large, square building bearing the sign proclaiming it the Devaen Inn. Where was it? Respectable towns had one on the outskirts, near the train station, business-minded towns built them near the inn. So what was this place?

"You lost?"

Roan jumped and spun around, banging himself in the knee with the edge of his suitcase. The dark skinned dracorian stared down at him from the porch of the sheriff's office, a shiny silver badge pinned to his chest. Roan swallowed hard under the unblinking scrutiny of those blue and gold eyes.

"I-I was looking for the-for the...whorehouse."

The drac made a scornful sound in his throat.

"You look a bit young to be seeking company of that sort," he said.

"I'm twenty-six," Roan muttered. "Could you just—"

"You should have stayed on the train," the drac said. "Nearest place like that is in Shesade." Roan felt the bottom drop out of his stomach.

"And-and when does the next train—"

"Next week." Roan stared up at him, speechless, and those strange blue and gold eyes narrowed at him. "Don't tell me you're another sex demon."

"No!" Roan said, taking a step backward. Dracs were fast, especially once they shifted from man form to dragon. "Wait, what do you mean, another?"

"Not really your business, is it?" the drac replied. "You want gossip, go to the inn."

"Yeah...I was on my way there anyway." Roan turned and hurried away, but he could feel the weight of those blue and gold eyes all way down the street to the Devaen Inn. As Roan stepped inside and shut the door behind him, he took a deep breath, drawing in the familiar scents of fragrant pipe smoke, fresh ale, and roasting meat. Right then, he could have been in any one of ten thousand inns scattered across a dozen worlds. The classic ones, the ones on technologically restricted worlds, they all had that same smell.

He strode over to the man behind the bar and set down his suitcase, absently flexing his cramped fingers as he waited for the man to draw a pint of beer and hand it to the pretty barmaid. She couldn't have been more than twenty, a tender flower of a girl, but with a woman's weary eyes. Roan jerked his head away, staring down at the polished wooden surface.

"What'll it be, young man?" the barkeep asked, taking a glass down from the shelf and wiping it out with a towel.

"I need a room, I guess," Roan said. He tensed as the barmaid stepped up beside him again, his eyes fixing on her tan, callused hand as she slid a stack of laenes across the bar.

"Did you say you wanted a room?" she asked, and his gaze traveled up her arm, lingered on a pale burn scar just below her elbow, his breath catching in his throat as she shifted and her sleeve pulled up, revealing a freckle on her upper arm. "Say, are you okay?" Roan drew a sharp breath and dropped his gaze to the bar again.

"Tired," he said. "Long trip."

"I'll bet it was," the barkeep said. "Nobody within five hundred miles of here would set foot in this town, on account of that—"

"Father, do *not* start that again," the barmaid said. "Really, you're as bad those old hens, clucking around the market all day—" She raised her voice in a passable imitation of an old woman. "Can you believe this tomato? When is that rotten Ishaan going to be hung? Did you see what *she* was wearing?" She shook her head and reached down for Roan's suitcase, her shoulder length blonde hair brushing the back of his hand. He leapt back, squeezing his eyes shut as he fought to maintain his human form. When he opened them again, the barkeep, his daughter, and several of the patrons were staring at him.

"Sorry," he said breathlessly. "I thought there was a spider...Hate spiders." A few people chuckled as they turned back to their drinks, but the barmaid was still looking at him funny. He needed to get out of there; he needed to be alone.

Before he could turn to leave, though, the barmaid said, "So, how long are you staying with us?" Her words pulled up the image of him tangled with her beneath the bed sheets, but he pushed it away.

"Till the next train comes through, I guess," he said.

"You guess? So no real schedule to keep to, then?"

"I-I guess not," Roan said.

"Would you consider sticking around a while?" Behind the bar, her father was shaking his head.

"Sezae, don't even think about it. This young man doesn't want to have anything to do with that demon."

Roan stiffened.

"Demon?" he asked. Sezae made a face at her father. "The sheriff said something about a demon; so did the train attendant." Sezae sighed and crossed her arms over her chest.

"Ishaan isn't a demon," she said, "he's sick."

"He's possessed," her father muttered. She just waved her hand at him to go away and stepped over to a large corkboard hanging on the wall, all kinds of advertisements pinned to it, most of them old and yellowed from the smoke.

"Really," she said, "he's the nicest guy, but when he falls asleep—"

"He rapes people," her father said, leaning over the bar and making no effort to keep his voice down. "He should be hung." All around the common room, Roan saw heads nod and heard murmurs of assent.

"He doesn't know he's doing it," Sezae replied, her face flushing with anger. Roan felt his own blood rise and forced himself to imagine his own hanging, which would no doubt be swift if he couldn't keep it together. "It's like sleepwalking," Sezae explained. "He does things, things he would never normally do, and he never remembers doing them, he just wakes up in strange places with people trying to hang him."

"And what does this have to do with me," Roan asked. This conversation was hitting uncomfortably close to home, except that he *always* remembered, even when he'd rather not.

Sezae reached up and pulled down a crisp, white notice. "He needs someone to lock his door every night and unlock it in the morning. The pay is ridiculous, but you get free room and board, and all you have to do is turn a key twice a day." She pressed the paper into his hand, her skin warm against his and he shuddered. "Please," she said, "he's been having to sleep in the jail and it's set the whole town on edge." Roan licked his lips and stared down at the paper. She was right, it was a ridiculous amount, but he was still tempted.

"I—He doesn't remember *anything*? Ever?" She shook her head. "Well...I suppose I could. For a while, at least."

"Great," Sezae said, flashing him a smile as she untied the strings of her apron and tossed it on the bar. "Grab your stuff. I'll drive you out there. Be back in an hour or so," she called to her scowling father. Roan couldn't really blame him. As he followed her out behind the inn to the stable and helped hitch the mules to the wagon, the fact that they were very alone weighed heavily on him.

"Are you always this trusting of strangers?" he asked. She glanced at him over the backs of the mules.

"Oh, I'm sorry, I didn't even ask for your name. I'm Sezae."

"That's not—I'm Roan, but that's not what I meant. You don't know me. I could be a-a killer, a monster—"

She laughed. "Please. I have a brother your age. All he ever thinks about is kissing girls." And then she winked at him. Roan turned away, that ominous chill racing over his skin. Not again. He just got here. He couldn't be chased out of another town this soon. "Hey, Roan, are you okay?" He heard the crackle of straw underfoot as she stepped in front of the mules.

"Fine," he said, staggering toward the rear of the wagon. "Not feeling well all of a sudden. I think I'll ride back here, if it's all the same."

"It's going to be rough," Sezae said, sounding confused. "That road—"

"It'll be fine," Roan said. He heaved himself up into the bed of the wagon, right next to his suitcase, and curled up into a tight, tense ball. After a few moments, he heard the wagon creak and begin to roll, the warm, close air of the barn replaced by a biting wind. He shivered, but it was the kind of distraction he needed. He felt his demon blood recede, still ravenous, but once again under control. That was too damn close.

"Feeling better?" Sezae asked. He glanced up at her and nodded.

"Sorry. I get these...spells sometimes."

She regarded him for a moment, then turned back to the road.

"Does that happen a lot?"

Roan sighed and rubbed a hand across his face.

"Not really. Just when I'm really tired." He leaned back against his suitcase and wrapped his arms around himself. "You were his friend, weren't you? I mean, before he—" Sezae reined in the mules and turned to frown at him.

"What are you really doing here?" she asked. "You're not one of those lawyers—"

"No," Roan said, shaking his head. "I got off the train by accident and—"

"Then how do you know so much about me and Ishaan?"

He opened his mouth, then closed it again.

"It wasn't that hard to figure out. You're obviously his friend, but your father hates him, so it was a pretty safe guess that he raped you. You don't strike me as someone who would become friends with her rapist after the fact, so you must have known him before—"

"Yes, we were friends," Sezae said, her blue eyes suddenly bright. "We grew up in the same town, went to the same school, helped each other with homework, told each other everything. He was my *best* friend. And when he told me his dark secret, when he told me he was sick, I told him that it'd be all right, the doctors would fix him." She reached up, wiped away a tear before it could fall. "And then one night I woke with him in my room, in my bed, on top of me. I was so scared and it hurt so much, but I couldn't make a sound or my father would come in and kill him."

"You couldn't wake him up?"

She shook her head. "My arms were pinned beneath me. When he was done, I was able to shove him off. He hit his head on the dresser and woke up. He started crying harder than I was. My father heard the noise and came in, dragged him out into the street, beat him nearly senseless, and then they threw him in jail. They would have hung him, too, but I said that it was consensual, that I let him into my room, and they had to let him go."

Roan shifted uneasily, fighting the urge to join her on the driver's bench, to kiss her tears away, to slide his hand up under her skirt—He looked down at his hands, folded in his lap.

"I don't know if I could be that forgiving," he said. "Even my best friend, even if it wasn't his fault..." She was silent for a moment, then she turned away and took up the reins again.

"I knew I had to forgive him," she said as the wagon lurched forward, "or I'd have ended up resenting our daughter."

Two

Ishaan raised the barrel of his rifle and took careful aim. He liked the lightness of the small caliber gun, but it meant his kill shot had to be perfect. More than one bullet was a waste and meant that the animal had to suffer while he loaded another round into the chamber. After watching this fat, gentle rabbit doe raise her young and raid his garden all spring, he had no desire to cause her pain.

The bullet went in one eye and out the back of her skull. She kicked once, twice, and then lay still, the chill evening air ruffling her fur. Ishaan leaned the rifle against the porch rail and headed out across the lawn toward the garden. After gutting and skinning the rabbit out behind the woodshed, he carried it back to the house, wrapped it in a clean towel. and placed it in the bottom of the fridge. He would have liked to have cooked it, slow roasted in the oven, with some young potatoes and fresh vegetables, but it was getting near dark and he needed to head into town soon.

He sighed and leaned against the counter. He couldn't blame Trydel, no matter how much he wanted to. The man had a right to get married and start a family. And he'd given plenty of notice. It wasn't *Trydel's* fault that no one within five hundred miles wanted to share a roof with him. Well, he couldn't say no one.

Ishaan grabbed a beer out of the fridge, dropped the cap on the counter with several others, and shuffled across the living room to his study. Cheery pictures of his 'daughter' stared accusingly at him, her round, pink face beneath a lacy white bonnet, blonde hair like her mother, but with his green-gold eyes. He fell into the old, heavy leather chair and took a long pull from the bottle, watching his flesh and blood grow up before his eyes. Sezae sent pictures every few months, all neatly labeled and dated on the back, but he didn't need to turn them over to know what it was that he wasn't there to see.

Red-faced, angry, like a little, wrinkled old man, wrapped in a pink blanket just minutes after she entered the world, crawling, walking, waving from the back of a fat gray pony, laughing in a pile of leaves, holding a small, spotted puppy, a look of pure joy in her eyes, running beside a spotted dog almost as tall as she was, and finally just smiling at the camera, a lavender bow in her hair. She was almost five now, the living, breathing evidence of his greatest sin.

His father had tried to make the problem go away, the same way he made all problems go away, but Sezae hadn't been interested in his money. She wanted the baby, she wanted them to get married and be a family. She wanted the impossible. He tipped back the bottle, drained it, and dropped it on the floor beside the chair. He listened to it roll under the chair and clink against the others. After a moment, it clinked again, melodiously, a continuous chiming sound.

Ishaan groaned and heaved himself out of the chair, wondering, as he headed out into the living room, if all outcasts eventually forgot the sound of their own doorbells. It was her; he knew before he left the study. She was the only person who would ever visit him. He just prayed she hadn't brought the child again.

"What?" he asked as he pulled the front door open. Sezae raised her eyebrows at his rudeness, but really, she was the last person he wanted to see, so why hide it?

"Are you still looking for somebody?"

"For the last time, Sezae, you're not—"

"No, I'm not, all right? That dream died years ago." He met her eyes, just for a moment, but it was still more than he could stand. To think about what he did to her—

"Ishaan, this is Roan." She gestured over her shoulder, to a young man he hadn't even noticed, standing out beside the wagon, suitcase in hand. He had a worn look about him, though he couldn't have been any older that Ishaan himself, his blond hair dull and tangled, his eyes pale blue or maybe gray. He didn't look happy to be there. "He got off the train by accident."

"I thought you ran the inn, not me," Ishaan said and he started to close the door.

"He's willing to work for you," Sezae said, planting her hand against the carved oak and shoving the door back open, "which is more than I can say about anyone else in town. Or do you like waking everyone up in the middle of the night with your screaming?" Ishaan turned and walked away, clenching his fists as Sezae's footsteps followed him across the room and into the kitchen. "You woke Isha—"

"Bad enough having the kid, but you had to go and brand her as mine, too." Didn't she realize the shit that little girl would suffer because she was *his*? He pulled another beer out of the fridge and she snatched it out of his hand.

"Don't even try and make this about Isha or me. You're not wallowing in self-pity, you're *drowning* in it, and I cannot watch you kill yourself like this."

"You know where the door is," he said and held out his hand. "Give me my beer and leave me alone." She threw the bottle into the sink, shattering the glass and spraying him with alcohol. "That's great. Thanks, Sezae. Now get out."

She stepped up into his face. "You are a worthless piece of shit, you know that, Ishaan?" She made it as far as the kitchen doorway before coming back. "I almost forgot, you daughter asked me to give you this." She jerked a folded piece of paper out of her back pocket and shoved it into his chest. He opened it as she stalked away, glanced down at the crude drawing, the misshapen letters, and then flung it to the ground.

"You're a sadistic bitch, Sezae!" he shouted after her. She said something, but he was already on his way out the back door and across the lawn. How dare she! He'd never even spoken to the kid, seen her just once outside of pictures, and then only for the second it had taken to slam the door shut again. He'd already made sure that she'd never want for anything, she could go to the finest college on any world, she'd never *have* to work a day in her life, so why did Sezae think it necessary to torture him with drawings of smiling suns and three-legged dogs and people with giant heads, *I miss you, daddy* scrawled across the top of the page. How could she miss him? She didn't even know him.

Ishaan reached the riverbank and stopped, staring down at the rushing black water as twilight fell among the great old trees. Why did she keep doing this to him? The girl he knew, the girl he loved, would never have been this cruel, sending him pictures, offering him the one thing he could never have. Didn't it occur to her that if he could attempt to rape his mother—and succeed in raping his best friend—what was going to stop him from raping his own daughter? He would rather die than do that.

And maybe that was the answer, the solution to everyone's problems. The river was deep and swift this time of year, and he'd never been a strong swimmer. Isha's money was in a trust, safe even from his father, guaranteed to her when she reached eighteen. Maybe this was the right thing to do. Maybe he should have been taken out and drowned the first night he wandered into his parents' bedroom.

"You're not thinking about jumping in there, are you?" Ishaan jerked his head around. The young man with the suitcase was standing behind him, only without the suitcase. "'Cause I can't really swim, but I'd feel obligated to jump in after you, and then we'd both—"

"What are you doing here?" Ishaan asked, turning away from the river. "I thought I told her to get out."

"Oh, you did," the young man said. "I tried to go with her, since you didn't seem in a real hiring mood, but she told me to stay. I guess maybe it was a good thing she did." His pale eyes darted to the river and then back to Ishaan.

"I wasn't going to jump," Ishaan snapped. He stood a moment, waiting for the young man to leave, and when that didn't happen, he stalked past him, back toward the house, the lights glimmering between the trees.

"So...I understand that this is a bad time, but—"

Ishaan stopped, the young man nearly running up on the back of his heels.

"I don't know what your game is, but no one 'accidentally' gets off the train in Devaen. Now go get your shit out of my house and meet me in the barn. I'll take you back to town since I'm headed there anyway, but that's all you're getting out of me, got it?"

"I-I—Yeah, I got it." Ishaan turned to head across the lawn to the barn. "You're sleeping in the jail, right?" Ishaan paused long enough to nod but did not stop, did not look back. "You don't suppose they have room for two, do you? 'Cause I spent all my money on a railroad pass and can't really afford to stay at the inn. Does the jail serve dinner, too, 'cause I'm star—"

"I'm sure that since Sezae brought you out and then stranded you here, they can afford to let you stay a few nights for free. I'm not going to pay you what it said on that notice. I didn't post it; she did."

"Oh. Well, that's okay. I'd like the job anyway, for whatever you are willing to pay."

"Fine. A coin a week. Deal?" He started toward the barn again. No one in their right mind would accept such a paltry sum.

"Okay." Ishaan glanced back, but he seemed completely serious. A little nervous, his trembling hands plucking at a loose thread on his shirt, but serious, so Ishaan turned and waited for an explanation. "I-I can see that you're wealthy, so I understand your skepticism, but honestly, I'm not trying to scam you or rob you. It wasn't even the money that made me consider taking the job."

"Oh, yeah? Then what was it?" The young man wet his lips and looked down at his hands, still pulling at that thread, and then shoved his hands in his pockets before glancing back up.

"Sezae told me about your...condition and—"

"Forget it," Ishaan said, his lip curling in disgust. "I don't need a whore." The young man's face flushed scarlet, obvious even in the failing light.

"That's not why I'm here," he said between his teeth. "I just thought that your life sounds shitty enough without having to ride into town and be locked in the jail every night. A human being deserves more dignity than that."

Ishaan opened his mouth, then closed it again.

"What was your name again?" he asked finally.

"Roan." He smiled hesitantly. "Roan Echarn."

"Ishaan Darvis. You don't mind if I run a background check, do you?" The smile vanished from Roan's face.

"Ah...no. No, go ahead. I mean, you won't find anything, but—"

"We'll just see about that." If there was one thing Ishaan knew, it was computers. "C'mon, I'll show you to your room."

"Really?" He sounded shocked. Ishaan couldn't help but wonder if there was a reason for that. "Thank you, Mr. Darvis, you won't regret it."

"We'll see about that, too, and don't call me Mr. Darvis. Ishaan will do."

"Oh. Okay." They climbed the steps up to the back porch. "You're not—I mean, the train attendant said something about a Mr. Darvis. That's not—"

"He was talking about my father," Ishaan said shortly as they stepped into the kitchen. He snatched Isha's drawing up off the floor and folded it carefully before slipping it into his shirt pocket. "So tell me, Roan, how does a man 'accidentally' get off of a train?" He glanced back, watching for signs of deceit, but the young man just colored and looked down at his hands, embarrassed.

"He—Well, he gets off thinking he'll find something that ends up not being there."

"Something like...?" Roan stepped past him and muttered something as he crossed the living room to fetch his suitcase from the foyer. "Sorry, I missed that."

"A whorehouse, okay?" Roan said, standing on the other side of the room and staring out the front window. "I was looking for a whorehouse."

"There isn't a whorehouse in Devaen."

"Thanks, but I already figured that out." He turned around. "Which one's my room?" Ishaan didn't move. If there was one thing he couldn't abide, it was a liar.

"I thought you said you didn't have any money. How were you going to pay—"

"I wasn't going to pay," Roan said and Ishaan raised his eyebrows. "I-I sometimes work freelance—"

"A freelance whore?" Ishaan said with a bark of laughter. "Now I've heard everything. Get out of my house." He watched Roan's face lose color.

"Mr.—Ishaan, please. You-you can't throw me out for that."

Funny, he thought he just had. He started forward, fully prepared to physically remove the young man from his property. "You don't think I like having to whore myself, do you?" Roan asked, and the desperation in his tone made Ishaan hesitate. "You think I like letting drunk men and lonely women paw all over me? I don't. I hate it. I want a respectable job, any job, so that I never have to do that again. Please, *please*, Ishaan, give me a chance."

"Why should I?" Ishaan demanded. When had anyone ever given *him* a chance? After Sezae, after the truth came out, he couldn't walk down the street without people crossing to the other side to avoid him. He wasn't allowed in school, Dr. Kennal refused to see him anymore, even the shopkeepers closed their doors to him, the richest kid on the planet, as if selling him gum would somehow make them a target. He stared across the living room at Roan, tangled blond hair falling across his brow as he looked down at the suitcase in his hands and turned to leave.

"Wait." Ishaan sighed. He was being stubborn and mean. It wasn't Roan's fault he'd had a shitty day. "You get one chance, okay? One night. Screw this up and I'll have you arrested for endangering and negligence. Do you understand?"

"Yes, yes," Roan said, nodding furiously. "I under—I won't let you down."

"You better not," Ishaan said, "because if I get out, the first person I'm coming after is you." Roan went white as a sheet again and shuddered, his whole body shaking. "Good, I'm glad you understand the severity of the situation. This way."

Across from the foyer was the guest bedroom, unoccupied since Trydel moved out. Ishaan pulled clean linens out of the cupboard and tossed the sheets and pillowcases on the end of the bed. Roan set his suitcase down and glanced around at the furnishings. It wasn't anything fancy; Ishaan preferred quality and functionality over aesthetic beauty. The dresser was pine, the desk and chair mahogany, and the bed frame oak. A well-worn high-backed chair, still upholstered in the original navy blue suede, sat in the corner beside a table and lamp.

"It's not much," Ishaan said, but Roan shook his head.

"I grew up in an apartment in the city and had to share a room with my brother. This is wonderful. Thank you." He stepped over to the desk and ran his fingers along the smooth, worn wood, then walked over to the suede chair and sank into it. "Really, this is—Hey, you have electricity!" He reached over and switched the lamp on, off, then on again. "I thought—"

"Planetary restrictions don't seem to apply where my father is concerned." Ishaan turned and left the room before Roan could ask the next logical question. "Come on," he called back, "I'll show you the rest of the house." Roan appeared a moment later.

"So that was a *real* refrigerator in the kitchen? Do you have a television, too?" Ishaan gestured across the room, to the transplasma screen hanging between the foyer doorway and his study, currently disguised as a scenic painting. "Oh, wow—but...how do you get reception if TV is outlawed?"

"The same way I get electricity," Ishaan said, already tiring of the conversation.

"Your father...Who—"

"Over here is the bathroom," Ishaan said loudly, opening the door between the guest room and the kitchen. He turned on the light, drawing back as Roan stepped past him. "Can I assume you know how everything works? Sink, tub, toilet?" He pointed to each.

Roan nodded.

"That's a big bathtub," he said. "You could fit two people in..." He fell silent, staring down into the tub. Ishaan rolled his eyes.

"I wouldn't know," he said and reached up for the light. "The kitchen's—" He stopped, hand held over the light switch, as Roan pulled his arms in tight to his body and bent nearly double, his shoulders heaving as he took short, hissing breaths. "Shit—" He started across the room. "Roan, are you—"

"Don't touch me!" Roan shouted, his voice startlingly deep and resonant. Ishaan stopped short, then took a step back. Perhaps he should have run that background check first and *then* shown him around the house. His mind raced out into the living room, across to his study, and jerked the rifle down off the wall. Shells were in the top drawer— "Please," Roan gasped, his voice back to normal, "I just need—catch my breath—"

"What are you?" Ishaan asked. As if in pain, Roan straightened up and slowly turned around. He was pale, his face shiny with sweat, and his eyes—dark, haunted, fearful. "Are you a werewolf?" Roan gave him a strained smile and shook his head.

"I-I—" He swallowed hard. "I get seizures, sometimes, when I'm tired. I'm okay."

"That didn't look like a seizure," Ishaan said. He should have fallen down, his eyes rolled back, convulsing, trying to bite his tongue off. Roan straightened his shirt with a sharp tug.

"Well, it was," he said, taking a hesitant step forward. "What do you want, a doctor's note?"

Ishaan ignored his sarcasm. "Do you get those often?" he asked.

Roan shrugged.

"Sometimes. They're stress related, and today hasn't been the easiest day for me. I'm fine, really."

"Great, but I'm more concerned that you're going to have an episode and die during the night, leaving me locked in my room for who knows how long."

"It hasn't killed me yet."

"Not comforting. This way." After pointing out the kitchen and pantry, Ishaan led Roan to the other side of the house—his side. "This is my room and my study," he said, gesturing to the two doors. That was as far as he intended the tour to go, but Roan stepped past him and opened his bedroom door, flicking on the light before Ishaan could even open his mouth.

"Nice," Roan said, glancing around. "I like the blue—Do I have the bigger room?"

Ishaan motioned for him to come out.

"Yes. The guest room—*your* room—was my parent's room. This one has always been mine." He stepped past Roan to turn off the light and close the door, and when he glanced back, Roan was already walking into his study. "Hey, no—Get out of there," he said, chasing after. "You have no reason to—"

"Oh, *hell* no," Roan said, crossing over to Ishaan's desk and running his fingertips across the chassis of his laptop. "Is this the new Cyberion III? Dual or quad cores?"

"Eight, actually." Roan's eyes grew wide and Ishaan couldn't help but smile at his excitement.

"What operating system does it run?"

"Windows Nebula. You know computers?"

"Just a bit," Roan said. "I had one back home—an old dual core Khessna my father bought when he started college, but I was looking to upgrade to a Cyberion I before—before I left. Now I wish I'd brought the Khessna with me, only they said no electronics. Customs even took my digital watch. Gave me a lousy coin and a half for it." He glanced around the room. "So...how *did* you get all this stuff here against regulations?"

"Space pirates," Ishaan said. "Do you think you could leave my things alone?"

Roan pulled his hands back.

"Sorry." Ishaan led him back out into the dining room end of the communal living space and showed him a silver ring with a single silver key on it, hanging just inside the door of the china cabinet.

"This will lock and unlock my bedroom door. There's a spare key in the woodshed, just to the left of the door, in case this one gets lost or something. Make sure it doesn't. I'll let you know when I'm ready for bed each evening. Typically, I'm up until between eleven and one. If you're asleep, I'll wake you. I wake up typically between eight and ten, when I've had enough sleep, as I've yet to find an alarm clock that can wake me." He checked to see if Roan was still paying attention. "I'll ask that you be up by nine every morning to let me out. Is that a problem?"

"Oh, no. I'm actually a pretty early riser."

"Fine. But whatever you do, never open the door without checking first that I'm awake. There's a slide in the door—" He stepped over and demonstrated, opening the little window. "Look in, call my name—if I'm not up you won't wake me. If I come over to the door, you need to look into my eyes. That's the only way to know if I'm really awake." He turned, stepping close to Roan and staring down into his eyes. Definitely gray, not blue. "Awake, my eyes are expressive, alert. Asleep, they are dull, empty, like the eyes of a corpse. Understand?" Roan nodded slowly and took a deliberate step backward. It seemed he didn't like having his personal space invaded. Or maybe he just didn't like being that close to a rapist.

"Good. I'll let you go unpack and get settled in then." He waited until Roan started to turn away. "Oh, one more thing." Roan glanced back. "Just in case it starts to seem like a good idea to wait until I'm locked up and then make off with my TV and computer, you should know that I can find anyone, anywhere, and I would not stop until I found you." Roan opened his mouth, but Ishaan stepped close to him again and followed as he backed up against the wall. "And when I did find you, I would not be happy." Roan's eyes grew very wide, his breath coming in short gasps. "Do you know what would happen to you if I tied you down and then fell asleep?" Roan slid sideways, along the wall, to get away from him.

"I'm not going to steal your shit," Roan said breathlessly. "I'm not interested in your damn money." He was thoroughly shaken, as pale and sweaty as after the seizure, his hands trembling. He shoved them in his pockets. "Can I go unpack now?" Ishaan dismissed him with a wave of his hand, watching as he disappeared into the guest room. After a moment, he heard the double *click* of suitcase latches being opened.

A freelance whore who suffered from seizures desperate for a job, but not interested in money and absolutely terrified to be within five feet of him? Who the hell was this guy and what was he hiding? Ishaan headed into his study to find out.

Three

As he hung his shirts in the closet and arranged his pants, socks, and underwear in two of the five dresser drawers, Roan couldn't stop his hands from shaking. That was too close. Way too close. Standing with the wall at his back, Ishaan towering over him, softly curled black hair falling across his brow, hanging in his hazel eyes, the heat of his body, the scent of his skin filling Roan's senses—

He shuddered and sank down onto the edge of the bed, cradling his head in his hands. The man was several inches taller and outweighed him by at least twenty pounds, but another few seconds and Ishaan would have found out how it felt to be overpowered and raped. Roan drew a long, slow breath and then turned back to his suitcase.

"So who are you really?" He jumped and glanced up at Ishaan standing in the doorway, his arms crossed over his chest. He did not look happy. "Because there are only three men named Roan Echarn currently registered with the League, and you aren't any of them."

Roan frowned.

"You ran the—How? That kind of paperwork takes weeks."

"Is that what you were counting on?" Ishaan said, stepping into the room. "That you'd be done doing whatever you've got planned before I found out who you really were?" He glanced down into the suitcase. "Surely you've got *something* in here with your real name on it."

Roan kneaded the edge of the mattress as Ishaan began to rifle through his possessions, tossing his three dog-eared books on the bed, dumping his hairbrush, toothbrush, razor, and nail clippers out of his toiletries bag, flipping through the stack of family photos and finally pulling out his battered black leather wallet. Roan grabbed for it, but Ishaan jerked it away. "Something in here you're trying to hide?"

"No," Roan said. "I mean—Not what you think. I can explain—"

"You had a chance to explain, Mr...." He pulled out the plastic ID card with a washed out picture of Roan on it, his eyes narrowing as he turned it to catch the light. "Jaren Axeris." He shot Roan a scathing look. "Nice to meet you. Says you're from Siva Delta, on Nethmalon. I've never heard of that world. Is it nice?"

"I wouldn't know," Roan muttered. Ishaan tossed the wallet down, but kept the card.

"Well, let's find out, shall we? You see this number, here above *your* picture? That's a license number. With those twelve digits, I can find out everything there is to know about you." Roan stared up at him and sighed. This man was determined to find something wrong with him, it didn't seem to matter what. Ishaan turned and strode from the room, heading toward his study.

After a moment, Roan forced himself to take a calming breath and go after him. Personally, he didn't care what Ishaan thought about him. The man was so sure that he was the only person in the universe suffering at the moment and he wanted to be sure that everyone else knew it and acknowledge him for that suffering. Roan hated that. But it was kind of hard to convince someone to let you lock them in a room overnight if they thought you were lying to them.

Roan stopped in the study doorway and watched Ishaan, his face blank as he scanned the glowing computer screen before him. "You have electricity, TV, *and* internet out here?" he asked. Ishaan's eyes shifted to him and grew hard. "What's the matter; didn't find what you were expecting?"

"Not exactly," Ishaan said, "though I will say you look pretty good for someone who died six years ago."

Roan shrugged.

"It's a fake ID. I would have told you that, if you'd have let me."

"Why do you need a fake ID?"

"Personal reasons," he said, "and frankly, it's none of your business—" He watched Ishaan bristle defiantly and open his mouth, no doubt to tell Roan to get out of his house. "But I'll tell you, 'cause I want you to trust me." He stepped into the room to better see the screen, but still left plenty of distance between him and Ishaan. "Run a search on Kethic Echarn, age twenty-nine, from Glavis on Inivon." The clicking of keys filled the room, followed by silence as they waited for the search to run. After a moment, the screen filled with writing. Ishaan leaned closer. Roan looked down at the ground and waited.

"Your brother," Ishaan said finally, his voice tight. "Your own *brother* pimped you out to his friends?"

"I was thirteen when it started," Roan said, "sixteen when he finally got caught. Our parents were mortified. They seemed to think I was as much to blame as Kethic and threw me out. Since I was still underage, I had to scrape up a fake ID in order to go off-world. A few months later, Kethic escaped from prison and as far as I know, he's still looking for me."

"Because?"

Roan shrugged.

"Not sure, but I doubt it's 'cause he misses me. My testimony was what put him away." It was the truth, more or less. Ishaan scrolled down the page, then closed the laptop and stood up.

"I'm sorry," he said, holding out the ID card. "I shouldn't have been so quick to jump to conclusions." Roan reached out and grabbed the card by one corner, making sure he came no closer than was necessary.

"Don't worry about it," he said. "It was suspicious, I'll admit it. Just...if something else comes up, ask me first before you launch an inquisition, okay?" The corner of Ishaan's mouth actually lifted in a sort of smile. "I'm going to go finish unpacking." At the doorway, he stopped, hesitated, then turned around. "Is your father a king or something? 'Cause I can't figure out how else you'd be able to get around all the restrictions."

"Yeah," Ishaan said, sitting back down at the desk, "he's the king of the universe." Roan stared at the back of his head, then sighed and walked away. Why was he so reluctant to talk about his father? Who was he? Roan had never heard of a Mr. Darvis before, and he would have thought, as important as he seemed to be, that he would have.

With his empty suitcase tucked away in the closet, Roan pulled the quilt off the mattress and grabbed up the folded sheet. This Ishaan was an interesting character, that was certain. He wasn't nearly as nice as Sezae had made him out to be, nor was he the raping monster that everyone else seemed to see. He was unpleasant and suspicious, but Roan supposed he had reason to be. He couldn't have had an easy life.

Roan shook out the sheet, the faint scent of lilacs wafting into the air as he spread it over the mattress, and wondered when Ishaan's condition had manifested. From what Sezae had said, it sounded like it wasn't until thirteen or fourteen—puberty—just like Roan. He ran his hands along the edge of the sheet, staring down at the creamy-colored cloth, remembering the night he finally discovered what he was.

Looking back, it was obvious, the way he'd been drawn to people kissing and groping in the theater, waking in the night and knowing his parents were having sex in the next room because he could feel the energy on his skin, hiding in the toilet at school and listening to some guy in the next stall jerking off, fighting the urge to reach under the partition and touch him...He knew that wasn't normal, but he also didn't know what to do about it.

And that night, waking up and glancing over to find a girl in Kethic's bed with him. They were trying to be quiet, the night punctuated by muffled giggles, groans, and the occasional *shhh*, but it wasn't the noise that woke him. He was *starving*, so hungry he felt hollow, and his entire body ached. He had tried to ignore what was happening on the other side of the room, even tried to pull his pillow over his head. That was when he had felt the horns.

He'd leaped out of bed, his legs tangling with his tail, and fallen to the floor, scaring the shit out of his brother's girlfriend. Kethic, though, hadn't seemed surprised. Apparently, incubism was genetic. Roan had spent the night sitting beside his brother's bed, one hand on that nameless girl's ankle, feeding on her sexual energy as Kethic made love to her.

She dumped him shortly after that—said she couldn't deal with the 'creepy little brother fetish'—but Kethic never had trouble finding girls. He was tall, handsome, with fair hair and sparkling eyes. Roan was thirteen. So Kethic found him willing partners. It only made sense to try and make some money in the process.

Eventually, the police found out and to save himself, Roan said it was all Kethic's idea. Sitting in that courtroom, telling lies under oath as his brother sat across the room and refused to look at him was, retrospectively, one of the lowest points in his life. Even after Kethic escaped from a seven year sentence, Roan knew he could never face his brother again. That was the reason for the hiding, that was the reason for the lies. Because he was a coward. He sighed and shook out the sheet again.

"He invented the outernet, okay?"

Roan jumped as Ishaan stepped into the room.

"He—Who?"

"My father. You asked who he was and...and I was a smart ass. I just don't like being treated like Verin Darvis's son."

Roan's jaw dropped.

"Verin Electromagic Technologies. *That's* your father?" Ishaan nodded and crossed his arms over his chest. "Wow, that's-that's—Wow." What else could he say? V.E. Tech developed the network of microgates allowing for the instant sharing of information between planets. Just like a world gate transported a person from one location to another, sometimes over millions of light years, these constantly open microgates transferred a continuous stream of information to and from anyone with a universal WiFi connection. It was the most significant technological breakthrough in a hundred years. And standing before him was the founder's son.

He cleared his throat.

"Well, that's interesting. Thanks." And he turned back to the bed, absently tucking one edge of the sheet under the mattress. He invented the outernet! Ishaan was right; he *was* the king of the universe—the digital universe, anyway.

"You want a hand with that?" Roan glanced up to find Ishaan standing at the end of the bed.

"Oh, no, I got it, thanks," Roan said. Ishaan raised one eyebrow and Roan looked down at his handiwork. He'd tucked it in crooked; one corner hung off the foot and the opposite didn't quite reach the head. "Well...it's been a while since I had to put sheets on a bed. I've been sleeping in inns and haylofts for so long—"

"First of all," Ishaan said, reaching out and jerking the sheet clean off the mattress, "this is the top sheet. See how the corners are flat?" He dumped the wadded up sheet into the blue suede chair and picked up its still-folded counterpart. "This one's fitted." He shook it out and showed Roan how to fit the gathered corners over the corners of the mattress. Then he spread the top sheet and they tucked it in along the bottom, each starting at a corner and meeting in the middle.

Roan had been doing a good job of ignoring his hunger—it was easier when he had something to distract him—but then the side of his hand brushed Ishaan's forearm, the sensation of skin to skin contact screaming through him like a guitar string wound too tight. He jerked back and turned away.

"Are you going to have another seizure?" Ishaan asked. Roan heard him take a step closer and quickly crossed the room.

"No." *Not as long as you stay away from me.*

"Then what's wrong with you? Are you afraid of me?"

Roan almost laughed.

"No," he said, turning back around and meeting those incredible hazel eyes, "I'm not afraid of you. I'm just tired and I don't like sharing my personal space with people I just met. No offense. You seem like a perfectly normal guy—"

"Well, I'm not," Ishaan said. He looked at Roan for a moment longer. "I'm going to go take a bath and get ready for bed. I'll let you know when it's time." Roan nodded, but Ishaan was already walking away. Maybe that could have gone better, but what was he supposed to say; the touch of your skin makes me want to rip your clothes off and bend you over the end of my bed? He shuddered and mentally slapped himself. He wasn't supposed to let himself have thoughts like that. Thoughts led to actions.

He finished smoothing out the sheets and spread the heavy quilt, then lay across the bed and stared at the wall for a while. That morning, when he woke up on that hard train seat, his only thought had been to find a whorehouse, to satiate the demon inside him for another two or three days. He never thought he'd be in a situation like this. He had never imagined that situations like this were possible.

A man who craved sex in his sleep and who would remember nothing of what happened. It was almost too good to be true. Roan rolled over and folded his hands on top of his stomach. What if it *was* too good to be true? What if he unlocked that door and Ishaan woke up? What if he remembered something in the morning? Roan was tired of running. He wanted to rest, even if it was only for a week.

But he also needed to feed. He was approaching his limits of self-control. If Ishaan touched him one more time...Not that that was likely to happen. The man was so easily offended. He sighed and sat up. He *had* to feed, but he would be as careful as possible, and if something went awry...this wouldn't be the first town he'd fled in the middle of the night.

He was sitting on the comfy old suede chair, rereading his favorite parts in one of the worn books when Ishaan stepped into the doorway, his hair damp and sticking to his neck and shoulders.

"You ready to do this?" he asked. Roan felt the blood leave his face, the demon in him clawing at the inside of his skin, trying to get out as the warm lamplight played across Ishaan's bare skin, glistening off the scattered droplets on his arms and stomach. He wasn't wearing a shirt. His thin cotton pajama pants rode low on his hips and Roan's eyes were inexorably drawn to the line of dark hair running south from his navel. Swallowing hard, Roan looked down at his book, took a deep breath, and set the book on the table next to the lamp.

"Ready when you are," he said, keeping his eyes fixed on the silver-gray carpet as he rose from the chair. It wouldn't be long now, he promised himself.

At Ishaan's doorway, he turned to Roan.

"I hope you don't think this is a game, or something to be taken lightly." Roan shook his head, his eyes still fixed on the floor. After a moment, Ishaan said, "The worst part of my day is lying down and wondering if I'm going to hurt someone that night. I need to know that you can be depended on." Hands tucked in his pockets to keep them from shaking, Roan licked his dry lips and raised his eyes, meeting Ishaan's green-gold gaze.

"Considering that it's my ass on the line," Roan said, "I'm taking this very seriously. You don't have anything to worry about."

Ishaan nodded.

"All right then. Good night." He stepped into his room and shut the door. Roan took down the key from inside the china cabinet, inserted it into the lock and turned it. The *click* of the tumblers falling into place seemed to echo through the living room. Roan reached out and tested the door. It rattled in his hand as Ishaan did the same. Mercifully alone, Roan sighed and leaned back against the wood. "Are you still out there?" Ishaan asked, his voice muted by the heavy door. Roan turned and slid the little window open.

"Yeah?"

Ishaan seemed to hesitate.

"I've been known to get loud," he said. "Yelling, banging on the door. I don't care what I say or do, don't let me out. And...and in the event of an emergency—fire, flood, dragon—you are under no obligation to try and save me. You'd probably just end up raped for your troubles." Roan drew a slow breath through his nose. This whole self-loathing act was getting old.

"I could never knowingly leave another person to die," he said, "no matter what the consequences were. Good night, Ishaan." Roan slid the window closed as Ishaan turned away. Did the man honestly think he was the only one on the planet with problems? Roan was tempted to unlock the door and go in there, to let the demon out and give Ishaan a little perspective. At least he didn't sprout horns and tail if he went too long between meals.

Speaking of eating, he was actually physically hungry, too. While he waited for Ishaan to fall asleep, he rummaged through the fridge, cupboards, and pantry. There wasn't much, but he made himself a sandwich and sat down in the living room to watch TV for a while. With almost six thousand channels to choose from, he would have thought finding *something* to watch wouldn't have been that hard, but nearly half the shows that he flipped past were in astaniko, the language of the gryphlians, which was funny, since he didn't think gryphs even watched TV.

He finally settled on some nature show, the cameraman following a couple of haggard-looking researchers across a snow-swept tundra as they tracked an injured wolf, pointing out the drops of blood on the snow, the shortening of the wolf's stride as it tired. The camera focused on the horizon and then zoomed in, filling the screen with the thin, bloody beast. It stopped and glanced back, and Roan slid to the edge of the couch, his half-eaten sandwich forgotten in his hand.

That was no wolf. And those were no researchers. Now he saw the guns, the swords, the silver shapes of the Ghost Hounds flitting in and out of the screen. Those were Huntsmen, and this was a Werewolf hunt.

He jumped and dropped his sandwich on the floor as something thumped against the inside of Ishaan's door, hard enough to rattle it. With one last disgusted look at the TV, he turned it off and scraped up the remains of the sandwich.

"Is something the matter?" he called as he walked to the kitchen to throw away his garbage. "Ishaan?" But Ishaan did not respond. Curious, Roan approached the door and slowly slid back the window. Green-gold eyes stared back at him, empty, lifeless, and he shuddered. Ishaan was right; he had the eyes of a corpse.

Roan leaned against the door and closed his eyes. He could feel Ishaan through the wood, feel his desire and frustration like hands sliding over his skin, pulling at him. His fingers brushed the doorknob, but he let his hand fall away. There were too many unknown factors. He didn't want to risk messing it up, not if he didn't have to. With shaking hands, he unbuttoned his pants and let them drop, a soft cry escaping his lips as the walls holding back the demon dissolved like smoke. His scalp tingled as his horns pushed up through the skin, a crawly sensation creeping down his spine as his tail extended from his backbone, and he fought not to gag as his throat adjusted to fit a tongue four times as long as before. Trembling, he took a step back and stared at his new shadow cast upon the door.

No wonder people called him a demon. He was horrific, a monster. He deserved to be shot—

Roan cleared his throat and stepped back up to the door. Apparently, Ishaan wasn't the only one prone to fits of self-pity. As grotesque as it was to watch, he couldn't believe he was indulging in it himself. He was easily five years older than Ishaan and ought to know better. Roan peered in the window again.

"Ishaan," he said, his voice deepened to a seductive rumble, "can you hear me?" Ishaan moved closer. Roan could hear his fingernails skitter over the inside of the door. "I know you want me," he said, watching flashes of desire, tension, and anger race across his face like lighting across the sky. "I want you, too. I want to be in there with you, touching you. You'd like that, wouldn't you? You'd like to feel my hands on you. I bet you'd like to feel my tongue inside you, too."

Ishaan threw himself against the door, his face pressed into the little window. Roan chuckled and stuck his tongue out, running the tip along Ishaan's bottom lip and Ishaan opened his mouth to him.

"That's not what I meant and you know it," Roan said with a smile. Ishaan seemed so out of it. Roan hesitated, then slid inside Ishaan's mouth, their tongues writhing against each other. Ishaan groaned and Roan gasped as the energy around him spiked. Ishaan was touching himself. Breathless, Roan drew back. "Yeah, that's what I want," he murmured. "C'mon, Ishaan, stroke it. Let me feel you enjoy yourself." Ishaan made a noise low in his throat and stepped away from the door, only to throw himself at it again.

"Easy now," Roan said. "I just need enough to get me through tomorrow. Now come on, you must do this nearly every night anyway."

"Gonna suck on you," Ishaan growled, his words barely intelligible.

Roan shuddered.

"I would love to let you," he said, "but I want to make sure you really don't remember anything first. So do me a favor, okay?" Ishaan pressed himself to the door again and Roan leaned close. "Come on," he whispered, flicking his tongue out to tease Ishaan. "Come on...come on, Ishaan...touch it, stroke it..." His eyes slid shut as Ishaan began to masturbate, the waves of sexual energy washing over him like a tropical sea. He drank it in, the heat filling his blood, pounding in his veins. Oh, yes. Like spring water, it eased his raging thirst, but could do nothing to slake the demonic hunger. That was harder to satisfy. Masturbation alone was not strong enough. But there would be time enough for that tomorrow night.

Roan opened his eyes, watching as Ishaan neared his climax, watching the sweet agony race across his face and lay his soul wide open. For an instant, the pleasure became the entire world—his lips parted in a soundless, breathless cry, his dead eyes flashed with something beyond wakefulness, beyond consciousness—and then a hoarse cry ripped from his throat.

Trembling, Roan leaned against the wood, listened to Ishaan's ragged breathing, and swallowed down the echoes that shuddered through his body. After a moment, he bent down and pulled his pants up. It wasn't enough—it was *never* enough—but it would keep him sane and safe for one more day, and really, what more could he ask? He brushed his sweat-damp hair back out of his face and staggered off to bed.

Four

Ishaan woke up cold and stiff on the floor in front of his bedroom door, his left shoulder aching. He sat up and leaned against the wall, rubbing his tender arm as he looked around for some clue as to last night's events. Nothing was broken, though with only the bed and dresser in the room, there wasn't much left to break. He glanced at the door, his lip curling in disgust at the sight of the thick semen, drying where it had dripped down the wood. He hoped Roan had been asleep before *that* had started.

He sighed and licked his dry lips. His mouth tasted funny, like strawberries and cinnamon. Frowning, he pushed himself to his feet. What had he eaten? The last thing he remembered putting in his mouth was that beer just before Sezae showed up. Which would explain his dizziness and hunger.

He picked up his pajama bottoms from off the floor beside the bed and turned them right-side-out again before making up his bed. For the first time in a couple of weeks he wondered if it wouldn't be easier to just forget the pajamas and go to bed naked. That's how he always woke up. But giving up that small token of modesty and respectability seemed like giving up something far greater—hope. It was like giving in, acknowledging that the sickness had won, and he would never do that.

Ishaan slipped into an old pair of black jeans and a blue T-shirt, and sat on the end of his bed to wait for Roan to let him out. Sitting alone in an empty room with only his thoughts for company was nothing new—Trydel never got up before nine, not once in the eight months he'd worked for Ishaan—but this morning he couldn't stop himself from glancing at the clock high on the wall every few minutes.

What had he heard? What would he say? Was he even still in the house or had he run off with all the electronics? He had probably invited all his friends over last night and they'd drunk all Ishaan's beer and smoked pot in his living room and made fun of him while he masturbated in front of the door. He scowled up at the clock again. Barely half past eight. With a sigh, he lay back on the bed and folded his hands under his head as he stared up at the ceiling. This was going to be a long half hour.

He sat up as the window in the door slid back.

"Ishaan," Roan called softly, "are you awake?" Praise the gods. Just hearing his voice put many of Ishaan's fears to rest.

"Yes," he replied, sliding off the bed and hurrying over to the door. He looked into Roan's pale gray eyes, watched the young man search his for conformation, and heard the key turn in the lock. Ishaan steeled himself for that 'first morning after' look. It was different each time, but every person who had ever unlocked that door for him had it. It said, 'You're a freak' or 'You're sick' or 'Why did I agree to this?'.

"Good morning," Roan said as Ishaan pulled the door open. He was barefoot, wearing a pair of baggy tan trousers and a tight black tank top. "I hope you don't mind; I'm making breakfast." He hung the key back up and headed for the kitchen. Ishaan watched him go, then crossed the room and shut himself in the bathroom. It was there, just for an instant, a darkness in Roan's eyes, a refusal to meet his gaze. He heard. Not for the first time, Ishaan wished he could remember what happened, what he'd said.

As he stepped back out into the living room, the scent of toasted bread wrapped around him and drew him toward the dining room table, where Roan was already eating. A plate of eggs and toast sat waiting for Ishaan, not at the opposite end of the table from Roan, as he might have expected, but just around the corner. Roan glanced up from his plate and Ishaan realized he was just standing there, staring at the young man while he ate. After last night, that had to be unsettling.

"You're not being paid to cook," Ishaan said. He hesitated, then sat down.

Roan took a bite of toast, chewed, swallowed and said, "It's toast and eggs. I'm not expecting to be paid. I just thought, after the night you had, a decent breakfast might be welcome." Roan glanced at him, that same look in his eyes. What did it mean?

"I'm sorry if I kept you awake," Ishaan said, picking at the toast. He was starving, but the thought of eating made him nauseous. He wasn't sure if it was from the hangover or from being reminded of what he couldn't remember.

"That was no problem," Roan said, stabbing a bite of egg and shoving it into his mouth. "I'm just wondering if you always shout those kinds of things at your employees?"

"I wouldn't know," Ishaan replied. He didn't want to ask, but he had to. "What kinds of things?"

"Oh, you know," Roan said, using the crust of his toast to mop up the liquid yolk on his plate, "I'm gonna suck on you. That kind of thing." Ishaan pushed his plate away.

"I don't know. I might have." The others never wanted to talk about it, which, Ishaan realized, was exactly what he wanted, too—to never talk about it. He shoved his chair back, but Roan wasn't finished.

"I wondered," he said, "if maybe my telling you that I worked as a whore sometimes didn't give this other you the wrong idea about me. You kept saying, 'Gimme some of that ass,' and 'Wrap those sweet lips around me,' and 'Do what you're paid to, you little whore'. And then you screamed and beat against the door, and finally jerked off and got quiet for a few hours. Then it all started again." Roan was watching him, fork poised before his lips. "You really don't remember that?"

Ishaan stood and leaned down, into his face.

"I don't remember crawling through my best friend's bedroom window and raping her. Why would I remember *that*?" He walked away from the table, but stopped at his study door and glanced back. "Don't ever talk to me about what I do when I'm asleep, understand?" He waited for Roan to nod, then stepped into the study and slammed the door.

There was no reason to discuss his illness. Talking about it wasn't going to fix him. The best thing for both of them was to pretend like nothing happened. That had always been the arrangement between him and his employees—he had assumed that Roan knew that. His mistake. Now things were clear and this wouldn't happen again.

He sat down and logged into his outernet account, sorting through and trashing the bulk of his e-mail. He had a message from his mother, full of false familial cheer as she once again asked him to come visit them sometime. In the three years since they moved off-planet to escape the shame of having a rapist for a son, he hadn't once gone to see them, or even said that he'd try. She probably thought it would make her a bad mother if she didn't ask anyway. He rattled off a polite reply, mentioning, for lack of other conversation, that Trydel had gotten married and that he had a new housemate. Not that either of his parents really cared. He'd be surprised if they actually read the whole message, once they saw that he wasn't going to darken their doorstep any time soon.

He logged off and stood up with a sigh. The thought of facing Roan again left a cold, heavy feeling in the pit of his stomach, but he had things to do. He opened the door to find the young man sprawled out on the couch across the room, the TV remote in one hand. Roan glanced at him and sat up.

"Is it okay that I watch the—"

"Fine," Ishaan said and headed into the kitchen. The room still smelled of toast, once again making his stomach rumble, but whatever dishes Roan had used were washed and put away. The broken beer bottle had been cleaned out of the sink, as well. Ishaan grabbed the dishrag out of the sink and turned to go clean off his door, but stopped short as Roan stepped into the doorway.

"Sorry," Roan said. "I was just wondering if there was anything for me to do around here. TV's great, but—"

"I'm sorry it isn't more entertaining around here," Ishaan said. "Excuse me; I'm in the middle of something." Roan stepped back to let him pass and then followed him across the room.

"That's not exactly what I meant," he said. "Do you have chores or something? I could dust. Or sweep."

"I'm not paying you to be my housekeeper, either," Ishaan said and closed the door in his face. He needed someone to lock him up and let him out. What they did on their own time wasn't any of his business. Trydel had always been off in town, courting his girl, and the one before him, Dek, had spent his time writing some sort of novel. He couldn't seem to remember what Tassic had done with himself all day, but Xeth had spent so much time on his smuggled palm computer that Ishaan had thought he'd had it implanted.

Now there was an idea. Roan had said he was familiar with computers and Ishaan did have that old Empirion Duo collecting dust in his closet. He finished scrubbing the semen off the door and opened it to find Roan leaning against the wall, waiting for him.

"I have something for you," Ishaan said. He tossed him the dirty rag, smiling to himself as confusion turned to disgust as Roan realized what he was holding. Ishaan left him standing there and went to dig the old laptop out of the back of the closet.

"I'm guessing it's not a puppy," Roan said and Ishaan glanced over his shoulder at the young man sitting on the end of his bed.

"You sure are making yourself at home," Ishaan observed.

Roan shrugged.

"You want me to get out?"

"I want to know what, besides the obvious, has changed since last night." Roan frowned and gave his head a small shake, as if he didn't understand. "Last night you could barely stand to be in the same room with me, now you're cooking me breakfast, following me all over the house, acting like you want to be friends? Do you really think it's going to get you anything?" Roan stared at him for a moment, then stood.

"First of all," he said, "I cooked *us* breakfast—there's a difference. Second, I followed you because there's nothing else to do. And third, it's not an act. I'm usually a friendly person. Yesterday was just a bad day. Today *was* shaping up to be a good day, until you woke up." He stormed out of the room. "I think I like you better when you're asleep!" he shouted from across the house and then slammed his door.

"Damn it," Ishaan spat. He jerked the Empirion out from behind a stack of boxes and stalked across the living room. He raised his hand to knock on the door, but grabbed the knob and shoved it open instead. This was still his house. Roan sat on the end of his own bed, lacing up his boots with sharp, angry jerks.

"What do you want?" he asked.

"You're not going anywhere," Ishaan said. "You entered into an agreement to work for me and if you violate that agreement I'll sue your ass for breach of contract, because I'll not live with the threat of you walking out hanging over my head. You'll leave when I say you can leave." Roan glared up at him and finished tying his bootlaces.

"I don't remember signing any paperwork," he said, rising to his feet, "and a verbal agreement is hard to uphold in court, especially without witnesses." He stepped over to the chair and picked up a battered red leather coat, carefully folding it over his arm before speaking again. "I'm going for a walk, Ishaan, I'm not deserting you, but if you ever again try to tell me what I can and can't do, I'll have you arrested for kidnapping and assault, and with your track record, I don't think that would turn out well for you. Do you?"

"You can't threaten me," Ishaan snapped.

"That wasn't a threat," Roan said. "It was a promise. Now get out of my way before one of us says something stupid." For a second, Ishaan considered knocking the defiance right off his face, but giving him a couple of black eyes probably wouldn't help the situation any. That damn dragon was looking for any excuse to lock him up and throw away the key; he probably shouldn't provide the physical evidence needed to do it.

He stepped back and Roan swept past him, stomping across the living room and out the front door. As the silent house pressed in on him, Ishaan clenched his fist and slammed it against the wall, putting a divot in the sheetrock. Son-of-a-bitch! He stalked into the guest room and dropped the Empirion on the bed, then turned and began pulling out the dresser drawers, dumping Roan's shit in a pile on the floor.

If that little bastard thought he'd won this fight, he was going to be unpleasantly surprised to find the doors locked and his crap scattered across the lawn. Ishaan didn't need him. Sleeping in the jail was miserable, but it wasn't the end of the world, and it certainly wasn't worth putting up with some cocky little prick who thought he had the upper hand.

It wasn't just the jail, though. It was walking past the people he used to know, seeing the way they looked at him, or refused to look at him, waking the town with his screams, waking his daughter...He stared down at the jumble of socks, underwear, and T-shirts. He hated waking in that cell, naked, cold, sticky, with the sheriff eyeing him like some diseased animal that needed a bullet between the eyes. Maybe he didn't *need* Roan, but having him around did make life easier.

With a sigh, he started gathering Roan's clothes back up and shoving them into drawers. He had no idea what went where, so he didn't even bother. It would guarantee a much needed discussion. He was out in the garden, transplanting the tomato seedlings, when he heard the back door open. He glanced over his shoulder, then returned to digging as Roan strode across the lawn, his long red coat whispering against the legs of his jeans.

"Did you find what you were looking for?" Roan asked. Ishaan dusted off his hands and stood.

"You tell me," he said. "I was looking for someone I could depend on, someone who wouldn't flake out and storm off at every little disagreement, someone who wouldn't try to use my sickness to get what they wanted."

"And you thought you'd find that in with my socks and underwear?"

"No. I was going to throw you out, but...I decided to give you one more chance."

Roan nodded slowly.

"I see. And this second chance is the result of you not wanting to sleep in the jail again?" Ishaan hesitated, then nodded. "Well then, I guess you did find what you were looking for. I'll be here, every night and every morning, no matter what. You have my word on that. And quit worrying about your stupid fortune. I'm not after your money." It was probably just his imagination, but Ishaan thought he heard something in Roan's voice, something that made him wonder what he *was* after, if it wasn't money.

Roan cleared his throat. "Now let me tell you what I'm looking for. I'm looking for someone who isn't going to accuse me of being a liar, thief, and con-artist every five minutes, someone who won't flip out of I decide to cook breakfast, someone who won't threaten to throw my belongings out onto the lawn at the drop of a hat, someone who isn't going sue me or have me arrested —"

"Fine," Ishaan said. "I can do that."

"Shake on it?" Roan held out his hand.

"A handshake is not legally binding," Ishaan said. Roan shrugged, but did not lower his hand. With a sigh, Ishaan wiped his dirty palm on the seat of his jeans and took the offered hand. Roan's grip was warm and surprisingly firm.

"All right then," Roan said. He shrugged out of his coat and hung it on one of the tall stakes that would support the beans in the coming months. "Planting tomatoes, are we?"

"Yeah, but—"

"I know, I'm not being paid to be your gardener. I just want something to do, okay?" Ishaan opened his mouth, then closed it again. It wasn't such a great thing to ask, he supposed. He picked up a tray of tomato seedlings and handed it to Roan.

"Plant them about a foot and a half apart, in these two rows, starting down there," he said, pointing to the far end of the garden. Roan looked down at the plants in his hands.

"This is a lot of tomatoes," he said.

"The animals eat a lot of them," Ishaan replied, kneeling down in the dirt again to get back to work.

"You could put up a fence."

"I like the animals."

"And the rabbit in the bottom of the fridge, was that one of the animals you liked?"

"Yep." He stabbed his hand trowel into the soil.

"Ah. I hope you never start liking me, then," Roan said with a chuckle.

"I wouldn't worry about it," Ishaan said. "If you don't want to put those in the ground, just set them down."

"Okay, okay," Roan said, heading for the other end of the garden plot. "Hey, do I get one of those little shovel things?"

"I only have the one," Ishaan told him. "Find a stick."

"Maybe I could use the one that's stuck up your ass," Roan muttered as he walked away.

"What?"

Roan glanced back, a look on innocence on his face.

"I was just wondering if you were planning on having that rabbit for dinner tonight, or if you were saving it for something." That *wasn't* what he'd said, but Ishaan suddenly didn't feel like fighting anymore. He just wanted to garden.

"You offering to cook it?"

Roan laughed.

"Me? I nearly burned the toast. But I'll help, if you want me to."

"Fine. We can start dinner as soon as these tomatoes get planted." With a nod, Roan knelt down and got to work. Ishaan watched him for a moment, using an old garden stake to loosen the dirt, then digging in with both hands to make a hole for the plant. Satisfied that he wasn't going to screw it up, Ishaan turned back to his own task.

The first few days were always rough, he reminded himself. Trydel hadn't wanted to be in the same room with him for almost a week. Xeth had nearly walked out twice. These petty arguments were nothing. They didn't like each other, plain and simple, and that was fine with him. Roan didn't have to like him to do his job.

"Hey," Roan called suddenly. Ishaan raised his head. "I was so pissed that you'd messed up my stuff, I completely forgot to ask what was in the leather satchel on my bed."

"It's just an old laptop," Ishaan said. "I thought maybe it would help entertain you. Do you have an outernet ID?"

"Yeah."

"Then you can log onto my network. The system password is 'iselda47'. And if you charge a bunch of porn to my account, I'll take it out of your pay, got it?"

Roan grinned and nodded.

"Thanks, Ishaan."

Ishaan snorted and went back to digging.

"It's not like I gave it to you," he said. "I'm just letting you use it so you'll leave me alone."

"Still," Roan said after a moment, "thanks."

Ishaan pressed the moist soil in around the tomato's roots.

"You're welcome," he said finally. He wasn't trying to make Roan like him, he was just trying to restore a little peace. After all, everyone knew that the most effective way to subdue any hostile entity was to give them unlimited outernet access.

Five

As soon as dinner was over and the dishes were washed, Roan hurried off to his room to hook up the laptop. It wasn't anything fancy, barely newer than his old Khessna, but it allowed him access to a world denied to him for too long. His inbox was stuffed with junk, which he sorted through with growing impatience. He didn't need blood-pressure medication, or the windows on his space cruiser fixed, and he certainly didn't need any male enhancement drugs. Thanks to the demon, if he was anymore 'enhanced' he'd be dangerous. Some people even complained that he was too big. Never during, strangely enough, but afterward when they could hardly walk. He couldn't exactly blame them.

He stopped, the pointer hovering over an address that he recognized. Kethic. Roan sat back in his chair and took a deep breath. What could he possibly want? The subject line read *Urgent!!*, but the message was dated more than a month ago. After a moment, Roan returned to trashing the spam, pointedly ignoring his brother's message.

It had been almost a year since he'd last heard from Kethic. Not nearly long enough, as far as he was concerned. After escaping from prison, Kethic had written to him, had sworn that he wasn't angry about Roan's betrayal, had wanted to meet and reconcile. Roan had agreed and they arranged to meet at a cafe on the concourse at the center of Invion's gating complex.

Kethic was waiting for him, but he wasn't alone. The men said they were scientists, studying incubism, and they wanted to help Roan, they wanted to cure him. Kethic looked like hell—pale, thin, dark circles under his eyes and fading bruises on his face and hands. Roan asked if that was the kind of help he'd be getting, too. The scientists had tried to grab him and he'd run.

At first, he'd been near panic, imagining what they were doing to Kethic, trying to plan some way to help him escape, but then he realized something. Kethic hadn't been under restraint and none of those scientists had a weapon or they'd have used it to stop him. Kethic had willingly led his little brother into a trap, had sold him out to be a lab rat. After that, Roan didn't worry about him so much.

And now this, an urgent message almost a year later. Maybe it was another trap, maybe he'd finally gotten around to apologizing, maybe he was begging for help, maybe he was writing to say that his scientist friends had finally found a cure. Roan tapped his fingers against the desk. A cure. He wondered what it would be like, to not have the empty, aching hunger inside him, to not live in constant fear that the demon would get loose, that he would be found out, that he would be killed.

Even if that was what Kethic's message said, could Roan ever trust him again? They had betrayed each other. That wasn't exactly something that could be forgotten. Roan closed the computer.

"I'm ready," Ishaan said from the doorway. He was wearing just his pajama pants again, only this time, Roan was able to enjoy the view. Ishaan was fit and lean, his skin tan, shoulders broad, arms well-muscled. Roan's eyes slid down his chest, lingering on his slender, compact hips, his arms suddenly longing to wrap around that slim waist, to pull him back against his body. Roan pushed his chair back and stood, feeling his jeans pull tight across his groin as he followed Ishaan across the house.

"G'night," Roan said as Ishaan stepped into his room and started to shut the door.

"Good night," Ishaan replied. Roan locked the door and leaned against the wood, absently running his hand over the bulge in the front of his pants. Soon, he told himself. Soon. He just had to wait until Ishaan fell asleep.

He flipped through a few hundred TV stations, watching the minutes creep by on the big clock on the back wall. How long did it take a man like Ishaan to fall asleep? Twenty minutes? Half hour? The night before he was standing at the door after about an hour. Roan wanted to be in his room before that happened.

Forty minutes after locking the door, Roan couldn't take it any longer. He slid open the window and peered into the pitch black room.

"Ishaan?" he said softly. No response. Louder, he said, "Ishaan, I need to talk to you. It's an emergency." Still nothing. "Ishaan, I think the barn's on fire." After a minute, he took the key off its hook and slid it into the lock. He licked dry lips and turned the key. As the door swung open, he returned the key to its hook and stepped inside, shutting the door behind him. Standing in the darkness, he listened to the sound of his own breathing, and across the room, Ishaan's gentle snores.

He turned on the light, blinking hard in the sudden brightness, and walked into the room, stopping at the side of the bed. Ishaan lay still and peaceful, his rugged, angry face softened by sleep. Roan reached out and brushed a lock of curly black hair back off his brow. He was handsome. To have this every night, to be able to stop running, would be worth all the rudeness and paranoia Ishaan could throw at him. This was a dream come true.

Ishaan's eyelashes fluttered and he moaned in his sleep, shifting beneath the covers. In one fluid movement, Roan stripped off his shirt and sank to knees, flipping back the quilt and sheet to expose Ishaan's lean body, his pajama's shoved down to mid-thigh as he touched himself.

The energy bathed Roan's skin like rays of spring sunlight melting away winter's chill, waking the demon from its reluctant slumber. It pressed against the inside of his skin, longing to come out, but Roan wasn't hungry enough to lose control. If he could help it, he'd never let himself reach that point again.

His fingertips slid over bare skin as he slipped Ishaan's pants down around his ankles. Ishaan stirred at his touch, inching closer to the edge of the bed. Roan slid one hand between Ishaan's thighs and Ishaan spread his legs like a cheap whore, lifting his hips off the bed as he pulled at himself. A soft sigh slipped between Roan's lips as he reached up, pushed Ishaan's hands away, and began to stroke that hard, hot flesh.

He fed, devouring the heavy, sexual energy that rolled off Ishaan. It was rich and heady, like a strong wine, but it lacked the substance of real sex. He slid his hands across Ishaan's skin, aching to climb into bed with him, to press him down into the mattress, to push deep inside him. He wanted it so bad, but if Ishaan woke up, if Ishaan caught him, Roan had a feeling he'd be lucky to escape with his life.

"Isn't that right?" he asked softly and Ishaan's empty, soulless eyes opened and turned his direction. "You'd kill me if you knew what I was doing to you." Ishaan growled something and started to sit up, but Roan leaned close and ran his tongue across the head of Ishaan's erection. Ishaan made a strangled sound and bucked his hips. "I thought you might like that," Roan said. "Now you lay back down and relax, and I'll let you come in my mouth. How does that sound?" For a second, he wasn't sure if Ishaan understood—those blank eyes just stared at him—then Ishaan sank back into the mattress and raised his hips off the bed. Roan chuckled to himself and then began to lick and suck at Ishaan once again.

Roan took his time, exploring every inch, every fold and crevice, every sound and movement Ishaan made. He wasn't in any hurry. The longer it took, the longer he could feed, and while pleasuring someone orally could never satisfy the demon like actual penetrative intercourse, it would keep it quiet for several days. Finally, Roan opened his mouth wide and swallowed Ishaan as deep as he could, until he felt the head tempting the edge of his gag reflex. He started to pull back, but Ishaan reached up and grabbed him by the hair, holding him still while he jerked his hips and thrust clear to the back of Roan's throat.

His eyes squeezed shut, Roan fought the urge to throw up, his throat muscles clenching as he tried to swallow and couldn't. He couldn't breathe, his hands grabbing at the bed to keep from leaving marks on Ishaan. If he left marks, he would be caught. Ishaan thrust again and cried out, and Roan felt the thick semen hit the back of his throat. Ishaan let go and Roan jerked back, choking, tears springing to his eyes as he swallowed. It felt like his throat was full of broken glass.

He grabbed his shirt and stood as Ishaan sank back into peaceful, oblivious slumber, his body damp with sweat. Roan turned and stalked out, flicking off the lights as he went. He locked the door and leaned back against it, still trying to catch his breath. That was unpleasant. He crossed over to the bathroom and took a look in the mirror. His face was red and his scalp hurt where Ishaan had pulled his hair, but none of that would show in the morning. He tried to remember if Ishaan had grabbed him or hit him, anything that would leave a bruise. He didn't think so.

Something would have to be done to keep that from happening again. Restraining Ishaan was the obvious solution, but with what? He was sure to struggle and rope burns would be awfully hard to explain. Roan slipped into bed and winced as he swallowed. At least he had a couple of days to come up with something; though not completely satisfied, his demon slumbered as peacefully as Ishaan.

Six

Sunlight streamed into the room, the barred windows leaving stripes across the bed. Groaning, Ishaan heaved himself up off the floor, his hands and stomach sticky with semen. His back and hip ached, and the heels of his hands hurt. He must have been pounding on the door again. Great. No doubt Roan would tell him all about it over breakfast.

That was something he'd have to stop. Did Roan really think he wanted to hear about his screaming and masturbating? Would Roan want to talk about his problems if, say, he wet the bed? Ishaan didn't think so. He slipped back into his pajama bottoms and sat on the edge of his bed, absently scrunching his toes into the carpet. He'd have to wash before he could get dressed.

It was almost nine. He considered knocking at the door since Roan was probably up, but he wanted to enjoy the peace while it lasted. Once that door opened, there was no telling what was going to happen.

He didn't actually dislike Roan—the young man was very friendly and likable—and that was part of the problem. He didn't *want* to like him. This was supposed to be a business relationship. Letting it become anything more was just asking for trouble.

"*No!*" Roan's shout echoed through the silent house. Ishaan jumped up and ran to the door, trying the knob even though he knew it was locked. Roan screamed again, wordless, anguished, and Ishaan pounded his fist against the door.

"Roan," he shouted. "Roan, what's wrong?" A thousand horrible visions flashed through his head as he rattled the doorknob again. Did someone get into the house? Did something happen in town? Was it something on the news? He pounded on the door again. "Roan, open the door!" And what if he couldn't? What if thieves had broken in, killed him, or worse, what if they were raping him? Ishaan pressed his ear to the door.

He heard the key slide into the lock and pulled back, jerking the door open as soon as he heard the lock click. Roan stood in the doorway, a sort of tight, empty look on his face.

"What happened?" Ishaan demanded. He didn't look hurt.

Roan turned and started back toward his own room.

"Nothing," he said, his voice flat. "Sorry if I disturbed you." Ishaan stared after him, then charged across the room and shoved his door open. Roan stood beside the bed, staring at the wall, and didn't even glance up as Ishaan stepped into the room.

"This is unacceptable," Ishaan said. "You can't scream for no reason. You scared the living shit out of me. I thought you were being raped, or Devaen had been attacked, or—"

"I got an e-mail from my brother," Roan said. Ishaan waited, but apparently, Roan thought that explained everything.

"What does he want?" Ishaan asked. "He hasn't found you, has he?"

Roan shook his head.

"He just wanted to let me know that our parents were dead." A painful emptiness opened up the bottom of Ishaan's stomach at the thought. He didn't have a very close relationship with his parents, but he couldn't imagine losing them.

"How? When?"

"Murdered," Roan said, his voice cracking, "over a month ago, executed in their home." He wrapped his arms around himself and began to cry, great ragged sobs that shook his entire body. Ishaan took a hesitant step toward him, not sure what to say or do. This was way outside the lines of strictly business, but he didn't feel right just saying sorry and walking away. He'd never seen a man hurt that much.

"It was my fault," Roan choked out suddenly, staggering forward and falling to his knees. "They killed them—my fault—looking for me—" He screamed and slammed his fists into the wall, again and again. Ishaan stepped forward and grabbed him by the wrists, but not before he'd cracked the sheetrock and smeared blood across the wall.

"Knock it off," Ishaan said, lifting Roan to his feet and shoving him back against the wall. "It wasn't your fault—"

"Yes it was!" Roan shouted, trying to pull away. "They were looking for me! They—I—" He seemed to collapse in on himself, to grow very small, and then he fell forward, against Ishaan's chest. Ishaan let go of his wrists and tried to step away, but Roan wrapped his arms around Ishaan and pressed his face into Ishaan's neck, clinging to him and sobbing brokenly.

"Ro-Roan," Ishaan said, standing rigid, his arms held out away from him. "Come on, man, get off me." But Roan was beyond either caring or understanding. Ishaan considered just shoving him away, but that was kind of heartless, considering. He sighed and tentatively placed his hands on Roan's back.

This didn't make them friends. This didn't change anything. This was one of those extenuating circumstances that didn't mean a thing. Once Roan calmed down, they'd both forget it ever happened. He hoped. Roan shuddered against him, his grip tightening, and Ishaan stiffened as Roan's lips brushed the side of his neck. He passed it off as an accident, until Roan did it again, and again, kissing him.

"What are you doing?" he demanded, his hands dropping from Roan's bare back.

"You're smart," Roan said, his voice hoarse and toneless. "Figure it out." His hands slid down Ishaan's back and tried to slip inside his pajamas.

"Hey!" Ishaan said, grabbing Roan by the arms and shoving him backward, against the wall. Roan looked up at him, his eyes dark with pain.

"Please, Ishaan, help me," he said. "I don't care what you do to me, just make it stop, make the pain stop, make me feel something else, anything else —" Ishaan regarded him for a minute, then turned and walked out. Behind him, he heard Roan slide down the wall and begin to cry again.

Ishaan locked himself in the bathroom, his hands shaking as he turned on the faucet and wet a washcloth. After he'd raped Sezae, and her father had dragged him out into the street and started beating the hell out of him, he'd welcomed the pain, he'd cherished every blow, every drop of blood, every broken bone, because it distracted from the intangible, inexpressible agony inside of him. He had raped his best friend. No words, no tears, no screams could relieve that pain.

So he understood Roan's actions, probably better than most. He wasn't angry at *Roan*. He raised his eyes and stared at his reflection, fighting the urge to slam his fist into the glass. Breaking the mirror wouldn't solve anything. It wouldn't change the fact that he almost hadn't walked away.

He closed his eyes and hung his head, leaning on the sink as the steam rose and clung, hot and sticky, to his face. What was he going to do? In that brief instant, he had wanted to grab Roan and spin him around, press his face against the wall and tear his pants off. It wouldn't matter, he'd told himself. Extenuating circumstances. They'd forget about it, like it never happened.

But some things just couldn't be forgotten. This was why they couldn't be friends. Friendship led to complacency, to carelessness, to people getting hurt.

"Ishaan?" He glanced toward the door, but didn't answer. "Ishaan, please, I need to talk to you."

"We have nothing to talk about," Ishaan said. He straightened up, turned off the water, wiped the moisture from his face. "Leave me alone."

"Please," Roan said, and he sounded desperate. "I'm sorry, I don't know what came over me. I wasn't thinking. I-I'll never do that again, I swear." Ishaan wasn't worried about that. He only had the one set of parents, after all. Ishaan steeled himself and opened the door. Roan looked up at him, red-eyed and pale-faced.

"Apology accepted," Ishaan said, brushing him aside as he headed for his room to get dressed. "Let's just forget about it, okay?"

"A-all right," Roan said, sounding confused. Ishaan supposed he had a right. His first thought *had* been to toss him out on the lawn, but they'd already settled that argument. Ishaan wasn't going to throw him out without just cause, and while sexual harassment probably qualified, there was always the damn extenuating circumstances to consider. This was a unique situation and would not be repeated. Ishaan would make sure of that.

Feeling better in a pair of soft gray slacks and a light, black button-down shirt, Ishaan strode out to confront Roan. He found him in the kitchen, trying to burn some toast. Roan glanced up from the toaster, a haunted look in his eyes, and Ishaan's carefully constructed rant died on his lips. He cleared his throat and decided to try a different approach.

"Did you want to leave for a couple of days?" he asked. "Sometimes it helps to visit the graves and say good-bye. I can sleep in the—"

"I can't," Roan said. The toast popped and he began to butter it as if his life depended on it.

"Why? Because your brother's still looking for you?" Roan nodded. "I would think, in light of the situation, that you could—"

"You don't understand!" Roan shouted, throwing the toast and butter knife down on the counter. "That's what they'll expect me to do. They'll be waiting for me!"

"Who?" Ishaan asked. Roan shook his head and turned away. "Don't give me that. Earlier you said 'they' killed—" Roan tried to leave the kitchen, to shove past him, but Ishaan grabbed him by the arms and pushed him back against the counter. "Damn it, Roan, if there are people looking for you, willing to kill your parents to find you, then I think I deserve to know about it!" Roan pulled away from him, but didn't try to run.

"*They* are some people my brother got involved with. They wanted me, too; I don't know for what, and when I refused, they tried to take me by force. I got away and have been running ever since."

Ishaan took a step backward. "Hang on a second, these people killed your parents so that they could catch you when you visited the graves, and you have *no* idea what they want you for?"

"No idea," Roan said with a shake of his head. "It was something Kethic got mixed up in, but that's all I know."

"Great," Ishaan muttered. "Just what I needed, drug dealers breaking down my door in the middle of the night."

Roan went back to making toast.

"Do you want me to leave?" he asked after a moment.

"No," Ishaan said, and then wished he hadn't. "I mean, if you want to go, I won't stop you—"

"I don't," Roan said. "I like it here, I like knowing where I'll be sleeping tonight, and tomorrow night, and the night after. It's been a long time since I could say that. And you don't have to worry—I've been very careful. Those people will never find me."

"Well, all right then," Ishaan said. He started to leave, but turned back and reached for a slice of toast. "Do you mind?"

"Help yourself." As Ishaan drew back, slice in hand, Roan grabbed his wrist. "And about earlier, in the bedroom—You have no idea how sorry I am. That will never happen again, you have my word."

"I already told you—"

"I know, I just want to be completely clear. I-I don't want there to be any weirdness between us."

Ishaan pulled out of his grasp.

"Look, Roan, I don't know what you think is going to happen here, but I'm telling you right now, we're not friends. We'll never be friends. Bad things happen to people who think they're my friends, okay? You work for me—let's just keep it that way. No one'll get hurt."

"Ishaan," Roan said, taking half a step toward him, "I'm not afraid of you."

"Well, you should be," Ishaan said, walking away. Nearly to his study, he stopped and turned back to find Roan standing in the kitchen doorway, watching him. "You should be," he said again, "and I'll tell you why. The first guy I hired to do your job, his name was Hektor. He was funny and friendly—a real nice guy, but one evening, we got drunk and passed out watching TV. When I woke up, he was packing his things. He kept saying, *I thought we were friends*, like that was supposed to have protected him from me. Friendship doesn't mean shit once I fall asleep, you got that?"

"Yeah," Roan said, his voice toneless, "I got it." He disappeared back into the kitchen and Ishaan shut himself in his study. This was for the best; this was how it had to be. Roan would see that. Or he wouldn't. Ishaan didn't really care, as long as he kept his distance.

Seven

Sitting alone in his room, Roan stared down at the quilt spread across the bed, his fingertips running back and forth across the ridge of a seam. His vision wavered and cleared, tears running silently down his face. Dead. The word kept ringing in his ears like the toll of a great bell, echoing, final. His parents were dead and it was all his fault.

The laptop sat open on the desk behind him, all the details not included in Kethic's message laid out in black and white online. His mother and father hadn't just been shot to death in their home, they'd been tied up, beaten, drugged, and then shot in the back of the head. His mother was killed first and then more than an hour later, his father. He'd had to watch her die.

Roan choked and buried his face in his hands, sobbing until he couldn't breathe. He curled up on the bed and pulled the pillow tight against his chest, squeezing with all his might. It hurt so much. He wanted to go there, to apologize, to say good-bye, and he couldn't. Kethic had warned him to stay away.

Roan didn't know what to make of that. In his message, Kethic had apologized. He said he honestly thought the scientists would help him and he had wanted Roan to be helped, too. He wasn't what they needed, though. He only had eight of the ten genetic markers for full incubism. They needed someone with all the markers, and they thought Roan might have them. Kethic didn't say what the scientists wanted to do to him, only that he'd finally escaped and was on the run, too. He said he'd try to keep in touch, but that had been more than a month ago. Had he been caught again? Was he dead, too?

A deep, hollow chill filled Roan at the thought. He dried his face on his pillowcase and scrambled off the bed, his fingers pounding the keys as he signed into his e-mail account. He opened a new message and addressed it to Kethic, then stared at the blank screen. He didn't know what to say. They hadn't spoken in so long. He tried to turn the jumbled thoughts in his head into words, erased it, tried again, erased that. Finally, he wrote: *Just got your message. Are you okay?* and sent it before he could second-guess himself. He stared at the screen, tapping his fingers on the desk, as if he could will a new message to appear. With a sigh, he closed the laptop and leaned back in the chair.

Ishaan cleared his throat from the doorway.

"You busy?"

Roan glanced over his shoulder and shook his head.

"Not really. Why?"

"I need to head into Devaen. I thought, if you wanted to come, we could get some food that you want to eat." Roan glanced at the computer. Hanging out with Ishaan was about the last thing he wanted to do, but if he stayed at the house, he'd just end up checking his e-mail every ten minutes and thinking about his family. He needed the distraction. "Or you could just tell me what you want—"

"Let me change my clothes and I'll be right out." Ishaan didn't respond and after a moment, Roan turned in his seat, half expecting him to be gone. He was still standing in the doorway, just staring at Roan. "Or were you only asking to be polite?"

Ishaan frowned. "When have I ever tried to be polite?"

Roan felt a small smile lift the corners of his mouth, not because Ishaan was trying to be funny, but because he was completely serious.

"Hurry up—I'll be in the barn."

He walked away and Roan took one last look at the laptop before rising from his seat and crossing over to the dresser. As he slipped into a tight black tank and a red button-down shirt, he wondered what his brother was doing. Was he telling the truth, or was it just more lies? He took a step toward the desk, then turned and sat on the edge of the bed to put his boots on. It was too soon; there would be no message. There would probably never be a message.

Roan cleared his throat and stood, blinking back the stinging in his eyes. He wasn't going to cry anymore. Crying wasn't going to bring them back, and since it didn't help with the pain much, there really wasn't any point. He'd thought about getting drunk, seeing if that dulled the pain like people said, but beer tasted like piss, and he'd either never gotten drunk enough to feel good, or he was doing it wrong—either way, he didn't feel like puking all night long. That wasn't the kind of distraction he was looking for.

He wanted to feed. The demon might not need it, but he did, he needed to drown his sorrow in sex, it didn't matter how or with whom. When he told Ishaan he'd let him do anything to him, he'd meant it. Nothing Ishaan could have done would have been too extreme, too humiliating, too painful. On the contrary, he had wanted to be hurt.

But Ishaan had pushed him away. He wasn't sure if he was now glad of it, or disappointed. Glad, he supposed. If something had happened, it would have only put more strain on their already tense relationship. The fact that Ishaan had hesitated was bad enough. Roan was pretty sure Ishaan thought he hadn't noticed, but even as distraught as he was, that moment's hesitation, the way his hands lingered just a little too long, the tightness in his body, the held breath—it was obvious.

The keys were hanging in the door as Roan stepped out, so he locked the house behind him and headed down the packed earth driveway toward the barn. The doors were open wide and as he approached, Ishaan rolled out into the sunlight in something that Roan had never expected to see on this planet.

"What the hell is this?" Roan asked, stopping as the vehicle pulled up beside him. "A car?" It was small and boxy, seats for two and space in the back for storage, and that was about it. It didn't even have a roof. Ishaan leaned across the passenger's seat and pushed the door open.

"Get in."

Roan dropped down into the plush seat and shut the door.

"How the hell did you smuggle a *car* onto this planet? Space pirates?" The car thrummed around him, a faint crackling sound coming from behind the seats.

"I didn't have to smuggle it," Ishaan said as they started rolling down the driveway. "I have a permit."

"Wow, must be great to have a father with connections," Roan said. "I bet daddy's little boy always gets what he wants, doesn't he?" He snapped his mouth shut, shocked by the bitterness and spite in his words. Ishaan stomped on the brake and the car lurched to a stop, almost throwing Roan face-first into the dash. "I'm sorry," Roan said immediately. "I don't know—That was uncalled for. I'm just—I'm sorry."

After a moment, Ishaan's scowl lessened and he began to drive again. Roan slumped down in his seat and stared over the top of the door at the trees rolling by. Attacking Ishaan wasn't going to make him feel any better, either.

"My father didn't have anything to do with it," Ishaan said suddenly. Roan glanced over at him, a slight frown on his face as he concentrated on the road. "I heard that this company was doing a study on a new kind of electric car, seeing what impact, if any, it had on the environment, and I signed up."

"And why do you suppose they picked you?"

Ishaan glanced at him. "What do you mean?"

"Well, I'm sure a lot of people signed up, but how many of them got picked?"

"I don't know how many people signed up," Ishaan said stiffly. "There were only six openings, and yes, I was chosen because I could afford the insurance. It's not a crime to have money."

"That's all I was wondering," Roan said, turning back to the forest flashing by. They had to be going at least twice as fast as Sezae in her mule-drawn wagon, and the road didn't feel nearly as rough. "Is it a lot?" Roan asked after a moment. "The insurance, I mean."

"This thing's powered by a ten thousand year old dragon pearl the size of your head. What do you think?"

Roan sat up in the seat.

"By a-a dragon pearl? They killed a—"

"They didn't kill anything," Ishaan said. "Do you really think a company trying to save the environment is going to do it by killing dragons? Don't be stupid." Ishaan glanced at him, then back at the road. "Dragon pearls aren't made by dragons, anyway."

"They're not? I thought—"

"So did I, but apparently, dragon pearls are made by colossal oysters at the bottom of the sea. The dragons dive down to find them and use them to generate electricity by slowly dissolving them with acid in a special pouch at the front of their throats. This thing works the same way. The company found a way to synthesize the acid and convinced the dragons to let them have six pearls, which, considering how possessive dragons are, was very generous of them."

"Sounds like more trouble than it's worth," Roan said. "What's wrong with a sturdy wagon and a couple of horses?"

"Nothing," Ishaan said and his voice was suddenly hard. "I liked having horses. I liked the mules and oxen and zebrulas, too, but they kept dying. Essaeli, Devaen's vet, said I wasn't caring for them properly and threatened to have me arrested for animal neglect." He glanced at Roan. "I wasn't neglecting them. I sent one of the bodies to Shesade for tests and they told me it was cantharidin poisoning."

"Someone was poisoning your animals?" Roan asked. That was beyond cruel.

"That's what I thought, but Shesade's vet said cantharidin came from blister beetles, which would get into the alfalfa and be eaten." He shook his head. "I searched every bale of alfalfa and didn't find a single beetle. I did, however, find crushed insect parts in the bags of grain."

"Crushed...in the grain...That sounds deliberate."

Ishaan nodded.

"I started buying feed from Shesade and my animals stopped dying. At least, until someone broke into the barn and shot them all." Roan's mouth fell open as he struggled to find words.

"How—Why would anyone—Who would do that?"

"I've got no proof," Ishaan said, "but I'm sure it was Gus Doras. He runs the feed store, so he had opportunity, and he had motive, too."

"Why?" Roan asked before he realized that he might not want to know. Ishaan was silent for a long time, so long that Roan had decided he wasn't going to answer. That was okay; he wasn't going to ask again.

"I raped his son," he said finally. Roan nodded. He had guessed it was something like that. He was just going to let the subject drop, but then a thought occurred to him.

"How many people have you raped?" Ishaan scowled at him, his lips pressed into a thin line. "I'm just asking," Roan said. "I'm not judging. I'd like to know, since we are going into town and we'll probably run into people who don't like you. I don't want to be surprised by anything they say."

"Five," Ishaan said, his knuckles whitening as he gripped the steering wheel. "Sezae, Rae Doras, Hektor, Dr. Vek's wife, and some traveler in the woods. I don't even know her name—I didn't recognize her—I just woke up beside her and ran off before she woke up and started screaming rape."

"She was sleeping beside you?" Roan asked. "That doesn't sound like rape to me."

"What would you know about it?" Ishaan snapped.

Roan shrugged.

"Nothing, I suppose, except that if it was me, I'd have run for the sheriff as soon as you finished and went back to 'sleep'." He made the quote marks in the air with his fingers. "I wouldn't have lain there beside you and fallen asleep." Except that he would have. If he thought he could get away with it—

"Are you trying to tell me she wanted it?"

Roan shrugged again.

"I don't know, but just because you had sex with her, that doesn't automatically make it rape. Random, meaningless sex in the woods isn't a bad thing. Sometimes, people just want that contact, that intimacy."

"No one would *want* to have sex with me," Ishaan said.

"I wouldn't say that," Roan muttered, turning away to stare out at the trees again.

"No one in their right mind," Ishaan clarified, "and not while I'm asleep." Roan didn't bother correcting him. They didn't speak again until the trees began to thin and then suddenly gave way to open farmland, the fields bright green with rows of knee-high corn. Roan sat up and glanced around. He didn't remember passing any farms on his way out to Ishaan's place.

"Where are we?" he asked.

Ishaan pointed to a stone marker set beside the road just ahead.

"About a mile outside of town. Why?"

Roan shook his head.

"Just wondering." He supposed he had been a little preoccupied, curled up in the back of the wagon. "Who lives out here?" He gestured to the gray farmhouse set back off the road, surrounded by a high, barbed-wire fence. Nice neighbors.

"A farmer and his husband. We've never spoken." After a moment, he added, "That used to be Sezae's house." Roan nodded. It made sense, then, why he went after her first; she was the closest. "Did she already tell you that?"

"I don't think so," Roan said with a shake of his head. "She might have mentioned it, but I wasn't feeling too well on the ride out."

"Yeah, her family lived on that farm for three generations, but after what I did, her father sold the farm and moved into town—took over running the inn, and instead of going to college like she wanted to, Sezae had that kid—"

"That kid is your daughter," Roan snapped. "Quit feeling sorry for yourself and take care of your family!" His voice broke and he slumped back in his seat, covering his face with one hand. Damn it, didn't he know how lucky he was?

"I tried to take care of them," Ishaan said after a moment, he voice low, dangerous. "She didn't want money and I didn't want them living with me. There wasn't anything else to do."

"I know," Roan said, "I just—"

"I understand," Ishaan said, much to Roan's surprise. A single tear rolled down Roan's cheek and he quickly wiped it away. He wasn't going to cry anymore.

"We're here," Ishaan announced a few minutes later and Roan sat up straight as the car rolled to a stop in front of a small produce stand. As they climbed out of the vehicle, Roan glanced around, finding faces in almost every window overlooking the street. People were coming out of the inn, Sezae among them, and standing on the wide wooden porch to stare. Roan had the sudden urge to ask who taught them manners, but followed Ishaan over to the stand instead.

"Afternoon, Ishaan," the man behind the stand said stiffly.

"Scott," Ishaan said, acknowledging him with a nod. He began to pick through a box full of ears of corn, every now and then setting one aside. Roan glanced over the array of fruits and vegetables. Most of these were growing in the garden, though they wouldn't be ready for harvest for more than a month. He reached out and picked up a large apple.

"Excuse me," he said, and the stand owner, Scott, turned unfriendly eyes on him. "I was just—Where do you get your produce from, that these would be ripe already?"

"Those are from last fall," Scott said with a scowl. Roan glanced down at the price scrawled across the front of their box.

"Really? 'Cause that's pretty pricy for a nine month old apple."

Ishaan cleared his throat and gave him a look that clearly said to shut the hell up. He ignored it. "That's more like what I would expect to pay for an apple grown off-world and imported through an unregulated world gate."

The scowl deepened.

"Maybe you ought to think about shopping elsewhere," Scott said, reaching out and snatching an ear of corn out of Ishaan's hand. With a furious look at Roan, Ishaan turned and started back toward the car, but Roan didn't move.

"We could do that, I suppose," he said. "We'd probably get better service in Shesade. And while we're there, we could visit the regulation authority and tell them about all these lovely apples that you don't have a permit for."

"Oh, like you've never ignored regulations," Scott said with a pointed look at the car.

Roan smiled, a malicious quirk of the lips.

"He's got a permit."

"What do you want?" Scott asked between his teeth.

Roan picked up two more apples.

"I want these, and I think he wanted that corn." He glanced back at Ishaan. "Anything else?" Ishaan shook his head. "I guess that'll do it." Scott gathered up the six ears of corn and thrust them toward Roan. "I don't suppose we could get a bag for these?" Scott looked ready to murder him, but he shoved the corn into a wrinkled paper bag and handed it over. Roan added his apples and then smiled at him. "Thanks. You have a nice day." He walked over to the car and placed the bag in the back.

"You're not really going to steal those, are you?" Ishaan asked. "He was one of the few people in town willing to do business with me."

"He still is," Roan said, opening the door and dropping down into the seat. "You're probably the only person willing to pay his outrageous prices. Go ahead, pay him—I haven't got any money—but I wouldn't give him more than half what he's asking. That's still more than a bag of corn and apples is worth."

Ishaan stood beside the car, tapping his fingertips against the plastic, then turned and walked back to the produce stand. Roan watched him hand over a stack of coins and smiled to himself as Ishaan took his advice. Scott frowned, but didn't say anything.

Roan could feel the eyes on them as Ishaan started the car and drove down the street, past the inn. Ishaan stared straight ahead, but Roan glanced over, smiled, and waved at Sezae. Her smile was hesitant, but genuine, probably one of the few they'd find in Devaen. Roan fought the urge to flip the rest of them off and folded his hands in his lap as they rolled a few buildings farther and pulled over in front of the general store.

"Stay in the car," Ishaan said as Roan started to open his door.

"What?" Roan said with a laugh. "You're kidding, right?" Ishaan frowned at him and climbed out of the car. "Ishaan—" Roan opened the door and got out, too. "You can't let people treat you like that. You need to stand up for yourself and if you won't then I will. You can't help what you are—what you do, and you shouldn't be punished for something you can't help. It's not fair."

Ishaan folded his arms across his chest. "You finished?"

Roan huffed and nodded.

"Good, because while I appreciate the pep-talk, if one of us doesn't stay outside with the car, the town children will throw rocks at it or fill the seats with horseshit. Okay?"

Roan opened his mouth, then closed it again. "Okay."

"When I'm done shopping, I'll watch the car and you can pick out anything you need, and then I'll pay for it. Is that going to work for you?" Roan nodded. Ishaan turned to head into the building, but Roan could have sworn he saw a hint of a smile on his face as he did. He was glad he could be so amusing. Leaning back against the side of the car, he stared at the peeling paint on the face of the general store, the grimy windows reflecting the afternoon sun and the faded buildings across the street.

He straightened up as something moved within the reflection and turned to see the curtains in one of the second floor windows swing back into place. Frowning, he leaned back against the car and tucked his hands in his pockets. He hated being watched. He knew it wasn't because of anything *he* had done, but it didn't stop him from glancing around, looking for the angry mob that would chase him out of town. After a few minutes, Ishaan came back out.

"Whatever you want, just give it to Iana behind the counter and she'll ring it up."

"I'll see if I can get us another discount," Roan said as he passed him.

"Don't," Ishaan said, a warning in his tone. "Iana's prices are fair enough."

Roan held his hands up in surrender and stepped inside the store. It smelled of dust and medicines, but he supposed that could have come from the old woman perched on a high stool behind the counter. She had a narrow, pinched face and dark eyes, her silver hair pulled back in a severe knot high on the back of her head, but as he walked in she gave him a polite smile. It didn't quite reach her eyes, but he supposed it was friendly enough.

Roan walked up and down the aisles, picking out soap and toothpaste and shampoo, and then he paused before the products of a more personal nature. He eyed the jars and bottles and tubes of lubricant. They all looked the same, and he supposed they all worked the same, so he reached up for a random jar when one of them caught his attention. It was blue, and priced almost three times as much as any of the others. He picked one up and stepped over to the counter.

"Excuse me," he said, holding up the jar, "but do you know, is this really worth six and a half coins a jar?"

"I wouldn't know personally," she said, in a way that made him wonder if she'd ever had sex in her whole life, "but I know people who refuse to purchase any other product."

"And that's why it's so expensive?" He set the jar down on the counter, a little apart from his purchases.

"It is expensive," she said, "because it's only made by a single mage in a small fishing village on a distant planet and by the time it gets to me it has the taxes and fees of three different governments added to the price. From what I've heard, you can buy it in Traxen for eight laenes."

Roan raised his eyebrows.

"I'll be sure to stock up if I ever get around that way." He tapped his fingers against the counter, and then slid the jar over next to his shampoo. "I'll try it. Why not, right? It's not my money."

"Always a good attitude to have," she said. "Anything else?" He glanced around the store.

"No, I—" His eyes fell upon a table of silk lilies in simple white vases. "Those flowers—Could you send them somewhere for me?"

"This isn't the post office," she said, but she didn't say no. "Where would you like them sent?" she asked after a moment. He faltered at that, then wrote down the address of the cemetery he'd found online. He knew he couldn't go see them, but that hadn't stopped him from committing the address to memory. "Do you want to write something on the card?" she asked, sliding a small piece of parchment and an envelope across the counter to him. There were so many things he wanted to say, but since no one would actually read the card—

He cleared his throat and wrote *Sorry I wasn't there*, slipped the card in the envelope and handed it back. "Thanks," he said and walked away. It wasn't much, but it was the best he could do.

Ishaan was scowling as he stepped out into the sunlight.

"Took you long enough," he said, striding toward him. He paused as he drew abreast of Roan. "Don't look now, but they sent the dragon to keep an eye on me." He jerked his head back in the direction of the inn and Roan leaned to one side to peer around him. The dracorian sheriff, conspicuous with his jet black skin and shiny silver badge, was standing between them and the inn, one hand resting lightly on the butt of the pistol hanging at his hip, watching them. "I'll be right back and then we can get the hell out of here."

After he disappeared inside, Roan leaned back against the side of the car. He could still hear the muted noise of the people gathered in front of the inn like a distant swarm of bees. Ishaan was lucky the sheriff was the only one menacing him—he could have the entire town down his throat—

Roan straightened and glanced over his shoulder at the drac, then at the crowd, then back to the drac. The sheriff gave him a slow nod and Roan turned away, slumping back against the car with a sigh. The law was on their side. Good to know. He should have guessed as much, though; he'd yet to meet a corrupt dracorian. Even the drac selling ice cream in the park across the street when he was a kid—

He drew a sharp breath and shook his head. Not here, not now. It hurt too much. He glanced up as Ishaan came out of the shop, carrying a large paper bag and wearing a bemused expression. Roan started to open the passenger's door, but Ishaan caught him by the sleeve, then set the bag in the back behind the seats and pulled out the jar of blue lubricant. Roan felt his face grow hot.

"What's this?" Ishaan asked.

Roan cleared his throat. "What does it look like?"

Ishaan arched an eyebrow and dropped it back into the bag. "And what do you need that for?"

"Use your imagination," Roan said, and just in case Ishaan was still having trouble, he made a loose fist and mimed jerking off. Ishaan rolled his eyes. "Oh, give me a break, you do it every night, two or three times—"

"That's different," Ishaan said. "It's not my choice."

"Fine," Roan said, turning away and pulling the door open, "you go ahead and pretend like you're some kind of sexless—"

"Who's pretending?" Ishaan asked, pulling the keys out of his pocket and stepping past Roan, toward the front of the car. "Nothing in the universe interests me less than manhandling myself."

"Well, not all of us are lucky enough to be you," Roan said.

Ishaan scowled at him from across the car. "Look, I understand that you're having a really shitty day, but I'm getting sick and tired of your little comments. I didn't invite you along so you'd have someone to verbally abuse."

"No, you invited me so you'd have someone to watch your fucking car!" Roan said, his raised voice echoing off the fronts of the nearby buildings.

"Roan," Ishaan said sharply, "get in the car. Now."

Roan slammed the door.

"Don't tell me what to do," he said. "You may be rich, but you don't own me."

"I'm leaving," Ishaan said between his teeth, his lips barely moving.

"Go ahead," Roan replied as he turned away, "I'll walk." He strode past the drac and down the street toward the inn, a dozen pairs of eyes darting between him and the car behind him. He heard Ishaan turn the car around in the middle of the street, the engine humming and the electricity crackling as he rolled up beside Roan, matching pace for several strides. Roan ignored him and after a moment, he zipped off, spraying Roan with loose dirt.

Coughing and choking on the dust, Roan stopped and watched him barrel out of town and disappear around a bend in the road. He spat grit on the ground, then turned and climbed the steps to the inn. The crowd drew back to let him pass and he shoved through the door into the nearly empty common room. Sezae, seated at the bar talking to her father, glanced at him as he approached.

"Roan, what—Are you okay?" she asked.

He shook his head.

"He hasn't paid me yet," he said. "I don't have any money. I don't suppose you'd let me pay you later. I really need a drink."

She glanced at her father.

"It's fine if you don't," Roan said, sliding onto the stool beside her. "You don't know me and I probably shouldn't be drinking anyway. I'll just sit here a while, if you don't mind. I don't really feel like walking back to his place just now."

"He left you here?" Sezae asked.

"Yep," Roan said, running his fingertips along a burn scar in the top of the bar, "just drove off and left me standing in the road. Threw a bunch of dirt in my face, too."

"Asshole," Sezae's father muttered. "What can I get you?"

Roan shook his head. "No, really, I—"

"Come on," Sezae said, nudging him with her elbow, "you need something to wash down all that dust."

He gave her a drawn smile. Across the room, people were starting to file back into the inn, but they didn't spare him much more than a glance.

"Well, all right. Anything but beer, I guess." He made a face and she laughed.

"A man after my own heart," she said. "Dad, make him a Toborran Moonrise."

"Oh, no," Roan said, "nothing fancy. Just ale or wine or something."

"No, no, you have to try this. It's my favorite drink."

Her father pulled a crystal tumbler down off the back shelf and poured an inch of some clear alcohol into it. From somewhere under the counter, he produced a bottle of thick pink liquid and added a single drop to the drink. The pink drop fell straight to the bottom and lay there like a rock. Roan reached for the glass.

"Hang on," Sezae said, "you have to wait for it to rise or it just tastes like alcohol." He arched an eyebrow and stared at the pink droplet stubbornly sitting on the bottom of the glass.

"Is it stuck?" he asked.

"Be patient," Sezae said with a laugh. "It takes a minute, but it's well worth—There is goes."

Roan watched as the pink drop lifted off and began to float up through the liquor, expanding as it went. It was almost as big as the tip of his thumb when it reached the surface and burst, staining the drink a faint, translucent pink.

"Pretty," he said. "Can I drink it now?"

"Yeah, but drink it slow," she said, hopping down from the stool as her father brought over three glasses of ale and a pitcher of beer, "you're too big to carry upstairs." She loaded the drinks onto a tray, but waited as he lifted the glass to his lips and took a hesitant sip, the alcohol cool on his lips but warm in his mouth. He swallowed. "Well, what do you think?"

"It's sweet," he said, surprised. "And smooth. What is it?"

"Vodka and pixie blood," she said as he took another sip. He almost choked and she laughed as she backed away with the tray of drinks. "Not real blood—concentrated pixyfruit juice." She delivered the drinks to a table in one corner and returned with the tray tucked under one arm, jingling a handful of coins, which she passed to her father. "So, regretting your decision to stay with him, eh?"

"Actually, living with Ishaan isn't that bad. It's everything else in my life that's shit right now." He took a long swallow, that smooth heat sliding down his throat and pooling in his gut, slowly warming his whole body. Maybe there was something to be said about getting drunk after all. He sighed. "I found out this morning that my parents are dead."

"Oh, Roan," Sezae said, reaching out to take his hand, "I'm so sorry. What happened?"

He shook his head.

"I-I don't really want—" He took another drink. "They were murdered." He stared down at the bar between them, at her hand holding his, and couldn't stop himself from relating the whole story. As he spoke, telling her all the same lies he'd told Ishaan, it felt like he was talking about someone else's screwed up life. She didn't say a word until he'd finished and raised his glass to his lips.

"I know it's not the same," she said, giving his hand a squeeze, "but I lost my mom to cancer almost two years ago." It wasn't the same, not even close, but he didn't say so. She was trying to be nice. "I do understand that empty feeling inside you, and I know it isn't much of a comfort now, but it will get better."

Roan swirled the pink alcohol in the bottom of the glass, then drained it in a single swallow. It was getting better already.

"Dad, get him another one—"

"No, no, thank you," Roan said quickly, pushing the empty glass across the bar. "I need to get back to Ishaan while I can still walk."

"You're going back?" she asked. "After what he did to you today?"

"That was nothing," Roan said. "You should have heard us yesterday. Finally, we agreed that he couldn't throw me out if I was there every evening and morning to lock and unlock his door. Besides, if I'm not there, he'll have to sleep in the jail, and I doubt anyone wants that." He stood, the room revolving slowly around him, and Sezae reached out to steady him as he swayed on his feet.

"Uh oh," Sezae said, pushing him back against the edge of the bar. "Stay here, I'll hitch up the mules—"

"No, it's okay," he said, straightening up and taking a deep breath. The room stopped spinning. "I can walk. I think the fresh air will clear my head." He took a hesitant step toward the door, but didn't stagger or stumble. "See, I'm fine. Thanks for the drink. And the company. I'll pay you back as soon—"

"Don't worry about it," she said, stepping close and rising up onto her toes to embrace him. He hesitated, then encircled her with his arms, turning his face into her hair and taking a deep breath. She smelled of pipe smoke, sweat, and jasmine and mint shampoo.

She tensed in his arms and he let go, taking a stumbling step backward and kicking the legs of an empty chair.

"Sorry," he said, grabbing the back of the chair as the room spun around him again. He shouldn't have done that. That was stupid. "I'm sorry, I don't—"

"It's okay," she said, reaching out and taking his hand again. "You just surprised me. I thought...Well, I thought Ishaan was more your type than I was." She gave him a crooked smile.

"Ishaan...Oh. No, I-I guess I don't really have a type." Sex was more important than food; he couldn't really afford to be choosy. After a moment, he slipped his hand out of hers. "I appreciate your understanding, but...I shouldn't have done that. I'll see you around." He turned away, pausing long enough for the world to settle back down, and then headed out the door and down the steps into the street.

It was later afternoon than he'd thought, the sun hanging just above the jagged black mountain peaks, its harsh bronze light reflected in every western-facing window. With a sigh, he shook his head and began walking into the sun. He tucked his hands in his pockets and ignored the baleful scowl on Scott's face as he passed the produce stand. Roan didn't care. Maybe he'd think twice before treating his customers like shit.

As Roan left the outlying buildings behind him and the trees began to close in on either side of the road, he regretted not accepting that ride from Sezae. He was tired, his arms and legs leaden, his eyelids heavy, and the road kept rolling beneath his feet every now and then. On second thought, he regretted accepting the drink. This was why he never got drunk.

"Hey." Roan glanced to his left, his head spinning as he turned too fast, and he staggered sideways before regaining his balance. Ishaan, seated in the parked car, was scowling at him from a wide spot just off the road. "Are you drunk?" he asked, opening the door and climbing out. Roan straightened up.

"No," he said, walking toward him. "I—have you been waiting for me?"

Ishaan crossed his arms over his chest.

"It's a long walk and I wanted to make sure you made it home in one piece."

"It's not that far," Roan said, "and I can take care of myself."

"Really?" Ishaan stepped toward him. "You *are* drunk. I've been sitting here for an hour while you were getting plastered."

"It was just one drink," Roan said, walking past him and fumbling with the handle on the car door. It wouldn't work. Ishaan must have locked the door. Irritated, he climbed over the door and fell into the seat, banging his elbow on the dash. "Dammit," he muttered, cradling his aching arm to his chest.

After a moment, Ishaan got back in the car and started it up. Roan slouched down in his seat and rubbed at his sore elbow, watching the trees roll by until he thought he was going to throw up. He closed his eyes and rested his head on the door, not even caring as he dropped off to sleep.

Eight

The late afternoon sunlight filtered through the trees and played across Roan's face as Ishaan turned off the main road. Ishaan envied him, sleeping peacefully, not a danger to anyone. The car lurched into a rut, bouncing Roan's head off the door and he groaned as he sat up, peering blearily around him. For a second, he looked confused, like he didn't know where he was, then he glanced over at Ishaan and it all seemed to come back.

"Stop the car," he said, his words still slurred. One drink. Yeah, right.

"We're almost there," Ishaan said as they rolled past the house and down the gravel tracks to the barn. Roan grabbed for the door handle.

"I mean it. I'm gonna puke." Ishaan hit the brakes and reached over, opening the door with one hand and shoving Roan out of the car with the other. He turned away as Roan vomited, staring out the windshield as Roan retched and choked.

"I hope you learn something from this," he said, raising his voice to be heard over the noise. Roan muttered something and rolled onto his back in the grass, his chest heaving. "You want to shut the door so I can go park?" Roan lifted his head enough to glare at him, then shoved the door shut with his foot. "Thank you."

He glanced in the rear-view mirror as he drove into the barn, watching Roan rise on unsteady legs and stumble toward the house. He had better not throw up on the front steps. Luckily, Ishaan had the house keys, so he didn't have to worry about the carpet.

He couldn't blame Roan for getting drunk—he couldn't really blame him for anything that happened that day, but it didn't stop him from being annoyed. He had enough problems without having to nurse his depressed employee through a hangover. One thing was certain, this had better not effect Roan's ability to perform his job. If someone got hurt because of him—

Ishaan pulled the bags out of the back of the car and tucked them both under one arm so he could shut and lock the barn doors. He hadn't had any trouble since the day he found his horses shot to death in their stalls, but it would only be a matter of time. The dragon hadn't done a damn thing to help him, and he had a feeling that Gus Doras wasn't finished yet.

Roan was seated on the front step, his elbows on his knees and his head in his hands, staring down at the ground. He didn't even move as Ishaan approached.

"Are you dying or something?" Ishaan asked, shifting the bags to his other arm so he could dig the keys out of his pocket.

"Feels like it," Roan muttered and then he groaned. "I think I'm going to be sick again."

Ishaan stepped back.

"What did you have?" Roan turned away and belched, quickly covering his mouth with his hand as his face went white, then green. "And how many?"

Roan took several short, desperate breaths and swallowed hard.

"It was just one. A Torboa Moonbeam—Sezae said—"

"A Toborran Moonrise? No wonder you're sick. Now come on, get up."

"Thanks, but I'll just sit here and finish dying if it's all the same to you."

Ishaan stepped past him and unlocked the door, leaving it open as he headed for the kitchen. He set the bags on the counter and placed the corn and apples in the fridge. Outside, Roan retched again and Ishaan shook his head. Served him right.

After a moment, Ishaan opened the cupboard beside the fridge and pulled out a small jar of yellow powder. Carefully, he measured half a teaspoon into a teacup and filled it with hot water from the kettle on the stove. He stirred it and then carried the steaming drink out to the front step.

"Here," he said, holding the cup down to Roan, "drink this. It'll help."

"I don't want help," Roan said, wrapping his arms around himself and turning away. "I deserve to suffer." He choked and started to sob again. Ishaan rolled his eyes and squatted down beside him.

"Knock it off," he said. "You can be as miserable as you want, but I need you straightened out before I go to sleep, okay? It's important."

"Oh, fine," Roan said, reaching out for the cup. Ishaan jerked back, splashing it across his hand. "What? I thought—"

"It's hot," Ishaan said, "but you need to drink it all in one swallow, even the gritty stuff in the bottom. Can you handle that?"

"I guess we'll find out," Roan replied, reaching for it again. This time, Ishaan let him have it. Roan sniffed the liquid, made a face, then drained the cup. "Ugh, that shit is bitter. What was it?"

"You don't want to know," Ishaan said as he took his teacup and went back inside. It was mostly ground roots and herbs, but even a little powdered dragon urine was usually too much for most people. He'd barely been able to stomach the thought when he found out, but the shit really worked. Not five minutes later, Roan rose from the step and came inside, still pale but no longer vomiting.

"Feeling better?" Ishaan asked as he walked from the kitchen to the bathroom, a package of razor blades and a bottle of shampoo in his hands.

"A little," he said as he sank onto the couch and closed his eyes. "Remind me to thank Sezae for trying to poison me."

"That's why you should never accept strange drinks from beautiful women," Ishaan said, placing his things in the cupboard beside the tub. "She actually *wasn't* trying to kill you," he said as he emerged from the bathroom. "She forgets that humans don't handle alcohol the same way athaenians do."

"Athae—She's not athaenian," Roan said. "She doesn't have silver hair, or purple eyes, or pointed ears."

"No, but her great-grandmother did. Which is why she can hold her liquor better than a man twice her size. Are you hungry?"

Roan groaned.

"I think that's being a bit too ambitious, don't you?"

"A little food will help settle your stomach. I'll heat up a can of soup. Chicken sound good?"

"Not really."

Ishaan ignored him and walked to the kitchen. He finished pulling his things out of the bag—a bottle of ground pepper, a bag of salt, a garden trowel—and carried the rest to Roan's room.

"I put your things on your bed," he said as he crossed behind the couch. He paused and looked down at Roan. "I hope I don't have to stress how much I *don't* want to hear you using that blue stuff on yourself." Roan's eyes opened halfway, then closed again.

"You won't," he said.

"Good. I'll go make that soup now." Ishaan was standing beside the woodstove, stirring the chicken soup when he heard Roan suddenly cry out. "What now?" he called, striding across the room with a dripping spoon in hand.

"Sorry," Roan called. He wasn't in the living room anymore. Ishaan glanced in the bathroom, but he wasn't there, either. "I just remembered that I forgot to check my e-mail when we got home," Roan said, stepping out of his bedroom.

"And are you expecting to hear from someone?" Ishaan asked, licking the cold soup off the back of his hand.

Roan shrugged.

"I wrote my brother. I-I wanted to know if he was all right, considering."

Ishaan nodded and turned to head back into the kitchen, but paused as he had a thought.

"You didn't tell him where you were, did you?" he asked. "You didn't mention the name of the town, or the planet, anything that he might use to find you?"

Roan shook his head.

"No, I just asked if he's okay, that's it."

"Well, make sure you don't, because if he shows up on my doorstep, I'll shoot him."

"Why?" Ishaan stopped in the kitchen doorway and glanced back. "What did he do to you?"

Good question. Ishaan opened his mouth, discovered that he didn't have a good answer, and shut it again.

"Because," he said after a moment, "he's an escaped convict. If he doesn't want to be shot, he should go back to prison, where it's safe." And Ishaan went back to stirring the soup. After they ate, Roan helped him clear the table and then stood and dried the dishes that he washed. Ishaan could feel him, standing at his elbow, gathering his wits and words like an impending storm preparing to break. He tossed the towel down on the counter and headed for his study.

"Hey, do you ever watch that expensive TV of yours?" Roan asked. Ishaan glanced back at him, standing in the doorway with the pan in his hands. He suddenly looked embarrassed. "I-I didn't mean—I just, I don't really feel like being alone right now." Ishaan frowned, not sure how that was any of his concern, and Roan started to turn away.

"Yeah, all right," he said. "It's not like I have anything better to do. What did you have in mind?"

"I don't care," Roan said over the clatter of pots and pans as he put the last of the dishes away.

Ishaan found the remote between the couch cushions and began to flip through the stations while he waited for Roan. Honestly, the TV was for whoever he had staying with him; Ishaan rarely watched it.

"How about a cooking show?" Ishaan asked as Roan crossed behind him and flopped down on the couch.

"How about a movie?" Roan suggested.

Ishaan hadn't really wanted to spend that much time out there, but there was no reason why he had to watch the whole thing. He opened the channel guide and found the page of movies.

"Not a chick flick, please," Roan said, leaning forward to take off his boots. He set them at the far end of the couch and scrunched his stocking feet into the carpet. "You like horror movies?"

"I hate horror movies," Ishaan replied. Just his luck. He probably liked car chases and big exploding shootouts, too. "A foreign film?"

"If I wanted to read the dialogue, I'd get a book," Roan said. Ishaan made a disgusted sound and threw the remote down next to Roan.

"Fine then, you pick something," he said, dropping down into one of the two armchairs. "I'll try not to fall asleep and rape you."

"In my current state of mind," Roan said, picking up the remote and scrolling down the list, "it wouldn't be rape."

Something in his tone sent a sliver of unease squirming through Ishaan's gut. What the hell did he mean by that?

"Hey, what about this one?"

Ishaan glanced at the screen. "Never seen it."

"You'll like it," Roan said. "It's a classic." It was only a quarter past the hour, so they hadn't really missed anything important and Roan quickly filled him in on the details. Ishaan wouldn't have gone so far as to call it a classic, but he didn't hate sitting there and watching the whole thing. In fact, the two hours seemed to pass rather quickly.

"Well, that was entertaining," Ishaan said as the theme music began to play and the credits rolled up the screen. He stood and stretched, then started toward his study.

"Want to watch another one?" Roan asked, grabbing up the remote.

Ishaan glanced at the clock. "Not tonight. I have stuff to do."

Roan looked disappointed, but he nodded.

"Yeah, all right. I've got things to do, too." But he just sat there flipping through the channels, the flickering light bright in his pale gray eyes. Ishaan stepped into his study and glanced back as he shut the door. Roan looked absolutely lost.

With a sigh, Ishaan sank into his desk chair and opened his laptop. Maybe he should have sat with him and watched another stupid movie. It wouldn't have killed him.

No. What was he thinking? They weren't friends. Yes, Roan had a shitty day. He'd probably have a lot more of them, but that wasn't Ishaan's problem. Roan didn't need to be coddled, he needed to suffer, to feel like shit, to cry, to feel sorry for himself, and then he needed to get over it. And the best thing Ishaan could do for him was to give him space.

Nine

Roan stared at the screen without really seeing it, bright flashes of color dancing before his eyes. He thought about getting up, going to the kitchen, and grabbing a couple of beers. Being drunk had been miserable, but it was a different, less painful sort of misery. It was distracting. As long as he had something to do, something to occupy his mind, he could pretend he was okay, but in the quiet, just him and the TV, he couldn't stop thinking that he should have been there. It wouldn't have happened if he'd been there. His parents would still be alive. The thought just kept running around and around inside his head, like mice on a wheel.

The door to Ishaan's study opened and Roan sat up. Maybe he'd changed his mind about that second movie. Ishaan glanced at him and then crossed to the bathroom and shut the door. Roan heard water running and glanced at the clock. Holy hell, almost two hours had passed since the movie ended. He flicked the TV off and shuffled into his room. He ached, probably from vomiting, and he considered just falling down on his bed and letting the world slip away, but Ishaan would need him to lock up once he was finished with his bath. Once he lay down, he didn't want to have to get up again.

He glanced at the computer, started toward it, then picked up the bag on his bed and dumped the contents out on the quilt. He reached for the shampoo, but grabbed the jar of lubricant instead. He held it a moment, then twisted off the lid and raised it to his face, taking a long, deep breath. It smelled cool, clean, herbal. He dabbed his fingers into the jar and rubbed the slick gel between his fingertips.

"What did I tell you about doing that when I was awake?"

Roan glanced over his shoulder at Ishaan, standing in the doorway, once again shirtless and dotted with drops of water from his bath. He quickly screwed the lid back on and dropped it on the bed.

"I was just smelling it," he said.

"With your fingers?" Ishaan asked, raising one eyebrow.

Roan ignored him.

"It's nice stuff," he said as he wiped his slippery fingers on the leg of his jeans. They needed to be washed anyway. "You want to borrow it? You know, since you're going to be—" He mimed jerking-off again.

Ishaan rolled his eyes and turned away.

"You ready to lock me up, or do you need a minute?"

Roan glanced down at the lubricant again, then followed Ishaan out into the living room. Roan grabbed the key out of the cabinet and reached for the door, but Ishaan held it open, a frown on his face as he looked down at Roan.

"You're going to be okay?"

Roan nodded. "I think so. I'm not going to kill myself during the night, if that's what you're asking."

"I wasn't asking," Ishaan said. "I was telling you; you're going to be okay. But it is a comfort to know you'll be here to let me out in the morning." For a second, a smile softened his features, then the scowl returned. "Good night." He shut the door.

"Good night," Roan replied as he locked it. He glanced at the clock, then headed back into his room. It was as if Ishaan was deliberately trying not to like him. The whole story about Hektor seemed like an excuse to be an asshole. So they'd been careless and someone got hurt. It wasn't the end of the world, but Ishaan acted like he'd done something unforgivable. Yes, raping his friend was horrible, but it wasn't his fault. Roan would have bet a month's pay that Hektor had realized that, after the shock wore off. No one could live in the same house as Ishaan and not see that this wasn't his choice.

Roan slipped into his chair and opened the laptop. Maybe he could find Hektor. It might not do any good—he might even be wrong—but if he could get Hektor to tell Ishaan that he for—

Roan had a message. From Kethic. He stared at the screen and felt like he was going to throw up again, his heart suddenly racing. Thank the gods, he wasn't dead, but what was he going to say? Nothing that Roan hadn't already said to himself. His hand shaking, Roan opened the message, his eyes jumping all over the short block of text, picking up a word here and there that made no sense.

Closing his eyes, he forced himself to take a deep breath and start at the beginning.

> It's good to hear from you, brother. I was afraid you were dead. I'm all right; hiding and hungry most of the time. I'm sure you know what I'm talking about. Good thing so many worlds have outernet cafes, eh? I imagine you don't trust me any farther than you could throw a dragon, but we need to meet up. Not now. I don't know if it's safe to talk this way, so we'll work something out later. Just know that I am more sorry than you can ever imagine. I hope you can forgive me someday for mom and dad's deaths. This is all my fault.
> I love you,
> Your big brother

Roan felt like a hand had reached inside his chest and squeezed his heart. He couldn't breathe. It wasn't Kethic's fault, it was *his*. They were-They were looking for-for him...because of Kethic. Roan squeezed his eyes shut as the tears began to fall, biting down on his knuckles to keep from sobbing aloud. It *was* Kethic's fault! He was the reason they were dead!

And he was still after Roan. Roan closed the computer and pushed the chair back, slamming his fists down on his knees. Well, two could play at that game. When the time came, Roan would tell Kethic exactly where he was, and let Ishaan shoot him when he showed up. Ishaan could shoot all of them.

Roan rose and began to pace, back and forth across the room. He couldn't take this any longer. He needed to feed, to glut himself on sex until he couldn't see straight, until the hollow ache within him was filled. The clock struck midnight and he ripped his shirt off over his head, discarding it in a pile on the floor. He snatched up the lubricant and strode out of the room.

At Ishaan's door, he paused, key in hand, and slid back the window, listening. The soft, distant sound of breathing reached his ears and he eased the key into the lock, turned it, and pushed the door open. The night was clear for once, pale blue moonlight streaming in through Ishaan's barred windows and pooling on the floor, revealing the shape and shadow of the man in bed, but hiding all else from sight. Roan turned on the light and stood beside the closet doors, staring at the side of Ishaan's face as he lay on his stomach, one arm under his pillow, the other crooked, his hand tucked beneath his chin, his hair swept back off his brow.

Roan stepped forward and pulled the covers off him, dragging them off onto the floor at the foot of the bed. Ishaan made a small sound and drew his arms closer to his body. The room was a little cold, but Roan barely felt it as he unbuttoned his pants and slipped out of them, dropping them in a pile near the door. He set the jar of lubricant on the end of the bed and then slowly crawled up Ishaan's body, straddling his legs as he reached up and grabbed the waistband of his pajamas.

As he drew them down around Ishaan's thighs, Ishaan raised his head and glanced over his shoulder.

"Roan?" he asked, his voice thick and sleepy. Roan froze, his heart fluttering wildly in his throat as Ishaan blinked and stared at him. "What...you doing?" Hardly daring to breathe, Roan leaned forward, close enough to see into Ishaan's empty eyes.

"You're asleep," Roan whispered in a relieved sigh. "Dammit, don't scare me like that." Ishaan didn't respond, but he pulled his arms underneath him and started to rise up. Roan threw his full weight on Ishaan's back, shoving him down to the mattress. He waited for the surprised exclamation as Ishaan woke, but Ishaan just lay there.

"All right," Roan said in Ishaan's ear, "here's how this is going to work." He wasn't sure if Ishaan understood anything he was saying, but it was worth a try. "You are going to behave or I'll walk out of here and you'll never touch me again. Unless you want to beat your own meat for the rest of your life, I'm in control, understand?" He didn't seem to, but after a moment Ishaan slowly nodded his head. Roan started to sit up, but hesitated. How much could you trust someone when they were asleep? He supposed it didn't really matter.

Roan climbed off and finished removing Ishaan's pants, then ran his hands up the insides of Ishaan's thighs, his eyes sliding closed as he savored the smooth skin, the hard muscle beneath, the energy that rolled off him like heat from a flame. Ishaan groaned and spread his legs, and Roan moved to kneel between them, his hands sliding from thigh to butt, gripping and kneading the flesh, making Ishaan writhe against the sheet.

He grabbed Ishaan by the hips, encouraging him to rise up on his knees, and then reached between his legs to grasp his erection. Warm and smooth as a Toborran Moonrise, the sex surged through him, making him feel heavy and buoyant at the same time, every nerve standing on end, and yet completely numb. He leaned down and bit one cheek, then the other, not hard enough to bruise, not hard enough to wake, just enough to draw a long, low moan out of Ishaan.

"Do you like that?" Roan asked, biting down again, leaving little red indentations in the shape of his teeth. "Do you like this?" He ran his tongue along the marks, his own length hardening at the sounds Ishaan made. "I bet you'll love this," Roan murmured, and he slipped his tongue between Ishaan's cheeks and stroked his opening.

Roan jerked back, gasping for breath, as the energy hit him like a kick in the gut and the room spun around him for an instant. It had been so long since he'd fed properly, he'd forgotten it could feel like that. A whore, lying there waiting for him to finish, could never feed him like someone who actually wanted it. And holy shit did Ishaan want it.

"More," Ishaan said in that guttural growl, raising his ass higher in the air and spreading his legs wider. Roan licked his lips, the heavy, salty taste of Ishaan lingering on his tongue, but it wasn't a bad taste. In fact, he kind of liked it. Roan braced himself this time, but was still hit by a wave of dizziness as he pressed his tongue to that tight ring of muscle, ran the tip around it, teasing him as he started to enter, then pulled back. Inside him the demon writhed, wanting to come out, wanting to shove that thick, four inch tongue in Ishaan's ass, but he ignored it. It was the reason for all his pain, all his misery. He hated it, and as long as he could feed, as long as it was kept sated, he would never let it out again.

Roan grabbed the jar of lubricant and twisted off the lid, dipped his fingers inside and spread the slippery blue stuff across both palms. He began to stroke and pull at Ishaan's arousal as he pressed his face into Ishaan's ass and drove his tongue as deep as it would go. Ishaan cried out and pushed back against him, his body trembling as Roan worked his tongue in and out of that tight, hot hole. He began to stroke himself, a shiver racing up his spine as he rubbed the lubricant across his skin.

The feeling was indescribable. He wasn't sure if it was hot or cold, but a faint tingling sensation made him grow even harder in his hand. The shit might be expensive, but it was worth every laene. Roan licked at Ishaan's entrance, groaning softly as he jerked himself off, nearly drowning in the energy that poured into him. It was so good. He needed it so much.

"Fuck me."

Roan gasped and pulled back. Ishaan was gripping handfuls of the sheet, his back damp with sweat as he lay with his chest on the bed and his ass in the air, his eyes closed and lips parted.

"Wha-What did you say?" Roan asked, but Ishaan didn't respond, except to groan and press back toward him again. Roan leaned down, licked him again, not sure if what he'd heard was what Ishaan had said. He drew back and regarded Ishaan's ass, already slick with spit and opened by Roan's tongue. He rubbed the slippery gel between his fingertips again. Ishaan would never know, not if he was careful.

Roan dipped his fingers back in the jar and smeared the gel across Ishaan's opening. Ishaan made a high, desperate sound in his throat as Roan slipped two fingers inside him. He was already so relaxed, so slick, that Roan hardly had to stretch him at all. As he rose up on his knees and rubbed the head of his erection across Ishaan's entrance, he wondered if Ishaan had ever had a man inside him before. Probably not, he decided, trying to ignore the strange feeling of guilt curling about in his gut like an eel, dark and slimy.

It wasn't like this mattered. He wouldn't remember it, so he could still go and find a nice guy to lose his virginity to, if he wanted. He'd never know any different. This didn't mean a thing.

Roan eased inside, watching the muscles in Ishaan's arms and shoulders bunch as he pulled at the sheet, feeling his abdomen and thighs tighten as he slipped deeper. Ishaan made a strangled sound, neither pleasure nor pain, but akin to both, and Roan paused, running his hands down and back up Ishaan's thighs, along his back, waiting for the discomfort to fade. He knew from experience, it usually hurt a little, being stretched, being filled, but after the initial pain, it transformed into a deep and satisfying kind of hurt, an ache that only made the pleasure more intense. At least, that's how it had been for him. Not every guy was the same, though. He'd met a couple in his travels who flat out refused to let another man inside them. Said it always hurt the whole time, no matter what. Roan hoped that Ishaan wasn't like those guys.

He didn't seem to be. After a moment, he began to push back against Roan, taking him deeper. Roan grabbed his hips and began to thrust into him, little short strokes to finish loosening him up. He gritted his teeth and tried not to let his fingers dig too deep into Ishaan's hips. That last thing he wanted to do was leave bruises. Of course, coming too soon was just one step above that. Everything in him wanted to drive deep and lose it inside Ishaan, but he couldn't. He couldn't.

He closed his eyes, leaned forward, and wrapped his arms around Ishaan's waist, one hand stroking Ishaan's shaft, the other squeezing and tugging at his balls as he rocked his hips and rubbed across Ishaan's prostate. Ishaan made the most delicious noises, breathless, moaning gasps and whimpers, shaking and shuddering beneath Roan until he finally cried out and came, spilling his seed across Roan's hands and the sheet beneath him.

Roan choked back a strangled scream, thrust deep, felt Ishaan tighten around him, and then pulled out, his seed splattering across the back of Ishaan's thigh. He took a shuddering breath, nearly a sob, and slumped forward, on top of Ishaan. He had wanted to come inside him, wanted to feel that tight heat surrounding him as he came, but it was just too hard to clean up. Semen on the bed would be nothing new to Ishaan, but if he found it inside himself? A little harder to explain.

After a moment, Roan sat up and screwed the lid back on the jar of lubricant. Ishaan was sleeping peacefully once again, faint red teeth-marks on both ass cheeks, and Roan reached out to run his fingertips across them. Ishaan drew away, mumbling something unintelligible into his pillow, and Roan climbed off the bed. He pulled the blankets back up onto the bed and covered Ishaan before grabbing his jar and his pants and turning out the light.

He shut and locked the door and then crossed to the bathroom to wash up, the demon quiet and sated inside him, but the hollow, empty pain in his chest still as deep and as raw as before. He turned on the faucet and washed his hands, staring down into the sink so he wouldn't have to look at himself in the mirror. How could he have done that? It was one thing to pleasure Ishaan and feed off the energy; he had to or he'd become dangerous, but fucking him, enjoying it? He closed his eyes and leaned on the sink, feeling like he was going to be sick.

He was a monster.

Ten

For a moment, Ishaan thought he was still dreaming, still lost in the ether, because he was warm and comfortable, lying in bed with his blankets over him, not curled up, naked on the floor, shivering in the chilly morning air. He opened his eyes, watched sparkling dust motes dance in the sunlight, drifting on lazy currents, and then his gaze dropped to the floor, to his pajamas piled beside the bed. So he wasn't dreaming.

He pushed back the covers, goose bumps racing across his skin as he sat up. He frowned. Something wasn't right. Hesitantly, he tightened his sphincter muscles...

Ishaan leapt to his feet, spinning around to shove the blankets off onto the floor. No blood. That was a relief, at least. He wrinkled his nose at the still damp stains upon the sheet, felt the semen on his stomach and thigh, stiff and sticky. Son-of-a-bitch, he was tired of waking up with this shit on him. And what in Cheyn's worst nightmare had he found in this room that would fit in his ass?

He'd been so careful to remove *anything* even remotely the right size or shape. He put his pajamas back on and shook out the blankets, ripped the sheet off the bed, lifted the mattress and looked underneath, jerked the drawers out of his dresser—There wasn't one single thing. He threw open the closet doors and began shifting the boxes inside, but they were all locked. He'd been so careful not to let it happen again. Which left only one explanation.

He heard the little window in the door slide open.

"Ishaan, are you awake?" Roan asked. Ishaan threw down the box he was holding and stalked over to the door.

"Roan, what the hell did you do?" he demanded.

Roan's eyes grew wide.

"What did I—Nothing! What do you—" He leaned closer to the window. "Are you even awake?"

"Of course I'm awake," Ishaan snapped, slamming his fist against the door. "Let me out of here."

"I don't know," Roan said. "You're acting weird. Let me see your eyes."

Ishaan pressed his forehead against the door and glared at Roan.

"Okay, I guess you are," he said, and Ishaan paced across the room and back as Roan got the key out of the cabinet and unlocked the door. "Now, what's going—"

Ishaan shoved the door back against the wall and grabbed Roan my the front of the shirt, slamming him against the wood.

"What? What did I—"

"You gave me something, didn't you?" Ishaan asked between his teeth. "Slipped it through the window? Did you think you could shut me up, or did you just want to see me shove something in my ass? Was it funny? Did it turn you on? What was it?" He slammed Roan against the door again. "*What was it?*"

"I-Ishaan, I have no idea—I didn't do anything, I swear." Ishaan turned away, stalking over to the bed and shaking out the blankets again. "Wh-what are you looking for?" Roan asked timidly. Ishaan flung the blankets down.

"I don't know!" he shouted. "Something...I woke up in bed this morning and my ass is sore, like I've been fucking myself with something, only—" He stopped, tensed, turned slowly to face Roan. "Did you come in here last night?" he asked. "Did you—Did you have sex with me?"

Roan recoiled.

"Hell, no! That's-that's just—disgusting."

"You didn't seem that disgusted when you came on to me yesterday," Ishaan pointed out. Roan stiffened and crossed his arms over his chest.

"I had just found out that my parents were dead—I wasn't in my right mind," he said. "Besides, I didn't want to have sex with you, I wanted you to beat the shit out of me, I wanted to suffer, I wanted to die. Sex was the farthest thing from my mind."

"Fine," Ishaan snapped, "you didn't have sex with me and you didn't give me anything. So why does my asshole hurt?"

"Well," Roan said, absently scratching at the side of his jaw, "I once knew a guy who could shove his entire hand in his ass—"

"Damn it, Roan, don't tell me shit like that," Ishaan said, holding up his hands and turning them back and forth in the light. Was that...Was that *shit* under his fingernails? He didn't want to know. He shoved past Roan and ran to the bathroom, turning on the hot water and letting it run until it was near scalding. His hands stung, red as lobsters, but it didn't help. He still felt filthy. He shut off the sink faucet and stepped over to the tub. He needed a bath.

With steam filling the room and the water as hot as he could stand, Ishaan slipped out of his pajamas and into the bath, drawing a hissing breath between his teeth as the water closed over his body. He shut his eyes and leaned back against the tub, teeth gritted as he washed himself, the pain erasing all traces of whatever he might have done.

What was he going to do, have Roan bind his hands to the bed frame each night? His parents hadn't known what to do with him, so they had tried tying him to the bed. He woke with his throat so raw he could barely talk, and they hadn't gotten a moment's sleep the entire night. It seemed that if he couldn't masturbate, he just screamed and screamed. He didn't want to go through that again.

"Hey, Ishaan—"

Ishaan jumped as Roan opened the door and stuck his head in. "What do—Oh. Sorry."

Roan's gray eyes lingered on him for a moment, then he looked down at the tile at his feet. "I didn't know you were—I was wondering what you wanted for breakfast."

"I'm not really hungry," Ishaan said. He needed to remember to lock the bathroom door from now on.

Roan nodded and started to withdraw, but then leaned back in again. "You know, I don't think it would kill you to relax a bit," he said. "I mean, have you thought about getting yourself some toys and lubricant? Might make things easier on you."

Ishaan just stared at him, hardly able to believe his ears. Roan was *not* suggesting—

"Wouldn't it be better than wondering why your ass was sore?"

"You—Get the hell out of here," Ishaan sputtered.

"Okay," Roan said, backing out of the room, "I was just saying—"

"Get out!" Ishaan shouted, grabbing the bar of soap off the shelf beside the tub and throwing it across the room. It hit the door and broke into three pieces, which bounced and clattered across the tile floor. Ishaan sank back into the water, his chest heaving, and clenched his fists. Roan had no idea what he was talking about. *This* was why he didn't want to be friends. Friends thought they had a right to poke their noses into business that wasn't theirs.

Ishaan heaved himself out of the tub and grabbed a towel off the rack, rubbing the stiff terrycloth across his skin hard enough to sting. Roan had no idea and no right to come in here and start offering advice, like he knew something about Ishaan's suffering. He knew nothing about it! Ishaan threw the towel down and glanced around before remembering that he hadn't brought any clean clothes to change into. Damn it. Well, he wasn't going to put his dirty pajamas back on. He grabbed the damp towel and wrapped it around his waist, silently praying that Roan was in his own room.

He opened the door to the flickering light of the television, Roan perched on the arm of the couch as he watched a weather report. A chance of rain this afternoon. Great. Roan glanced at him as he stepped out into the living room, those pale eyes traveling unnervingly down his body.

"Get off of there," Ishaan snapped as he walked toward his room. "You're going to break the arm."

Roan shifted to the seat.

"So, do you want to work in the garden this morning before the rain comes?"

Ishaan stopped in the doorway, then turned and stalked over to the couch.

"Don't *ever* talk to me about my sickness again. You have no idea what I've been through, what I go through. If you're tired of listening to me, you're free to leave—"

"I'm not going anywhere," Roan said, pointing the remote past him to turn off the TV. "That's not what—I just don't think you should have to suffer like you have been."

"And why not?" Ishaan demanded. "Don't I deserve to be punished for the things that I've done? I'm an animal, a monster, a demon—I don't even deserve to live."

Roan leapt to his feet, standing chest to chest with Ishaan, and Ishaan had to force himself to stand his ground.

"That's not fair," Roan practically shouted. "You can't help what you are. You try not to hurt anyone. You have as much right to live and be happy as anyone else."

"And you think a handful of sex toys are going to make me happy?" Ishaan asked. Roan seemed to suddenly realize how close he was and sank back onto the couch.

"Maybe...maybe you could find someone who understands—"

Ishaan laughed, the sound harsh and echoing in the silent house. "You think there's anyone out there who would let me rape them—"

"You can't rape the willing," Roan said, but Ishaan ignored him.

"I don't want a whore in my house," Ishaan said. "I will not pay someone for that."

"But if you could find someone who wanted to—"

"No, Roan!" Ishaan shouted. "No one would *ever* want to."

Roan stared up at him, opened his mouth to say something, but Ishaan didn't want to hear it. "I don't want to talk about this anymore," he said. "You could never understand what it's like to be hated for something you can't help, so don't pretend like you understand what I'm going through. This is how it has to be and if you don't like it, you know where the door is. Now excuse me while I go put some clothes on." It was chilly in just a damp towel.

He took his time dressing and putting his room back together, postponing the inevitable moment when he'd have to go back out and face Roan again. Did Roan really think it would be that easy to find someone willing to have sex with him? Did he really think Ishaan had never looked? Yes, she'd been a whore, but that had just made it worse. Not even his money had convinced her to spend a second night with him. She'd said he was rough, almost brutal, and insensitive, concerned only with his own pleasure. He swore he'd never use anyone like that again. It was inhuman, and it made them nothing more than a convenient hole to fuck.

He glanced up from smoothing his quilt for the third time to find Roan standing in his doorway, watching him.

"What?" he asked. He so did not want to have this discussion again.

"I'm making eggs," Roan said. "You want some?"

"I said I wasn't hungry." Roan shrugged.

"That was earlier. I thought you might have changed your mind." He started to leave. "You should eat something," he said over his shoulder. "Or is starving yourself part of your punishment?"

"Fine," Ishaan called after him, "let's eat eggs. Eggs will fix everything, won't they?"

"They won't hurt," Roan replied. Ishaan stomped around his room for a few more minutes, tugging on his sheets, punching his pillow into different shapes, and then he realized how childish he was being. He couldn't avoid Roan. They lived in the same house, ate at the same table. Ignoring him was even proving to be difficult. It seemed like they were either fighting, or getting along too well. There was no middle ground, no polite, disinterested indifference. Roan was one of those all or nothing guys; either they were friends or enemies. Friends was out of the question, but enemies wasn't all that much better of a choice. Why couldn't they just get along civilly?

When Ishaan finally ventured out into the living room, he heard the crack and sizzle of eggs being broken into a hot pan. After a moment's hesitation, he headed for the kitchen. Roan was standing beside the woodstove, turner in hand and sweat sticking his blond hair to his brow. He glanced up, then looked back down into the pan and poked at the whitening edges of the eggs.

"I hope eggs are enough," he said. "You're out of bread and I don't know how to cook anything else." Ishaan noted that he'd said *You're* out of bread, not *We're* out of bread. He drew a slow breath, letting that turn over in his mind.

Finally, he said, "Well, we have been eating a lot of toast. Did you check the freezer?" He stepped over to the fridge and opened the freezing compartment, a package of freezer burned trout leaping out at him. He shoved it back in. "I usually keep an extra loaf in here..." But aside from the trout and a few packages of venison burger from the buck he'd shot last fall, the freezer was empty. "I guess not."

"I guess you should have bought some in town yesterday," Roan said, using the *you* again. Ishaan was finding that he didn't like it much.

"I don't buy bread in town," Ishaan said, closing the freezer door. "We can make our own."

Roan glanced at him, his choice of words apparently not lost on the young man. Good. Roan needed to know that as long as he lived in the house, he was responsible for half the work; half the cleaning, half the gardening, half the cooking...Okay, maybe not the cooking. Ishaan stepped over to him and took the turner from his hand, quickly flipping the eggs over before the edges got any blacker.

"I was just about to—That stove is hotter than I thought," he said in his defense.

Ishaan shook his head and sighed. "Get the plates and silverware out, would you? And maybe after we eat, you can help me burn some bread, too."

"What about the garden?" Roan asked, taking two plates down from the cupboard. "I went out there while you were in the bathroom and there's all kinds of little weed things sprouting up between the rows."

"That happens," Ishaan said. "We can do the gardening while the bread bakes. If you want." Maybe he was trying too hard to be polite. He almost seemed nice.

"Sounds good to me," Roan said.

Ishaan didn't reply. He pulled the pan off the stove and stepped over to the counter, deftly scooping the eggs up and delivering them to their plates without breaking the yolks. On second thought, the yolks might have cooked too long to break. He almost always broke one.

Roan took his plate into the dining area as Ishaan sprinkled his breakfast with salt and pepper. He took a seat across from Roan and neither spoke as they began to eat. That was fine, until Ishaan realized that Roan never looked up from his plate, then it became uncomfortable, oppressive. Damn it, he didn't want to feel like this in his own home.

"So," he asked finally, because Roan was obviously not going to break the silence, "got any ideas for dinner?" Roan just shook his head, but that might have been because his mouth was full. "I've got some venison burger in the freezer. I could cook that up, make it into a gravy, and put it over potatoes."

"Sounds good to me," Roan said again. Ishaan stared at him, but he continued to watch his plate.

"Is something bothering you?" Ishaan asked as calmly as he could manage. Roan glanced up at him, then looked away.

"You could say that," he said, poking at his eggs. A dribble of thick, bright yellow yolk oozed out. "Doesn't really matter, though—I'm not allowed to talk about it."

"Hasn't stopped you yet," Ishaan said. Roan opened his mouth, but Ishaan didn't give him the chance to speak. "Why are my problems so fascinating to you? Am I some kind of social science project? Or is it just a convenient distraction from your own miserable life?"

Roan shoved his chair back from the table and started to get up, but Ishaan slammed his fist down on the table hard enough to bounce the silverware off both their plates. "Sit your ass back down," he said. "You started this; you don't get to run away now."

"Why not? It's what you'd do."

"*Neither* of us is leaving this table until this gets settled. Now sit down and answer my questions."

Roan dropped into the chair and crossed his arms over his chest.

"Your problems aren't *fascinating*," Roan said scornfully. "It's like watching a train wreck; horrifying, and I want to help, I just don't know what to do."

"I never asked for your help," Ishaan said, pushing his plate of eggs to the side. "I never would—"

"I know," Roan said, combing his fingers back through his hair, "and you wouldn't accept my help even if I knew what to do. You enjoy suffering—"

"I do not," Ishaan said.

Roan rolled his eyes.

"Oh, please. If you weren't miserable, you wouldn't be anything."

"What does it matter to you?" Ishaan asked. "Why do you care?"

"Because I like you," Roan said and Ishaan watched in horror as his face colored. "I don't mean—Not like *that*, Ishaan. I barely know you, but when you're not *trying* to be an asshole, you're nice and-and you remind me of my brother."

Ishaan raised his eyebrows.

"I remind you of the guy who pimped you out as a child and destroyed your family? *Thanks*." Roan drew a slow breath and bit the inside of his lip, staring down at his plate as if the eggs held some kind of secret.

"I haven't been completely honest with you," he said at last. "Kethic didn't force me to become a whore." He glanced up, but Ishaan just sat back in his chair and crossed his arms over his chest, waiting. "We didn't have a lot of money growing up," Roan said. "It was always paycheck to paycheck, and then our father got laid off and the bills started piling up—We were going to be evicted.

"And then Kethic found this job and started bringing money home every night. He saved us. I was only thirteen, but I wanted to help, too, so one evening I followed him to 'work' and saw him blowing some guy in an alley and getting money for it. He was so mad at me. Made me swear not to tell mom and dad, and tried to send me home, but I still wanted to help. We found out that word spread fast among those kinds of people and that they'd pay ten times as much to be sucked off by a thirteen year old."

"That's despicable," Ishaan said, shaking his head. He felt nauseous. Roan cleared his throat and shifted uncomfortably in his seat.

"That's why I didn't tell you in the first place. It was a horrible situation, but we didn't really have any other choice. Dad couldn't find work, mom was losing her sight, we were—"

"Roan, that's not what I meant," Ishaan said. "I meant those kinds of men were despicable. I wasn't judging you." He wasn't sure *why* he wasn't—he had a teenage prostitute sitting at his table—but for some reason, it didn't matter. "Was it just oral or did you have sex with them?"

Roan's eyes seemed to search his face, then he looked away again.

"Not at first. Kethic did, but he said I was too young. He made me wait until I was almost fifteen and then—" He laughed, but not like it was funny. "He had this idea to let word slip that I was looking to sell my virginity to the highest bidder."

"How much did you get?"

"Ten thousand."

Ishaan raised his eyebrows.

"Ten thousand coins? Damn."

Roan shook his head.

"Not coins—ilea."

"You're kidding. My house isn't worth ten thousand ilea."

For a second, a smirk flitted across Roan's face.

"He could afford it. He was this rich older guy—owned a couple of big apartment buildings. Might have owned ours, come to think of it. He was actually really nice, aside from his lusting after teenage virgins. He was one of the few who seemed to care as much about how I felt as he did himself." He fell silent for a moment. "Honestly, I don't regret that night. It could have gone so much worse."

Ishaan didn't know how to respond to that. He was right, but it felt wrong to agree.

"So, if your brother isn't some monster who forced you into prostitution, does that mean you're not really on the run from him?"

"No, that part's true, unfortunately. That's another reason that I lied. It's hard to admit that when we got caught, I turned on him and let him take the fall for me. I'm a coward and I lied to save my ass, and I am ashamed of myself."

It seemed like there was more he wanted to say, but he just stared down at the half an egg on his plate. Ishaan reached across the table and slid the plate aside, catching and holding Roan's gaze when he looked up.

"You were a scared kid and you did what anyone would have done, and if your brother can't see that, then it's his problem. You need to let it go."

Roan laughed again, humorlessly. "It's easy to say that, isn't it? Just let it go, get over it, quit blaming yourself, it wasn't your fault—but it's a whole 'nother thing to actually do it. Isn't it, Ishaan?"

Ishaan stood and Roan rose with him. "I thought we weren't leaving this table until things got settled."

"I was just clearing the dishes," Ishaan said, grabbing his plate and reaching for Roan's.

Roan snatched it up first. "I'll help."

They carried the dishes to the kitchen and scraped them into the trash before setting them in the sink.

"You want to start on that bread now?" Ishaan asked, opening the cupboard and pulling down a large mixing bowl.

Roan crossed his arms over his chest and leaned against the counter. "I'd rather finish this conversation. We dragged my shameful past out into the light, now it's your turn. Why are you so damned determined to be alone?"

"Because it's easier," Ishaan said, jerking open the fridge and pulling out the butter and eggs. "You have no idea what it's like to wake up and realize that you've hurt someone you care about. I can't be sure I won't hurt someone in my sleep, but I *can* be sure that no one I care about is near."

"That's why you don't want Sezae or your daughter around..." Ishaan turned away, fighting tears at the thought. He swallowed hard and blinked them away. "And that's why you won't let yourself like me."

Ishaan laughed. "What's to like? You're annoying and clingy and always sticking your nose where it doesn't belong."

"Ishaan," Roan said quietly, "I won't ever let anything happen, but if something did, if you got out of your room and came after me, I wouldn't blame you. I mean, who could resist this ass, right?" He chuckled and was still smiling as Ishaan turned to face him, but then grew dead serious again. "In fact, I don't see why you'd ever have to know. Unless you wanted me to tell you, that is."

Ishaan opened his mouth, then closed it again. He felt like he should say, 'Yes, tell me' but if he was honest with himself—

"I don't want to know," he said, turning away again. He felt like a coward for saying it, but it was the truth. "If you think you could hide it from me—"

"I could."

Ishaan nodded and headed for the pantry, but a sudden thought chilled him to the bone. He glanced back at Roan.

"Are you?" he asked. Roan frowned. "Hiding something from me?"

"Oh. No, I'm not," Roan said.

Ishaan studied those gray eyes, that youthful face. He looked like he was telling the truth. But then, he always looked like he was telling the truth. Maybe it wasn't such a good idea to agree to being lied to. Now he would wonder if everything was a lie. Ishaan slipped into the pantry and switched on the light, standing for a moment in the middle of the tiny room.

If he was going to believe anything Roan ever said to him, he would have to trust that Roan wouldn't lie to him without a good reason. Could he do that? Could he trust him? He supposed he'd have to.

Eleven

Once the bread was baked and the garden weeded, Ishaan surprised Roan by pulling a pair of old cane fishing poles out of the pantry. He'd been uncharacteristically nice ever since he'd come out of the pantry with the flour, sugar, and baking whatnot, but it was beginning to get alarming. Roan kept waiting for the bad news.

"What do you think, you want fish for dinner tomorrow?" Ishaan asked as he handed one of the poles to Roan. Roan looked dubiously at the old pole.

"I suppose," he said. "You really think we could catch something with these?"

"I do it all the time," Ishaan replied, bending down to dig into the cupboard to the left of the sink. "The fish don't care what sort of pole you've got, all they're interested in is—Aha!" He stood and shut the cupboard, a small jar of something pink in his hand, which he held out to Roan. "The bait."

"Dehydrated Kalgaxian Tipsid Shrimp," Roan read off the faded label. "Irresistible to 99% of fish tested. Satisfaction guaranteed." He glanced up at Ishaan. "This shit really works?"

"Satisfaction guaranteed," Ishaan said, pointing to the words on the label. "Don't you think that if it didn't I'd have gotten my money back?" Roan shrugged. If he was that rich, it would probably be too much of a hassle to go through for a couple of coins. He glanced at the price tag still stuck to the lid.

"Holy shit!" For six ilea, yeah, it'd be worth the hassle.

"And that was on sale," Ishaan said as he headed for the door. Roan shook his head and followed, waiting at the edge of the woods while Ishaan dumped the weeds out of a tin bucket. Roan glanced up at the sky, blue now, but with dark gray clouds bunched up to the east.

"The weather guy said it was going to rain," Roan said as Ishaan led him through the trees.

"It isn't raining now."

"Yeah, but it could start."

"What, are you afraid you'll melt?" Ishaan asked with a laugh.

"No, but...I don't really want to get all wet and cold. Why can't we do this tomorrow?"

"Weather could be worse tomorrow," Ishaan said. "Around here, once it starts to rain, it usually lasts three or four days." He glanced over his shoulder. "Why? You got something better to do?"

"No," Roan said, "I just—"

Ahead of him, Ishaan stopped, looked around, and then headed off again, though not on the same path. Actually, there wasn't a path. Roan hurried after him, a knot of unease growing in his gut as he realized that he hadn't been paying attention and had no idea in which direction the house lay.

"Ishaan," he asked after a moment, "you're not mad at me, are you?"

Ishaan stopped short and turned, a frown on his face. Roan swallowed hard.

"Why would you ask that?" Ishaan asked.

"Well, I— just—" He forced a laugh. "I mean, it's not like I thought you were leading me out into the woods to kill me and then dump my body in the river."

Ishaan just stared at him, which, under the circumstances, wasn't comforting. Roan licked dry lips. "You-you're not, are you?"

Ishaan rolled his eyes. "No, you idiot, I'm not going to kill you. I thought, after our conversation, that I'd try to be a little nicer, but that's obviously been a waste of time—"

"Oh, don't start that," Roan said with a laugh. "I was only kidding. C'mon, let's go catch some fish before it starts raining." He motioned with his pole for Ishaan to keep going and after a moment Ishaan turned and began walking again. Roan let out a relieved sigh. For a minute there, he'd really wondered. He shook his head. It was absurd; Ishaan wouldn't hurt him. He hurried to catch up.

Ishaan led him to a place where the bank dropped off sharply down to the water and the river flowed slow and deep. Both sides of the river were lined with great drooping willows and tall, spindly blue cottonwoods, a carpet of rotting leaves broken only occasionally by a patch of grass or a fading elisade, the pink petals tattered and curling under.

"We should have brought a blanket or something to sit on," Roan said, glancing around at the damp ground. Ishaan laughed and set the tin pail down.

"We're not going to be here that long," he said and held out his hand for the jar of bait. The desiccated shrimp looked like shriveled pink cashews with spiky legs and Ishaan handled them like they were made of glass. He shoved the barbed fish hook in under the shell, starting just behind the head and emerging in the middle of the back. Roan started to bait his own hook, but Ishaan took it from him. "If you don't do it just right, they can wriggle right off the hook."

"Wriggle?" Roan asked, looking down at the dried up shrimp. "Right. And how many years have you had these things?"

"About ten," Ishaan said, handing Roan his baited pole.

"Ten years. I don't know about you, but after ten years in a jar, I wouldn't feel all that wriggly." Ishaan started to frown and say something, but he just shook his head and chuckled.

"Tipsid shrimp are found in the wild in only place—Bralikt' Sashali."

"Sounds pretty," Roan said, holding the skewered shrimp up to a narrow beam of sunlight. With the light shining behind it, he could see all the organs and chambers inside.

"The name means *Never Rain*," Ishaan said. "It's a giant desert valley." Roan glanced from his shrimp to Ishaan and then back again.

"A desert?"

"Yeah. It only rains every fifteen or twenty years."

"So...these are like, dust shrimp?" Ishaan stepped over to the riverbank and swung his baited hook out over the water. He dipped the dried shrimp into the river, then pulled it back out. Roan raised his eyebrows as the shriveled shrimp swelled up and began to kick its little spiky legs.

"They can wait in the sand for thirty years or more for the rain to come," Ishaan said, casting his line for real this time. "When it does, the valley floods—a foot or two of water that might last a couple of weeks. Everything that has been lying dormant bursts back to life: insects, algae, plants, and tipsid shrimp. They pop out of the sand, spawn and die. The eggs—Aha, got one!" Roan watched, mouth open, as Ishaan reeled in a speckled trout as long as his forearm. Ishaan pried its mouth open, a slightly busted, but still kicking shrimp on the hook as he pulled it out. He dropped the fish in the bucket and glanced at Roan. "That's one for me, none for you."

"I didn't know we were keeping score," Roan said, stepping up to the edge of the bank. He flipped the baited hook out into the middle of the river.

"You'll never catch anything like that," Ishaan said, and he cast out to the far bank. "Anyway, the eggs hatch after a day and a half and the shrimp eat the algae until the water dries up, and then they burrow into the sand and dry out and wait for the next rain."

"Wow," Roan said. "So, somebody has to go out and sift the desert to—"

"Used to," Ishaan said. "Now they have big tipsid shrimp farms all over the universe. My father took me to one when I was a—"

"Oh! Oh, I got a bite," Roan shouted as the rod nearly jumped out of his hands. He reeled in a big, ugly fish with a gaping maw and yellow spines down its back. "What is it?" he asked as it danced on the end of the line, flipping icy water on both of them.

"A barbed hautfish," Ishaan said, reeling in his own line and leaning his pole against the trunk of a cottonwood. "Careful—just put it on the ground."

Roan lowered the tip of the rod and the fish began to flop across the ground. Ishaan stepped forward and planted his boot on the fish's tail, then leaned down and carefully extracted the hook. Roan's shrimp wasn't as lucky as Ishaan's, but it was still alive. Ishaan hooked his fingers in the hautfish's mouth and lifted it out of the leaf litter. "These spines," he said, pointing, "are mildly poisonous. Won't kill you, but it causes severe swelling of the area, fever, nausea, body aches—"

"So, a real nasty fish," Roan said. Just his luck. Ishaan dropped it into the bucket. "What are you—"

"They may be nasty, but the flesh has a rich, buttery flavor. It's probably the tastiest fish on the planet. Nice job." Roan stood in shock as Ishaan smiled at him, but he quickly smiled back. This was going to take a while to get used to, but if Ishaan was sincere...They grabbed their rods and cast together.

Ishaan reeled in two more trout before his shrimp finally kicked the bucket. Roan got one, but it was the largest of all of them. The clouds had finally blanketed the sky in ominous gray and the wind blew gusty and cold between the trees as Ishaan led the way back through the woods. Before long, Roan noticed the first patter of rain on the leaves overhead.

"I told you it was going to rain," he said, hurrying ahead of Ishaan.

"I never said it wasn't," Ishaan replied. Roan glanced around, looking for a trail or some sign of habitation, but all he could see were the trunks of oak and maple. "You better wait for me or you're going to get yourself lost."

"Well, then hurry up," Roan said, glancing up at the thick canopy above his head. A heavy drop of water splashed across his cheek and ran down his neck, under his collar, making him shiver.

"You really don't like the rain, do you?" Ishaan asked, drawing up beside him.

"I don't mind the rain so much," Roan said, turning up his collar, "it's the thunder and lightning that can come with it that I don't much care for."

"We don't get thunderstorms in the spring," Ishaan said, heading off to their left. Roan chased after him.

"Never?"

"Well, maybe once that I can remember. Thunderstorms tend to be a summer occurrence, so—Wait, what's that?" Roan froze, listening, and the hair on the back of his neck stood on end as a distant growl rumbled through the trees, steadily growing louder.

"Come on," Roan said, grabbing at Ishaan's arm, "we've got to get inside. It's not safe—Why are you laughing?"

"It's the train," Ishaan said, still chuckling, "coming back from Shesade. The tracks run just a few hundred yards beyond the river. I can't believe you thought it was thunder." And he started laughing again.

"You know what, Ishaan? Go to hell. Thousands of people are killed each year by lightning." He strode away, in the general direction that they'd been heading. They couldn't be far from the house.

"And thousands more choke to death on their food," Ishaan called after him, "but you're not afraid to eat, are you?"

Roan stopped, turned, planted his hands on his hips.

"I have to eat," he said. "I don't have to stand around and wait to be hit by lightning." He walked away again, trying to look beyond the trees, trying to see the garden, the back lawn, something.

What did Ishaan know? Had he been playing on the apartment roof the day that lightning had struck the rusted fire escape? Had he seen the blue-white arcs slice through the bricks and melt the steel? Had he smelled the air burning?

"Head left," Ishaan called and Roan glanced left to see a thinning patch of trees, and beyond that, the neat rows of beans and lettuce and tomatoes. Finally. He emerged from the woods only a few steps ahead of Ishaan, and a few seconds behind the rain. It began to sheet down into his face, his blond hair sticking to his forehead and slapping against the back of his neck as he broke into a run. His feet pounded up the steps to the porch and he shoved the back door open.

"Hey, hey—don't track mud all over my house!" Ishaan shouted after him.

Roan stopped just inside the door and kicked off his muddy shoes. He leaned his fishing pole against the counter and pulled his shirt off over his head. The shoulders and front were soaked, but the back was still fairly dry, and he wiped the rain from his face and toweled some of the water out of his hair. Ishaan came trudging up onto the porch a moment later, not seeming to care that his black hair was dripping all down his shirt, the thin blue cloth plastered against his muscular upper body—

Roan turned away, almost tripping over his shoes as he moved aside to let Ishaan into the kitchen. What was wrong with him? His demon was fed and sleeping peacefully. He shouldn't be having these kinds of feelings and thoughts, it wasn't healthy, it wasn't safe. What if those scientists came looking for him? What if someone found out about his condition? What if Ishaan found out? He couldn't bear to see *that* look on the face of someone he cared too much about. They could be friends—he wanted to be friends—but he didn't expect that much from a friend. He could still walk away from a friend.

"So, you got all wet and you didn't turn into a toadstool," Ishaan said as he peeled his shirt off his body. "You going to stop acting like a freak now?"

"I was not," Roan said, perhaps a bit too vehemently for the conversation. He colored and turned away again. "I mean—I told you, it wasn't the rain that was bothering me." He threw his wet shirt at Ishaan and headed for his room. "Hey, I thought you were going to be nice to me."

"I was nice to you all afternoon," Ishaan said, his voice moving across the house as he walked to his own room. "I took you fishing. We did the whole guy-bonding thing. What more do you want?"

"Dinner would be nice." Roan smiled to himself as he shrugged into a loose, short-sleeved, button-down shirt. He started to button it, then said forget it, it was too much work. Roan kicked off his wet pants and pulled a pair of sweats out of the drawer.

"Can you clean fish?" Ishaan asked suddenly. Roan slipped into the pants and stepped out into the living room.

"I think anyone over the age of eight could manage to gut a fish," Roan said. "It isn't rocket sci—" He glanced toward Ishaan's room, his sentence dying on his lips as he watched Ishaan struggle out of his heavy, wet jeans, standing on one foot with his back to the door, his black briefs doing more to accentuate his ass than cover it. Roan realized he was staring and headed into the kitchen. "Yes," he said after a moment, because he couldn't remember if he'd ever answered Ishaan's question, "I can clean the fish."

"Good," Ishaan said, and Roan heard him grunt and then a thump, probably from him losing his balance. Roan was sorely tempted to go see if he was okay. Before he could, Ishaan said, "You in the kitchen?"

"Yeah," Roan said, leaning forward and resting his elbows on the counter, his head held in his hands. He shouldn't be doing this; he was just asking for trouble.

"Could you put the little frying pan on the stove?" Ishaan asked, "and wash up a few potatoes? Four or five, unless you're real hungry, and then make it six. They're in the pantry." Roan shoved himself away from the counter, lifted the pan down from its hook and set it on the stove, then stepped into the pantry. The cool, dusty room seemed to close around him, barely larger than his outstretched arms, and he dug into the potato sack quickly, loading his arms with five of the little tubers.

Ishaan was in the kitchen when he came back out, wearing a pair of black sweats and a gray T-shirt. He glanced at Roan.

"Nice," Ishaan said. Roan stopped short, taken aback and after a moment, Ishaan frowned at him. "Those are nice potatoes; not shriveled, equal sized, no eyes sprouting out of them—Are you all right?"

Roan turned away and dumped the potatoes into the sink. "I'm fine. A little tired, maybe. I couldn't sleep last night."

"Sorry," Ishaan said, his tone cold.

"No, not because of you. I-I got an e-mail from Kethic." He turned on the faucet and began to scrub at the rough, dirty potato skins. "He wants to see me."

"What is he—stupid?" Ishaan asked. "Like you would ever—"

"I want to," Roan said, startling himself. He hadn't really thought about it, but now— "He apologized for everything. He even took the blame for our parents' deaths."

"Nice of him," Ishaan said, "considering that it *was* his fault. Fine, do whatever you want, but don't bring him here. I don't want him in my house."

Roan turned off the water and grabbed a knife.

"I won't," he said as he cut the potatoes into quarters. "I don't want him in *your* house, either."

Ishaan took a breath, like he was going to say something, but then he didn't.

Roan placed the potatoes in a saucepan, covered them with water and carried the pan over to the stove. "I figured I could take the train into Shesade next week, stay a couple of nights, if that's okay."

"I can stay in town," Ishaan said, but he didn't sound happy about. "Did you salt the potatoes?"

"Oh, no, I forgot."

Ishaan stepped past him, grabbed the salt off the back of the counter, returned. Neither spoke for a moment, that heavy silence seeming to suck the air out of the room.

"Ishaan, I—He's my brother. I have to give him a chance."

"No, you don't," Ishaan said, "not after what he did. If he was any kind of brother, he never would have turned you into a whore."

"I told you, that was my choice—"

"You were a kid, Roan. It wasn't your choice to make. He was older, he should have protected you—"

"You don't know anything about it," Roan said, turning away. Kethic *was* protecting him, keeping his demon fed, keeping the really creepy guys away. What he was wasn't Kethic's fault. "Thank you for your concern, but I have to deal with this."

"It is your life," Ishaan said with a shrug. "I left the bucket on the back porch. Watch out for the hautfish."

They made idle conversation as they worked, the smell of raw fish and cooking venison filling the kitchen. Dinner was delicious, though the mood was rather somber and tense. After they cleaned up and Ishaan went to his study to do whatever it was that he did, Roan sat down at his desk and opened the laptop.

He started to log into his e-mail account to tell Kethic where he wanted to meet, but an ominous thought made him pause. What if his e-mails *were* being watched? What if he showed up in Shesade next week and the scientists were waiting for him? What would Ishaan think if he never came back?

So what was he going to do, use a code? He loved his brother, but the scientists would probably crack any code he used faster than Kethic. Roan tried to think back to the notes Kethic would leave for him before he left for school. None of them were in code, they just said where and when. It hadn't exactly been hard to keep what they were doing a secret from their parents. They either knew, and knew it was the only way, or they suspected, and didn't want to know. There was no need for a code; nothing ever went wrong.

Well, that wasn't true. He remembered one afternoon, walking from school to meet up with Kethic on the trashier side of town, and unbeknownst to him, the police had set up a sting to catch all the underage whores in the area. Kethic had found out in time, but hadn't had a chance to warn him, so he had waited in an alley a few blocks away, on the path he knew Roan would take, and had intercepted him before he could get caught.

What if he did something like that; told Kethic to go somewhere and then grab him halfway? What was the name of the town beyond Shesade? Roan pulled up a map of the area and a train schedule. This might actually work. He finished logging into his account and discovered a new message from Kethic.

> Brother,
> I know you're angry and don't want to see me. I understand. I think it's best if we don't meet right away. I'm going to go see some friends so I'll be out of touch for a few days, but I wanted to get some flowers for mom and dad's graves. Do you remember what her favorite flower was? I think it was lilies. I'll talk to you in a couple of days.
> Love,
> Your brother

Roan balled his fists and fought not to slam them down on the desk. What an idiot. He didn't even wait for a reply. Well, Roan could still tell him of his plans, even if he wouldn't get the message until after he got back from visiting his friends. And since when had Kethic had any friends? He was always such a loner. Roan supposed time changed everyone. He was glad one of them could afford that luxury. With quick, sharp taps on the keys, he pecked out his reply.

Brother,
You don't know anything about me. I think we should meet in Lorexan on Eshaedra. Let me know when and I'll have further instructions for you. And you should know better than anyone, mom's favorite flowers were lilacs, afinas, and bachelor buttons.
Your brother

It wasn't much of a letter, but it said what he wanted to say. Well, almost. He sent it quickly before he could add a *P.S. I hate you* at the bottom. That wasn't true, even if it was what he felt like saying. After a moment, he closed the computer and leaned back in the chair. Damn, he was tired. He glanced over at his bed, then up at the clock. Ishaan would be up for at least another hour. Maybe he could just take a little nap.

He knocked on the study door and then eased it open. Ishaan glanced at him as he stuck his head in.

"Sorry to bother you," Roan said. "I'm going to lie down. Just wake me up when you're ready for bed, okay?" Ishaan nodded and turned back to his computer. What was he doing? Online stock trading, gambling, multiplayer gaming, having cyber sex—Roan withdrew and shut the door before he started to laugh. He could just see straight-laced Ishaan typing dirty things with one hand to some stranger while he jerked off. Never.

Roan shed his shirt and stretched out on his bed, pulling one corner of the quilt over his bare back. He lay a moment, listening to the rain beating on the roof over his head, then sighed and closed his eyes. Did he hang out in chatrooms? Did he pretend to be someone else? Did he have a blog, chronicling their lives for all the universe to read?

The sound of the rain drifted away and he sank deeper into the mattress, his body heavy and warm. He opened his eyes and got up as Ishaan sauntered into the room, wearing just his black briefs, his body glistening with drops of rain. Roan reached out, running his hands over Ishaan's skin, collecting the drops of water on his palms. He drew his hands back, twin mirrored pools reflecting Ishaan's face back at him.

"Roan," Ishaan said, his voice echoing up out of the mirrors. He stepped closer and Roan watched the mirrors fall from his hands and shatter on the floor, blood oozing out of the broken pieces. He looked back up at Ishaan.

"Roan," Ishaan said again, reaching out to place his hand on Roan's shoulder. Roan leaned toward him, their lips brushing, warm, soft—

"Hey!" Roan jumped awake, blinking hard as his blurred vision snapped back into focus. Looming over him was Ishaan, red-faced and angry looking.

"What-What happened?" Roan asked, looking around. "Ishaan, what—"

"You kissed me," Ishaan growled between his teeth. Roan's eyes widened. The rain, the mirrors. He glanced around. No, it was a dream. How could Ishaan know what he'd been dreaming? Unless...

"You mean, kissed you, really?"

"Yes, really," Ishaan snapped. "I came in to wake you up, said your name, gave you a shake, and you sat up and kissed me on the mouth."

He seemed to realize that he was still leaned over the bed and straightened up. Roan ran his hands back through his hair, his heart pounding as he searched for an explanation that wouldn't get him shot.

"I-I was dreaming," he said. That was honest and safe enough. "About a-a girl I used to know."

Ishaan raised one eyebrow.

"A girl?"

"Yeah," Roan said, frowning, "why is that so hard to believe?"

"Well—" Suddenly, Ishaan seemed embarrassed. "Don't take this the wrong way, but I thought you liked guys."

"Sezae said the same thing," Roan said. "Do I really give that impression?"

"Sometimes. I've noticed you looking at me."

Roan felt his face turn scarlet, burning from the middle of his chest clear to his ears.

"I-I—Well, you're a good looking guy, Ishaan, and you've got a great body—" Now it was Ishaan's turn to color. "But it's just a physical attraction that will pass. Don't worry, I know better than to sleep with boss." He laughed, but Ishaan remained serious, staring at him with dark, thoughtful eyes. The laughter died on Roan's lips and he cleared his throat. "Unless, of course, the boss is interested..."

Ishaan snorted and walked away. "You going to lock this door, or not?"

Roan sighed and climbed off the bed. That was stupid. He hurried across the living room as Ishaan started to close his door and stopped it with his hand. "I was just kidding, you know," he said.

Ishaan pulled the door open enough to frown at him. "No you weren't," he said. "You may think you can lie to me, but I'm not as dumb as I seem. If I gave the slightest sign that I'd allow it, you'd be all over me."

"No, I—"

"Which makes me wonder what *really* happened last night," Ishaan said, his eyes never leaving Roan's face.

Roan tried to keep his expression blank, perhaps slightly confused, but inside his heart was racing and his stomach churned. He was dead. He was so dead. "You came into my room, didn't you?"

"No," Roan said, just sure his voice was going to crack or waver and give him away. It didn't. "Look, just because I'm mildly attracted to you doesn't mean that I would rape you in your sleep!" That was the truth, at least. His attraction had nothing to do with it. Ishaan just kept watching him, but Roan kept his mouth shut. He knew that guilt often drove people to fill uncomfortable silence with things they didn't want to say.

Finally, Ishaan nodded. "All right, fine," he said, but he didn't sound like he was really convinced. "Good night, then."

"Good night," Roan said and pulled the door the rest of the way shut. He locked it, hung up the key, and returned to his room, where he fell down upon his bed and covered his head with his pillow. He felt like he was going to be sick, his stomach filled with nervous butterflies. He couldn't do that again—stare down Ishaan and lie to his face, not like that.

He got back up, changed his clothes and turned out the light before slipping between the sheets. He never should have had to. He should have known better than to have sex with him. Of course he was going to notice! Roan groaned and pressed the heels of his hands to his closed eyes until light exploded in the darkness. He was so stupid. Well, never again. He could feed just fine sucking him off—even just touching him. As long as he did it frequently enough, and every other day would do fine, he shouldn't have to engage in penetrative intercourse. Everything would be fine and Ishaan would eventually forget all about last night. Roan rolled over and drifted off to sleep.

He woke with a start, feeling like no time had passed, but a glance at the clock revealed that more than an hour had gone by. So why was he awake? The answer came from across the living room, a pounding at Ishaan's door and a hoarse scream. Oh. He'd forgotten that Ishaan would do that every night that he wasn't there. Roan pulled his pillow over his head and tried to go back to sleep, but he could still hear Ishaan's frustrated cries. Finally, he pushed the pillow aside and sat up, listening as Ishaan stroked himself to climax and fell silent.

He ran a hand across his face and yawned, but didn't lie back down. Ishaan would be quiet for a couple of hours, and then he'd get back up and do it all again, and again, and perhaps even a fourth time if he was feeling particularly unsatisfied. Roan did not want to be woken up to *that* every two hours all night long. After a moment, he threw back the covers and padded barefoot across the living room. Apparently, he'd have to feed every night, just to get a little peace and quiet.

Roan listened at the window, then unlocked the door. Ishaan lay curled up against the wall, shivering slightly. Roan shook his head and sighed. This was no way to live. He bent down and grasped Ishaan's arm, tried to pull it across his shoulders, but Ishaan was as heavy as he looked. Roan stepped away and ran a hand back through his hair. He didn't want to leave him on the floor, but he didn't quite have the upper-body strength needed to lift him. He supposed he could drag him over to the bed, but rug-burns on his ass might lead to more unpleasant questions.

Not sure what else to do, Roan took a seat on the edge of Ishaan's bed and pulled the quilt up around his shoulders to wait for him to stir. As soon as he could coax Ishaan to his feet and back into bed, he could blow him and go back to his own room. His bed would be cold by then. Damn. He drew his feet up and wrapped a corner of the quilt around them. It was really chilly. He needed to get up and put more wood on the stove, but that would mean exposing his bare skin to the air again. Not a real appealing thought. But if he did, Ishaan might not be so uncomfortable, over there on the floor.

"Ah, shit," he muttered, and threw off the blanket. It was warm in the kitchen, his arms and chest bathed in the heat of the glowing coals as he fed more dry fir into the flames. With the fire crackling, he stood a moment and warmed his hands over the cast iron woodstove, then returned to Ishaan's room, which of course only seemed colder. Roan slipped under the covers of Ishaan's bed, goose bumps prickling his arms, and glanced at the clock. It wouldn't be long now, he told himself.

Roan ran down the empty street, searching for something. Trees lined the street, great spreading branches meeting above his head to form a long cathedral hall, the leaves glowing like stained glass in the sunlight, but not one of them was the *right* tree. Where was it? Ahead, the ground rose in a small hill, but the road remained level, cutting right through the hill. The trees followed the contour of the ground, rising up to tower over his head, and there it was, the third tree up the slope from him. Roan left the road and climbed through the grass to the base of the gnarled giant.

His eyes scoured the scarred, knobby trunk, looking for the right knot. He reached out, ran his fingers over the rough lump, and pushed. The trunk of the tree swung inward, like a door, and he stepped inside, descending a flight of narrow spiral stairs. His heart beat faster as he neared the bottom, as he drew closer to that thing he'd been searching for.

He stepped out into an empty room, white walls and polished hardwood floors, windows without curtains looking out into endless yellow fields. He heard a sound and turned, looking through an open doorway into an adjacent room, where a tiny child stood beside a large basin of water. The child opened his mouth and gray water poured out into the basin, then he bent over and shoved his head under the water. Roan leapt forward to stop him before he drowned, but something grabbed him from behind, strong hands roaming across his chest, down his stomach, pulling at his pants. He tried to push the hands away, but they wouldn't let go, and then he felt a sharp pain a something tried to enter his butt—

Roan jerked awake, his head reeling as he struggled to remember where he was, what he'd been doing. Ishaan! Shit, he'd fallen asleep. Hands gripped his hips and he cried out as the pain came again, sharp, burning—he pulled away, slipped free of the grasping hands, scrambled to get off the bed, but Ishaan caught him by the ankle and dragged him back. Roan clawed at the mattress, feet kicking, his sweats and underwear bunched around his ankles, but it was no use; Ishaan was so much stronger. He felt Ishaan climb on to the bed, straddle his legs, and Roan cried out in desperation.

"Ishaan, please, don't do this!" Fingers dug into his hips, holding him down. "Ishaan, stop!" But it was no use. Ishaan couldn't hear him. Roan squeezed his eyes shut and gathered all the spit his dry mouth could manage onto his fingertips. He reached back and smeared it across his opening, for all the good it would do. Saliva was hardly an ideal lubricant, but it would help. He hoped.

The head of Ishaan's erection pressed against Roan's entrance, hot, hard, trying to breach his defenses, and that horrible pain splintered through his body again. He gritted his teeth and tried to relax as Ishaan forced himself inside. Every breath caught in his throat, his whole body shaking as Ishaan slid deeper, not even pausing to let him adjust.

Roan buried his face in the blankets and cried out, a hoarse, ragged sob. Why was Ishaan doing this? Why was he hurting him? Ishaan began to thrust, driving deep, rubbing across Roan's prostate, and the mingled pain and pleasure was just short of sickening. It hurt too much to feel good, and the pleasure stuck in his gut, hot and heavy as molten lead. The energy pressed in on him, choking, smothering.

After only a few minutes, Ishaan began to hammer into him, his breathing growing louder, more ragged as he neared his climax. Roan pulled at handfuls of bedding, praying for Ishaan to hurry up and come. Ishaan grunted, his hips jerking, and then he fell still, his hands sliding off Roan's hips. Roan cried out and scrambled away from him, off the bed and onto the floor. He pressed himself against the wall, his body shaking so hard he couldn't stand. He stared up at the bed as Ishaan slumped forward and stretched out, breathing hard, but otherwise quiet and peaceful.

A horrible, irrational anger flared inside him. How could Ishaan be so brutal, so uncaring? What had Roan ever done to deserve that? He wrapped his arms around his body and leaned his head back against the wall, a single tear rolling down his cheek. Now he understood the town's anger and why Hektor had left.

Roan was no stranger to sex—he didn't even mind having a rough partner —but he'd never been forced before, he'd never been unable to stop it. That was the worst part, worse than the pain, that helplessness. After a moment, Roan pulled his legs under him, pulling his sweats and underwear up as he stood. Ishaan lay across his blankets, his arms and legs drawn up to his body as he shivered in the chill air. Roan stared at him, his hair damp with sweat and sticking to his forehead, and that initial anger faded.

It wasn't Ishaan's fault. He didn't know he was doing it. Wasn't that what Roan had been saying since he got there? Ishaan was right; it was easy to say, but harder to understand, especially in the face of such apparent cruelty. Roan pulled the quilt out from under Ishaan and started to cover him, but the bottom fell out of his stomach at the sight of blood smeared along Ishaan's shaft. He drew a shuddering breath and walked to the bathroom, returning with a warm washcloth. It really wasn't that much blood, he assured himself as he cleaned

Ishaan up, and it wasn't that surprising, considering how much it hurt, but it made it impossible to avoid the truth of the matter. He'd been raped.

Roan tucked Ishaan in and locked the door once more, and then headed back to the bathroom to draw himself a bath. He needed to clean up and pull himself together fast. When he made that offer to Ishaan, to keep this sort of thing from him, he never actually expected it to happen, but now that it had, he understood exactly why Ishaan could never find out.

Twelve

Ishaan stepped out of the nearly empty woodshed, his arms loaded with fir. Summer was coming, but not fast enough. The nights were still damn cold. As he crossed the lawn toward the back porch, he paused, listening to the low rumble and clack of the train on the other side of the river. He climbed the steps, stomping the mud from his boots, and Roan opened the door for him, a greasy fork in one hand.

"How's that meat coming?" Ishaan asked as he dumped the wood in the box and brushed the slivers off his shirt.

"It's getting there," Roan said. "Some of it still looks a little pink." Ishaan took the fork from him and stirred the ground venison on the stove. This was the last package. Except for that icy block of old trout, which needed to be tossed out, the freezer was empty. Ishaan glanced over his shoulder at Roan, chopping onions and celery fresh from the garden.

"I heard the train going by out there," Ishaan said.

Roan nodded.

"That's the train to Shesade, you know."

"I know," Roan said. He brought over the veggies in a small bowl and Ishaan dumped them in with the meat. "I never heard back from Kethic," Roan said, watching Ishaan stir the pan.

"Well, not that I think your brother deserves any more chances, but it has only been four days. You did say he was visiting friends. He probably hasn't even gotten your message yet."

Roan shrugged.

"Maybe. You ready for that sauce now?" The meat was nicely browned, the onions starting to turn golden and glassy.

"Yeah, just about. It's on the back shelf—"

"I know where it is," Roan said with a grin as he headed into the pantry.

Ishaan shook his head and lifted the lid off the saucepan, a cloud of steam billowing up into the air. Once the sauce was added to the meat, he'd—He jumped, almost dropping the lid, as the house filled with a brittle, musical chime.

"What the hell was that?" Roan called from the pantry.

"The doorbell," Ishaan said with a frown. He set down the lid and fork. "Put the sauce in the pan and stir it, would you? Then move it to the trivet and the water to—"

"I know," Roan said, stepping out with a dusty jar of tomato sauce in one hand, and a little jar of something in the other. "I found these mushrooms in the back. Can we throw them in, too?"

"Let me see them," Ishaan said, reaching out, but the doorbell rang again. "Damn it. Go ahead and open them, but don't add them to the sauce. I don't remember canning mushrooms last year, so they might be bad."

"I think I could tell the difference between a good mushroom and a bad one," Roan said, laughing as he gestured toward the door. "Go see who it is and yell if you need help chasing them off."

"And what are you going to do, flirt them to death?" Ishaan said as he headed into the living room.

"Hey!" Roan said, trying to sound offended. "I can be scary when I want to."

"I know you can," Ishaan said. "I've seen you, just out of bed, haven't brushed your hair or your teeth—" He fell silent as he reached the door, threw back the deadbolt, and jerked it open. On his porch stood a man in his late twenties, white-blond hair pulled back in a tight braid, wire-rimmed glasses and gray-blue eyes, neat dress shirt and slacks and a long, black leather coat. He looked strangely familiar.

"What do you want?" Ishaan demanded. The man on the porch didn't seem the least surprised by his rudeness.

"Sorry to bother you," the man said, "but I'm looking for Ishaan Darvis. Would that be you?" He had a deep, pleasant voice and an educated, officious attitude that immediately set Ishaan's teeth on edge. Not another lawyer.

"Maybe," Ishaan said. "Who's asking?"

"Detective Aris Kalavon," the man said, flashing a shiny silver shield. Ishaan stiffened. "Are you Ishaan Darvis?"

"Er, yes, Detective, I am. What is this about?"

"I was hoping we could discuss this inside," Detective Kalavon said, glancing past him into the living room. "It's about your roommate, Roan Echarn."

Ishaan's heart nearly stopped. He licked suddenly dry lips.

"Has he done something?" he asked, his voice tight, but level.

"Oh, no," Detective Kalavon said with a shake of his head. "He's not a suspect. I just need to ask him a few questions concerning his parents' deaths." Kalavon adjusted his glasses, his gray-blue eyes seeming to search Ishaan's face. "You were aware that his parents had been murdered?"

"Yes," Ishaan said, nodding. He stepped back out of the doorway. "Come in, please. I'll tell Roan that you're here." As Kalavon stepped past him, Ishaan couldn't shake the feeling that he'd seen this guy somewhere before. Not someone he'd met, more like from a picture—That was it.

Ishaan shut the door, then locked it. Kalavon was standing just inside the foyer, his hands in his pockets, looking around the living room. Ishaan stepped up behind him, grabbed him by one arm and the back of his neck, twisted his arm up behind him and shoved him against the wall.

"Hey!" Kalavon shouted. "What the fuck are you doing? You just assaulted an officer."

"Give me a break," Ishaan said, leaning against him as he began to struggle. "If you're a cop, then I'm a cheese pizza."

"Ishaan, what's going on?" Roan called. "The water's starting to—"

"Roan," Ishaan said, "come in here a minute."

"What about the—"

"It'll be fine," Ishaan said. "Get in here." He glanced toward the kitchen as Roan stepped into the doorway.

Roan's jaw dropped. "What are you—Who is that?"

"I thought I told you," Ishaan said between his teeth as he spun Kalavon away from the wall and around to face Roan, "that I didn't want your brother in my house." Roan's eyes grew wide and for several seconds, no one spoke.

"Hey, Roan," Kethic said finally. He turned his head and spoke over his shoulder. "How'd you know?"

"Roan's got pictures of you," Ishaan said, still watching Roan. "Besides, you've got the same eyes."

Kethic laughed. "That's what mom always said. Remember that, Roan?"

Roan stepped farther into the room.

"How did you find me?" he asked, his voice barely louder than a whisper. "I never told you where I was." His eyes darted to Ishaan. "Never, I swear."

"What do you mean, how? I followed the flowers. Isn't that why you—"

"What flowers?" Ishaan asked. Roan looked confused, then a look of horror spread across his face.

"The lilies," he said. "That's why—mom's favorite flower—"

"I was trying to tell you that I'd gotten your message. Didn't you read my e-mail?"

"What flowers?" Ishaan demanded, twisting Kethic's arm a little farther. He grunted in pain.

"Roan sent a vase of lilies to our parents' graves," Kethic said between his teeth. "I traced the delivery company back to Devaen, and a little asking around sent me out here. Your drac sheriff is an asshole, by the way." He glanced over at Roan. "So, little brother, I don't suppose you could call off your boyfriend before he breaks my arm?"

"He's not my boyfriend," Roan and Ishaan replied in one voice. Their eyes met for a moment, then Ishaan looked away.

"Whatever," Kethic said, sounding irritated, "could you get him off of me?" Roan stood for a moment, then turned and headed back into the kitchen.

"Ishaan, let him go," he said as he left. "I need your help in here. The sauce is going to burn and the water is boiling over."

Kethic tried to pull away again, but Ishaan held tight.

"What makes you think I'll listen to him?" Ishaan asked. "This is *my* house."

"Must be nice not having to worry about not getting any," Kethic said. Ishaan dug his fingers into Kethic's shoulder.

"What the hell's that supposed to mean?"

"I mean, you don't have to worry about sleeping on the couch, since he's a—"

"Kethic!" Roan snapped, suddenly standing in the kitchen door, his face white as death. "Why the hell are you here? Haven't you done enough to me? Ishaan, please, let him go!"

Ishaan shoved him forward, watched him stumble and almost fall on his face. Kethic straightened up and turned, his jaw set and eyes flashing with anger.

"Real funny," he said, wincing as he rolled his shoulder. "Let's see how tough you are when you don't get the jump on someone." He took a step toward Ishaan.

"Kethic, you take one more step and I will never speak to you again," Roan said. Kethic glared at Ishaan, then turned and walked toward Roan. "Don't come near me, either. I'm still pissed at you. I don't know what I was thinking when I agreed to see you."

Kethic stopped, glanced around like he wasn't sure what to do with himself, and then flopped down into one of the green armchairs. Roan stared at the back of his head for a minute, then looked at Ishaan. "The water's ready for the pasta," he said, as if his estranged brother had never invaded their home.

Kethic ignored them both as Ishaan walked into the kitchen and pulled Roan to one side.

"When did you send flowers?" Ishaan asked. "Last week, in town, with my money?"

Roan nodded.

"Stupid. Didn't you realize someone could track that?"

"I wasn't thinking real clearly at the time," Roan said. "Maybe if you'd been with me, instead of outside guarding your precious car—"

"So this is *my* fault?" Ishaan asked.

Roan threw up his hands and walked away. "No, it's mine. You're right, everything is my fault."

Ishaan watched him pace across the kitchen and back. He shook his head.

"I'm not doing this," he said, stepping over to the fridge and grabbing a beer. "I'm not going to fight with you. Deal with your brother. Leave me out of it." He opened the back door and strode down the stairs and across the lawn.

"What about dinner?" Roan called after him.

"I've got mine," Ishaan said, raising the brown bottle into the air. He heard the back door slam, but kept walking. This wasn't his problem and he sure as hell wasn't going to try and fix it. He reached the riverbank and stopped, staring down into the swift, rushing water as he popped the cap off his beer. His family lived on another planet. *That* was how he solved problems. He took a long pull from the bottle and sighed.

So now what? If Kethic could find them, so could anyone else, if they had a mind to. Roan had to know he wasn't safe anymore. If he and his brother made up, they would leave together, and when the killer drug dealers came looking for him, Ishaan would be tortured and executed just like Roan's parents. *And* he'd have to start sleeping in the jail again. He couldn't decide which was worse.

Ishaan raised the bottle halfway to his lips, then lowered it again. Would Roan really leave? It was the smartest thing he could do, but he wasn't exactly known for his brains; the flowers had proven that. Was he, at that moment, packing to leave? Would Ishaan return to an empty house, dinner unfinished, burning on the stove? He started to take a drink, but the beer tasted like bile. He spit it out and flung the bottle into the river, his hands shaking as he shoved them into his pockets. If that was what he had to look forward to, maybe he wouldn't go back.

Thirteen

Roan watched Ishaan stalk across the backyard, beer in hand, and enter the trees. He slammed the door, but Ishaan didn't even glance back. Bastard. Roan turned to the stove, grabbed up a large wooden spoon, and lifted the lid off the saucepan. A cloud of steam enveloped his wrist and he jerked back, the lid hitting the floor with a clatter. Boiling water splashed onto the stovetop, spitting and hissing as it evaporated. Roan picked up the long box of hair-like pasta, searching the back and sides for instructions in a language he could read.

"Need some help?"

He glanced at Kethic, standing in the kitchen doorway, then turned away.

"What are you doing here?" Roan asked. He heard Kethic step into the room.

"I've been wondering the same thing myself," Kethic said. "I didn't figure you'd be too thrilled to see me, but this—What did I do?"

"You showed up *here*," Roan said, pulling a handful of the long, thin pasta out of the box, "and now Ishaan's pissed at *me*."

"So you're the one who'll be sleeping on the couch," Kethic said, reaching over his arm and taking the pasta from him. "You don't need that much." He handed about half back and Roan carefully fed it into the bubbling water.

"Thanks. And nobody sleeps on the couch. He's not my boyfriend."

"What then, friends with benefits?"

"No, I just work for him."

"So you're his whore."

Roan glared at his brother.

"I am *not* his whore. This is a respectable job."

"What, you do his cooking and cleaning?" Kethic said. He grabbed Roan by the arm and turned him to look in his face. "You can't tell me you're not feeding off him regularly. I've never seen you so healthy looking."

Roan pulled away and went back to stirring the pasta.

"You can't mention in the incubism in front of him. He doesn't know, and...he'd kill me if he found out."

Kethic walked around him, to the other side of the stove, and stirred the simmering sauce.

"Let me see if I have this straight," Kethic said after a moment. "You live with this guy, but you're not his boyfriend, you work for him, but you're not his whore, and you have sex with him, but he doesn't know about your condition. What am I missing, because that doesn't make any sense to me."

Roan glanced at the clock.

"How long does this cook for?" He switched hands to give his tired wrist a break.

"About twelve minutes," Kethic said, sounding impatient. "Are you going to answer my questions, or should I go ask him?"

"If I tell you, you can't say anything to him, understand? He's really sensitive about it."

"About what?" Kethic asked, leaning closer. "Is he deformed or something?"

Roan rolled his eyes.

"No, dumbass, he's not deformed. He—I don't know what you call it, but he has a disorder, kind of like sleepwalking, only he has sex."

"In his sleep?" Kethic raised his eyebrows. "You mean he doesn't wake up, right?"

"No, I mean he gets up and walks around and has sex with the first person he finds, whether they want it or not."

Kethic didn't say anything for a long moment.

"So...he rapes people."

"He has," Roan said slowly.

"Does he know he's doing it?" Roan shook his head. "Does he remember when he wakes up?" He shook his head again. Another long pause. "Has he hurt you?"

Roan stared down into the bubbling pan.

"No," he said.

"You're lying," Kethic said. He reached out, hesitated, then placed his hand on Roan's shoulder. "Roan, what did he do?"

Roan shook his head.

"It was my fault. It was—it was stupid. I should have been more careful."

"That son-of-a-bitch," Kethic hissed. He dropped the fork into the pan, splattering tomato sauce onto the chimney pipe, and turned toward the door.

"Kethic, no!" Roan shouted, grabbing him by the arm. "You can't tell him."

"You mean he doesn't know?" Kethic asked.

Roan shook his head.

"Look, it's not a great situation, but it is what it is, and I don't want to lose it, okay? He needs someone to lock his bedroom door every night and unlock it in the morning so he won't hurt anyone. It's not his fault that I fell asleep on his bed waiting for him get restless so I could feed off him."

"So-So that's—" Kethic pulled away from him. "You have sex with him while he's asleep. You take advantage—You rape him!"

Roan recoiled.

"No! No, I-I—"

"Did he give consent?"

"Part of him did," Roan said, and even in his own ears it sounded like a lame excuse.

"Was it the part that was able to give consent, or was it his dick?" Kethic asked. "Because the two are not the same. Damn it, Roan, how could you do this?"

"Kethic, I-I'm not hurting him. He doesn't remember. It's like it doesn't even happen—"

"Is that what you tell yourself? Does it make it easier to do?"

"Don't judge me!" Roan shouted. "You're not perfect. Mom and dad are dead because of you." Kethic's face grew twisted and ugly, his hands balling into fists.

"You should be glad they're dead," he said, "because having a rapist for a son would have killed them." He stepped closer, leaned into Roan's face. "Do you honestly see nothing wrong with what you're doing?"

"I'm not hurting him," Roan said again. "If anything, I'm helping him. He gets relief and no one gets hurt."

"Then why don't you tell him?" Kethic asked. "Let him choose to have you screw him in his sleep—"

"I don't screw him," Roan said. "That happened once, and it was a mistake and I'll never do it again." Roan glanced at the clock, then grabbed the bubbling saucepan off the stove and dumped the pasta in the colander sitting in the sink. He turned his face away as steam billowed up. "And when was the last time you told someone what you are? How'd *that* turn out?"

Kethic's narrowed eyes never left him as he shook the excess water out of the pasta and tipped it into a large bowl. Roan rinsed the colander, dried his hands, and then turned to face his brother. "No, what I'm doing isn't right, but when has a normal person—not a mage, or a scientist, or a doctor, but a normal person—when have they ever understood what we are? They see us and we are monsters, demons, evil. I don't want him to look at me like that."

"He sleeps quieter after I've been with him. And I don't *screw* him; I use my hands or my mouth—I get no pleasure from it—and if it keeps him from beating off four times a night, I don't see the harm."

"The harm," Kethic said quietly, "is that he didn't agree to it. But—" He held up his hand to forestall Roan's protest. "You're right; it is hard to make someone understand, and I can see why you don't want to risk losing this. I won't say anything to him about what we are, but you really should. You can't build a relationship on lies and secrets."

"Kethic," Roan said, rubbing wearily at his jaw, "we're not in a—"

"Maybe not now," Kethic said, "but in a month or two? Who can say?"

"I can," Roan said. "You said it yourself; you can't build a relationship on lies and secrets and I *can't* tell him the truth. I won't start something that's doomed to fail."

"Then you need to be careful," Kethic said, "because things like this have a way of sneaking up on you, and you'll fall in love with him before you even realize it."

Roan sighed and shook his head.

"Thanks for the advice, but I'm not going to fall in love with him. The situation is mutually beneficial, that's all. If it starts becoming anything else, I'll leave. I've done it before."

"As long as you know what you're getting into," Kethic said with a shrug. He fished the fork out of the sauce, burning himself, and licked his fingertips clean. "This is good. Is it ready to eat?"

"Yeah, but...I think we should wait for Ishaan."

"I don't want to wait," Kethic said. "I haven't eaten since this morning." He looked out the window. "Where is he?"

"Probably by the river. It's about a hundred feet into the trees."

"I bet that's nice. Have you gone fishing?"

"Once." Roan tapped his fingers on the counter, then headed for the door. "I'm going to go find him and tell him that dinner's ready." He paused with his hand on the door. "Maybe you ought to come with me. He's a little protective of his stuff and might not be too happy with me if I left you here alone."

"Paranoid?" Kethic asked with a crooked grin.

Roan grinned back.

"Just a little." They strode across the lawn and into the woods. The trees weren't thick there and Roan could see clear to the riverbank, but he didn't see Ishaan. They reached the edge of the river and stopped, Kethic glancing into the swift water as Roan bent down and picked up a shiny bottle cap. "Well," Roan said, "he *was* here, at least."

"I still am here." They turned to see Ishaan leaning against the trunk of a gnarled oak, his arms crossed over his chest. "What do you want?"

"Dinner's ready," Roan said. Ishaan looked angry. His eyes slid from Roan's face to Kethic.

"I told you, I already ate." Angry *and* intoxicated. Great.

"Beer is not dinner," Roan said. "Quit being an ass and come back in the house. Unless you still want to fight, of course."

Ishaan turned away, staring out over the rushing river.

"No," he said at last, "I don't still want to fight."

"Good. Then come on, the pasta's getting cold." The three of them started back toward the house and Ishaan glanced past Roan at Kethic.

"Is he eating with us?"

"I hope you don't mind," Roan said, nodding. "We had a nice talk and got everything sorted out."

"Good for you," Ishaan said and Roan frowned. Why was he still so pissed? "So when are you leaving?"

"Er, tomorrow?" Kethic said. "I was hoping, maybe, that I could stay here tonight. I can crash on the floor, I don't mind—"

"No," Ishaan said, "absolutely not. Go back to Devaen, stay at the inn."

"I can't afford—"

"I'll pay for it," Ishaan said. "You're not sleeping in my house." Roan shot a glance at his brother, trying to convey a strong sense of shut-the-hell-up, but Kethic kept pushing.

"If this is about hiding your condition, don't bother. Roan already told me."

Roan groaned as Ishaan glared at him.

"It just sort of came up," Roan said with a shrug.

"I bet it did. 'Hey, wanna sleep over and laugh at the freak?' Maybe you should both go stay at the inn."

"Don't start that," Roan said. "You know I wouldn't—"

"And try to get over yourself," Kethic said. "As far as your condition goes, it's not even interesting. I know people with problems ten times as bad as yours."

Ishaan stopped walking in the middle of the lawn.

"Like what?" he demanded. Roan felt his life crumbling around him; this couldn't be happening. *Don't say it,* he begged silently. *Kethic, please don't—*

"Like incubism," Kethic said. Roan's eyes darted to Ishaan, but he only frowned.

"What's that?"

"Nothing," Roan said quickly. "Come on you two, I'm hungry—"

"It's a genetic condition," Kethic said, shooting Roan a dirty look, "that causes a person to crave sex—more than that, even—it makes them have to feed on sexual energy, and if they can't feed, they'll starve and die, slowly, horribly, painfully."

"Do they rape people without knowing it?" Ishaan asked, his tone bitter.

"Oh, they know it," Kethic said, "they just can't stop it. Once an incubus reaches a certain point they lose control and will do anything, to anyone, in order to feed." Ishaan seemed to think about that.

"Okay," he said with a grudging nod, "that's a little worse. You know a lot of these incubus people?"

"Just two," Kethic said, and out of the corner of his eye, Roan saw him glance his direction.

"Can we finish this conversation over dinner?" Roan asked, turning and striding toward the porch. "I'm starving." The thought of eating actually turned his stomach, but he had to do something to get them to stop talking. He stopped at the door and glanced back.

"So these two incubuses you know—"

"Incubi," Kethic corrected.

"Whatever. Do people bother them a lot? Or are they pretty much left alone?"

"They do a lot of moving around," Kethic said. "They try to keep what they are a secret and they're always afraid someone will find out. A lot of ignorant people mistake them for demons and try to kill them."

Roan opened the door as they climbed the steps, locking eyes with Kethic as he passed.

They dished up without another word about it and sat together at the table, Ishaan across from Roan and Kethic to his left. After only a few bites, though, Kethic had to open his mouth again.

"Hey, Ishaan, I just had an idea," Kethic said. "Maybe you should meet one of my incubus friends." Roan almost choked on his pasta.

"What for?" Ishaan said, frowning. "So we can compare notes on the horrible things we've done? To decide which of us has had the shittier life?"

Kethic shook his head, finished chewing, and swallowed.

"No. I thought, if you liked him, he could live here. It would give you someone to do at night and he wouldn't have to worry about finding someone to feed off of."

Ishaan's fork fell to his plate with a clatter.

"You want me to—No! I'm not going to let some *thing* feed off me in my sleep, like a—like a parasite. You're disgusting!"

"I was just asking," Kethic said with a shrug. Roan grabbed his plate and headed for the kitchen. "Where are you going?"

"I'm done," Roan said. "I'm going to take a walk."

"But you hardly touched your food!"

Roan ignored him, threw his plate in the sink, and stalked out into the backyard. If Kethic was going to ruin this, he didn't want to be there to watch. He headed for the river.

Fourteen

Ishaan stared down at his plate as the door slammed behind Roan, leaving him alone with Kethic. He glanced up at Roan's elder brother, who gave him a sheepish grin.

"I guess that was my fault," he said. "He asked me not to bother you."

Ishaan pushed his spaghetti around on his plate, then set his fork back down.

"Aren't you going to go after him?" he asked.

Kethic paused with his fork halfway to his mouth. "What for? He doesn't want to talk to me. Besides, I'd end up getting lost out there."

Ishaan sighed.

"And so will he, probably." He stood and leaned forward, down into Kethic's face. "You clean out my house while I'm gone, you touch *anything* and I'll not rest until I see you back in prison where you belong."

"Told you about that too, did he?" Kethic said, his mouth full of half-chewed pasta. He swallowed. "No wonder you tried to break my arm."

"You should have taken better care of him," Ishaan said, straightening up. "You were his brother—"

"You don't know half of what you're talking about," Kethic snapped. "I did what I had to. I did the best I could. I tried—"

"You still let your brother sell himself in an alley. He was a kid. You weren't. You should have stopped him."

"We didn't have a choice!" Kethic shouted, slamming his fist down on the table. "I kept him safe. I never let the creeps touch him, no matter how much they offered. It was the best solution to a problem that was royally fucked. So don't tell me what I should have done. You have no idea." He shoved his chair away from the table, rose and stalked away, but instead of storming out the door and out of their lives forever, he flopped down on the couch and began flipping through the TV channels.

"Fine, I'll go find your brother, then," Ishaan said. Kethic waved the remote in a vaguely dismissive gesture. "It'd be a shame if you left while I was gone and never came back."

"Don't worry," Kethic said, his eyes never leaving the television, "I'm not going anywhere."

Ishaan clenched his fists, then turned and headed out back. It was starting to get dark and chilly, and Roan had been wearing just a thin, short-sleeved shirt. Not that Ishaan was dressed any better. He shivered as he entered the trees, his head raised as he searched the shadowy woods.

While the path from the river to the house was easy to follow, and anyone with half a brain would think to find the river and follow it back to the path, Ishaan knew that being lost was a frightening and disorienting experience. He'd been ten or twelve—before all the trouble started, anyway—and he thought he knew his way around the woods pretty well. He'd been going hunting and fishing with his father for several years by then.

But as the afternoon wore on and the shadows changed, the forest began to look quite unfamiliar. He panicked, rushing around in random directions, when all he would have had to do was use the moss on the trees to find north and head that way until he reached the river. Instead, he ran in circles for three hours and had to be rescued by his father.

Ishaan reached the riverbank and glanced around. Roan was nowhere to be seen. Damn it. Which way had he gone? He wandered upstream a few dozen feet, looking for footprints, signs, then turned and searched the ground downstream. He didn't find anything, which was a little odd, considering the ground was still soft from the rain a few days ago. He didn't consider himself an expert tracker, by any means, but the only footprints he could see were his own, just now and from before, leading to the great twisted oak.

He stepped over to the tree, frowning at the sight of fresh, dark mud smeared on the knobby trunk. After a moment, he raised his eyes to the branches. Roan was watching him from a branch about ten feet above the ground.

"Hey," was all he said. Ishaan stared up at him and had the sudden urge to just walk away. He wasn't lost, and since he was just going to take off with his brother in the morning anyway, what did they have to talk about?

"Having fun?" Ishaan asked. "Sitting up there, watching me look for you?"

"I didn't know you were looking for me," Roan said. "Besides, I wasn't sure I wanted to be found." He seemed to hesitate. "What do you want?"

"I want to know how soon you and your brother are going to get the hell out of my house," Ishaan said, angrier than he'd intended. He hadn't intended to say anything, it just sort of came out. Roan's whole body tensed, his expression turned stony, and he dropped down out of the tree.

"So that's it then, you're just going to throw me out? I don't have any say in the matter? I don't get to tell my story? You're just going to take the word of my lying, escaped-convict brother!"

Ishaan took a startled step backward.

"I'm not throwing you out," he said.

"That's not what you said," Roan shouted.

"I assumed you would leave since you and your brother were reconciled," Ishaan shouted back. "It's not like I want you to go!" He regretted that as soon as it was out of his mouth. Roan just stared at him, face unreadable, but Ishaan could just imagine the things running through his mind. Ishaan cleared his throat. "And what did you mean, *your story?*"

"Oh. I-I meant—I thought Kethic told you I was going with him. That's all." They stood facing each other for a moment, then Roan looked away. Ishaan continued to regard him, a tightness in his gut. Roan was lying, he was almost certain, but he didn't care. Roan would not lie to him without a good reason. He wanted to believe that.

Roan glanced back up at him. "Was that all you wanted—to see when I was leaving?"

"Yeah," he said, "that was it. And...and you should come back inside. It's getting dark and cold out here, and you're not dressed very warm." He reached out and tugged at one of Roan's short sleeves, his knuckles brushing against Roan cold skin. "Damn, you're freezing," he said, pressing the back of his hand to Roan's arm. "C'mon, let's go in."

"Is my brother still here?" Roan asked as they started toward the house.

"As far as I know," Ishaan said. "He was watching TV when I left."

"Great," Roan said, shoving his hands in his pockets as he stumped along beside Ishaan. "I was hoping he'd either leave or you'd toss him out."

"I still could, if you want me to," Ishaan offered, nudging Roan with his elbow. Roan gave him a crooked grin and shook his head.

"No, we probably shouldn't. He *is* the only family I have left."

Ishaan's arm twitched as he considered putting it around Roan's shoulders to comfort him, but that was pushing things a little too far. If Roan wanted a hug, he could get one from his brother. That's what brothers were for. That and selling your virginity to the highest bidder, apparently.

"I'm sorry he said all that stuff to you," Roan said suddenly. "I shouldn't have told him about your condition, but—"

"It's all right," Ishaan said. "It's not exactly a secret and he seemed to understand better than most." He drew a slow breath, debating. "So," he said finally, "have you ever met the incubi your brother was talking about?"

"Yes..." Roan said after a moment. They reached the porch steps and Ishaan stopped to let him go first, but Roan just leaned against the rail and picked at a knothole in the board. "They're just normal people," Roan said. "You could meet one and never even know it. They certainly aren't monsters, or demons, or parasites. They're just people."

"I...I know," Ishaan said. "I shouldn't have said that. It was horribly hypocritical, considering, it's just...the thought of someone doing anything to me while I'm asleep, let alone feeding off me like some kind of sex vampire, and I can't stop them, I can't even remember..." He shuddered. "It just gives me the creeps."

"Oh, yeah," Roan said, still picking at the wood, "it's creepy, disgusting."

"Besides," Ishaan said, reaching out and mussing up Roan's golden hair, "what do I need anyone else for? I've got you."

Roan didn't respond for a second, then he looked up and grinned.

"Threesomes can be fun," he said and Ishaan rolled his eyes, though to be honest, that didn't sound like such a bad idea.

"Come on," he said, "let's see if we can get the remote away from your brother. There's an old pirate movie on tonight that I wanted to watch."

"Sounds good," Roan said, heading up the stairs. "If Kethic has his choice, he'll watch porn all night long."

"I have porn channels?"

"Yeah, thirteen of them...Not that I've ever watched porn on your TV."

"Oh, right, I believe that."

"Okay, maybe once."

"Get in the house."

Fifteen

With Kethic on the other end of the couch and Ishaan seated in the armchair just beyond Roan's reach, both of them trying to talk to him while ignoring each other, the two hour movie felt more like a four hour root canal. When the credits finally began to roll, Roan jumped up off the couch.

"Well, I don't know about you guys, but I'm exhausted. C'mon, Kethic, I'll make you up a bed on my floor. I'll be out to lock you up in a minute, Ishaan."

"I'm not tired," Kethic said, reaching for the remote.

Ishaan rose from his chair. "I'm going to go take a bath."

Roan watched him disappear into the bathroom. As soon as the door was shut, he stepped over to his brother and smacked him in the back of the head.

"Hey!" Kethic said, scowling up him.

"That was for bringing up the incubism," Roan said through his teeth.

"I know what it was for. I was doing you a favor."

"A favor?" Roan hissed. He dropped onto the couch beside Kethic, grabbed the remote out of his hand, and turned the volume up to drown out their voices. "And-and what? If he'd said *Sure, let me meet your incubus friend,* you'd have pointed at me and said *Surprise!"*

Kethic shrugged. "Hadn't really thought that far ahead. It's good to know, though, isn't it?"

"Oh, yeah, it's great. He thinks I'm a parasite, Keth, a freaking sex vampire. If he ever finds out, he's going to *hate* me."

"And why would that matter?" Kethic asked. "I thought you weren't falling for him."

"I'm not," Roan snapped. "But that doesn't mean I want him hating me. His father is very rich and he could cause me—us a lot of trouble."

"You think he'd do that?"

"He might. I don't know. I don't want to find out. Just stop doing me favors, okay?"

Kethic didn't respond, just grabbed the remote back and went back to flipping channels. Roan started to get up, but a screen filled with naked, tan, sweaty flesh caught his eye, and his jaw dropped as Kethic stopped his surfing.

"Hey, now this is what I'm talking about," Kethic said with a grin. Two men, one with short, honey gold hair and the other with a long, silver and black streaked braid, were going at it in what appeared to be a large dining hall, the blond shoving his partner back onto the long table. "Is that how you and Ishaan do it?"

Roan jumped, felt his face color, and lunged for the remote.

"Gimme that," he said, but Kethic held the remote over his head and leaned away, keeping it out of Roan's reach. "Keth, knock it off." But Kethic just laughed.

"C'mon, Roan, give me a hint; is he bigger than that guy?"

Roan refused to look at the screen again, but the groaning and moaning and overacted breathless cries of ecstasy that filled living room were still making his pants uncomfortably tight across the front. In fact, not looking just made things worse, made it easier to imagine him and Ishaan making those noises.

Watching the TV, Kethic's eyes grew wide. "Holy hell," he whispered. "You ever do something like that?"

Roan almost looked, but made another grab for the remote instead.

"Kethic, I mean it, turn this crap off." He pulled at Kethic's arm, trying to bring the remote within reach, but Kethic stretched out, practically lying back on the couch, laughing his damn head off and holding Roan off with his free arm.

"Is that the best you can do?" Kethic asked. "'Come on, sissy boy, you want it, come and get it."

"Kethic!" Roan hissed. "This is not a game, damn it. I'm going to—I'm—I—" He shoved Kethic's arm out of the way and lunged at him, lying on top of him and pinning him to the couch as Kethic continued to laugh and hold the remote beyond his head. Roan reached for it, but Kethic quickly pulled it in and shoved it beneath his back. Roan slipped his hand between the couch and his brother's body, groping for the remote, but Kethic pulled his hand free and tried to throw Roan off onto the floor.

"Hey!" Roan shouted as he lost his balance. He clutched at Kethic to keep from falling, but only succeeded in pulling him off the couch, too.

Roan lay on his back on the carpet, Kethic on top of him, both of them laughing as they tried and failed to untangle themselves and get up. Roan reached for the remote, sitting on the couch cushion, but Kethic pushed his arm away.

"Okay, Keth, I mean it this time," Roan said, out of breath. "If Ishaan comes out here and sees this, he's going to—"

"Wish he'd stayed in the bathroom," Ishaan said, leaning on the back of the couch as he frowned down at them. "You couldn't have waited until I was asleep?"

Roan tried to scramble out from under his brother, but for some reason, Kethic grabbed him by the upper arms and pinned him to the floor.

"You're just jealous," Kethic said and Roan stared up at him in horror. "You want to join us?" Ishaan glanced at the TV, his face expressionless, and then back down at Roan. Suddenly, Roan's earlier threesome joke didn't seem that funny. Ishaan picked up the remote and turned the TV off before heading for his room.

"Roan, when you're finished playing with your brother, I'm ready for bed." He left the living room and Roan glared up into Kethic's grinning face.

"That wasn't funny," Roan said through his teeth.

"I thought it was hilarious," Kethic said. He sat up, but remained straddling Roan's hips, and raised his eyebrows. "Oh, what's this?" He wiggled his hips, rubbing his butt against the bulge in the front of Roan's pants. "Do I detect a bit of a woody going on there?" He laughed again and slid off of Roan. "Hurry up, then. Ishaan is waiting for you to tuck him in." Roan sat up.

"I think you need to leave," he said quietly, but Kethic just laughed and climbed to his feet, offering Roan a hand up. Roan knocked his hand away and stood on his own. "I mean it, Kethic, I want you to go."

He walked past him, over to Ishaan's room, opened the door and slipped inside. The bedroom was barely lit by the light of the waning moon filtering in through the window and Roan could make out little more than Ishaan's silhouette standing near the side of his bed.

"Roan?" Ishaan asked.

Roan licked his dry lips.

"Yeah," he said. For several moments no one said or did anything, then Ishaan's dark figure lunged across the room and shoved Roan back against the door. For a split second, panic, swift and choking, rose up in Roan's chest. Ishaan was going to kill him. Roan raised his hands to push him away, but Ishaan caught his wrists and pinned them to the door above his head. A single, startled cry escaped his lips, and then Ishaan covered Roan's mouth with his own in a hard, breathless, bruising kiss.

Surprised, Roan couldn't move as Ishaan's tongue slipped into his mouth, exploring him, claiming him. This was wrong. Something about this was wrong. Then Ishaan's lean, strong body pressed against him, his erection evident through his thin cotton pajamas, rubbing against the aching bulge in the front of Roan's pants. Roan kissed back, body arching away from the door as he sought contact. Ishaan let go of Roan's wrists and began to pull at his clothes, shoving his T-shirt up, fumbling with the button on his jeans.

Roan gasped as Ishaan unzipped his jeans with a jerk. Ishaan began to bite and suck at Roan's neck as he slipped his hands down into Roan's pants. Roan clutched at his arms, his knees weak and shaking as Ishaan stroked him. He closed his eyes, dug his fingers into Ishaan's muscular shoulders, and turned his face into Ishaan's neck, damp hair brushing his face, the scent of sweat and shampoo surrounding him.

Ishaan pulled back suddenly, grabbed Roan by the shoulders and pushed him down to his knees. Roan clawed at the waistband of Ishaan's pajamas, dragging them down his thighs as he leaned forward and took Ishaan into his mouth, running his tongue around the head as he stroked the shaft with one hand and slipped the other into his own pants. He freed his erection and began to jerk off, the thought of losing it as Ishaan filled his mouth making his balls tight. Ishaan reached out, resting his hands on the top of Roan's head, and began to move hips, thrusting into Roan's mouth.

Moaning, Roan sucked, his tongue caressing that hot, slick skin as it slid in and out of his mouth, his body tensing as drew near his climax and then backed off, waiting...waiting...Ishaan made a low, guttural sound in his throat, his grip on Roan tightening as he thrust harder, deeper. Roan almost choked, but Ishaan eased up and Roan suddenly realized why this was so wrong: Ishaan was awake. He was awake.

Ishaan cried out and a flood of warm, thick semen filled Roan's mouth. Roan closed his eyes, swallowed, and came across his hand and the carpet. His head spinning, he remained kneeling on the floor before Ishaan, the darkness filled with the sound of their ragged breathing. After a moment, Ishaan reached down and pulled up his pajamas, then stepped away from Roan and walked to his bed. Roan climbed to his feet, the orgasmic euphoria quickly turning to nausea as he watched Ishaan lie down and pull his blankets up over himself without so much as a single word. As quickly and quietly as he could, Roan fixed his clothes and opened the door.

Kethic leaned against the wall just outside the room, his eyes bright and face flushed. He moved back as Roan stepped out, took down the key, and locked the door, but as Roan turned and headed for the bathroom, Kethic followed and caught him by the arm.

"That felt incredible," Kethic said. "What did you guys do in there? Did he fuck you? How was it? I could hardly hear—" Roan whirled around and slammed his fist into Kethic's face, a sharp pain shooting up his arm as Kethic stumbled backward and fell over the arm of the couch into the seat. Roan watched blood well up from two gashes on his knuckles, then raised his eyes and took a step toward Kethic.

"I thought I told you to leave," he said. Kethic swung his legs off the arm and sat up, blood rolling down his chin and dripping onto his shirt.

"I thought you were joking," he said, wincing as he touched his split lip. "You really hit me."

"I'll hit you again if you don't get the fuck out of this house," Roan said.

Kethic raised his eyebrows.

"That's some pretty serious cursing," he said, rising to his feet. "What did I do?"

Roan's jaw dropped.

"What did you do? *What did you do?* You've ruined my life!"

"Oh, please," Kethic said, rolling his eyes. "Don't get all melodramatic on me. All I did was help you. I mean come on, would you have ended up in there, with him, *awake*, if it hadn't been for me?"

"No," Roan said, "I wouldn't have."

"So you should be thanking me, not throwing me out." Hands shaking, Roan lunged at him, grabbed him by the front of the shirt and yanked him up off the couch.

"Thanks to you," Roan hissed between his teeth as he shoved Kethic backward across the living room toward the door, "he's going to wake up tomorrow so disgusted with himself and with me that he'll make me leave."

They were nearly to the door before Kethic managed to stop and pull away from him.

"He won't—"

"Yes he will!" Roan shouted. "You don't know him. I'll be lucky if he even *looks* at me while he's telling me to pack my shit and get out." Roan felt like he was going to throw up. He unlocked the front door and jerked it open. "Get out."

"Roan," Kethic said, reaching out to put his hand on Roan's shoulder, "he's not going to make you leave. He likes you."

Roan shrugged off his brother's hand.

"No, Kethic, he doesn't, and after tonight, he probably hates me. Now get out."

Kethic made an exasperated sound.

"C'mon, Roan—"

"*Get out*," Roan said, and he balled his already bloody hand into a fist again.

"All right, fine," Kethic said, holding his hands in front of his face as he stumbled through the door. "I'll just go sleep in the woods—try not to freeze to death. Great way to treat your brother, Roan," he said as he walked away, heading down the driveway toward the road. "The only family you have left, and you turn him out into the cold." He was practically screaming now. "Mark my words, little brother, you shut that door and you will *never* see me again. I'll be out of your life forever, gone, vanished, like I—" Roan shut the door and locked it, then ran to the bathroom and threw up.

This could not be happening—this could not have *happened*. Why did he go into the room? Why didn't he just lock the door and walk away? He leaned back against the cabinet under the sink, gasping for breath as he fought the tears rolling down his face. How could he have been so stupid, so weak? He ruined everything.

Sixteen

Ishaan opened his eyes and groaned into the carpet, his body cold and stiff. Son-of-a-fucking-bitch. He squeezed his eyes shut and slammed his fist against the floor, choking back a sob. What the hell had he done?

Opening the bathroom door to find two naked, sweaty men fucking on television, and then seeing Roan and his brother wrestling on the couch, clearly fighting for the remote, but it didn't take a lot of imagination to picture them doing something else, his heart had been pounding, his body already aching when Kethic had invited him to join them. The thought of stripping down and lying in a tangled, writhing, sweaty ball of sex was almost more than he could take. He fled the room.

And then Roan had come to him. Ishaan pounded his fist into the floor again. He should have told him to get out—he should have made him leave! Instead, he shoved him against the wall, kissed him, touched him, made him suck on him—Worse! He'd fucked his mouth, fucked him like he was some filthy whore! Roan didn't deserve to be treated like that.

How could he be so stupid? His life was looking good for the first time since his condition appeared and he had to screw it up for a lousy blow-job? He shook his head as he shoved himself to his knees. That wasn't fair. After everything else he'd done to him, he was denying Roan the credit he deserved. It wasn't a lousy blow-job; it was the best one he could remember getting, not that he'd gotten that many. After the townsfolk tore down the whorehouse to try and dissuade him from coming to town, he had sort of given up on sex. Looked like he should have had himself castrated, too.

Ishaan dressed and then sat on the edge of his bed, waiting. Roan had to hate him. He was probably packing his bags that very minute. No, he'd probably packed up last night. He could have even left already. Ishaan listened for a sound, a footstep, anything, but the house was silent. Ishaan was trapped in his room...and he deserved it. Sezae would probably show up in a few hours to let him out—he couldn't see Roan leaving him to die. He'd probably never see Roan again.

A noise outside the door brought his head up and his muscles tensed. The little door slid open and Ishaan held his breath.

"Ishaan?" Roan said and Ishaan closed his eyes, his breath escaping him in a sigh. "Are you awake?"

"Yeah," Ishaan said and then he realized it probably would have been easier if Roan had left. He rose and shuffled to the door, his eyes downcast as he leaned against the wood. He couldn't do this—he couldn't look Roan in the eyes, not after what happened. He swallowed hard and looked out the window. The pain darkening those blue-gray eyes was almost too much to bear. It was his fault, all his fault. He heard the key slide into the lock and turned away.

He waited for Roan to leave, listened for the closing of the front door, but after a moment, Roan pushed his bedroom door open.

"Are you coming out?" he asked, a hesitancy in his voice. "I've got bacon cooking."

Ishaan frowned.

"Yeah, I'll be right there," he said and listened to Roan's footsteps head for the kitchen. He wasn't leaving. Well, maybe he was waiting until after breakfast, but that didn't seem real likely. After what Ishaan had done, he wasn't leaving. Why? Ishaan was barely paying him, aside from room and board, and not even a whore would let someone do what he had done without expecting something in return.

His lips parted in a soundless cry as he realized Roan's game. Roan expected him to feel guilty about what happened, guilty enough to offer something of monetary value to make up for it. He straightened up and squared his shoulders. Well, he was going to be disappointed. Ishaan strode to the bathroom to take care of business and wash up and then he joined Roan in the kitchen. Roan glanced at him, then back down at the pan.

"Where's your brother?" Ishaan asked. He wouldn't be surprised to find that this was all Kethic's idea.

"He left," Roan said.

Good riddance, as far as Ishaan was concerned. Kethic had started it, even if Ishaan was the one who had been too weak to stop.

"You want to split an omelet?" Ishaan asked.

Roan raised his head, a look of surprise and then relief on his face. "Sure," he said with a hesitant smile. "You want vegetables in it? I could go see what's in the garden."

"You watch the bacon," Ishaan said, frowning again. "I'll look in the garden." He went out barefoot, his toes cold and pant legs soaked with dew by the time he reached the garden. Roan didn't seem to be playing him. He acted like he thought Ishaan was upset with *him*. Why would he think that? Roan hadn't shoved him against the wall and made him suck his dick. Of course, it wasn't uncommon for victims to blame themselves, to somehow think they invited the assault. Ishaan felt nauseous just thinking it, but it wasn't an unreasonable assumption.

If it was more than an assumption, though, if it was the truth, Ishaan couldn't let Roan go on blaming himself. That wasn't right, either. He found a small Barandian pepper and a handful of green onions, but nothing else was ready for harvest yet. It'd be another couple of weeks. As he turned and began the wet walk back to the house, Roan stepped out on the back porch and stood at the rail, waiting for him. Everything in him screamed to run the other way, but he had to face this. As he drew up to the porch, he cleared his throat.

"Roan, about last night—"

"I thought we didn't talk about what you did when you were asleep," Roan said, his tone too light and careful to have been sarcastic or cruel. He wanted to pretend that Ishaan had been asleep and remembered nothing. Their eyes met for a moment, that pain returning to Roan's face. He did, he blamed himself. Ishaan opened his mouth, tried to find the words and the will to tell him the truth, but it was just too hard. He licked his dry lips, cleared his throat again, and then nodded.

"You're right," he said. "We don't need to talk about it." Roan's relieved smile did nothing to relieve Ishaan's guilt, though. He had done something terrible, again, and suffered no consequences for his actions, again. One day, the punishments for his crimes would catch up with him and kill him.

"Sometimes," Roan said after a long, tense moment, "friends can overlook mistakes that other people might not be able to. I know you said we'd never be friends, but...I would like to think that maybe we are."

Ishaan stared down at the dewy grass growing up around the bottom porch step and drew a slow breath. He was asking for so much trouble, but he wanted so badly for Roan to overlook his mistake. He nodded.

"Yeah," he said, raising his eyes to Roan, "I think we are, too." If Roan could overlook this, forgive him for his mistake, then he would make certain that it was the last such mistake he ever made.

Seventeen

"So, what you think," Ishaan asked as he headed into his room, "hunting tomorrow, or fishing? What do you want to do?"

"I dunno," Roan said from the kitchen. He opened the freezing compartment and peered inside. "We've got lots of—"

"I can't hear you," Ishaan called. Roan rolled his eyes and walked to Ishaan's doorway. It had been almost a week since that awful night and though everything was back to normal, save for a few awkward moments every now and then, Roan hadn't again set foot in Ishaan's room. Not while Ishaan was awake, at least.

"I said, there's plenty of fish in the freezer, and a couple of whole pheasant, so it doesn't matter to me."

"You ever had kelret meat?" Ishaan asked, glancing at him. If he noticed that Roan was lingering in the doorway, he didn't say anything.

"I don't think so. What is it?"

"Kind of like a rabbit, but with shorter ears and a longer tail, climbs trees, about this big." He held his hands up about a foot apart. "They taste real good barbecued," he added with a crooked grin as he slipped into bed.

"Sounds good to me," Roan said, reaching for the door. "Good night."

"Hey, Roan—" Roan stopped, his heart suddenly racing as he waited for Ishaan to speak. "Could you turn off the light?"

"Sure," Roan said, taking a single step into the room to hit the light switch. He wasn't sure if he was relieved or disappointed—he wasn't even sure what he thought Ishaan was going to say. He pulled the door shut and locked it, then crossed the room and collapsed onto the couch with a sigh.

What was wrong with him? Life was almost normal again, so why did he keep thinking about that night, about the way he'd felt as Ishaan's hands slid down his pants? He could blow Ishaan every night for the rest of his life and his demon would be sated, but he needed more. He needed human contact. He needed to be touched, even if it was a mistake.

That was the part that scared him; the thought that he would risk screwing up his life just for five minutes of desperate pleasure. It wouldn't take much to get it, either. All he had to do was push the right buttons and Ishaan would lose control. Roan closed his eyes and clenched his fists. He knew just what buttons to push, too. A little incidental contact, some accidental porn on the TV, maybe walk in on him in the bath—

Roan surged to his feet and went to his room, wanting to slap himself. He sat down at the desk and logged into the e-mail account, but there was no message from Kethic. He'd been trying all week to get a hold of him, to apologize, but with no luck. He wasn't sorry for getting angry, or for throwing Kethic out—Kethic's little jokes could have ruined everything—but he did regret hitting him.

He was changing into his pajamas when he heard a noise in the living room. It sounded like Ishaan tapping on his door. Roan glanced at the clock as he crossed the room. It hadn't even been forty-five minutes. He reached up to slide the little window open, but the sound came again—from the front door. What the hell? It was almost midnight.

Roan hurried to the door, his hands hesitating on the locks. What if this was a trap? What if it wasn't someone he wanted to let into the house? He leaned close to the door.

"Who is it?" he asked, trying to sound tough and angry—trying to sound like Ishaan. He failed.

"Roan, it's your brother. Please, let me in." He sounded tired and in pain—he sounded like his demon was trying to get out. "Please, Roan, I'm sorry for—" Roan unlocked the door and jerked it open. Kethic, pale and haggard, stood on the doorstep. "Thank you," he whispered and Roan reached out to steady him as he staggered into the house.

"Keth, what happened to you?" Roan asked, helping him over to the couch. "Where have you been?"

"In town," Kethic said. "At the inn. I was going to try bartering my services for a room, but when I mentioned I was your brother, Sezae just let me stay. She's really nice." Roan stiffened and stepped back from Kethic. "Not *that* nice," Kethic clarified. "That's what's wrong with me. No one in that entire town is willing to fuck me."

"You haven't fed in a week?" Roan asked. "I'd be dead or someone would be hurt."

"That's why the scientists couldn't use me," Kethic said with a laugh. "I'm not incubus enough. And that's why I think you are. You could hold the key to a cure, little brother, you could end all this."

"Kethic, I-I can't. I can't let them—"

"I know," Kethic said, leaning back on the couch and closing his eyes. "I know. I'm sorry. I'm not thinking straight." He sat up suddenly. "Have...have you...finished with him already?" Roan felt something cold and slimy knot up in his gut. Kethic needed to feed.

"You can't," Roan said. "You're the one who told *me* it was rape, remember?"

"A bit's changed since then," Kethic snapped. "I overreacted."

"That's easy to say now," Roan said, "now that you need him." He shook his head. "I'm sorry, I can't let you."

"Let me?" Kethic asked, struggling to his feet. "What, is he yours? Does he belong to you—your private sex toy? Cheyn take you, Roan, I'm not asking to fuck him, I just want to feed while you do whatever it is you do. Either that, or I can go back to town and wait for the demon to pick somebody. Maybe Sezae—"

"All right," Roan said, wanting to vomit at the thought. "You can feed, but it won't be much. All I do is suck him off."

"It'll be enough," Kethic said, sinking back down to the couch. "The train comes through tomorrow and I'll be fine once I'm back home. I've got more than enough people willing to take care of me there."

"I thought you said you were still on the run," Roan said, frowning.

Kethic drew a slow breath.

"I lied," he said finally. "I didn't want you to think it was safe to come home."

"Aren't they still after you?"

"No," Kethic said, shaking his head. "They know I'm not full-blooded, or whatever."

"But Keth, they *murdered* Mom and Dad. Aren't you afraid that they'll do the same to you?"

"It would serve me right if they did," Kethic said, "but I don't think they're going to. They were at the funeral and they've been at the cemetery every time I've gone to visit, but they're not after me. They're waiting for you."

"You've seen them?" Roan asked. "And you didn't do anything about it? You didn't kill them?"

Kethic rolled his eyes.

"Don't you think I wanted to?" he asked. "But I've got no proof that they killed our parents and I'd probably get caught and thrown in jail, and then everyone would find out what I am. And anyone with a brain would figure out that you're one, too. So, no, I didn't kill them."

"Sorry," Roan said, sinking down next to his brother. "I wasn't thinking." He didn't know how Kethic could be so damn logical about it. If Roan had seen those murdering bastards hanging around the graves like vultures, he'd have killed them—or died trying—and jail be damned.

"So," Kethic said after a moment, "were you going to—"

"Oh, right," Roan said, standing up. He glanced at the clock. "Oh, shit."

"What is it?"

"It's been more than an hour. He could be up already. He could be waiting for me."

"What does that mean?" Kethic asked, reaching out for a hand up. "What would he do?"

"Rape me," Roan said, pulling Kethic to his feet. Kethic stared across the room at Ishaan's door. "And don't even think about it. It's not pleasant, at all. He made me bleed."

"Were you prepared?" Kethic asked.

Roan stared at him.

"What part of rape don't you understand?" Roan asked. "Of course I wasn't prepared. He just grabbed me and fucked me."

"So, what if you *were* prepared?" Roan started to turn away in disgust, but

Kethic grabbed his arm. "Just listen to me, okay? I don't know what's happened since you threw me out, but you're living here, so I guess he wasn't too upset. He could have stopped what happened, but he didn't. He could have made sure it would never happen again, but he didn't. So on some subconscious level, he's okay with it, if not actually *wanting* it."

"Your logic is convoluted," Roan said.

Kethic gave him a tired smile.

"Maybe, but it makes sense to you, I can see it in your face. Let's just try something, okay? Prepare yourself this time and then let him fuck you, see if it's different, see if I'm right. Because if I am, he won't rape you, he won't just mindlessly plow your ass to satisfy his own bestial urges."

"Don't use that word—bestial. It make you sound like you know what you're talking about."

"Come on, Roan, you know I'm right."

"You just want to feed on real sex."

"That, too."

Roan hesitated.

"What if you're wrong; what if he hurts me?"

Kethic draped his arm over Roan's shoulders and pulled him into a hug.

"I won't let him," Kethic said. "That's my job, remember, to look after my stupid kid brother. I'll admit, I haven't done a real great job lately—"

"That wasn't your fault," Roan said. He sighed and stepped away from Kethic. "I guess if we're going to do this, we better hurry before he starts beating on the door and masturbating."

"Oh, but that sounds like so much fun," Kethic said, chuckling as he followed Roan. Roan fetched the blue lubricant out of his bedroom and headed for the bathroom.

"I can do this on my own," he said, closing the door on Kethic.

"You sure?" Kethic asked. "I wouldn't mind lending a hand. How about three fingers?"

Roan laughed.

"Not interested, sorry." Back when they'd been whoring in alleys, they'd been paid handsomely to do things to each other, but it was never something he enjoyed. He and Kethic grew up together, they'd seen each other naked a thousand times, they were best friends, but the sexual stuff just felt forced. For him, at least.

"Are you almost done?" Kethic asked. "I'm *starving*. Are you sure you don't need help? My fingers are longer than yours." Roan leaned on the sink, his body twisted as he thrust his fingers deep inside himself. It probably would be easier with Kethic's help, but he managed on his own. He washed his hands and started to open the door, but grabbed a towel and wrapped it around himself first. Kethic, leaning against the back of the couch, took one look at him and arched an eyebrow. "Did you find modesty in your ass, because you never had any before."

"Sorry," Roan said as he headed for Ishaan's room. "I haven't preformed for an audience in a few years. I'm feeling a little weird."

"Hey, it's just me," Kethic said, stepping up behind him. Roan felt Kethic's breath on his neck and pulled away.

"Quit it, okay?" he said. "I'm trying not to freak out at the thought of what Ishaan might do to me and you're not helping."

"Sorry," Kethic said, his voice tight, strained. "The demon is making this real hard. You're not a little boy anymore, Roan."

"Kethic," Roan said softly, "I can't do this if I can't trust you to stop him if he's hurting me. Do you understand? I need to know that you're in control, that you'll help me."

"I won't let him hurt you," Kethic said, sounding almost normal. "I'll take your place before I let that happen." Roan stood before the door, key in the lock, his hand trembling. This was such a bad idea. Finally, he swallowed hard and unlocked the door, pushed it open, and stepped inside.

"No matter what happens," Roan said over his shoulder, "don't wake him up. Being raped wouldn't be as bad as being caught." He reached out, turned on the light and stopped dead. The bed was empty. "Shit!" Roan hissed. He spun around.

Standing next to Kethic was Ishaan. They'd stepped right past him in the dark. Ishaan turned his empty, lifeless eyes from Kethic to Roan and then stepped forward. Roan backed away, his eyes darting past Ishaan to Kethic, standing in front of the door, a look of helplessness on his face.

"What do I do?" Kethic asked.

Roan didn't answer. He didn't know. Roan scrambled away from Ishaan, crashing against the closet doors as he tried to run past him, to get out of the room. Ishaan caught him around the waist, practically lifted him off the floor, and threw him face down on the bed. Roan screamed as Ishaan climbed on top of him. Not again. This could not be happening again.

"Kethic!" Roan shouted as Ishaan ripped the towel away from his body. Ishaan's large, warm hands grabbed his hips, then slid down and spread his cheeks apart. "Ishaan, please," Roan begged. "Kethic, help me." He screamed again as he felt the head of Ishaan's erection touch his opening—

"Get off him, you son-of-a-bitch," Kethic said, leaping onto the bed and grabbing Ishaan's arm, trying to pull him off. "Why don't you fuck somebody your own size?" Roan glanced over his shoulder as Ishaan shoved Kethic away, sending him crashing against the wall. Kethic groaned and tried to get up, but he was too weak. Roan twisted, kicking, fighting, but Ishaan caught one flailing arm, pinned it to the mattress, then lay on top of Roan, breathing hard on the back of his neck. Roan could feel Ishaan's erection pressed against his ass and he closed his eyes, choking back a sob.

"Shhh," Ishaan whispered and Roan froze, his heart thundering in his chest. "It's all right." A thrill ran through Roan; hope, fear, he wasn't sure, but he was suddenly shaking, barely able to breathe. Ishaan let go of his arm and raised himself enough to guide the head of his erection back to Roan's opening.

"I'm gonna...kill him," Kethic grunted, stumbling back over to the bed.

"Wait, wait," Roan said, breathless, as Ishaan eased inside him. It hurt, a little, but no more than with any other guy. "He's not hurting me. Y-you were right. He's not hurting me."

Beside the bed, Kethic sank to his knees, one hand reaching out to touch Ishaan's shoulder and he sighed in relief.

Ishaan pushed deeper and Roan groaned into the mattress. Ishaan fell still, pressed his lips to the back of Roan's shoulder, and then began to move, slowly, easing in and out. The pain faded, each slow stroke twisting it into a deep, aching pleasure. This was what he wanted, this was what he missed. Ishaan's body covered him, hands sliding beneath him, caressing his chest and stomach, moving down between his legs.

"Oh, Ishaan," Roan moaned. He'd wanted this so much, for so long. "Harder—Please, Ishaan, harder. Fuck me." Ishaan didn't respond. He continued his languid strokes, drawing a frustrated groan from Roan.

"Does he talk to you?" Kethic asked.

"Sometimes," Roan said through his teeth. "He sure doesn't listen, though." He tried to raise his hips off the bed and force Ishaan deeper, but he was pinned. "Damn it."

Finally, Ishaan began to thrust harder and Roan bucked against him. Ishaan drove into him, stroking him, and Roan stiffened as he came on the sheet with a strangled shout. He tried to pull away, but Ishaan wasn't finished, thrusting into his trembling, sensitive body again and again. Roan writhed, whimpering, as Ishaan continued to fuck him. It was too much, it felt too *good*, he couldn't take it—

Ishaan slammed into him, driving him into the mattress, and they both cried out as Ishaan came, jerking his hips and sending another splinter of pleasure deep into Roan's body. Roan lay, trembling, gasping, almost sobbing, beneath Ishaan as he waited for the agonizing ecstasy to fade.

"That," Kethic said in a whisper, "was amazing."

Roan turned his head to look at his brother, sagging against the side of the bed, breathless, with a wet stain on the front of his pants.

"You came?" Roan asked.

Kethic looked down at himself.

"Looks like it." He laughed. "I'm not surprised. That was better than most of the actual sex that I've had. I *told* you he liked you."

"No, he doesn't," Roan said with a grunt as he tried to shove Ishaan off of himself. "That's just because of his sickness. It's always been intense."

"Or maybe he's always been attracted to you." Kethic stood and helped roll Ishaan over.

Roan climbed off the bed and grabbed his towel off the floor.

"He can barely stand me," Roan said, even though he knew Kethic was probably closer to the truth than he was. They didn't speak as they cleaned Ishaan up and tucked him back under the blankets, not until Kethic caught him as he headed for the bathroom.

"Thank you," Kethic said. "I know that was strange and uncomfortable for you, and if I hadn't been so desperate, I never would have—"

"It's okay," Roan said. "How many times did I freak out your girlfriends growing up? I'd say we're even."

"Sounds good to me," Kethic said, stepping past him and heading for Roan's room. "I'm going to borrow a pair of pants, if that's okay."

"Better than you running around naked," Roan said with a grimace as he shut himself in the bathroom. He ran himself a bath, sinking into the hot water with a gasp and a sigh. He ached, but it was a good, fulfilling sort of ache, and every now and then another ghost of a shudder ran through him. That had been the most incredible sex he'd ever experienced. It was the most incredible *experience* he'd ever had. How could he go back to those impersonal, nightly blow jobs? He couldn't. Not *every* night, anyway.

Kethic could be completely full of shit and Ishaan might not want to have anything to do with him, but he didn't really care. It was wrong, it was immoral, but he was only human. He was weak, he was selfish, and Ishaan never needed to find out.

Eighteen

Ishaan heard the back door open and glanced up from weeding the cucumber beds as Roan came bouncing down the steps and running across the lawn. He recognized that grin.

"How's Kethic?" he asked, thrusting the shovel into the hard, dry ground.

"He says hello," Roan said, stopping on the other side of the corn and peering over the long, green leaves. "He also has some...interesting news. You remember I told you he had a new girlfriend?"

"No."

"Yes, I did," Roan said. "He met her on the train after he spent the night here. I told you."

"Yeah, I guess I remember," Ishaan said, grinning to himself. He remembered, he just liked giving Roan a hard time. "What about her?"

"She's pregnant, so they're going to get married."

"What?" Ishaan asked, stabbing his trowel into the ground and standing up. "That was...What, two months ago?" Roan shrugged and nodded. "They're crazy. It'll never work out."

"Tell me about it," Roan said. "I told him he should get her to end the pregnancy, but he said he wouldn't. He's so selfish, he wants a kid so badly, he's willing to risk that it—" Roan shut his mouth, his brow furrowed and eyes tight.

Ishaan wiped the sweat from his forehead and regarded Roan. He knew that look.

"Risk that it...what?" Ishaan asked. Roan glanced up and Ishaan could see him grasping for an answer.

"That it won't work out, of course. That's all I meant." They looked at each other for a moment, then Roan turned away, walking down the long row of corn.

He was lying again. Ishaan drew a slow breath, then sighed and knelt back down in the dirt. He didn't care. He trusted Roan. The man was entitled to a few secrets and as long as they didn't come back to bite Ishaan on the ass, he didn't care.

"So, when's the wedding?" Ishaan asked after a while. He glanced down the rows at Roan, shirtless in the baking sun, his skin tanned to a wonderful gold and hair pulled back in a tight braid, snapping beans off the vines and dropping them in a big metal bowl.

"Some time in the fall," Roan said with a shrug. "They want to wait a while, but she wants to be able to fit into her mother's wedding dress, so...It's not like it matters," Roan said after a minute. "I can't go."

"Those people?"

Roan nodded.

Ishaan jabbed at a thistle with his trowel. "I wouldn't worry about it," he said. "They'll be divorced within two weeks."

"If that long," Roan added, but he wasn't convincing. And why should he be? Unable to attend his only brother's wedding; Ishaan would have been pissed. He set down his hand shovel and stood, the sweat rolling down his back and sticking his hair to his neck.

"Hey," he said, drawing Roan's attention. "Want to help me with the watering? Then I'll give you a hand with the beans and we can get out of this sun."

"Sounds good," Roan said, nudging the bean bowl into the shade under the vines. They grabbed the buckets from beside the tomatoes and headed for the river. Usually, the shade of the woods was a welcome relief, but the air was so still and muggy, it was like walking through a tropical jungle. Only at the river's edge was the air noticeably cooler. Ishaan dipped out a bucket of water and set it on the bank, then bent down and splashed the chill water on his face and chest. He shivered and sighed appreciatively.

"I can't believe how hot it is," he said as he straightened up. "This kind of heat isn't healthy. It makes people act a little crazy." Roan glanced at him and raised one eyebrow, but Ishaan just reached out and took his bucket from him.

"What—" Roan asked, but Ishaan just grinned and shoved him backward into the river. Roan burst to the surface, gasping in shock and pawing the water from his eyes. "Ishaan! What the hell?" Roan asked. The water came up to just above his navel and his slick skin gleamed in the dappled sunlight filtering through the trees.

"I don't know what came over me," Ishaan said. "Must've been the sun."

Roan stared up at him, stunned, then he laughed and backhanded the water, flipping it onto Ishaan. With a shout, Ishaan leaped off the bank, drawing his knees up as he plunged into the river.

It was cold! He came up gasping, his entire body screaming, awake, alive, his skin prickling, tingling. He swept his hair back out of his face and grinned at Roan.

"You're insane," Roan said. "We've got work to do."

"We've been working all summer," Ishaan said. "Relax for five minutes, would you?" He slid forward into an easy breast stroke, swimming against the current and losing ground, but not much. This time of year, though the water came straight from the last lingering pockets of snow clinging to the shadows on the mountains, it wasn't very swift or deep.

Ishaan heard a splash and glanced toward the bank, figuring it was Roan climbing out of the river, but Roan wasn't in sight, in or out of the water. He stopped swimming and planted his feet among the smooth, round river rocks, searching the trees.

"Roan?" he called. "Ro—whoa!" Something grabbed him by the back of his shorts, kicked him in the back of the knees, and jerked him over backward as his knees buckled. The chill water closed over his head. He thrashed his arms and kicked his feet, his heels slamming into the rocky bottom. He pushed off, thrusting himself back to the surface, gasping and choking as Roan laughed.

"Gotcha," Roan said. Ishaan flipped his wet hair back and glared at Roan. "Uh oh," Roan said, but he was still laughing as he struggled through the water toward the bank, swinging his arms and splashing water back at Ishaan.

Ishaan took a deep breath and dove under, slicing through the water faster than Roan could run. He grabbed Roan's legs and pulled them out from under him. Roan fell on him, wrapped one arm across Ishaan's chest, and held him down as he tried to pull away, but only for a second. Roan let go and they both shot to the surface, gasping and laughing. Roan lunged at him, but Ishaan caught him by one arm and sidestepped the feeble attack. Roan stumbled through the water, caught himself on the bank, and spun around. Ishaan grabbed him and shoved him back against the riverbank.

"Surrender," Ishaan demanded, but the laughter died in his throat as he suddenly felt Roan's thigh pressed against his, their bare stomachs separated by an inch of water. A thought flashed through his mind; he was doing it again. Something inside him drew tight, trembled, threatened to snap. Ishaan leaned closer, Roan gasped and they stood, skin to skin for one fleeting second.

"Please," Roan whispered, his hands trembling, his eyes dark and frightened. Ishaan pulled back, hardly able to breathe. *What* was he doing?

"I-I'm sorry," Ishaan said, turning away. He was sorry. He'd almost molested his friend again and he was *sorry*. He grabbed at the bank and hauled himself out of the water, his head spinning. No, not molested, not raped or fucked—that wasn't what he'd wanted to do. Ishaan closed his eyes and clenched his fist. He couldn't, he wouldn't, ever. Roan was understanding, Roan might even let him, like he'd let him before, but Roan could never love him.

Ishaan choked, swallowed the sound before he could make it, and lunged to his feet. He could *not* do this here. He heard a sound and turned, looking down at Roan as he felt along the slick, muddy bank for something to grab on to. Ishaan hesitated, then reached down, offering Roan his hand. Honestly, he expected Roan to refuse. He was ready for that sting, but not for the hollow ache that opened in his chest as Roan took his hand.

"Thanks," Roan said, his feet on dry land once more.

"No problem," Ishaan replied and he bent down to finish filling the buckets.

Roan cleared his throat.

"You know, Ishaan, I don't know what—"

"I don't know what I was thinking, either," Ishaan said. "I wasn't, I guess. I'm sorry. It won't happen again."

Roan was silent for a long moment.

"Well, okay then," he said and grabbed his two buckets before heading for the garden. They watered in silence and when he was finished, Roan grabbed the bowl of beans and went in the house. Ishaan didn't blame him at all.

When Ishaan finally followed, Roan had already changed into a pair of dry black shorts and a white tank, which made his tanned skin glow like bronze. He was standing at the counter, snapping the tips off the beans, and didn't look up as Ishaan passed.

Ishaan locked himself in the bathroom and peeled off his wet cutoffs and briefs, one hand sliding along his hardening dick. Roan would never know how much he had wanted to kiss him, hold him, slide his shorts off, and make love to him. He could almost feel that hot, tight body wrapped around him amid all that cold, rushing water, almost hear Roan's breathless gasps and moans, his cries of ecstasy.

He was crazy if he thought Roan could ever love him. He was a monster, a demon, an insatiable beast, and not just when he was asleep. If Roan ever knew the things he thought, the way he felt, when he looked at him, when he thought about touching him, Roan would hate him. Sweet, kind, understanding Roan would hate the sight of him, because he had no excuse for his urges and desires. He was awake. He should be able to stop it, but he couldn't.

With a sob, Ishaan sank to his knees and leaned against the cabinet, his eyes closed as he masturbated silently. He was weak, but Roan would never know.

Nineteen

Roan lay on his bed, staring up at the ceiling, listening to the ticking of the clock on the wall. It seemed to be slowing down. Every time he glanced up, it seemed that less time had passed than before. Once, he even could have sworn the hands had moved *backward*. With a frustrated sigh, he got up and stalked out into the living room, grabbed the remote, then threw it back down. He went to the kitchen and looked in the sink, but the dishes were all washed. So he grabbed the dish rag and began scrubbing down the counter top. He just needed something to do before he went crazy thinking about what had almost happened.

Ishaan had almost kissed him. He groaned and scrubbed harder at a stain. He was sure of it; standing in the river, barely a breath between them, Ishaan had come *that close* to kissing him. And then he'd just walked away. *Oops, my mistake. Sorry, not interested after all.*

Had he known? That close, had he somehow, subconsciously, sensed that Roan wasn't quite normal? Had to be. Nothing else stopped him. Roan had even whispered please—*please*, begging him, and he'd just turned away. *I'm sorry*, he'd said. Like that was supposed to mean something. Why couldn't he say what he was really feeling? *Hey, I wanted you, 'till I realized what you were, now you just creep me out.*

It wasn't a stain, it was a dark vein in the marble. Roan threw the cloth into the sink and stormed back into his room. He'd waited long enough. He dug his lubricant out of his underwear drawer and headed into the bathroom.

Yes, it was weak and disgusting and selfish, and he couldn't stand the sight of his own reflection as he worked his slippery fingers deep inside himself, but he needed Ishaan, needed his touch, his smell, needed to feel his weight on top of him, his hard cock inside of him. Maybe it wasn't real, maybe Ishaan had no idea what he was doing, or with whom, but Roan couldn't forget how Ishaan had pushed Kethic aside that night, had come straight after him. Roan could pretend that he knew. He could pretend that Ishaan wanted him. It didn't hurt anyone.

Roan eased Ishaan's door open and slipped inside, hesitating against the wall before turning on the light. Ishaan didn't move, lying quietly on his back, one arm above his head, his hair hanging across his face. Roan walked to the bed, staring down at him, and then reached out to brush his hair back. He slid beneath the covers and up against Ishaan's warm, muscular body, just lying beside him for a moment before rolling onto his stomach to wait. He rested his chin on his folded hands and sighed.

The first few times after Kethic had gone home, Roan had been afraid, entering Ishaan's room, but Ishaan hadn't attacked him, hadn't hurt him. Was it simply because he'd been taking care of Ishaan every night and Ishaan didn't have that frustrated rage anymore? Or did Ishaan know it was him? He wanted it to be the latter.

Before long, Ishaan became restless, both arms sliding under the blankets, and Roan could tell he was working his pajama pants off. A tight, fluttery feeling settled in Roan's stomach, his heart pattering against the inside of his chest. Almost time. Ishaan's hand touched the small of his back and he groaned, his eyes sliding shut. It was real. It was as real as he was ever going to find.

Ishaan's hands moved across his skin, making his whole body tingle and he felt himself grow hard. He raised his hips and one of Ishaan's hands slid beneath him, brushing against his shaft and he gasped.

"Ishaan," he said through his teeth, "stop teasing me. Please, I need you."

"Roan," Ishaan said, a deep, rumbling growl in his chest. Roan felt him rise up on his knees, those strong hands gripping his body. Roan shuddered in anticipation. Then Ishaan grabbed him by one arm and tried to roll him over.

"What are you doing?" Roan asked, trying to pull away. He tried to get his knees under him, but Ishaan was so much stronger. Ishaan rolled him onto his back and Roan looked up into those cold, empty, lifeless eyes. He turned his face away, unable to pretend anything with Ishaan's blind, dead eyes staring through him.

Ishaan slid his hands between Roan's thighs, spread his legs and climbed between them. Roan tried again to pull away, to turn over, but Ishaan held him down. Roan felt Ishaan brush across his opening, press against him, push inside, and he cried out, a sound of mingled pleasure and sorrow. It wasn't supposed to happen like this. He wanted to be fucked from behind, so he couldn't see that it wasn't really Ishaan.

His eyes turned up to the ceiling, Roan drew short, gasping breaths as Ishaan's hands caressed the insides of his thighs, gently spreading them wider, then eased beneath him and lifted his hips off the sheet. Ishaan sank into him in one slow, smooth stroke and Roan's breath caught in his throat as the pleasure shuddered through him. He couldn't remember ever having anyone so deep inside him.

Without drawing back, Ishaan began to grind his pelvis against Roan, rocking his hips and pressing against Roan's prostate, a deep, unbearable, aching ecstasy gathering in the middle of him, tight and heavy. Roan squirmed, trying to ease that pressure, but every movement just made it worse. He reached up, grabbing at the headboard, and tried to pull away. He just needed Ishaan to not be quite so deep, but Ishaan wouldn't let him go. Strong hands gripped his thighs, slid down to his waist, holding him tight against Ishaan.

With a frustrated cry, Roan grabbed the pillow beside him and hurtled it at Ishaan, hitting him in the head. Ishaan barely even blinked, but he drew back, just a little, just enough for Roan to be able to breathe without feeling like he was on the verge of coming the whole time. Ishaan ran his hands back up Roan's thighs, his touch making Roan shiver, and then he leaned forward, bracing himself on his forearms, his body covering Roan's.

Roan arched his back, pressing his own hard arousal against Ishaan's stomach, and Ishaan groaned as he lowered his head and pressed his face into the crook of Roan's neck, each ragged breath, each brush of lips and tongue drawing another gasp from Roan. Roan gripped the headboard, eyes squeezed shut as Ishaan's hands slid beneath his back and shoulders, clutching at him, holding him too close.

Ishaan began to work his hips, long slow strokes, and Roan cried out, his legs wrapping around Ishaan's waist of their own accord. How could this feel so good when it hurt so much? Choking on a sob, Roan let go of the cold headboard and wrapped his arms around Ishaan's shoulders, his fingers digging into his back.

"I wish you loved me," Roan whispered, turning his face into Ishaan's hair, breathing deep of his skin and sweat and shampoo. He would have given anything at that moment to have Ishaan say something, anything—Ishaan raised his head and Roan's eyes snapped open, his breath a stuttering gasp as he looked up into Ishaan's face, hoping, searching for some sign that Ishaan knew what he was doing...

Empty eyes stared back at him without seeing, a deep and terrible ache growing in Roan's chest as Ishaan continued to fuck him, just like he would have fucked anybody else. Roan choked back a sob and shut his eyes again. It wasn't fair. He hadn't done anything except be born different, and for that crime he was doomed to a lifetime of nights like this, held in the arms of the only man he'd ever let himself love, who would not, could not, ever love him in return.

Soft, warm lips pressed against his and he turned his face away, a sob catching in his throat, choking him. Ishaan kissed the back of his jaw, just below his ear, his lips moving along Roan's jawbone, then lingering at the corner of his mouth. Roan shook, torn between ecstasy and agony, his body aching, heart breaking. He wanted it to be real. A low sound escaped him, a sound of pain and despair, and he turned his head back, capturing Ishaan's mouth in a hungry, desperate kiss.

Roan lifted his hips to meet Ishaan's thrusts, moaning into Ishaan's mouth, and Ishaan began to pound into him. Roan pulled away, his head falling back as he gasped for breath, shuddering and shaking, his body taut as a drawn bow about to be released. He cried out as he came, his seed slick between their bodies as Ishaan continued to drive into him. Roan clung to him, every breath a helpless cry as the pleasure raced through him like electricity in his veins. Ishaan tensed, gasped, and moaned as he spilled himself inside of Roan.

"Love...you..." Ishaan muttered into Roan's shoulder as he sagged and grew limp, completely asleep once more. Roan lay beneath him, trying to catch his breath, but Ishaan's words echoed in his head, tearing at his soul.

Ishaan didn't know what he was saying, or to whom. He didn't mean it, he couldn't. Roan shoved Ishaan off of him and turned away, drawing his knees up and wrapping his arms around himself as he stared across the room and shivered.

The worst part of it all was that he wanted to believe it. He knew better. He was smarter than this. It could never work and yet he'd let himself fall in love anyway. With a sob, he rolled over and wrapped his arms around Ishaan, crying against Ishaan's shoulder, too weak to fight anymore. Ishaan shifted in his sleep and Roan started to let go, but rather than pulling away, Ishaan brought his arm up across Roan's back, drawing him closer. Roan tensed, holding his breath, but Ishaan just let his cheek rest against the top of Roan's head.

Roan sighed and closed his eyes. This could have been the most perfect moment of his life; instead, it cut like a knife into his heart. He couldn't do this anymore. He shrugged off Ishaan's arm and sat up, the ache in his chest deepening, but he didn't have a choice. He couldn't live like this. It hurt too much. The next time he and Ishaan went into town, he'd ask Sezae to post the notice back on the board. He would find a replacement and then he would leave. It was the only answer.

Twenty

Ishaan leaned back in his chair and let his arms hang at his sides, giving his fingers and wrists a break. He'd been typing for the better part of three hours, replying to threads on the half dozen forums he helped moderate. Had it really only been three hours? He glanced over at the windows, already dark even though it was high summer and the sun shouldn't even have set for another hour or more. A faint ticking against the glass answered his unasked question—it was raining, and with the sky that dark and the wind blowing the rain against the eastern windows, they were in for a storm. Ishaan reached over and turned on his desk lamp, then went back to his computer.

A while later, he was startled from his typing by a heavy *whoomph* against the side of the house, hard enough to rattle the glass in the window casings. The wind had picked up. Good, they'd need firewood for the coming winter.

"Ishaan?" Roan called from the living room where he was watching television.

"Hmm?"

"Where's the Livaen Valley?"

"You're living in it," Ishaan said. "Why?"

"The TV has one of those streaming ticker things running across the bottom of the screen," Roan said. "It says, '...has issued a weather advisory for the Livaen Valley from eight pm to six am, calling for strong wind, heavy rain and hail, and isolated severe thunderstorms—' Ishaan?"

"Don't worry about it," Ishaan said. "The garden will be fine. The wind might blow down a tree or two, but none of them are close enough to hit the house and we could use the wood."

"Oh. Okay," Roan said, his voice small. Ishaan started to ask if there was a problem, but a bright flash of blue-white light lit up the room, followed some moments later by the low rumble of distant thunder. Ishaan tapped his fingers against the edge of his desk, remembering the fit Roan had thrown when they'd been fishing and it had started to rain. If he really hated thunder that much...

Ishaan powered down his laptop and unplugged it from the outlet. It wasn't likely that the house would be struck by lightning, but he didn't need the hassle of getting a new computer. Rising from his chair, he stepped over to the doorway of his study and looked out. Roan was sitting on the couch, his knees drawn up to his chest and his arms wrapped around his legs, staring fixedly at the television, his face pale. Another flash whited out the shadowy corners of the room and Roan jumped, his shoulders hunching up about his ears as he waited for the thunder. Ishaan watched him shudder as the rumble filled the room. The storm was still some miles off, but with the wind out of the east, it was bound to pass right over them.

"You okay?" Ishaan asked.

Roan glanced at him, swallowed hard, and nodded.

"Fine."

Ishaan hesitated, then walked over and sat down beside him, but not too close. Ever since that afternoon in the river, he'd been careful to keep his distance.

"I don't think you ever told me why you dislike thunder so much," he said. "Did something happen?"

Roan nodded.

"When we were kids, Kethic and I used to play on the roof of our apartment building. One hot, muggy summer afternoon, a bolt of lightning struck the iron fire escape not twenty feet from where were standing. Bits of white-hot metal burned holes in our jeans and sneakers and we were both damn near deaf for days."

"You shouldn't have been on the roof in the first place," Ishaan said, frowning.

"Where were we supposed to play?" Roan asked. "The street? Our apartment was tiny and the nearest park was five miles away. Besides, we liked watching the dragons fly past on their way to their rooftop dwellings. Our building was too old and not up to code for dragon habitation."

"That should have been your first clue to stay off it," Ishaan said with a chuckle. Roan didn't seem to think it very funny, though. He just stared at the television.

"Want to watch a movie?" Ishaan asked after a moment.

"Aren't you busy?"

"No, I need a break," Ishaan said. "Besides, I don't want my laptop getting fried if lightning hits the house."

Roan whipped his head around, a look of horror on his face.

"Could that happen?"

"There's a possibility, yeah," Ishaan said, mentally kicking himself. "It's just a small chance, though, and we'd be okay. Just don't take a bath."

"I'm going to go unplug your computer," Roan said, his tone flat and bleak as he unfolded himself from the couch and headed for his room. Ishaan watched him go, feeling a stirring of compassion as the windows lit up again and Roan cringed. Poor guy. Ishaan grabbed the remote and began paging through the channel guide, looking for something to watch that they would both enjoy. He found an old movie that he'd seen years ago, but it was good enough to watch again. It was based on the true story of the first team of planetary explorers to visit Rachalia, who were hunted, captured, and killed by the native inhabitants —a race of large, insect-like beings. The second expedition found only the first team's gear, including their journals and recording devices documenting much of their ordeal. Then they got the hell off Rachalia and petitioned to have it declared a restricted world. As far as Ishaan knew, it still was.

Another flash danced through the room, followed by a swift and sharp crack of thunder. The leading edge of the storm was almost there. From Roan's room came a startled yelp and a hollow thump. Ishaan started to get up and go see if he was okay, but Roan hurried out and dropped back down onto the couch, rubbing the back of his head with one hand and leaving almost no space between them. Ishaan shifted uncomfortably, but didn't move away.

"This looks interesting," Roan said, grabbing the remote and turning the television up. "What's it about?"

"Why the Department of Exploration no longer sends manned expeditions into unsurveyed worlds," Ishaan said. While the movie played and the thunder rolled and Roan continued to jump and cringe, Ishaan did his best to ignore Roan's proximity, but it was hard when Roan's elbow brushed his arm and when Roan's leg rested against his. On the screen, the last three members of the expedition had walled themselves off inside a dark cave. They could hear the Rachalians beyond their fortifications, shifting the rocks aside with unhurried, relentless determination. The doomed people were somberly passing around their only pistol, taking turns putting the gun under their chins and pulling the trigger to see who would get their last bullet and be spared the horrific fate of being turned into an incubator for the Rachalians' eggs and later into food as the larvae hatched and ate their way out.

Ishaan knew the shot was coming and he steeled himself not to jump, but he wasn't prepared for the blinding flash of lightning and the deafening crack of thunder that exploded over their house, close enough to disrupt the reception on the TV for a moment. Roan screamed and grabbed at him, fingers digging into his arm. Ishaan pulled away, then felt bad about it and against his better judgment, he put his arm around Roan's shoulders.

"It's okay," Ishaan said.

"I know," Roan said, drawing away "Sorry, I don't mean to be a—"

"You're not," Ishaan said, shaking his head. "You're not."

When the movie finished, Roan picked up the remote and began flipping through the channels.

"What do you want to watch now?" he asked.

Ishaan stifled a yawn and glanced at the clock.

"It's about time for me to go to bed," he said. It *was* late, but Ishaan had the feeling that if they had a few more claps of thunder, he'd end up with Roan sitting in his lap, which would *not* be a good idea. It was already too comfortable just to have him sitting so close, warm against his side. He wanted nothing more than to put his arms around Roan and comfort him, but he stood instead. "Will you be okay?"

"Oh, sure," Roan said, drawing his knees back up to his chest. "It's just a little noise, right?" He looked ready to jump out of his skin, but Ishaan headed into the bathroom. He couldn't take his usual pre-slumber bath, but he washed up and brushed his teeth, glancing out into the living room as another crack of thunder rumbled through the house. Roan looked so small and fragile, hunched on the couch. Ishaan spat toothpaste foam into the sink, wiped his mouth on a towel, and turned off the light.

"Are you sure you'll be okay?" Ishaan asked, stopping at the end of the couch and looking down at Roan. "I could stay up for a while longer."

"I've imposed on you enough already," Roan said, "but thanks for the offer." He set down the remote and stood, following Ishaan over to his bedroom. "If it gets too bad," Roan said as he took the key down off its hook, "I'll just come crawl into bed with you, like I used to with Kethic when I'd get scared." He chuckled, but it sounded forced, and Ishaan didn't find the joke funny at all.

"There are worse things than thunderstorms," Ishaan said, shutting his door.

"I know; I'm sorry," Roan said over the clicking of the lock. "Good night."

"Night," Ishaan replied, running his hands back through his hair as he was walked to his bed. Would that man never learn?

Lying in bed, Ishaan stared up at the ceiling, waiting for the next flash and rumble. He pictured Roan, sitting all alone on the couch, scared and vulnerable, Roan clinging to him, trembling as Ishaan wrapped an arm around his shoulders. Roan had pulled away, but what if he hadn't? When the next flash came, would he have let Ishaan hold him? Would he have allowed Ishaan to kiss him? Would he have followed Ishaan to his room and let Ishaan make love to him?

Pressing his hands over his face, Ishaan groaned into his palms, but it came out sounding more like a sob. What was it about Roan that made him different from the others? Ishaan had never wanted Hektor or Trydel or Dek or any of them like he wanted Roan. Roan was just so...so nice and friendly and compassionate and *understanding*. And so unafraid. It was like he truly understood what Ishaan went through and what he did, and he wasn't afraid. None of the others had. They did their job and avoided him as much as possible, which was what he had encouraged. He didn't blame them.

Ishaan couldn't decide if Roan's attitude was an asset or a liability. His stupid jokes seemed to indicate the latter. Not being afraid was one thing, but did he have to be so careless? The more Ishaan cared about him, the more it would hurt when everything fell apart.

Tossing and turning, Ishaan lay awake, blue-white light piercing his eyelids every time he closed them, the thunder rattling the marrow of his bones. Poor Roan.

Ishaan raised his head, frowning into the darkness. That noise—it sounded like the little window in his door being opened, but why—

"Ishaan?" Roan said softly.

"Yeah, what is it?" Ishaan asked, throwing back the covers and starting to get out of bed. "What's wrong?"

"Oh," Roan said, sounding surprised. "Are you awake?"

"Yes. What's wrong?"

"Nothing," Roan said quickly. "I-I just...wanted to apologize again for what I said earlier. I'd never come into your room without your permission."

"Oh," Ishaan said, a little confused. "Okay. Thanks."

"Good night," Roan said and shut the window again.

As Ishaan lay back down, he rubbed a hand along the stubble forming on his jaw, replaying Roan's voice in his head. He had sounded surprised, like he hadn't expected to find Ishaan awake. But why try to get his attention if he thought Ishaan was asleep? Unless he *wanted* Ishaan to be asleep. Had he wanted to apologize to a sleeping man who wouldn't remember, who wouldn't respond? Was this the first time Roan had tried to clear his conscience in such a way? Ishaan doubted it. Did Roan talk to him about other things? His frown eased and a soft smile pulled at his lips as he pictured Roan standing outside the door, rambling on like he had a tendency to do, making inane comments about what was on TV, saying all the things he couldn't say to Ishaan when he was awake...

Ishaan sighed into the darkness and rolled over, tucking his arms up under his pillow and closing his eyes. It was a nice thought, anyway.

Twenty-one

Roan sat in the armchair in his room, the laptop balanced on his knees as he scrolled through his e-mail. He hadn't heard from Kethic in a couple of weeks and the wedding was growing steadily closer. *If* they were even still going through with it. Roan trashed the accumulated junk mail and clicked over to a local weather site. No storms in the forecast. He sighed in relief. Last week's had just about been his undoing. He had waited long enough for Ishaan to fall asleep—on a normal night, he *would* have been asleep. If Roan had gone in without checking...

A soft knock on his half-closed door roused him from his thoughts and he glanced up as Ishaan stuck his head into the room.

"What's up?" Roan asked.

"Payday," Ishaan said, tossing a handful of coins onto Roan's bed.

"Thanks," Roan said as Ishaan started to withdraw. Roan opened his mouth and started to speak, then hesitated. He wanted to just let Ishaan walk away, like he'd been doing for days, but it had to be done. "Hey, Ishaan?"

"Yeah, what is it?" Ishaan asked, stepping back into the doorway.

"Do you need to go to Devaen any time soon?" Roan asked, the words flat and lifeless on his tongue, almost spoken a hundred times. "I've got some errands to do and I could walk, but I thought if you needed to go—"

"Yeah, I'll give you a ride," Ishaan said. "I can get a few things at the store."

"Thanks," Roan said, a sick sort of weight settling in his gut. Closing the laptop, he stood and set it in the seat of the chair before changing his clothes. He had to do this—he wanted to. It was the best thing for both of them, really. He'd overstayed his welcome and it was time to move on before anyone got hurt.

Roan sighed. Too late for that.

"Are you about ready?" Ishaan called from the other side of the house as Roan sat on the end of the bed, tying his boot laces.

"Just about," Roan replied. He gathered up the coins off the bed, took the rest of his savings out of his sock drawer, and grabbed his jacket. He was standing at the front door jingling the money in his pocket when Ishaan came out of his room. Roan's gaze devoured him from head to toe—the raven black hair falling carelessly to his collar, the tight blue T-shirt, the faded jeans—

Roan looked away before Ishaan noticed. He shouldn't have been staring; there was nothing unusual about the way Ishaan was dressed. He silently followed Ishaan out to the barn and helped roll the cloth cover off the car. As

Ishaan drove the five miles into town, Roan sat slumped in the passenger's seat, staring out the window and trying to think of something to say to break the silence, but he was afraid anything that came out of his mouth would just sound fake.

When they finally reached Devaen, Ishaan slowed to a crawl and stopped in front of the general store.

"This going to work for you?" Ishaan asked. Roan nodded. For a moment, neither of them moved. "You can go on in first," Ishaan said. "Just put what you want on the counter and—"

"Right, I know the drill," Roan said, opening the door and climbing out of the car. He started to close the door.

"Is everything all right?" Ishaan asked him, looking up at him. "You've been really quiet lately. More news from Kethic?"

"No news from Kethic," Roan said. He shook his head. "I've just been a bit distracted, that's all." He closed the door and hurried into the store. It only took a few minutes to pick out what he needed—shampoo, deodorant, and a couple pairs of knitted socks. His were getting a bit worn in the heels and winter was coming. If he was going to leave, he'd need to be able to keep his feet warm. Or maybe he'd take a world gate to a place where it was summer. There was no reason why he couldn't.

Roan went back outside and waited with the car while Ishaan did his shopping and paid. When Ishaan returned, carrying the paper bag in one hand and his change in the other, Roan plucked at imaginary lint on his shirt.

"Ishaan, I-I need to go talk to Sezae," he said. "Do you mind waiting a few more minutes?"

"Sezae?" Ishaan repeated, glancing toward the inn as a frown knitted his brow. "What for?"

"I owe her for that drink she tried to kill me with," Roan said with a tight laugh. "And I need to repay her for letting Kethic stay for free."

"And you're only now getting around to that?" Ishaan asked, glancing at him. Had he guessed?

"It took a while to save up the money," Roan said, avoiding his gaze. "My boss is a cheap-ass who pays me slave wages."

"You want a raise?"

"No," Roan said.

"I'd have loaned you the money if you had said something," Ishaan said.

"I know," Roan said, "but I wanted to do it myself. You understand."

Ishaan nodded.

"Yeah. Don't take too long, though, and if she brings up me and that kid, try to change the subject."

"All right." For once Roan didn't feel like correcting him. He had done all he could. If Ishaan didn't want to think of 'that kid' as his daughter, it was his choice, one Roan had a feeling he'd come to regret. Hands tucked into his pockets, Roan headed for the inn, ignoring the suspicious and hostile looks from the townsfolk he passed. That was one thing he wouldn't miss about this place. One of only a few.

Stepping into the inn, he drew a slow breath, savoring the sweet herbal pipe smoke and the savory scents of roasting meat and baking bread. He glanced around for Sezae, but she wasn't wiping tables or waiting on the guests like usual. A young man with short, dark hair was working in her stead, looking rather frazzled as he slipped behind the bar to draw three tankards of ale from the cask on the back counter. Roan hesitated, but walked over to the bar anyway; he didn't want to keep Ishaan waiting too long.

"Excuse me," he said. "I'm looking for Sezae."

"She's busy," the guy said, coming out from behind the counter with his hands full. "What do you want?"

"I want to talk to Sezae," Roan said, wondering why anyone would put this guy in charge—his people skills needed a bit of work. "I'm a friend of hers."

"Sezae!" the guy shouted over his shoulder. "Somebody's here to see you!" Roan sighed and walked away, letting the guy get back to work. He stood at the bar, running one hand back and forth across the smooth, worn wood and polished brass while he waited. After a minute, Sezae appeared, strands of her long, blonde hair stuck to the sweat on her brow. She looked exhausted, but she smiled when she saw him.

"Hi, Roan," she said, wiping her hands on her apron, which was unusually smudged and smeared. "How are you?"

"I'm fine," he said. "How are you? You look tired."

"Father had an accident in the kitchen yesterday," she said. "He spilled some oil on the leg of his pants and it caught fire."

"Great Maele," Roan said. "Is he all right? Did you take him to the doctor?"

"Dr. Artic took a look at him," she said, shaking her head. "Gave him some medicine for the pain and some bandages to keep it clean. He said Father will be fine, but it's a bad burn. If Joryn wasn't due in on the next train, I'd toss him in the wagon and take him to Shesade myself. They have a proper clinic up there."

"Who's Joryn?"

"A traveling healer," Sezae said. "He passes through once a month or so. He's expensive, but he does good work. But until then, I'm in charge and— Oh, crap, the roast is going to burn." She turned and headed back through the doorway behind the bar.

"Sorry, I didn't mean—" Roan started.

"I can't hear you," Sezae called. "Come back here; it's okay."

"Are you sure?" Roan said, glancing at the guy waiting on the customers, but he was too busy to stop Roan as he stepped behind the bar and ducked through the doorway. The long room was the biggest kitchen Roan had ever seen, with a giant oven against one wall and a sizzling grill beside it. Roan stood back as Sezae opened the oven, clad to her elbows in thick, blackened mitts to shield her from the heat. She pulled out a large, cast iron slow-cooker and set it on an iron trivet on the adjacent stove.

"That's better," she said, closing the door of the oven before removing her mitts and wiping the sweat from her brow. "I don't know how father does this all. So," she said with a smile, "to what do I owe the pleasure of your company?" Her smile faltered. "It's not more trouble with Ishaan, is it?"

"No, no," Roan said, shaking his head. "Nothing like that. I just wanted to pay you back—"

"You don't have to do that," Sezae said.

"I want to," Roan said, pulling the handful of coins out of his pocket. "It's been a long time since anyone was willing to do me any favors and I would like to do something to repay your kindness."

"Goodness, Roan," she said with a laugh, "it was just a drink."

"And you let my brother stay here for free," Roan said.

"But that's not your responsibility," she said.

"Yes, it is. He's my brother." And she wouldn't have had to if Roan hadn't thrown him out in the middle of the night. Of course, Kethic had deserved that. "No more arguing," Roan said, grabbing her hand and forcing the money into it. "You have no idea how much your generosity means to me."

"Okay, fine," she said, glancing down at the coins. "This is much more than you owe us, you know."

"Well, I-I need to ask you for another favor," Roan said. "I need you to post that notice again—the one looking for someone to take care of Ishaan—"

"Oh, Roan—No, you can't go," she said. "Whatever it is, whatever he did, please reconsider. Please, let me talk to him—"

"No, you can't," Roan said, unable to keep the pain and desperation out of his voice. "Sezae, I-I—" He took a deep breath. "I'm falling in love with him, but he-he—"

"He won't let himself be loved," Sezae said. "Oh, Roan, I know how you feel, I do..." She closed the distance between him and pulled him into a hug. He clutched at her, fighting to keep the burning at the back of throat from turning into tears.

"Then you understand why I have to go," Roan said. After a moment, he pulled away. "I'm not going to abandon him, though. I won't make him sleep in the jail again. I'll stay until you find someone else, which is why you can't say anything to him. It'll make him horrible to live with."

"All right," she said. "I'll try to find someone."

"Thank you," Roan said. He took a step toward the doorway. "I should go; he's waiting—"

"Does he know?" Sezae asked. "That you love him, I mean."

Roan shook his head.

"No, I don't think so. If he does, he doesn't care."

"You should tell him," she said. "Before you go, just to be sure. You're the best thing that's ever happened to him. I can see it when I look at him—he's happier than he has ever been."

"So am I," Roan admitted. If it wasn't for that one little thing...

"So tell him. Give him a chance; he might surprise you. Don't throw this away if there's a chance."

"All right," Roan said. "If there's a chance." Which there wasn't. Happy endings were reserved for better people than him.

Hands tucked into his empty pockets, Roan left the inn, his boots thumping hollowly on the wooden porch. He hadn't expected to feel happy about what he had just done, but he was a little surprised by the weight and sense of loss that settled over him. He almost went back inside to tell Sezae that he had changed his mind. Instead, he squared his shoulders and marched over to Ishaan's car. As he drew near, the driver's door opened and Ishaan climbed out.

"All done?" he asked. Roan nodded. "Everything go okay?"

"Yeah," Roan said, frowning. "Why?"

"You look...resigned," Ishaan said.

"Oh," Roan said. "I guess I'm just tired. Are you ready to go home?" *Home.* For the first time in years, he had a place to call home and he was about to lose it because Ishaan couldn't see past his own misery and self-imposed isolation. He was a selfish bastard and Roan would be better off without him.

"Actually, I was hoping you'd do me a favor," Ishaan said. "It'll just take a minute. Do you see that store over there?" Roan looked where he was pointing, to a whitewashed little building with faded pink window trim and a tattered golden awning over the door. "That's Daella's ice cream shop. She makes the best strawberry ice cream on the planet—at least she used to. I haven't been welcome in her shop in almost six years."

"So you want me to buy you ice cream?" Roan asked.

Ishaan frowned.

"Not if it's too much trouble." He started to get back in the car.

"Quit being a dick," Roan said, walking around the front of the vehicle. Ishaan straightened up, a mix of confusion and anger on his face. Apparently, he didn't like being called a dick. Roan quickly checked himself; now was not the time to pick a fight. "It's not too much trouble. I was just making sure I understood what you wanted. Now, are you going to give me some money—I gave all mine to Sezae."

Ishaan regarded him for a minute.

"All right," he said finally, digging a couple of coins out of his pocket. "Here. Just a single scoop of strawberry on a cone." Roan nodded and started to walk away. "Oh, and you can get yourself something if you want," Ishaan called after him.

"Thanks," Roan called back, but he wasn't in the mood for ice cream. He hurried across the street and past half a dozen little stores and houses before reaching the ice cream shop. As he pushed open the door, a cluster of tiny bells hanging over the entry chimed, announcing his arrival.

"I'll be right with you," said a feminine voice from behind the counter. Roan crossed the room and peered over the counter, at what appeared to be a young man sorting through a crate of strawberries on the floor. His blond hair was cut very short, his skin a natural bronze, his short-sleeved shirt crisp and brilliant white, his black trousers held up with black suspenders. He glanced up, his pale blue eyes almost colorless against his dark skin, and smiled.

"How can I help you?" he asked in that distinctly feminine voice, wiping bright red berry juice on a rag before climbing to his feet. He was slender and willowy, pretty, but not enough to be a faerie—not a full-blooded one, anyway.

"I'd like a strawberry cone, please," Roan said.

"Did you know that's my specialty?" he asked, bending down and plucking a handful of dark, ripe berries from the crate.

"So I've heard," Roan said, watching as he used a delicate knife to remove the green tops and tough cores. "I believe the exact words used were, 'the best strawberry ice cream on the planet'."

"Well, I don't know if I'd go that far," the young man said, his cheeks turning a rosy pink. "Who told you that?"

"Oh," Roan said, for a moment drawing a blank. "Um...Sezae."

"Sezae?" he repeated, giving Roan a funny look. "I haven't seen her in my shop in years."

"Well, she was probably repeating what her guests had said, then," Roan said. "I don't know—I didn't ask." That seemed like a good enough explanation for the ice cream maker. He diced the strawberries and dropped them into a clean, white soapstone mortar, using the matching pestle to render them into a thick, sticky mash before adding a spoonful of fine, white sugar. Roan arched an eyebrow as the young man turned and opened a tall, metal cabinet, the inside coated with glittery frost crystals. He pulled out a small jar of heavy white cream and carefully poured some into the mortar.

"You have a refrigerator?" Roan asked, curious as to what connections *this* guy had. "I didn't know they were allowed on this planet."

"They're not," the young man said, putting the cream away. "This is an ice box. It uses magic to keep things cold."

"Neat," Roan said. "I bet one of those is expensive."

"I got a rebate from the government," he said with a crooked grin. "They appreciate efforts to avoid impacting the environment." He grabbed a slender brush with short, stiff bristles out from under the counter and began to stir the cream and strawberry concoction. It looked very...pink, but certainly nothing like ice cream.

Placing his empty hand against the side of the mortar, the young man closed his eyes, a pale blue light blossoming beneath his skin. Roan could feel the chill coming off of him, a fine white mist, like warm breath in the dead of winter, swirling in the air as he began to stir the mortar faster and faster, the cream thickening, whipping up into frosty peaks. After a minute, he stopped, the light fading away.

"You're a mage," Roan said. That explained the voice and the pretty face— mages were notorious for using magic to alter their voice and appearance.

"An air mage," he said, scraping the brush clean on the rim of the mortar, "but not recognized by any council, so don't address me as M'Lord or anything." He chuckled and grabbed a large, golden brown cone off the back shelf, the seam where the edges met sealed with a drizzle of chocolate to keep the ice cream from leaking out. Using a spoon, he packed the ice cream inside and then handed it across the counter to Roan. "That'll be six laenes, please."

Roan set one of the coins on the counter and headed for the door.

"Hang on, sir—your change—"

"Keep it," Roan said, the bells chiming as he opened the door. "Ishaan can afford it."

"Ishaan Darvis?"

Roan slipped outside and closed the door behind him, smirking to himself. He shouldn't have said anything, but he couldn't help it. Looking up and down the road to make sure he didn't get run over by a horse, he crossed the street and hurried toward the car. The ice cream was already starting to melt, thick, sticky pink drips oozing down the back of his hand. Ishaan was standing beside the vehicle, arms crossed over his chest as he rested his butt against the door.

"You didn't want anything?" he asked as Roan approached. Roan shook his head and handed him the cone, licking the melted ice cream off the back of his hand. Ishaan was right—it was excellent. "Did she give you any trouble?"

"Who?"

"Daella, the owner."

"No, she wasn't there," Roan said as Ishaan licked the drippy edges. "It was a young man—"

Ishaan laughed.

"Blond hair, blue eyes, air mage?" Roan nodded. "That was her. And she's a lot older than she looks. My father used to buy ice cream from her when he was a boy."

"Wow," Roan said. "Must be nice to have magic."

"I imagine it's a bit like having money," Ishaan said, a thoughtful crease in his brow as he regarded his ice cream. "Everyone who doesn't have it thinks how wonderful it must be." Roan pondered that while Ishaan enjoyed his ice cream, licking around the edge, his tongue gliding over the frosty treat, leaving trails and teasing lumps of berry out, the juice staining his lips pink.

"Quit staring and go get one of your own," Ishaan said and Roan looked away, but not soon enough, apparently.

"No, that's okay," he said. "I was just thinking about something else."

"Here, you can have a taste of mine, then," Ishaan said, holding the cone out toward him. Roan stared at it in disbelief.

"Are you sure?" he asked.

"Sure. Why? Are you sick?"

"No," Roan said shaking his head. He hesitated, then leaned over and ran his tongue over the soft, sweet ice cream. Drawing back, he licked his lips and moaned. "Great Maele, that is the best ice cream I've ever tasted." Ishaan took another lick, then offered it to Roan again.

"It's melting faster than I can eat it," he said. "If you don't help me finish it, I'll just have to throw it away."

"All right, you don't have to twist my arm," Roan said with a grin. The late summer sun was warm against the side of his face as it crept low in the sky over the jagged mountains, but the ice cream was cold and the moment almost too perfect to be real. Roan glanced up at Ishaan, the tall man's gaze lost in the distance. Maybe Sezae was right, maybe Roan could take a chance on Ishaan, maybe he was wrong.

A noise behind him drew his attention and he glanced across the car where a man had come out of the general store. As the man walked away, a brown paper bag in his hands, he kept looking over his shoulder at them, glancing back every few steps. And he wasn't the only one. Everywhere he looked, every porch, every window, someone was watching him. It was different than the first time, though. Those faces had been hostile. These were shocked, appalled, like what Roan would expect to see looking out through the bars of a circus freak show.

"They're all watching us," Roan muttered, taking the cone from Ishaan and dipping his tongue down inside to get at the remaining ice cream.

"Yeah, I see them," Ishaan said. "This'll give them something to gossip about for weeks." Stunned, Roan just stood there and let Ishaan take the cone back from him. He was just doing this to give the people something to talk about? Maybe he hadn't changed at all.

When he tried to hand the nearly empty cone back, Roan shook his head. "I've had enough," he said. "I know, how about when you finish it, we sit in your car and make out for a while? That'd really give them a show."

"What?" Ishaan asked, but Roan just walked around to the passenger's side of the car and climbed in, slumping down in the seat with his arms crossed over his chest. He was not a side-show attraction and he didn't appreciate being used to shock people. He suddenly remembered the look on the ice cream maker's face when he mentioned Ishaan's name. But that was different...wasn't it? He supposed not. After a minute, Ishaan slipped in behind the wheel. "Mind telling me what that was all about?" he asked as he started the car.

"It's nothing," Roan said, staring out the window. "It was my mistake. Just forget it."

"You know, you've been acting real moody lately," Ishaan said, an edge to his tone as the car began to roll. "If there's something wrong, you need to tell me. Maybe I can fix it."

"You can't fix this," Roan muttered. Louder, he said, "It's personal. Don't worry about it. I won't let it interfere with me doing my job, and that's all that matters, right?"

"Right," Ishaan said after a moment. Roan fought back tears, blinking hard as they left Devaen. The sooner someone answered that notice, the better.

Twenty-two

From across the room, Ishaan heard the key turn in the lock and he froze as the door swung open.

"Do you want breakfast?" Roan asked, a scowl on his face. "'Cause I'm not hungry, but I'll cook some—"

"What the hell are you doing?" Ishaan asked, stepping around the end of the bed. "You didn't even look in here. I could have been asleep."

"It's not like I would have disturbed you," Roan said, turning away. "If you're not hungry, I think I'll just go back to bed." He had been moody and distant for weeks now, ever since he learned the date of his brother's wedding. It was the big day, which explained why he was worse than usual, but it was no excuse for his careless disregard of the rules. They were there for *his* protection. Ishaan followed him across the living room.

"I wasn't worried about being disturbed," Ishaan said, stopping in Roan's doorway as Roan climbed back into bed and pulled the covers over his head. "I don't want anything to happen to you."

"Oh, who cares," Roan grumbled. "Just shut the door and go away, would you?"

Ishaan tapped one finger against his lips, his brow furrowed. This was going to be harder than he thought. "I don't think so," he said at last, walking into the room and jerking the covers off of Roan. Roan raised his head and glared at him. "Get up, get dressed; we're going for a drive."

"I'm not going anywhere," Roan said, reaching for the blankets.

Ishaan pulled them completely off the bed and onto the floor.

"You're next," he said. "Now get up—I don't have all day. And put on something nice," he called back as he headed for the kitchen. "I need you to make a good impression, even if all you do is sit there and look pretty."

A few minutes later, Roan stuck his head into the kitchen.

"Why? What's going on?"

"I have to meet with some lawyers from a big magitech corporation," Ishaan said, staring down into the toaster as the bread browned. "They want to buy out my father's company and since he won't deal with them, I have to, and it would be nice if I had someone there for moral support."

"But why me?" Roan asked. "Why not—"

Ishaan glanced at him, arching an eyebrow as he waited for Roan to pull the name of some imaginary best friend out of his ass. As much as he hated to admit it, Roan was his friend, as close as Sezae had ever been. If he allowed himself to dream, maybe they could be more than friends—but he couldn't do that. Dreams were for fools.

"I'll go change my clothes," Roan said as he turned and left the doorway.

When the toast popped, Ishaan spread them with butter and dusted each piece with a sprinkle of cinnamon. He supposed this went beyond simple friendship, but it was too late to change his mind. The check was already in the mail, as the saying went. He took a bite out of one slice and carried the other into the living room.

"You want a slice of this toast?" Ishaan asked.

"No thanks," Roan called from his room. "Why am I only just now hearing about this?" He stepped into the living room in socks, jeans, and a short-sleeved, sky blue, button-down shirt over a white tank.

Ishaan raised his eyebrows.

"I thought I said to dress nice," he said.

Roan looked down at himself. "What's wrong with what I'm wearing? I'm gonna button the shirt."

"Don't you have a suit?"

Roan gave him an incredulous look. "A suit? What the hell would I need a suit for? I'm a whore on the run, remember?"

"Good point," Ishaan said. He took another bite of his toast, then stepped over and handed the untouched slice to Roan. "Eat that. We won't be having lunch until late and I don't want to have to listen to you complain about being hungry." Roan tore a bite out of it as he turned and stalked back into his room, grumbling something unintelligible as he went.

A second later he reappeared, swallowed, and asked, "So are these clothes all right? They're the nicest ones I have."

"They're fine," Ishaan said. "I'm going to go get dressed and then we'll go, all right? About twenty minutes?"

"Whatever," Roan said, heading back to his room. Ishaan shook his head, a crooked smile on his face, and turned toward the bathroom. Fifteen minutes later, he was standing at the front door, keys in one hand and a garment bag over his shoulder, wearing faded gray jeans and a red T-shirt under his black leather jacket.

"Are you coming?" he called. "It's hot in here."

"I'll be—dammit—right there."

Ishaan took a step toward the open bathroom door.

"What's taking so long? I thought you just had to put your shoes on."

"Yeah, but...somebody wants me to look *pretty* for the damn lawyers...and I can't get my damn hair to...lay flat."

Ishaan almost laughed aloud.

"I really don't think they'll be looking at your hair," he said. "Now come on. You'll have time to play with it after we get to Shesade."

"Shesade? I thought we were doing to De—" He stepped out of the bathroom, his arms above his head as he tried to tie back his blond hair, and fell silent as he stared at Ishaan. Ishaan could almost feel Roan's eyes moving over his body and he cleared his throat. Roan's gaze jumped to his face and he let his arms drop, his hair swinging back down to brush his shoulders. "So why aren't *you* wearing a suit? This is your meeting, isn't it?" Ishaan's lips twitched, but he didn't think Roan noticed.

Ishaan held up the garment bag.

"What do think this is, my dry cleaning? I'm not wearing my good suit for the three hour drive just to get it all wrinkly—"

"Three hours?" Roan said with a groan. He reached back into the bathroom and turned off the light. "Why couldn't they meet you in Devaen?"

"I didn't want them that close to our house," Ishaan said, rolling his eyes as Roan went into his room again. He should have waited until they were outside to put his jacket on. "If those scumbags find out where I live, next thing you know, they'll be camped out on our lawn."

Roan came out of his room, his long red coat in one hand a slight frown on his face. "Did you say *our* house, *our* lawn?"

Ishaan thought back, heard himself say those words, and shrugged. "Yeah, I did. Is that a problem?"

Roan actually seemed to be considering it. "No, I guess not," he said finally and motioned toward the door. "Are we going?"

The morning air was chill and damp, a thin mist creeping just above the bed of fallen leaves. Ishaan pulled the front of his jacket closed, Roan slipping into his as they walked down the gravel driveway to the barn. Ishaan shoved open the double doors and the gray light fell across the car.

Roan glanced at him.

"When did you put the roof on?"

"Yesterday," Ishaan said. "Why?"

Roan shrugged and climbed into the car as Ishaan hung his suit from a hook in the ceiling.

"If you knew yesterday," Roan said as Ishaan dropped down into his seat and slipped the key into the ignition, "why did you only just tell me about it? I mean, how long has this thing been planned?"

"A couple of months," Ishaan said, turning in the seat to look out the rear window as he backed out of the barn. "I didn't tell you about it, because it wasn't any of your business and I hadn't planned on taking you, but considering how depressed you've been the last few weeks, I didn't think it safe to leave you home alone. The last thing I want to come home to is you in the bathtub with your wrists slit."

Roan snorted.

"Like I'd do that," he said and Ishaan felt a sense of relief he hadn't been expecting. Had he really been worried that Roan was going to hurt himself? Apparently. "No, if I was going to kill myself, you'd find me hanging in the barn. No mess, and if you do it right, no pain—just *snap* and you're dead."

Ishaan stopped the car and looked at him.

"I take it you've done a bit of thinking on the subject?"

Roan shrugged again and looked down at his hands.

"A bit, I guess. It's not like I sit in my room and practice tying hangman's knots all day or anything, but it's been a rough year. First my parents, now Kethic's wedding—"

"That's right," Ishaan said as he finished backing up and turned onto the road, "that's next week, isn't it?"

"It's today," Roan said, slumping in his seat. "Thanks for paying attention."

"Considering that it's not *my* brother and I don't even like him, I think I was pretty close," Ishaan said. He could hear the mud splashing and splattering up underneath the car and grimaced. What a wonderful day for a drive. "It's not fair," he added after a moment. "You should be allowed to attend your only brother's wedding, even if you can't be his best man. Why didn't you just go in disguise? Color your hair, wear glasses, grow a beard—" Roan shot him a withering look and he laughed. "Okay, fine—we could have stuck on a fake beard or something."

"I wanted to," Roan said, "but Kethic wouldn't tell me where the wedding was going to be. He said they were going to *her* home world, but he wouldn't tell me what it was. I know he's just trying to keep me safe, but—"

"You wouldn't be in danger if it wasn't for him," Ishaan pointed out. "He probably figured your murder would ruin the honeymoon."

Roan laughed, but he didn't sound amused.

"You'd probably be right," he said, "if they could afford a honeymoon. They can barely pay rent."

"And they think they can raise a kid? Do they have any idea how expensive those things are?"

"Oh, how would you know?" Roan asked, scowling out the front window. Stung, Ishaan didn't answer. Shutting Sezae and their daughter out of his life wasn't his choice. It was what had to be, what was best for the child. After a minute, Roan said, "I'm sorry, Ishaan. That was cruel. I know you love your daughter a lot more than you let on."

"I don't even know her," Ishaan said, perhaps a little sharper than need be. "All I have are pictures."

"You could get to know her," Roan said, shifting in his seat, sitting up straighter. It seemed he wasn't so depressed when distracted by someone else's problems. Ishaan sighed. "When she's older, I mean," Roan added. "The two of you could have lunch once in a while, or go fishing—"

"And what happens when she asks why I don't live with her and her mother? Or why they can't live with me?"

"Tell her the truth," Roan said and Ishaan laughed.

"The truth? Are you insane?"

"No. I'm not talking full disclosure with all the gory details—just that you have an illness that makes you dangerous when you're asleep and you don't want to hurt her. That's simple enough, isn't it?" It was too simple. It almost made *him* sound like the victim.

"Roan, I know you're just trying to help," Ishaan said, "but I'd rather you just left it alone. I'm trying to do what's best for the child—"

"And you think not knowing her father is best for her?"

"Yes, I do. The less she has to do with me, the better. I don't want her being treated differently because she's my kid. So just drop it, okay?"

Roan was silent for several minutes. "Is your condition hereditary?" he asked suddenly. "I mean, could your daughter—"

"Oh, shit," Ishaan whispered, his gut clenching. "I never even thought about that. I have no idea." Could he possibly ruin any more people's lives? Why couldn't his father have just taken him out and shot him and saved everyone a lot of pain and misery?

"Shesade has a doctor, right?" Roan asked. "Maybe we could stop and ask someone about it, as long as we're there."

"Those idiots don't even know what I have," Ishaan said, "and in six years, they haven't been able to find out. I doubt they could tell us anything."

"Did you look it up online?"

"I just told you, I don't know what it's called."

Roan turned in his seat to stare at him. "You're kidding, right?"

Ishaan scowled at him.

"You look up the symptoms and it'll tell you what it's called," Roan said. "You never thought of that? I thought your father was some kind of computer genius."

"And if my father had been a brain surgeon, would you let me operate on you?" Ishaan snapped.

"Good point," Roan said.

"Besides, my father just came up with the idea for the outernet. He didn't create the technology or magic that allows it to work."

"All right," Roan said, sinking back into his seat, "point taken. When we get back home, we can look it up and see. Until then, there's no point in worrying about it. I shouldn't have even brought it up; you need to concentrate on your meeting."

"What meeting?" Ishaan asked and Roan gave him a funny look. Oh, shit. He forced a laugh. "Just kidding. I was trying to take your advice. I won't worry about it." But how could he not? He had already ruined Sezae's life and now that innocent girl could have inherited his curse. The thought made him want to be sick.

"You're a terrible liar," Roan said after a minute. Ishaan fought the urge to glance at him. His face would give him away completely.

"What makes you say that?" he asked, staring at the road ahead.

"You're still worrying about it," Roan said, and Ishaan almost sighed in relief, "I can see it in your face. I never should have said anything; I'm sorry."

"You shouldn't have said anything *now*," Ishaan said, "but that's something I need to know. I can't believe it never even crossed my mind."

"Well, it isn't something you usually have to think about," Roan said.

"You did," Ishaan pointed out, "and you don't even have kids." Roan didn't say anything and Ishaan suddenly realized that he didn't know that for sure. "Do you?" he asked, glancing over at Roan. "I never even asked."

"No," Roan said, shaking his head, "I don't have kids, thank Maele."

"You don't want kids?"

Roan hesitated.

"I would love to be a father someday," he said, "but I don't want to have children." Ishaan frowned as he tried to figure that one out. He wanted to have kids, but he didn't want to have his *own* kids...and he was the one to think of the hereditary thing...

"Is there something wrong with you?" Ishaan asked. "Something you don't want to pass on to your children?"

Roan slouched in his seat and stared out the passenger's window.

"You could say that," he said.

With just short glances at the road to keep from driving into a tree, Ishaan studied Roan as if he'd never seen him before. Roan caught him looking and scowled. "It's not obvious, asshole. Quit gawking at me."

"So what is it?" Ishaan asked.

"None of your business," Roan said.

Ishaan laughed.

"Sorry, pal, but you lost the right to say that when you wouldn't stay out of mine." A slight frown creased his brow as he thought of something. "Does this have anything to do with that seizure you had?" Roan's lips moved, mouthing the word *seizure*, and then he shifted in his seat.

"Right, the seizure. Yeah, that has a lot to do with it."

"Really? Because it doesn't seem like that big of a deal to me. You've been here almost six months and you've only had the one."

"It was worse growing up," Roan said. "A lot worse. I never knew when one might happen, or around whom, or how bad it would be. It was terrifying and embarrassing, and I felt so alone, so isolated, like no one else in the universe, not even my brother, could ever understand what I was going through. And then I met you."

Ishaan raised an eyebrow.

"Me? Let me guess: your life doesn't seem so bad compared to mine."

"That wasn't what I meant," Roan said. "Just that...finally, someone understands how hard it is to be different." He was staring out the window, his hands resting on his thighs, and Ishaan almost reached over and took his hand, but reached up and turned on the windshield wipers instead, the stiff, dry rubber scraping the six raindrops off the glass with a chattering squeal.

Ten minutes later, the rain was falling in earnest, the wipers hissing across the windshield as Ishaan peered through the glass at the road ahead, lit by the weak beams of his headlights. It wasn't even noon yet, but underneath the trees, with the thick clouds hanging above, it might as well have been dusk. Ishaan made a mental note to complain about the lights the next time he had to send a report back to the car company.

"Can you pull over somewhere?" Roan asked, his back popping as he sat up taller in his seat. "I gotta take a piss."

"Now?" Ishaan asked, glancing over at him. "We only left home twenty minutes ago."

"I forgot," Roan said with a shrug. "What's the big deal?"

"It's pouring rain," Ishaan said. "You'll get soaked."

"I don't care."

"Well, I do," Ishaan said. "You'll ruin my upholstery. Just sit still for ten more minutes, would you? We're almost to Croatoan Cathedral; we'll—"

"Croatoan?" Roan repeated, turning in his seat to face Ishaan. "You had a Croatoan here?"

Ishaan raised one eyebrow. "I have no idea what that means. It's a rock formation, a great vaulted tunnel that the road passes through, probably carved by the river thousands of years ago. Somebody carved Croatoan into the rock so that's what it's called; Croatoan Cathedral."

Roan just stared at him for a moment, then let his head fall back against the seat.

"I can't believe this," he said with a laugh. "You really have no idea. Are we almost there?"

"I told you," Ishaan said, scowling, "about ten minutes. Now, are you going to tell me what I don't have any idea about, or am I going to pull over and kick you out?"

"It's one of those stories that every planet has, but no one believes, kind of a modern legend, like Sasquatch or ferrian ghouls."

"I still don't know what you're talking about," Ishaan said, looking for a wide spot in which to dump him.

"Unexplained phenomena," Roan said with a grin. "It's been a hobby of mine since I was a kid, especially the legend of the Croatoan." He settled back in his seat and cleared his throat. "According to legend, the Croatoan are a super-advanced species of people who live out on the dark edge of the universe, well beyond explored space. They mostly keep to themselves, except when they need new slaves, and then they raid small colonies, taking everyone back to their slave-farms, leaving no evidence behind, save for a single word, carved into wood or stone: Croatoan." Ishaan couldn't help himself; he snorted with laughter. Roan gave him a dirty look.

"I'm sorry," Ishaan said, fighting hard to regain a straight face. "You actually believe this crap?"

"It's not crap. There have been more than three dozen documented cases of 'lost colonies' bearing the Croatoan name, from one side of the universe to the other. I never thought I'd actually get to see one, though. How far back does it date?"

"How should I know?" Ishaan said. "This road was built a hundred years before I was even born."

"No wonder it's so rough," Roan muttered. "Is that it up ahead?"

Through the thinning trees, a pale wall of stone rose up on the right hand side of the road. On the left, the ground sloped away, a few stunted trees growing up from cracks in the rocks, before dropping sharply to the river below.

"Not quite," Ishaan said. "You'll know when we get there." The road grew steeper, rivulets of brown rainwater racing down the wagon-wheel ruts, and the deep channels carved into the granite cliff were full and roaring. Roan leaned forward in his seat, staring out the front window—sometimes leaning into Ishaan's lap to stare out his window at a particular waterfall or rock formation.

"Wow," Roan whispered, leaning close for the third or fourth time, his hand braced against Ishaan's leg as they drove past a wide, white sheet of water cascading down from somewhere unseen.

"They call that the Bride's Veil," Ishaan said and Roan tensed, obviously only just realizing how close they were. Without a word, he withdrew to his side of the car. Ishaan wished he'd kept his mouth shut as he absently rubbed at the cold spot just above his knee where Roan's hand had been. Those little moments—the brush of an arm as they moved past each other in the kitchen, the touch of a knee under the table as they ate, the warmth of a hand when they both reached for the remote at the end of the movie—it was as close to a romantic relationship as he was going find, and though he knew better, he enjoyed them. Roan, on the other hand, grew silent and distant and moody when he realized they were sitting too close or laughing too much. Ishaan hated that.

He cleared his throat.

"This is the last bridge before the Cathedral," he said. "We're passing Zai Falls, the third highest waterfall on this side of the mountains." He slowed as they rolled across the wide stone bridge and Roan looked out at the thundering cascade of water roaring down the cliff face—but he looked from his own seat and he didn't say anything. With a sigh, Ishaan sped up again.

Less than a mile later, the car reached the top of the pass and as they rounded one last corner, Roan gasped and sat forward in his seat. The great gaping maw of the Cathedral rose before them, twice as wide as their house and three times as tall, with the road leading straight through it. Ishaan drove into the gloomy passage, the patter of the rain on the roof ceasing instantly as the stone ceiling arched overhead. He pulled off the road, into a wide, flat area, and shut off the engine.

"So," he said as he opened the door, "what do you think?" Roan climbed out and gazed around in awe. It wasn't hard to figure out why they called it Croatoan Cathedral; long, narrow slits carved into the outer wall let thin, gray light filter in and crystal stalactites hung from the ceiling, glittering faintly from the shadows. Ishaan made a note to bring Roan back on a sunny day. Now *that* was a sight to behold.

"This is incredible," Roan said, his eyes sweeping all around the cavern. "Where's the carving?"

Ishaan almost rolled his eyes.

"It's up here," he said, heading for the interior wall.

"Hey, are those stairs?" Roan ask, hurrying past him. "They are! And they look old." He dashed up several steps before stopping to wait for Ishaan. "I don't suppose you know who cut the steps?"

Ishaan shrugged. "I think they were here when the surveyors came through with the road." They reached the top of the steps, to a wide platform up under the curved roof of the cavern. A stack of firewood sat back against the wall and a blackened circle of rocks marked an old fire pit.

"What is this?" Roan asked, stopping to tap a burned tin can with the toe of his shoe. Glass and scorched bones littered the ground and an old, torn blanket sat piled beside a log worn smooth by countless asses resting upon it.

"What does it look like?" Ishaan asked, kicking the can back into the fire pit. "Travelers camp here on their way to Shesade, especially in weather like this." Actually, he was surprised no one was there.

"But-but this is an historic site," Roan said, "not a-a-a rest stop!"

"Your carving is over here," Ishaan said, fighting not to laugh. It was no wonder he couldn't keep his distance; Roan was just too cute sometimes. He led Roan to the back wall and Roan cried out in dismay at the sight that greeted them. Carved all across the stone were names and dates, *Fuck the Universe* and *Jimi Was Here*, a hundred years of graffiti in a dozen different languages. Ishaan stepped back, his eyes sweeping the stone in the dim light as he tried to remember exactly where the word was. Not surprisingly, he couldn't find it. He had been just a boy, after all, when his father had brought him up here—

Frowning, he squatted down and looked up at the wall, as he had done nearly fifteen years before. "There it is," he said, rising up and reaching out to run his fingers over the deep grooves. Roan stepped up next to him, once again oblivious of his proximity, and traced one of the elegant symbols.

"Are you sure?" Roan asked. "I mean, it looks older than the rest of this crap, but...What language is it?"

"Beats me," Ishaan said with a shrug. "From what I understand, they had to bring a linguistics expert in—"

"A gryph?"

"Of course."

"Well, okay then. Gryphs aren't often wrong."

"Try never," Ishaan said with a laugh as he turned away from the wall. "C'mon, we need to get going. We've got things to do before the big meeting."

"Like what?" Roan asked, following him toward the stairs.

"Like have my pants let out," he said. "I can't believe they don't fit anymore."

"You have put on a little weight," Roan commented.

Ishaan glanced over his shoulder.

"Look who's talking."

"It's a healthy weight, though," Roan said. "You were too skinny before—all bone and gristle. It was disgusting, to be honest."

"Didn't stop you from looking." He'd lost track of all the times he'd caught Roan staring at him. It was probably just morbid curiosity, but sometimes he couldn't help wondering, hoping that it might mean something more.

"Yeah, well...When you get to be my age—"

"Your age?" Ishaan repeated with a snort. "You're what, a year older than me?"

"I turned twenty-seven last month, thank you very much."

Ishaan stopped and turned to face him.

"Your birthday was last month? And you didn't say anything?"

Roan sort of shrugged and looked away. "I didn't want it to sound like I was fishing for a present, or something. Besides, I haven't really celebrated a birthday in years."

Ishaan got a guilt-induced e-mail every year, but otherwise, his birthdays passed without mention, as well. He'd never admit it aloud, but he hated that. "C'mon, tubby," Roan said, thumping Ishaan in the gut as he passed, "let's go have those pants let out." Ishaan smiled to himself and headed for the car while Roan walked to the entrance to answer nature's call.

As they rolled smoothly into Shesade, down the wet, paved streets, every head turned to watch their approach. Roan shifted uncomfortably in his seat, but Ishaan didn't mind. These people were simply curious, not hostile. A gang of kids standing on the porch of a candy shop broke away from the display window and began to run after the car, laughing and shouting as the rain quickly plastered their hair and clothes to their bodies. After a couple of blocks, they began to fall back, until only one lanky girl in a blue T-shirt and jeans continued to chase them.

Ishaan glanced at the dark windows of the *Golden Unicorn* restaurant as they drove by, at the large *Closed* sign in the window, and fought to keep a straight face. Being rich did have its advantages. He pulled up about a block down the road, in front of the men's formalwear boutique, and they climbed out as the girl came stumbling to a halt beside the car, red-faced, dripping wet, and gasping for breath.

"You again?" Ishaan said as he dug into his pocket. "This is the third time, isn't it?" She nodded and straightened up. "What's your name?"

"Sara," she said, flipping her brown hair out of her eyes. She glanced at Roan, standing up under the cover of the shop's porch. "That your boyfriend?"

"Not exactly," Ishaan said, reaching out and pressing a fat platinum ilae into her hand. "Here, go buy some candy for your slow friends."

She grinned and shoved the coin into her pocket.

"Thanks, Mr. Ishaan," she said and ran off, back to the waiting huddle of children. Ishaan walked around the back of the car and up onto the shop's wooden porch, his hair dripping rain onto his face. He ran his hand back through it and glanced at Roan.

"What?" he asked as Roan stared at him.

Roan shrugged.

"Nothing, I guess. You do know you just gave that girl what would be five month's wages for me?"

"Yeah, so what?" Ishaan said as he reached through the passenger's side door for his garment bag. "You want a raise?"

"No," Roan said, shaking his head. "I don't mind working for one tenth the minimum wage, I just...Just when I think I have you figured out, you surprise me." Ishaan swung the garment bag up over his shoulder, trying to ignore the way Roan was looking at him—and the way that look made his heart beat faster.

"Well, don't be too surprised," Ishaan said, stepping past Roan and pulling the shop door open. "If those little gremlins are stuffing themselves with sweets, they won't be messing up my car." He motioned for Roan to enter the shop. Roan kind of grinned and shook his head, then stepped through the door. Ishaan took a moment to collect himself before following.

The shop was quiet and lit only by the light from the front window. Headless mannequins displayed various styles of suits and tuxedos, but Ishaan strode straight for the back of the shop, to the dark doorway and the mirrored corner. "Lira?" he called, leaning through the doorway and looking up the long, narrow flight of stairs. "Are you up there?" Something thumped above their heads, then footsteps tramped over to the stairway.

"Is that you, Ishaan?" Lira called, leaning into the stairway and peering down at him.

"Of course it's me," Ishaan said. "Who else shops here?"

"Oh, ha ha ha," she said, her steps heavy as she descended the stairs. "If you were my only customer, I'd have packed it in years ago. How've you been?"

"Not bad. You?" He moved back as she reached the bottom of the stairs and stepped out into the shop, a red-faced, round woman about the same age as his mother, with fine black hair and dark brown eyes.

"Could be better," she said, gesturing toward the front of the shop. "I hate this damn rain. Why can't it just—" She caught sight of Roan, standing out of the way next to a rack of suit jackets. "Well, my day just got brighter. Who're you?"

"This is Roan," Ishaan said. "He's my..." My *what*? Employee, roommate, friend...

"Ah, I see," Lira said, nudging him in the ribs. "No wonder you look so good. So, how can I help you gentlemen?" Ishaan could feel Roan's gaze on him, moving across his skin like a caress, and he kept his eyes stubbornly averted.

"I just need a few quick alterations," Ishaan said, "but my friend here is looking a whole new outfit."

"Oh, but why?" Lira asked. "That hobo look is quite fetching on him."

Ishaan glanced at him and Roan's cheeks pinked as he looked down at himself.

"What's wrong with my clothes? Ishaan, you said I looked fine."

"For a hobo," Lira said with a laugh and Ishaan could see the embarrassment turning to anger in Roan's face.

"He doesn't look like a hobo," Ishaan said, shooting Lira a look. "Our engagement simply requires a more formal attire."

"How formal?" she asked, raising one pencil-thin eyebrow.

"Very formal," Ishaan replied and out of the corner of his eye he saw Roan frown. "Now, about my pants—"

"Yes, yes, get in the back and change so I can see what I'm dealing with. I'll help your friend look for something less hobo-ish to wear." Ishaan hesitated to leave Roan alone with Lira. Not that she do anything, but the gods only knew what she might say. "Oh, go on," she said, hustling him into the back changing area, "I'm not going to eat him. Unless you think he'd like that. You said you were just friends, didn't you?"

"We're...complicated," Ishaan said, looking over her shoulder at Roan. He grinned to himself as Roan looked at the price tag of one cheap-looking suit coat, his eyes widening as he dropped the tag and stepped back. "Help him find something nice, in black, with burgundy or silver accents, but not too much color—and of course, money is no object."

"It never is with you," she said and headed out into the shop. Ishaan stepped into one of the two changing booths and quickly shrugged out of his traveling clothes. His pressed black pants almost fit; he could button them if he didn't breathe, but they felt too tight across his ass and his white dress shirt was tight through the arms and shoulders. Had he really put on that much weight? He turned back and forth in the full-length mirror, but he couldn't really see it. Roan was right—it was a healthy weight.

"You're insane!" Roan said, sounding like he was standing just outside the back room. "I-I can't put this on—it's worth more than I am!"

"Oh, come on," Lira said, "I just want to look at you. Humor an old lady?"

Roan started to protest again.

"Roan, just shut up and put on the clothes," Ishaan said, his voice loud within the small, enclosed space. Roan didn't respond, but after a moment Ishaan heard the door of the adjacent booth slam shut. He rolled his eyes and opened his own door to find Lira waiting for him.

"You got fat," she said, looking him over with a critical eye.

"Thanks," Ishaan replied. "Can you do something about it?" She motioned for him to follow and he made his way out to the mirrored corner of the shop, the vest and jacket in hand. Lira turned on three glaring lights and began fiddling with the front of his pants, sliding her hand down underneath the waistband. "Watch those fingers, you dirty old woman," Ishaan said as her knuckles brushed his groin. He knew her better than to think it was accidental.

"Aw, you know I only keep this stupid shop open so I can feel up handsome young men."

"I know, which is why I'm saying keep your hands off me. And my friend."

"About that..." Lira said, stepping up onto a stool to tug at the shoulders of his shirt. "Since when have you ever let things get complicated? And with a guy, no less."

"It's not that sort of complicated," Ishaan said, rolling his shoulders and feeling the material pull taut across his back.

"You just wish it was," Lira said. Ishaan started to protest, but couldn't. "That's what I thought." She poked him in the ribs with a finger. "All right, let's see the rest. I can't do anything about the shirt—just buy a new one." Ishaan had figured as much. He slipped into the vest and tried to button it. "Forget it," Lira said. "I'll move the buttons. Jacket?" That had the same problems as the shirt, though not quite as severe.

"Well?" Ishaan asked as she felt along the shoulder seam.

"Give me an hour."

Ishaan glanced at himself in the mirror and turned his head to one side, frowning as his hair brushed along his shoulder.

"If you can do it faster," he said, "I'll make it well worth your while."

"In a hurry, are we?"

"We have an appointment we shouldn't be late for."

"Then go change so I can get started. And where's your cute friend? Did he get lost?"

Ishaan sighed.

"Probably." He headed for the back room, and nearly ran into Roan in the doorway. "There you are. What's the...hold up?" He took a step back and ran his eyes down Roan, to his stocking feet and back up again. Black dress pants, crisp white shirt, dark, dark burgundy vest with antique silver buttons, a black tuxedo jacket and a burgundy bow tie untied around his neck. "Well," Ishaan said and cleared his throat. "You don't look half bad."

"You—you're wearing one, too," Roan said, frowning. "What sort of meeting is this?"

"A fancy one," Ishaan said. He leaned closer, grabbed him by the arm, and turned him first one way, then the other. "It seems to fit. How does it feel?"

"Hot, stiff, tight—And I can't figure out what this is for."

"It's a cummerbund," Ishaan said with a smile. "It goes around your waist." Roan glanced down and tried putting it on, but he kept twisting it. Ishaan reached out to help, then pulled his hands back. "Later," he said, stepping past Roan and into his changing booth. "Go put your other clothes back on."

"What? But I just—"

"We've got a half hour to kill and I don't want you ruining it. Now hurry up." He shut the door and leaned against it, drawing a long, slow breath. Roan didn't look half bad. That was like saying the rain didn't feel half dry. With a shake of his head he began to undress.

Roan was waiting for him out in the shop, watching as Lira neatly replaced his tux on the hangers. Ishaan handed her his pants and jacket and then headed for the door. "Thanks, Lira. Pick me out a shirt, too, would you? No ruffles."

"Do you see anything in here with ruffles?" she called after them. Ishaan stepped outside and held the door for Roan, who kept glancing at him out of the corner of his eye, a tight, nervous expression on his face.

"Now where are we going?" Roan asked as they climbed into the car.

"There's a barber a few blocks over and I don't know about you, but I'm in desperate need of a haircut." Ishaan pulled away from the tux shop and turned down the next cross-street, splashing through a puddle at the corner.

"I can't afford all this," Roan said after a moment. "If I worked for you for the rest of my life, I couldn't earn enough to pay you back."

"So you *do* want a raise."

"No! Ishaan, that's not what—"

"I know," Ishaan said, laughing. "I was teasing you. Relax, okay? You don't have to pay me back. Consider it a...late birthday present."

Roan was silent for a moment.

"So when's *your* birthday?"

Ishaan glanced over at him.

"In the spring," he said evasively. He pulled up in front of the barber and they climbed out. Roan was uncharacteristically quiet while the barbers trimmed their hair and gave Ishaan a shave, and he didn't say a word on the drive back to Lira's shop. Ishaan couldn't help but wonder if he suspected something.

"Is something bothering you?" he asked once they were closeted away in their separate changing booths. Roan took so long to answer, Ishaan began to wonder what he'd done to earn the silent treatment.

"We're not really here to see any lawyers, are we?" Roan asked finally. Ishaan opened his mouth, then closed it again. Lies and secrets were so much trouble.

"How'd you figure?" he asked.

"You don't wear penguin suits to a business meeting."

"Oh, and how many business meetings have *you* attended?" He stepped closer to the mirror and adjusted his bow tie, waiting for Roan to respond with a smart remark of his own, but he didn't. Ishaan sighed. "You're right. There is no meeting. Sorry I lied; I just wanted it to be a surprise."

"I'm surprised, all right," Roan said. He sounded like he was in shock.

"Well, save some of that for the restaurant," Ishaan said, grabbing his black jacket and stepping out of the booth. "Speaking of which, we don't want to be late. They might give away our reservation." He chuckled to himself. "How's it coming?"

"Could you ask Lira for a clip-on bow tie? I can't seem to get this."

Ishaan rolled his eyes and pushed open the door to Roan's booth. Roan jumped back, a startled look on his face. Ishaan hesitated, but Roan was fully dressed, except for his shoes and the tie, which was knotted crooked around his neck.

"Clip-ons are for little kids and guys with one arm," Ishaan said, succeeding in drawing a small smile to Roan's lips. "I'll do it for you." As he untied the knot and worked on tying the bow, his knuckles brushed across the soft skin under Roan's chin. Like a match being lit in a dark room, Ishaan suddenly saw Roan trembling, backed into the corner of the booth, and his mouth went dry and his heart started beating fast. This was wrong.

He moistened his lips and watched Roan's eyes follow the movement, then dart back up to his own. Ishaan looked for fear or disgust in those stormy, blue-gray eyes, and when he didn't find it, his hands began to tremble at Roan's throat. This couldn't be; he was imagining it. Slowly, Roan reached up and touched Ishaan's wrist, his fingertips sliding across the back of Ishaan's hand, and Ishaan jerked back, his heart pounding.

He cleared his throat and turned away, pretending not to see the hurt and disappointment on Roan's face. "C'mon," he said, grabbing his jacket and exiting the booth. "We're going to be late." He paid Lira and headed for the door, the small shop suddenly smothering. He needed fresh air.

Outside, the rain beat against the porch roof, drowning out the thundering of his heart. Roan stood beside him, silent, and they watched the rain fall for several long, tense moments before Ishaan raised the plastic garment bag over his head and ran out into the street. Neither spoke as they drove back through town and pulled up under the gilded awning in front of the *Golden Unicorn*.

"It's closed," Roan said, his voice tight as they walked up to the frosted glass doors.

"Not to us," Ishaan replied, opening one side of the double doors for Roan. They stepped into the quiet restaurant foyer, the carpet dark and thick under their muddy dress shoes. Roan started toward the seating area, but Ishaan caught him by the sleeve and handed him a towel from off a shelf beside the door. "For your shoes," he said as Roan stared at him blankly.

As they cleaned up, Ishaan kept glancing at Roan, at the frown on the young man's face. Not only had he spoiled the surprise, but he'd managed to piss him off, too. He tossed his muddy towel into the bin and turned to Roan.

"I know I pretty much ruined this," he said, "and I'm sorry."

"You didn't ruin anything," Roan said softly. "I just—I can't believe that you'd do something like this...for me."

"Why not?" Ishaan said, forcing a laugh. "You're my friend."

"Yeah, but this is..." Roan wet his lips. "This is more than you'd do for a *friend*. This is...driving three hours to dress up and have dinner in a closed restaurant, Ishaan. This is...more than I deserve." He took a bracing breath and looked down at the carpet. "If-if this is your way of trying to tell me something, you didn't need to go to so much trouble. You could have just asked. I would have said yes."

"Asked?" Ishaan said with a slight shake of his head. "Asked what? I don't—"

"Ah, Mr. Darvis!" Ishaan turned as the owner, a tall man in a fine suit, stepped into the foyer and gestured to them. "Come, come, your party is waiting for you."

Ishaan glanced back at Roan.

"Your party?" Roan said, frowning. "Who else is here?"

Ishaan's jaw dropped.

"Who—I thought you knew." Roan shook his head. "Then what did you think we—" It was like all the air had been sucked out of the room. "You thought this was a date?" Roan's face flushed and he looked away. A date... didn't have to go to so much trouble...just had to ask...Ishaan felt the bottom drop out of his stomach. Roan had offered himself and Ishaan had been too dense to see it.

Roan turned on his heel and shoved open the door, but Ishaan grabbed him by the arm and pulled him back inside.

"Get off of me," Roan snapped, jerking away. "Go have your party. I'll wait in the car."

"It's not *my* party," Ishaan said, catching him again. For a second, they just stared at each other, then Ishaan turned Roan bodily and hustled him over to the seating area. The owner was giving them a funny look, but gestured toward the banquet table on the east side of the room. Roan's head turned and then his whole body stiffened as Kethic rose from the table and walked toward them.

"K-Kethic," Roan whispered. "What's going on?"

"What do you think?" Kethic asked with a grin as he grabbed Roan and pulled him into a tight embrace. Ishaan felt a strange, unwelcome stab of jealousy and glanced away. "I couldn't get married without my stupid kid brother as my best man, now could I?"

Roan pulled away.

"How did you do this? I mean, this is—this is unbelievable."

"Well, I'd love to take the credit," Kethic said with a laugh, "but it was your boyfriend's idea." Roan turned, their eyes met, and neither spoke, neither said a word to correct Kethic. Kethic stepped past Roan and cleared his throat as he looked up at Ishaan. "Which, by the way, I really appreciate. You have no idea. We were going to be married in a magistrate's office, and I couldn't even afford to *rent* a tux, and now we have all this, and my brother, and the honeymoon—" He broke off, choking back tears. "You have no idea," he said again and then stepped forward and wrapped his arms around Ishaan. Ishaan stiffened and awkwardly hugged Kethic back.

"It-it's no big deal," Ishaan said, glancing at Roan. Was it wishful thinking, or did he see a flash of jealousy in those blue-gray eyes? He pulled away from Kethic. "You're welcome. Just...make it work and be happy."

Kethic looked over his shoulder at his brother.

"That reminds me; I need to talk to you later. Remind me. Right now, I'd like to introduce you to your future sister-in-law and her family." He threw his arm over Roan's shoulder and headed for the table, but stopped and glanced back after a few steps. "C'mon, Ishaan, you too."

Twenty-three

Roan leaned forward in his seat and stared out the front window at the low, gray sky overhead. Those looked like snow clouds. The air smelled like snow. The wind was biting cold and he could see the slopes of the mountains beneath the clouds, the tall conifers dusted with white. Last week's storm had blown out a few days after Kethic's wedding and this bitter chill had come racing down the flanks of the mountains right behind it.

"Is it going to snow soon?" he asked, glancing over at Ishaan. Ishaan just shrugged. He'd been quiet since they left Devaen and headed for home. Roan tried to think of what he could have done, but nothing jumped out at him. "When I was a kid, I used to love the snow," he said, hoping to coax a bit of conversation into the silent car. "After I left home, snow meant being cold and wet and hungry most of the time. This is the first winter I'll be able to enjoy it again."

"Well, maybe," Ishaan said, staring ahead at the road.

"Wh-why maybe?" Roan asked, frowning.

"You never know," Ishaan said, his tone clipped. "Somebody could answer your ad."

"What ad?" Roan asked.

Ishaan glanced over at him, scowling.

"Don't play dumb. I talked to Sezae while you were shopping. She told me you asked her to put that notice back up. If you wanted to leave, you should have just said so." Roan felt the bottom drop out of his stomach. He'd forgotten all about that.

"Ishaan, I-I did that months ago, right after...after I heard about Kethic's engagement."

"And that made you want to leave?" Ishaan asked. "Are you sure it wasn't because I almost molested you in the river?"

"You didn't al—"

"And at the wedding, you wouldn't even look at me after what almost happened in the back of Lira's shop."

"That's not—"

"If you want to leave because you're afraid of me, just say so. It wouldn't be the first time."

"I'm not afraid of you," Roan said, raising his voice so Ishaan couldn't interrupt him again. Ishaan turned down the driveway and pulled into the barn, shutting off the car and turning in his seat to face Roan.

"Then what is it?" he demanded. "I deserve the truth."

"You don't want the truth, remember?" Roan said as he opened the door and climbed out of the car. Ishaan followed.

"Is that it?" Ishaan asked, his skin turning an ash gray. "Is that why you—"

"I don't want to leave," Roan said, his stomach churning. "Posting that notice was a mistake, an error in judgment. I'll have Sezae take it back down the next time I see her. Now will you just let it go?" He grabbed their groceries out of the back of the car and headed for the house.

His heart pounding, he waited on the front step while Ishaan locked the barn doors. The truth. He wanted the truth. Roan had been agonizing ever since Kethic had pulled him aside at the wedding reception and told him that his new wife, Merra, knew about his condition, and she didn't care. She knew he was an incubus and she loved him anyway. *That* was why Roan had avoided looking at Ishaan, because he didn't want to be caught staring, imaging what Ishaan's reaction to such news would be.

Roan looked down at the ground as Ishaan came up and opened the door. He took one of the heavy bags and they went inside. Roan locked the door and then followed him to the kitchen. How could life be so comfortable one minute and like chewing broken glass the next?

They didn't speak as they put the groceries away, walking past and around each other as if they'd been doing it their whole lives. Ishaan was perfect for him, and not just because he kept the demon fed. If Roan told him the truth, if Ishaan could accept him...Roan just wished he had more to offer.

He was sitting in his room, reading in the blue suede armchair, when Ishaan stepped into the doorway and knocked lightly on the door jamb. He was dressed in boots, jeans and a sweatshirt, so he wasn't ready for bed. Roan set the book aside and raised his eyebrows.

"Get some shoes on," Ishaan said. "I think I saw a light in the barn."

"You left a light on?" Roan asked as he rose and stretched, his spine crackling.

"No, you idiot, I didn't," Ishaan said. "Now hurry up."

"Do you think it's the guy who killed your horses?" Roan slipped into his shoes and grabbed his coat out of the closet.

"Could be," Ishaan said as he turned and headed across the living room.

Roan glanced around.

"Where's your rifle?" he asked. "Shouldn't we be armed?"

"I don't think we'll have any trouble," Ishaan said as he unlocked the front door. He pulled it open and a blast of icy wind swirled into the house. Roan stepped past him, out into the cold, and flinched as icy snowflakes stung his face. His shoes crunched in several inches of fresh powder, all the leafless trees glowing with a mantle of white. "You said you liked the snow," Ishaan said, stepping up behind him.

Roan didn't move, not even to draw breath. Ishaan was doing it again, so close Roan could feel him though they weren't touching, just like the river, just like the changing booth, only this time, Roan wasn't going to speak or move and screw it up. He stood, trembling, waiting, as Ishaan's warm breath slid through his hair, across his cheek, under his collar. *Touch me*, he begged silently. *Don't make me wait anymore.*

Ishaan stepped past him and the breath left him in a rush, his whole body cold and shaking. What had he done this time? He turned just as Ishaan slipped on the flagstone sidewalk. Roan reached out, grabbing Ishaan's arm, but Ishaan landed on his back in the snow anyway, with Roan lying on top of him.

"Sorry," Roan gasped as he scrambled to get up. "I tried to—Are you okay?" He looked down into Ishaan's face, his cheeks pinked by the cold, his lips parted as he fought to catch his breath. It couldn't be easy, with Roan practically lying on his chest. Roan started to push himself upright, but Ishaan grabbed the front of his coat. Roan stared at him, waiting, but Ishaan made no further move. What kind of game was this? His hand red and nearly numb with cold, Roan reached up and brushed a wayward curl back out of Ishaan's eyes. Ishaan tightened his grip on Roan's coat, but did nothing to stop him.

This was a bad idea. Roan knew it. He knew that Ishaan would just pull away at the last second, shove him off, get up, and leave him in the snow. He knew it, but he couldn't help but pray that he'd be wrong. He leaned closer, hesitated, his eyes searching Ishaan's. He saw fear and uncertainty and pain, but also a deep longing, a need that mirrored his own. This was going to hurt so much. Roan closed his eyes and pressed his lips to Ishaan's.

Ishaan didn't respond, his mouth tight and hard, and a deep, immeasurable ache tore the soul out of Roan's chest as he realized that he'd just made the biggest mistake of his life. A sob rose in his throat, hot and choking, but before he could pull away, scramble to his feet and run, Ishaan made the tiniest sound, barely more than a whimper, and clutched at him, his lips softening, parting. Surprised, Roan jerked back with a gasp, his breath pluming white in the freezing air. Ishaan tensed beneath him, let go of his coat, and Roan could see a kind of panic rising in his eyes.

Roan didn't think, he just leaned down and kissed Ishaan again. *Don't freak out*, he begged. *Please don't freak out.* Hesitantly, he brushed his tongue against Ishaan's and felt him shudder. Ishaan's large hands, cold as ice, slid up to Roan's face, cupping his cheek, tangling in his hair, drawing him closer. Breathless and light-headed, Roan shifted his body, pressing against Ishaan, his blood burning as he felt Ishaan's hard arousal against his thigh.

Another sound escaped Ishaan, but this time it sounded more like the cry of a trapped animal. Roan pulled back and Ishaan turned his face away, his skin flushed as he tried to catch his breath.

"It's...cold out here," he said. "We're going to...catch cold." Roan pushed himself to his knees, sitting back on his heels as Ishaan sat up and combed melting snow out of his hair. Roan could feel a gulf opening between them, a dark emptiness that chilled him to the bone. He shivered.

"Ishaan..." he whispered as Ishaan climbed to his feet. Ishaan started for the house, his sweatshirt and jeans soaking wet, but then stopped. He just stood there for a moment, then turned and offered his hand to Roan.

"C'mon," he said, his eyes on the trampled gray snow between them, "let's go inside."

Roan's heart soared like a bird in the spring sky as he reached up and let Ishaan pull him to his feet. Up onto the front step and through the door they held hands, frozen fingers entwined, but in the foyer Ishaan let go. He pulled off his boots, stripped off his sweatshirt, and headed across the living room, toward Roan's bedroom.

Roan kicked off his shoes and shrugged out of the coat as fast as he could, dropping it in a wet pile in front of the door. He couldn't breathe, he couldn't think. His head felt full of pixies, flitting and giggling and chasing each other in circles. He stepped into the living room and stopped short as the bathroom door closed with a bang.

After a second, Roan shook his head and continued into his room. Ishaan was just washing up. He had to be one of the most fastidious men Roan had ever met. Shutting himself in the bathroom wasn't a bad sign. Roan changed out of his wet shirt and jeans and into a pair of soft cotton pajama pants. He pulled the blue lubricant out of the drawer and tossed it on the end of the bed.

Was Ishaan taking a long time or did it just seem that way? Roan glanced at the clock, but he hadn't noticed what time it was when Ishaan went in. He picked up the jar of lubricant, opened it, and dipped his fingers inside. Pajamas around his ankles, he leaned on the bed and prepared himself, his fingers still chilled as they entered him, spreading the gel as deep as he could. He wiped his hand on his wet shirt and stepped over to the wall his room shared with the bathroom, holding his breath as he listened through the wall. He could hear water running. It sounded like the tub being filled. Roan paced back and forth across the room, then marched out into the living room and tapped on the bathroom door.

"Ishaan?" he said. "Ishaan, are you—"

"Leave me alone," Ishaan replied, his words like a knife in Roan's heart. "I'm sorry. I shouldn't have done that."

"Done what?" Roan asked. "You didn't do anything. I did. I kissed you." He waited, but Ishaan didn't say anything. Damn it! He couldn't believe this had happened again. He banged his fist against the woodwork. "Do you enjoy doing this?" he called. "Is it funny to get me all worked up and then walk away?" He grabbed the doorknob and twisted, but it was locked. "Ishaan, if you don't open this door and talk to me, I'll...I'll leave!"

"No, you won't," Ishaan said. He sounded like he was just on the other side of the door. "Just go away. I-I need to think."

"What's to think about? I want you, and-and I thought you wanted me."

"It's not that simple."

"Yes, it is," Roan said, turning away in exasperation. He leaned on the back of the couch, let his head hang, and sighed. Maybe he should leave. Ishaan was just stubborn enough to keep himself locked in the bathroom all night—Roan straightened up and stepped back over to the door. "You can't stay in there forever," Roan said.

"Watch me," Ishaan replied.

"And what happens when you fall asleep?" Roan asked with a bitter smile. "Do you really think you won't open the door then? Do you really want me waiting out here when that happens?" There was a long silence.

"You wouldn't."

"Watch me," Roan said. He heard the lock rattle and stepped back as the door opened. Ishaan, his hair wet and tangled, shirtless, his skin red from the cold, stared at him with dark, haunted eyes.

"Tell me you wouldn't," he said, his voice tight. "Roan, please, tell me you would never—"

"I would," Roan said, "if it was the only way I could have you." There it was, practically the truth. Now Ishaan would hit him, or lock himself back in the bathroom, or toss him out on his ass—Ishaan lunged at him and Roan tensed, raising one hand to ward off a blow, but Ishaan grabbed him by the shoulders, almost shoved him over the back of the couch, and kissed him. The intensity, the urgency in Ishaan's kiss took Roan right back to that evening. It was happening all over again. Ishaan's hands slid down the front of Roan's pajamas and he gasped into Ishaan's mouth as cold fingers wrapped around his shaft.

Roan pressed his hands against Ishaan's chest, his fingertips kneading the hard muscles, savoring the warm skin as his hands slid down Ishaan's stomach. He fumbled with the button on Ishaan's jeans, tugged the zipper down, and rubbed against Ishaan's erection through the cotton of his briefs. Ishaan jerked back, his flushed face filled with hunger and desire as his eyes traveled down Roan's body. Roan reached for him, but Ishaan caught him by the wrist and spun him around, shoving him forward and bending him over the back of the couch. Roan dug his fingers into the upholstery as his pajamas were dragged down around his ankles and he watched over his shoulder as Ishaan shoved his jeans down to his thighs.

"Please," Roan whispered as Ishaan grabbed him by the hips. Ishaan seemed to hesitate, then pressed against Roan's opening. Roan groaned and pushed back, shouting hoarsely as Ishaan slid inside him in a single swift thrust. He gritted his teeth against the slight pain and watched Ishaan's faded reflection in the dark TV. He was awake. Finally, he was awake. Pleasure shuddered through him as Ishaan drove deep and hard, again and again, grunting, his breath fast and ragged.

With a strangled cry, Ishaan jerked his hips, and Roan stood stunned as he felt the heat of Ishaan's seed deep inside him. In the dark TV, he watched Ishaan step back and look down at him, an expression of horror and disgust on his face, and then turn and disappear back into the bathroom. Roan flinched as the door slammed shut.

Twenty-four

What had he done? Ishaan stumbled over to the tub and kicked off his jeans before throwing himself into the steaming water. He felt filthy. His hands shaking, he scrubbed himself, the hot water searing his chilled skin. This was *exactly* why he'd never wanted to let this happen. He was too rough, too insensitive. He hurt Roan. Closing his eyes, he choked on a sob. He'd tried not to, but he wanted him so much, and the tightness, the heat of Roan's body, the fever in his eyes, the supple softness of his skin was just too much, and now Roan knew him for what he truly was—a monster.

Ishaan waited to hear the front door slam as Roan left him, shivering in spite of the heat, his heart pounding, aching. *What had he done?* Ishaan raised his head and looked across the room as the doorknob rattled. He'd locked the door, though. Good. The last thing he wanted to do was face Roan—

Crash! Ishaan jumped as the door burst inward, the door jamb splintering. Roan stepped into the room, naked, breathing hard, his fists clenched, limping slightly as he favored his right foot. He'd kicked the door in. Ishaan started to get out of the bath, but Roan just stared at him and he sank back into the water, his whole body tied up in cold, trembling knots. What did he want?

Roan walked across the room and swung one leg over the edge of the tub. Ishaan drew his legs up, staring down at his knees as Roan climbed into the bath and stood in front of him. He did not have a good feeling about this, but whatever Roan wanted, it was no more than he deserved. He wouldn't stop him.

"Don't sit there looking like somebody's puppy who just peed on the carpet," Roan said. "Just say you're sorry." *Sorry.* What an inadequate, meaningless word. It could never express the depth of his regret.

"I-I'm sorry," Ishaan whispered. "I'm so, *so* sorry, Roan."

"Good," Roan said, stepping forward and straddling Ishaan's bent knees, "then you won't mind doing me a little favor." He wrapped his hand around his soft dick and gave it a couple of strokes. "What do you say, Ishaan? Is it my turn yet?" Ishaan didn't answer, he just swallowed hard and didn't move. "What's the matter, you never suck on a guy before?" Ishaan shook his head. Roan took another half step closer, still stroking himself.

"If you don't want to," Roan said after a moment, "I won't make you, but... I'd like you to. I think you owe me this much." Ishaan swallowed again, his mouth as dry as if he'd been eating ashes. Roan was right, though; Ishaan owed him. He took a bracing breath and sat up, his lips parting as he leaned forward. "Slowly," Roan said, breathless and hoarse as Ishaan took him into his mouth. He tried to remember the handful of blow-jobs he'd been given, but his mind was blank, focused on the warmth of Roan's skin, the weight on his tongue, the soft skin against his lips.

"Use your tongue," Roan instructed. "Suck and lick. C'mon, Ishaan." Ishaan hesitated, then began to move his tongue, rubbing it against the underside of the head and a long, low moan escaped Roan's lips. Ishaan shuddered as the sound crawled over his skin, making his own dick twitch. He began to suck, sliding down Roan's length, taking more of him into his mouth, and Roan moved his hand from his shaft to the back of Ishaan's head, his fingers working into Ishaan's tangled curls. Ishaan tensed, waiting for Roan to grab a handful and start thrusting into his mouth, but Roan's touch was so gentle, his fingertips pressing against Ishaan's scalp and making his whole body tingle. Ishaan closed his eyes as tears slipped down his cheeks.

"That's enough," Roan said suddenly, pulling back. Ishaan opened his eyes and looked up as Roan sank to his knees in the water, straddling Ishaan's waist. Ishaan shifted, afraid that Roan would notice how hard he'd gotten while sucking him, but Roan just took Ishaan's face between his hands, his thumbs brushing across Ishaan's cheeks as he wiped away the tears. "I'm sorry," Roan whispered, "I shouldn't have made you—"

Ishaan shook his head.

"You didn't—That wasn't—I-I hurt you, I used you—"

"You lost control," Roan said. "It happens. You apologized. Now just—" His voice broke and he looked down at Ishaan's chest. "Just do me one more favor and I'll never ask for anything again."

"What?" Ishaan asked. In response, Roan reached behind him, his fingers finding Ishaan's erection. Ishaan tensed, the breath catching in his throat as Roan rose up on his knees, positioned the head of Ishaan's arousal at his entrance, and began to ease himself down. Ishaan curled his toes against the bottom of the tub and grabbed the cold porcelain sides as Roan gripped him, tight and hot. He trembled deep inside as he fought to keep still. Never again. He would never be that person again.

With a groan, Roan sank down, moving his hips from side to side as he took Ishaan as deep as he could. Ishaan couldn't take his eyes off of Roan's face; his parted lips, his flushed skin damp with sweat, his fine, fair hair clinging to his brow and neck as he arched his back. He was so beautiful. Ishaan started to reach up, to touch him, but dropped his hand back to the edge of the tub. This wasn't about what he wanted, it was about what Roan wanted, and Ishaan doubted Roan wanted him touching him. Roan wouldn't even look at him.

Ishaan gasped as Roan began to move on top of him, slowly rocking back and forth, riding him, each breath ending in a soft moan of pleasure. Tears burned the back of his throat as Ishaan remembered the sounds *he'd* forced from Roan; cries of shock and pain. He deserved this. He deserved every agonizing second, seeing what could have been, but wasn't, all because of him, all because he couldn't control himself. He sat there, the water lapping against his chest, and let Roan have his revenge.

After a moment, Roan reached out and braced his hands on Ishaan's shoulders, his fingertips digging into Ishaan's muscles as his breathing quickened, his whole body tensing. Roan's skin glowed, the lingering tan of summer lit from within by a rosy blush, glistening with water and sweat—Ishaan couldn't take it any longer. He could do better—he could do it right.

Roan made a startled sound as Ishaan grabbed him by the hips, soft skin and firm muscle flowing like silk over stone against his hands, but Roan didn't stop, he didn't pull away. Ishaan leaned forward, pressing his lips to Roan's collarbone and drawing a long, breathless moan from him.

That was the sound Ishaan wanted to hear. He began to rock his hips, pushing up into Roan as he sank down, the water sloshing all around them, splashing out onto the floor, but he didn't care. He'd do anything to hear Roan make that noise again. Ishaan kissed the side of Roan's neck, his hands sliding down to grip and knead Roan's butt, and Roan cried out, his fingers digging into Ishaan's shoulders.

Ishaan leaned back, bracing his feet against the bottom of the tub as Roan arched his body, one hand stroking himself as he cried out and came into the water. Ishaan had never seen anything so erotic. He lifted his hips, thrusting up into Roan, making Roan's whole body jerk.

"Ishaan!" he gasped, trying to rise up on his knees, but Ishaan held him tight and lifted his butt, pounding and grinding into Roan, shuddering as he neared his own climax. Roan shouted, hoarse and wordless, and collapsed forward onto Ishaan's chest, one hand clenched into a fist against Ishaan's shoulder, the other gripping his arm. Roan's ragged breaths against Ishaan's neck made him shiver and he clutched at Roan's butt, spreading his cheeks as he drove deep and lost it, coming hard inside of him.

With a groan, Ishaan relaxed into the warm water, his heart pounding, every now and again raising his hips and forcing another soft cry from Roan. His hands slid up Roan's back, his arms wrapping around the smaller man, and for one desperate, selfish moment he held Roan against his body, his eyes closing as he turned his face into Roan's hair and pressed his lips to the soft skin behind his ear.

Roan tensed in his arms, drawing back, and Ishaan realized he'd done something stupid again. He started to let go and turn his face away before he had to see the look in Roan's eyes, but Roan's strong, warm hand cupped his cheek, Roan's thumb tracing his cheekbone as he turned Ishaan's head back and leaned down to kiss him. Their lips met and Ishaan felt a great weight lift from his body, as if gravity suddenly no longer applied to him. He flew.

After a moment, Roan pulled back and sat up, his eyes still downcast, and Ishaan felt himself falling, lost and empty.

"That was much better," Roan said, his voice nearly toneless. "Thanks." He rose up, letting Ishaan slip out of him, and then climbed to his feet. Something inside Ishaan was screaming, writhing, dying, as he watched Roan turn and start to climb out of the tub.

"Wait." Ishaan heard his own voice before he realized he'd spoken, saw his hand gripping Roan's wrist before he'd realized he'd moved. Roan glanced down at him, trepidation in his eyes, and Ishaan found himself at a loss for words. "What...What *was* this?" he asked finally, letting his hand slip off of Roan's arm. "What did it mean?"

"Why does it have to mean anything?" Roan asked, glancing away. "Sometimes guys just have sex."

Ishaan licked his dry lips.

"Roan, that wasn't just—"

"What then?" Roan demanded. "What do you want it to mean? Do you—do you want to be...to be—"

"Yes," Ishaan said, "I want to be...with you." It was ridiculous. He felt like an idiot just for saying it, never mind meaning it. What was he thinking? As if Roan could ever want him for more than an occasional fuck. He was barely even worth that.

"Thanks for trying to make me feel better," Roan said after a moment as he climbed out of the tub, "but I would rather have this mean nothing, than have you pretend it meant something it didn't. I'm a whore, remember; I've heard more meaningless 'I love you's than ten guys twice my age."

"I didn't say I loved you," Ishaan said.

Roan paused, then grabbed a towel and wrapped it around his waist. "You're right, you didn't."

Ishaan watched him walk out of the room, his gut twisted up into a cold, tight knot, his heart hammering in his throat as he climbed to his feet, shivering slightly in the chill air. As he toweled dry, he kept hearing himself say, over and over, 'I want to be...with you.' It wasn't just meaningless words to make Roan feel better. If that was all he was trying to do, he could have come up with something a lot better than *I want to be with you.*

Ishaan wrapped the towel around himself and started across the living room, but a sound from Roan's room drew his head around—the scrape and rattle of drawers being jerked open and slammed shut, one after another. Roan was packing. The thought of watching him walk out the door filled Ishaan with a sick kind of despair. It felt like waking up on Sezae's floor and realizing what he'd done to her. He thought he'd made sure he would never have to feel that way again.

Anger flared inside him, sudden and dizzying, and he stalked across the room and through Roan's doorway, his fists and teeth clenched. This was all Roan's fault, and if Ishaan had to suffer, then he was going to make sure Roan hurt just as much. Standing before his dresser in his pajama pants, Roan glanced at Ishaan and then turned away, but not quick enough. Ishaan had seen the glistening tear-tracks on his face.

"I'll be there to lock your door in a minute," Roan said and Ishaan watched him dry his eyes on the backs of his hands. Ishaan's anger bled out of him as he took another step into the room.

"Roan..."

"I said I'll be right there!" Roan shouted, grabbing a T-shirt off the end of his bed. Ishaan watched him struggle with it, searching for a sleeve and shoving his arm out the neck hole instead. With a frustrated cry, he flung the shirt to the floor and sank down on the edge of the bed, his shoulders shaking as he hid his face in his hands and sobbed. Ishaan stood in the doorway, ashamed that he'd ever thought that Roan wasn't hurting just as much as he was. How could he have been so stupid, so blind? Without a word, he walked to the bed and sat down beside him.

"Don't," Roan said as he started to rise. Ishaan caught him by the arm and pulled him back down. "Ishaan, please—"

Ishaan kissed him, tasting the salt of his tears as he opened his mouth and slipped his tongue between Roan's lips. Roan made a muffled sound and pressed his hands against Ishaan's chest. For a moment, Ishaan feared Roan would push him away, but those soft hands slid across his skin, caressing, exploring. With a groan, Ishaan wrapped one arm around Roan's shoulders and cupped the back of his neck with the other, exploring his mouth as he eased Roan back onto the quilt and leaned over him, his bare chest pressed to Roan's.

Roan pulled back suddenly, breathless.

"Why? Why are you doing this?" he asked, closing his eyes as more tears slipped free. "You've never been this cruel to me before. What did I do?"

"You didn't do anything," Ishaan whispered, kissing him again. He responded, almost desperately, but choked on a sob when Ishaan drew back. "All this time, you didn't do anything, you didn't say anything—"

"Of course I didn't," Roan said, turning his face away. "You made it perfectly clear you didn't want to have anything to do with me. The only time you'd touch me was when you lost control and it didn't matter who you were with."

"Is *that* what you think?" Ishaan asked, brushing Roan's hair back out of his eyes. "I couldn't stop myself *because* it was you. I've never wanted anyone as much as I want you."

Roan wiped at his tears and glanced at him.

"Then why didn't *you* say something?"

Ishaan lowered his eyes.

"I'm not exactly the kind of guy most people want lusting after them. I-I never thought—"

"That someone could love you?" Roan said softly. Ishaan nodded. "Well...I do...if that means anything."

"It does," Ishaan said, leaning down and pressing his lips to Roan's, his fingers sliding along Roan's jaw, caressing his face. Ishaan drew back and gazed down into those bright, blue-gray eyes. "Roan, it means *everything*."

Twenty-five

"Why do you have to pick movies with such ugly heroes?" Ishaan asked, reaching into the bowl of popcorn in Roan's lap. His other arm was stretched out along the back of the couch, his fingers absently combing through Roan's hair. "I mean, look at that guy," he said, gesturing at the TV with his handful of popcorn. "His teeth are crooked, so's his nose, and there's no way that's his real hair color."

"I'd still fuck him," Roan said with a shrug.

"If he's got a pulse, you'd fuck him," Ishaan said with a laugh. "I've never met anyone as horny as you."

"I don't hear you complaining," Roan replied. He set the popcorn bowl aside and leaned against Ishaan's shoulder, one hand resting on his thigh as they watched the movie.

"I got an email from your brother the other day," Ishaan said after a while.

"Oh, yeah?" Roan said. "What did he want?"

"He told me you were an incubus." Roan felt the world around him grind to a halt. Nothing in the universe moved as he held his breath and waited.

"I don't care," Ishaan said. "I love you and *are you asleep?*"

Roan frowned.

"What?"

"Hey—" Something poked him in the ribs. "Wake up." Roan opened his eyes and glanced around. He was still cuddled up against Ishaan, Ishaan's arm around his shoulders. Disappointment flooded through him as he realized that it was a dream, just a stupid dream.

"Sorry," Roan muttered, sitting up.

"No problem," Ishaan said, but his tone was clipped, tense. That was the one thing they still fought about. Ishaan hated it when Roan was careless around him. For the thousandth time since that first snow, Roan opened his mouth, then closed it again.

"I'm going to...go put some wood on the stove," Roan said as he climbed to his feet. "It's getting chilly in here." He could feel Ishaan's eyes on him as he headed for the kitchen. Why couldn't he just tell him?

"Good thing spring's almost here," Ishaan called after him. "I was out in the woodshed yesterday and—aw, shit."

"What?" Roan asked, but then his eyes fell upon the nearly empty wood box. "Oh. Don't worry, I got it."

"You sure?" Ishaan asked. "It is sort of my job."

"Since when?" Roan said, grabbing Ishaan's old coat from behind the door.

"I don't remember writing up a chore chart. I'm borrowing your coat. And your boots."

"They'll be too big," Ishaan warned as Roan slipped one foot into the oversized boot.

"I just have to walk across the backyard," Roan said with a laugh as he opened the door. "I'll be right back. Don't eat all the popcorn."

"Too late," Ishaan said as Roan stepped outside. Light snow fell around him, large, heavy flakes that muffled the sound and magnified the light, giving the backyard an eerie, pearly silence. He pulled Ishaan's coat tight around him and picked his way down the slippery stairs and along the hard-packed snow path leading out to the woodshed.

It smelled like him. Roan buried his nose in the heavy cloth and breathed deep. Why couldn't he just tell him? For nearly three months they'd been living as lovers, making love almost every evening, but when it was over, Roan still had to lock Ishaan in his room. He'd have given nearly anything to fall asleep in Ishaan's arms and wake there in the morning. He knew Ishaan wouldn't hurt him, but to convince Ishaan of that fact, he'd have to tell him the truth, and that scared him more than anything.

Sure, he had dreams where Ishaan just held him and kissed him and said he didn't care, but he also woke from nightmares just as often, horrible dreams of Ishaan chasing him through the woods, calling him a demon and a monster as he shot at him with his rifle. If that did happen, Roan knew he wouldn't run. Some things just weren't worth surviving.

Roan kicked away the crust of frozen snow in front of the woodshed door and pulled it open, musty, freezing air hitting him in the face and making him shiver. It was pitch black inside as he felt around for the dwindling stack of firewood. A few more cold weeks like the one they were having and spring wouldn't get there fast enough. As he loaded up his arms, he glanced back toward the house, warm electric lamplight glowing in the kitchen windows and spilling out onto the backyard, his trampled trail a dark, ugly scar across the pristine snow.

Just like his secret—a scar across their perfect life. He had never been happier, never felt safer, even with those murdering scientists out there somewhere. That all felt very distant and unreal. Ishaan was the only real thing in his life now and he would die before he did anything to jeopardize that.

His arms full, Roan stepped back and nudged the door closed with his foot before turning back toward the house. He heard a soft *pop* from the direction of the trees and his head snapped around as something whistled out of the darkness and stung him in the side of the neck. He yelped and dropped the wood, his hand darting up to pluck something out of his skin. His vision began to blur even as he held up the red-fletched dart, his head spinning as his eyes rolled back. He felt himself falling, but everything went black before he hit the ground.

Twenty-six

As the screen blacked and went to commercial, Ishaan glanced into the popcorn bowl, grimacing at the hulls and unpopped kernels, and then up at the clock on the wall. The movie was only half over. Assuming Roan could stay awake through the rest of it, he probably ought to make another batch of popcorn. With a sigh, Ishaan rose to his feet and grabbed the bowl. How could Roan fall asleep like that? What would have happened if Ishaan had dozed off, too? They had to be more careful.

Ishaan stepped into the kitchen and dumped the hulls in the trash before setting the bowl on the counter. He leaned against the cold marble and rubbed at his tired eyes. On one hand, it was nice having someone this comfortable around him, but on the other, he wondered what made Roan think he was immune to Ishaan's sickness. Did he think he was safe because they were lovers? Ishaan kept trying to tell him that it wouldn't matter. Every time Roan cuddled up to his side after they made love, his presence so warm and comforting, every time Ishaan was tempted to just wrap his arms around his lover and fall asleep, he remembered the pain in Sezae's eyes, the betrayal on Hektor's face, and he knew that he couldn't live with himself if Roan ever looked at him like that.

Yes, it would be the most wondrous thing in the world to wake up with Roan in his arms—it would be nothing short of a miracle—but it wasn't a chance he was willing to take. As he reached up to open the cupboard where the bag of popping corn was kept, his eyes strayed out the kitchen window, to the alabaster blanket of snow covering the backyard. He glanced at the still empty wood box. Where the hell was Roan? It didn't take this long to bring in an armload of firewood.

Struck by the sudden horrible image of Roan slipping on the icy stairs and breaking his neck, Ishaan stepped to the door and pulled it open. Nothing but Roan's footprints, already dusted with a thin covering of new snow. With an uneasy feeling growing in his gut, Ishaan stepped out onto the back porch, the ice burning his bare feet, and peered into the eerie blue-white darkness. His eyes followed the track out to the woodshed, his heart climbing into his throat at the sight of the dark mound lying motionless beneath the falling snow.

He leaped the porch steps, his feet stinging, screaming as he raced along the path of frozen snow. All he could see was Roan, dead or dying in the cold, until he was practically standing over the dropped armload of wood. His heart thundered, the sound seeming to echo from the bleak, black trunks of the nearby trees as he stared down at the trampled snow. What happened? Where was he?

Ishaan wrapped his arms around himself and ignored the pain in his feet as he stepped around the jumbled pile of firewood. He stopped dead at the sight of three distinct sets of footprints approaching from the river side of the woods and then heading away toward the barn, walking three abreast, but it couldn't hide the marks left by Roan's feet as they dragged him away. Ishaan followed, stumbling and tripping as he ran through the deep snow alongside the tracks, around behind the barn and then to the road, where the footprints ended at a set of fresh wagon tracks, heading up toward Shesade.

Shivering so hard his teeth chattered, Ishaan started up the road, but only took a handful of steps before he stopped. This was insanity. Here he was standing in the middle of the road, barefoot, unarmed, without even a coat. The gods only knew how long ago Roan had been taken. Five minutes? Ten? Ishaan couldn't remember how much more of the movie he'd watched before getting up. They could be a mile away by now. Ishaan had to think logically. Panicking would only waste more time.

He turned around and headed for the house. He needed warm clothes. Too bad Roan had his boots. He might have an old pair in the closet, though. He'd need his rifle and extra shells. He couldn't imagine drug dealers, or whatever flavor of criminal they were, going anywhere unarmed. He should get the car, too. Maybe not. It could outpace any vehicle on the planet over smooth roads, but it was shit in the snow. He kept asking the developers for some better tires, but his e-mails were always met with a polite *Your suggestion has been duly noted* automated reply.

Besides, in this weather, not even tessarsan caribou could pull a wagon over the pass, which meant they probably weren't going far—just far enough so no one would be able to hear Roan scream—

Ishaan choked and fought not to throw up. Nothing was going to happen to Roan. He wouldn't let it. Hands clenching into fists, he began to run.

Twenty-seven

Like swimming up through thick, black water, Roan struggled back to consciousness. He could hear voices and feel people touching him, but his eyes felt as though they were glued shut. Someone grabbed him by the chin and pried his mouth open. He tried to turn away, but hands grabbed either side of his head and held him still as something slender and dry slipped into his mouth and scraped along the inside of his cheek. He tried to raise his hand to push it away, but he couldn't move.

"I think he's waking up." The voice behind him sounded familiar. Why would it sound familiar? The hands released him and his head fell forward before he realized he'd have to hold it up himself. Where was he? What was going on? Roan forced one eye open, brilliant white light searing clear to the back of his skull, and closed it again. He tried to swallow, but his mouth was hot and gummy and tasted of metal.

"Just take it easy," that alarmingly familiar voice said. "The drugs will wear off in a minute." Drugs? Roan never did drugs. What was he talking— The dart! Roan was getting wood and—his eyes snapped open, his whole body tensing as he remembered. Blinding shapes swirled before his eyes and he gave his head a shake, as if that would clear his vision. All it did was make him nauseous. As his surroundings slowly came into focus, he realized he was in some really deep shit.

Wide straps held his wrists and ankles to the arms and legs of a heavy wooden chair with a thick, padded belt across his chest. Not rope, not tape. This wasn't some spur-of-the-moment kidnapping. He could hear several people moving around behind him, as well as the click and whir of machinery and the ticking of a keyboard being used. The lights making his head throb were electric. No one on Eshaedra had electricity...except Ishaan. But why—

"Roan?"

Slowly, Roan raised his head, the figure before him dancing in and out of focus.

"You," Roan whispered, his eyes narrowing.

"Don't look at me like that, little brother," Kethic said, holding a small paper cup to Roan's lips. Warm, bitter water trickled into his mouth. "This is your own fault, you know. If you had just cooperated—" Roan pulled back and spat the water in his brother's face.

"Cooperated? These fuckers murdered Mom and Dad."

A tall man with dark hair stepped over beside Kethic.

"I am afraid your parents' deaths were a tragic and regrettable accident," he said, his voice almost musical with some off-world accent. "Our sole purpose is to help people."

"Help people?" Roan repeated. "How is this helping anyone?" He pulled against his restraints. The tall man reached out like he was going to put his hand on Roan's shoulder. Roan pulled away from him, as far as the strap across his chest would allow, and the man let his hand fall back to his side.

"We have taken a sample of your DNA and it is now being examined by our computers. If you possess the complete genetic sequence, it may be possible to isolate and alter the incubus genes in others, essentially curing the condition."

"And if I don't have all of them?" Roan asked. "Are you going to kill us like you killed our parents?"

Kethic dropped to one knee beside the chair and took Roan's hand.

"No, Roan," he said as Roan tried to pull his hand out of Kethic's grasp. "Dr. Saucher promised me you wouldn't be harmed. As soon as they have what they need, they'll let us go."

"Then why am I still tied up?" Roan asked. "They have my DNA. What more do they need?" Kethic didn't seem to have an answer for that and glanced up at the doctor.

"Just a precaution," Dr. Saucher said. "The results should be back in a few moments."

"You're so full of shit," Roan muttered. Dr. Saucher didn't respond. He turned away and stepped over to a brown-skinned man working at a laptop. Roan looked around the tent, but unless someone was standing right behind him, it was just the four of them. He glanced over at his brother. "So what are you getting out of this? How much am I worth to you?" Kethic had the nerve to look hurt.

"They didn't bribe me," he said. "I went to them."

"And is that supposed to make me feel better?" Roan asked. "Why, Keth? Tell me why you would do this to me. What changed?"

"We had tests done," Kethic said, looking down at the muddy canvas floor between his shoes. "On the baby. She has four of the known incubus markers."

"Four?" Roan said. "But that's good, right? You said you have eight—"

"It's still too many," Kethic said, shaking his head. "They said there's a twelve percent chance that some form of succubism will manifest."

"Twelve percent?" Roan said. "You had me gunned down in my backyard for twelve lousy percent?"

"Oh, shut up," Kethic said. "Wait'll it's your kid."

"I'm not going to be stupid enough to have kids," Roan snapped. "You should have made her get rid of it."

"My daughter is not an *it*," Kethic said between his teeth. "Her name is Kerrali and I *was* going to ask you to—" One of the machines crowding the make-shift tables began chattering and spitting out reams of paper. Kethic stepped past Roan as Dr. Saucher read over the printout. "Well?" Kethic asked.

Dr. Saucher cleared his throat.

"Would you like the good news first, or the bad?"

Roan's heart dropped to the pit of his stomach. Bad news.

"Um...bad, I guess," Kethic said, glancing back at Roan.

"Your brother does not possess the complete sequence."

Kethic's shoulders sagged.

"Then what's the good news?"

"He has only seven of the markers."

"How can that be good news?" Kethic asked, frowning. "How can that even be possible? His condition is so much more severe than mine. It has to be a mistake."

"No mistake," Dr. Saucher said, folding up the printout and setting it on the table. "Roan has seven markers, leading me to believe that the one you do not share is responsible for controlling the severity of the symptoms. This is very good news indeed. It puts us one step closer to understanding this condition and discovering a cure for it."

Kethic turned and gave Roan a sheepish smile and shrug.

"Not quite the news we were hoping for, but...you'll still forgive me, right?"

"Get me out of this chair and I'll consider it," Roan said through his teeth. He'd consider it...as soon as he was finished beating Kethic senseless. Kethic stepped over and began unbuckling the strap holding Roan's left arm down.

"Unfortunately," Dr. Saucher said, "there is more bad news."

"What now?" Kethic asked, still working with the stiff leather strap. Roan glanced around his brother at the doctor, just as Dr. Saucher pulled a slim black pistol from inside his white lab coat and pointed it at Kethic's back.

"I am afraid I cannot trust you not to go to the authorities now that you know my name and have seen my face," Dr. Saucher said, "so I am going to have to kill you now." He took a step toward them and raised the gun to the back of Kethic's head. "I do apologize." Roan's eyes darted to the assistant sitting silently at the computer, watching with evident unease, but there was too much fear in that dark gaze when the man looked at him.

Crack. The sound was almost unreal, echoing in the silence, but the hot blood that splattered across Roan's hand and cheek was too real. He screamed and looked up at his brother, a look of shock on Kethic's face. Kethic turned as Dr. Saucher's body hit the floor and Kethic's back was dark with blood and other, thicker things. For an instant, no one moved, then the assistant leaped to his feet. Kethic dove to the floor and grabbed the doctor's gun, raising it as the assistant shoved open the tent flap and vanished into the darkness.

Kethic scrambled to his feet just as the assistant came stumbling back into the tent, and right behind him, rifle in hand, strode Ishaan. Roan couldn't breathe as their eyes met, his chest filled with such a powerful, trembling warmth he thought he was going to explode. It was just like in a movie, that moment where the hero saves the girl and the triumphant music plays—Roan began to laugh, a high, hysterical sound that brought a frown to Ishaan's face.

"Nice to see you, too," Ishaan said, stepping over and finishing freeing Roan's arm with a tug on the strap. "Are you all right? Is he all right?" he asked Kethic. Kethic had the assistant seated back in his chair and was keeping him there at gunpoint.

"They tranquilized him," Kethic said. "I don't know if it's worn off yet."

The laughter died as swiftly as it had come over him as Roan watched Ishaan move about the tent. He was looking around. He could be pretty dense sometimes, but even he had to realize that something unusual was going on here. Any second and he was going to ask...and Roan wasn't sure he could keep lying to him. Ishaan glanced down at him, his hazel eyes shadowed by a frown, but he didn't say anything. He turned to Kethic.

"Are *you* all right?" he asked.

"Never better," Kethic said, perching on the edge of one of the tables as he kept the pistol trained on the assistant. "How'd you find us?"

"Followed the wagon tracks," Ishaan said.

Kethic nodded.

"Not exactly the best weather for sneaking around, is it?" He glanced at Dr. Saucher. "Nice shot, by the way. You saved my life."

"Don't get all choked up over it," Ishaan said. "I didn't know it was you. All I could see were silhouettes and I just shot the guy with the gun."

"I guess I'm twice as lucky to be alive, then," Kethic said. "What do you suppose we ought to do with this guy?" Ishaan eyed the assistant, then squatted down and unstrapped Roan's legs.

"Here, put him in this thing," Ishaan said as he slipped an arm around behind Roan and helped him to his feet. Roan's head spun with the sudden rise in elevation and his knees buckled with the first step he tried to take, but Ishaan didn't seem to mind holding him up. His big hands moved possessively over Roan's arms and chest. "So, what is this?" Ishaan asked and Roan felt the bottom drop out of his stomach. "Who are these people? What did they want with you?"

Roan glanced at the assistant, whose dark eyes darted back and forth between them as Kethic tightened the straps across his wrists. If he said anything—

"Can we talk about it later?" Roan asked. "I just want to go home."

Ishaan hesitated, then took Roan's hand and gave it a squeeze.

"Of course," he said, then looked over at Kethic. "Think you can handle this guy if I take Roan home and then run into town and wake the sheriff?" The sheriff. Questions. Interrogations. And then the truth would come out. Everyone would know about Roan. Ishaan would know...

"No problem," Kethic said, tightening the strap across the assistant's chest and stepping back. "Just don't be gone too long, okay?" He glanced down at the dead doctor, at what was left of his face, and quickly looked away again.

"I'll hurry," Ishaan said, grabbing his rifle. Roan could have managed the walk by himself, but he needed to feel Ishaan's arm around him. He wasn't sure if it was the drugs still lingering in his system, or just the realization that he was about to lose the only man he'd ever loved, but he felt numb and foggy, like his brain had been disconnected. All he could think was that it was all about to fall apart and there was nothing he could do. They stepped outside, into the snow, and Roan shivered.

"Where are we?" he asked, glancing around at the dark forest surrounding them.

Ishaan pointed to the left. "The road is just beyond those trees. We're about a mile and a half from the house."

Roan started to take a step down the narrow track of packed snow, but Ishaan caught him by the arm and pulled him back. He wanted answers; he wanted the truth. Roan felt like he was dying.

"Ishaan, I—" A hot, fierce kiss silenced him, stealing his breath and leaving him trembling.

"Don't ever do this to me again," Ishaan said, his strong arms wrapping around Roan, nearly squeezing the air right out of him. "I couldn't bear to lose you."

Roan sobbed and clung to him. How could he do this to Ishaan? How could he just pretend like nothing was wrong while he waited for their world to end? It was cowardly and it was cruel, and if it had to end, why drag it out any longer? Besides, maybe it would mean something if Ishaan heard it from him instead of reading it in a police report.

Roan drew back, his heart pounding.

"Ishaan, I-I'm sorry," he whispered. "I—" Roan jumped as two shots rang out, his eyes widening as he gripped Ishaan's arm. Kethic. They turned and shoved through the tent flaps, drawing up short at the sight of the assistant, motionless on the floor beside Dr. Saucher. Kethic stood over them, his face pale as he stared down at the gun in his hand.

"What happened?" Ishaan asked, stepping forward and kneeling down beside the assistant. Kethic didn't answer, he just watched as Ishaan checked for a pulse. "He's dead," Ishaan said as he stood up. "Kethic, what happened?"

Roan walked farther into the tent, his hands shaking as he placed them on the back of the chair he'd been strapped to. A cold, uneasy feeling twisted through his gut.

"He-he got free," Kethic said. "I must not have—the straps were too loose, maybe—he came at me—I just pulled the trigger—" Roan swallowed hard as Kethic raised his head and their eyes met. "I've never killed anyone before."

"It was self-defense," Ishaan said, but Roan knew better. Kethic had the same dark, detached look in his eyes that he'd get when turning tricks in the alley. A necessary evil, he used to say. He didn't have any choice. Kethic glanced away as Ishaan reached out for the gun. He hesitated, then pressed it into Ishaan's hand.

"I guess there's no reason to rouse the dragon tonight, then," Kethic said.

Ishaan stared down at the bodies, sighed, and shook his head.

"No, we should report this as soon as possible. Waiting makes it look like we have something to hide and we don't need to give that dragon any more reason to crawl up our asses." He turned and reached for Roan. "Come on, I'll take you home and we'll get cleaned up, and then I'll go into town and wake the sheriff."

Roan stepped into his one-armed embrace, shaking from the inside out. The assistant was dead. The only other person who knew the truth about them was dead. Roan tightened his grip on Ishaan. He wasn't going to lose him after all.

He supposed he owed Kethic his thanks, but that seemed evil, thanking his brother for killing someone. It really was self-defense, but not like Kethic was telling it. Roan fought the urge to glance back at his brother as they made their way through the snow to the road. There would be time to talk later.

Once clear of the trees, they found the scientists' wagon, their huge, shaggy horse dozing under a light dusting of snow. Roan was glad when Ishaan helped him up into the back of the wagon; he didn't think he could have made the mile and a half walk back to the house, especially in Ishaan's too-large boots. Kethic climbed into the driver's seat and took the reins as Ishaan swung up over the side and settled down beside Roan. It was like he thought Roan would vanish if he wasn't holding him. Roan didn't mind in the least.

As they rolled away down the rutted road, Roan remembered the printout and tensed.

"What is it?" Ishaan asked.

Roan shook his head.

"Nothing. I'm just—I'm glad you found us."

"Me, too," Ishaan said, his breath warm on Roan's face as he leaned in and brushed his lips against Roan's forehead. Roan sighed and lay his head on Ishaan's shoulder. Did that paper have his name on it, or was it just a random sequence of DNA? How much was in that computer, and how much of it would the sheriff be able to understand? He wished he could have had just five minutes to burn those papers, delete those files. Too late now.

Kethic stopped the wagon in the middle of the driveway and jumped down from the driver's seat.

"Should we put the horse in the barn?" he asked as Roan and Ishaan clambered down out of the back.

Ishaan shook his head.

"No, the stalls are full of boxes and I'll need the wagon to get into town, anyway. Besides, he doesn't seem that bothered by the cold." Ishaan paused to rub the big horse's nose before they headed inside, a look of longing in his eyes.

"What will happen to him?" Roan asked as Ishaan unlocked the front door. "I mean, do you think the sheriff would let you keep him?"

"I doubt it," Ishaan said. "He's evidence, or a witness, or something. C'mon, let's get that blood washed off you."

"Me first," Kethic said, pushing past them. "I think I've got that guy's face in my hair. I won't take long."

"I'll find you something to change into," Roan said, kicking off Ishaan's boots as he headed for his room. While Kethic washed up, Roan stood in various doorways, watching Ishaan as he gathered the dropped firewood, brought it inside, loaded the stove, discovered a withered carrot in the bottom of the fridge, and filled a pan with water for the horse. Roan just couldn't bear the thought of losing sight of him. He stood at the front door and leaned against the door jamb, his arms wrapped around himself as Ishaan offered the carrot to the horse and scratched him behind the jaw as he ate.

"Tub's all yours," Kethic said, making Roan jump as he stepped up behind him. He was wearing a pair of Roan's old sweatpants and no shirt, the cold winter air raising goose bumps up his damp arms.

"Thanks," Roan said and he started to step back out of the open doorway. He glanced at Ishaan, still petting the horse, and then he closed the door and headed for the bathroom. While the tub filled with steaming water, Roan peeled off his blood-splattered clothes and dropped them on the tiled floor. His reflection stared back at him like the survivor of some gruesome battle, his face dotted with smeared droplets of blood, his eyes dark and shadowed. He rubbed at the blood on the back of one hand, feeling it ball up against his palm.

He had almost died. His breath shuddered through him as he realized just how close that had been. If Ishaan had been a second or two later, Kethic would be dead, and shortly after that, Roan, too. He'd been through some awful things, escaped some hairy situations, but nothing like that. Hands shaking, he shut off the faucet and climbed into the tub. The heat prickled across his near-frozen skin as he scrubbed at the blood on his hands.

He glanced up as someone tapped on the door.

"It's not locked," he said, his voice loud and hollow in the empty room. He was disappointed when Kethic stuck his head in.

"I'm going to lie down on your bed for a while," Kethic said. "Wake me when Ishaan goes to get the dragon and I'll sit up with you while you wait for him, if you want."

"All right," Roan said, nodding. It would give them a chance to talk. From the look in Kethic's eyes, he was thinking the same thing as he nodded once and withdrew from the doorway. Before the door latched, however, it swung back open and Ishaan stepped into the room. Roan caught a glimpse of Kethic's worried frown before Ishaan shut the door on him. Roan sank farther into the water as Ishaan walked toward him. Now he would start with the questions. Now it would start to fall apart.

"Are you feeling better?" Ishaan asked as he stripped off his shirt. "Have the drugs worn off?"

"I still feel a little woozy," Roan said. "I'm not sure if that's the drugs, or just...what happened."

"It could be shock," Ishaan said and Roan watched him unbutton his jeans. "You mind if I join you?"

"I don't mind," Roan said. On the contrary, he felt empty without Ishaan's arms around him. He slid forward as Ishaan climbed in behind him.

Ishaan hissed in pain as he stepped into the tub.

"Shit, that hurts," he muttered under his breath and Roan looked over his shoulder at him. "My feet," Ishaan explained and Roan glanced down at them, as red as lobsters beneath the water. "When I realized something was wrong, I didn't think to put shoes on, I just went looking for you."

"Barefoot?" Roan asked. "You're lucky you don't have frostbite, you idiot."

"You'd been kidnapped," Ishaan said, sinking down into the water. "I wasn't real worried about my feet." He stretched his legs out on either side of Roan, his big hands rubbing at Roan's shoulders. Roan groaned and leaned back against him, enfolding himself in the warmth of Ishaan's embrace. For a long time, neither of them spoke.

Finally, Roan sighed.

"Well, they weren't drug dealers, I guess."

"No," Ishaan said softly, "I don't think they were. They looked like researchers, scientists. Did they say what they wanted you for?"

Roan hesitated, then nodded. "They seemed to think I was an incubus."

Ishaan went very still beneath him.

"That's ridiculous," Ishaan said. "You—you couldn't be one of those... things. Could you?"

Roan swallowed hard, suddenly feeling very cold and small inside.

"When I was sitting there, waiting for them to run my DNA, I was so afraid the test would say I was one, I was so afraid you wouldn't love me anymore if you found out I was an incubus—"

"But you're not," Ishaan said, holding him tight and kissing the side of his face.

"But-but if I was," Roan said, blinking hard as tears stung his eyes, "you-you wouldn't love me—"

"Oh, Roan," Ishaan whispered. "If you found out you were an incubus, I would too love you. I'm not going to stop loving you for something you can't help." Roan almost sobbed with relief. "Now, if you'd always known you were an incubus and you'd been lying to me this whole time, I'd toss you out in a heartbeat." And then he laughed, like it was some kind of joke. Roan tried to laugh with him, but nearly choked on the sound. "Are you sure you're all right?" Ishaan asked. "You're shaking. Maybe I should take you to the doctor."

"No, I'm fine," Roan said. "Really. I don't want to see a doctor." Ever again. "I just want to put this behind us and forget about it."

"Soon," Ishaan said, his lips brushing the shell of Roan's ear as he spoke. "The sheriff will probably want to talk to you about it. Speaking of, I should probably go—"

"No," Roan said, clinging to his arms as Ishaan made to let go of him, "please stay—just a little longer."

Ishaan relaxed with a sigh. "All right, but we can't stay in the tub all night."

He took Roan's wrist and held his hand up in front of them. "See, you're already getting all wrinkly." Ishaan chuckled into Roan's hair, raising goose bumps down his neck. They lapsed into silence, but Roan could barely hear the quiet over the voice screaming inside his head. Why did Ishaan say that? Did he know; did he have any idea?

"So what do I tell him?" Roan asked after a minute. "The sheriff, I mean. About what happened."

"Tell him the truth," Ishaan said. "We didn't do anything wrong."

Roan nodded, feeling sick inside. Maybe Kethic would know what to do. They sat in the bath, not saying much, until water had gone almost cold. "That's enough," Ishaan said with a sigh. "I'm cold and wrinkled and tired, and I still have to go to town before I can sleep, so c'mon, get up."

The air was freezing on his wet skin and Roan toweled off as quickly as he could. He'd forgotten to bring clean clothes in with him, so he wrapped the towel around his waist and reached for the doorknob.

Ishaan caught him by the hand.

"I know this isn't how it's traditionally done," Ishaan said, their fingers entwining as he pulled Roan toward him, "and we've both have quite a scare tonight, so neither of us is thinking clearly, but I was wondering if maybe... maybe you might want to marry me." For an instant, Roan wondered if he'd fallen asleep in the tub. This had to be a dream. It couldn't really be happening, could it? Ishaan squeezed his hand, waiting for an answer, and Roan drew a startled breath.

"No." The word was out of his mouth before he realized it. "I mean yes!" he said quickly, but now Ishaan just looked confused. Roan swallowed hard. "Yes, I want to marry you. I just...can't."

"You're already married, aren't you?" Ishaan said, frowning.

"No," Roan replied, "I'm not married. I just...I have something I need to do first, something I should have done a long time ago, but I'm such a fucking coward..." He looked down at the floor and shook his head.

"Maybe I can help," Ishaan said, reaching out and brushing his knuckles along Roan's cheek. Roan almost laughed.

"I wish you could," he said. "This is something I have to do myself and after I do, you can ask me again. If you still want to, that is."

"Of course, I'll still want to," Ishaan said as he drew Roan up against his chest. "I love you." Roan looked up into his eyes as he brushed a lock of blond hair back from Roan's face.

"I love you, too," Roan said, closing his eyes as Ishaan leaned close and kissed him. His heart fought to beat in the crushing grip of misery, his soul aching. He did; he loved Ishaan more than anything, but it wouldn't matter, not once Ishaan found out. Ishaan drew back and Roan turned away before he could see the tears caught in Roan's eyelashes. "I thought you were in a hurry to get out of here," Roan said with a forced laugh as he opened the bathroom door. "A proposal isn't exactly a quick conversation."

"It could have been," Ishaan said, following Roan out into the living room. "I ask, you say yes, we kiss—"

"Ishaan, I'm sorry—"

"No, it's okay," Ishaan said, reaching out and placing his hand on Roan's shoulder. "Really. Do what you need to do. I'll be here when you're ready."

"Thanks, Ishaan," Roan whispered. "I appreciate it." Ishaan gave his shoulder a squeeze, then headed for his room. Roan watched him go, then fled to his own room. He pulled open a drawer and grimaced as the dry wood squeaked. Kethic was sleeping, and right then, his brother was the last person he wanted to talk to. Kethic had warned him that this would happen. *You can't build a relationship on lies*, he'd said, and he was just the kind of ass to remind him of that fact, and throw in an *I told you so* for good measure. Roan didn't need that on top of everything else. He glanced at his bed, at the still and quiet lump beneath the quilt, and sighed in relief as he turned away and dug into his drawer for a pair of sweats.

He threw on sweat pants and a T-shirt, and slipped out without rousing his brother. Ishaan was already in the foyer, kneeling down to tie his boots. He glanced up as Roan crossed the room.

"Kethic still asleep?" he asked. Roan nodded. "Wake him up. I don't think you should be left alone, especially with your condition."

"My condi—oh, the seizures." For a second, his heart had almost stopped. "Right. I don't think we have to worry about it," Roan said, but Ishaan shook his head.

"You don't know that and I'd feel better if I knew someone was with you."

Roan sighed.

"All right, I'll wake him up." For all the good *that* would do.

"I shouldn't be gone for more than an hour," Ishaan said. "I don't know if the dragon will want to take our statements tonight or wait until tomorrow—" He shook his head and stood up. "At this point, I'm so tired, I can barely even remember what happened." Roan wished he could say the same. The whole nightmare was permanently etched into his mind. Ishaan grabbed his coat off the hook and gave Roan a quick kiss before opening the front door. Icy wind swirled in, but thankfully the snow had stopped falling.

"Be careful," Roan said, stepping into the doorway as Ishaan headed out into the cold, dark night.

"I will," Ishaan said. "Now go back inside before you freeze. And lock the door." Roan didn't move, watching as Ishaan climbed up into the wagon and took up the reins. He gave them a flick, the heavy leather straps thumping against the horse's rump. The massive beast snorted, a plume of white billowing up around his face, and shook the snow off his back before starting forward. "I mean it," Ishaan called as the wagon rolled past, the snow crunching beneath the wheels, "lock that door. I love you."

"I love you, too," Roan said, stepping back inside the house. He didn't shut the door, though, until Ishaan had turned up the road and disappeared from sight. With a sigh he slid the deadbolt into place and headed for the couch. Even though he'd told Ishaan that he would, he didn't want to wake Kethic. Not yet. He needed a few minutes to himself, to sort through all the shit that landed in his lap.

As he sat down, though, there came a soft tapping at the front door. With a groan, Roan heaved himself back to his feet and crossed the room. "What did you forget?" Roan asked as he unlocked and opened the door. But it wasn't Ishaan standing on the front step. Roan jumped back as Kethic darted into the house and shut the door behind him.

"Shit, it's freezing out there," Kethic hissed, rubbing his hands together, his skin red and raw looking. "I thought he'd never leave. Is the fire going?" He kicked off his wet shoes and headed for the kitchen.

"Hey! Hang on a minute!" Roan said, chasing after him. "I thought you were asleep."

"Good," Kethic said. "If anyone asks, I've been asleep this whole time." They entered the kitchen and Kethic stepped over beside the stove. "I had something I needed to do."

"What?"

Kethic chewed at the inside of his lip, his brow furrowed as he stared down at his hands.

"It might be best if you don't know. Just trust me—"

"Trust you!" Roan shouted. "Why the hell should I? You sold me out—"

"They told me they weren't going to hurt you," Kethic said. "I was desperate and I believed them. I'm sorry. I've been trying to fix it."

"Is that why you murdered the assistant," Roan asked, "to try to 'fix' your mistake?"

"I didn't have a choice," Kethic said, his voice hardly louder than a whisper. "He threatened to expose us. He said if I didn't let him go, everyone would find out what we were. So I agreed and I freed him, and then I shot him. The first bullet didn't kill him, though, it just knocked him down. He looked so...shocked. And then I shot him again and he was dead." Silence filled the little kitchen. "I didn't want to," Kethic said after a minute. "I didn't think I had a choice."

Roan didn't know what to say.

"It's okay," he said finally, but they both knew it wasn't. "So, where did you go?" Kethic started to shake his head. "Just tell me, Keth. How can I help cover your ass when I don't know what we're covering up?"

"All you gotta do is tell them that I was asleep and that I never left the house." Kethic walked away from the stove, like that was the end of the conversation, but Roan grabbed him by the arm and spun him back around.

"Damn it, Kethic, what the hell did you do?"

Kethic jerked away from him.

"I burnt it, okay?" he said. "I went back to the tent and I made it look like the heater was too close to some papers and I burned everything—the computer, the bodies—all the evidence is gone. We're safe. No one will ever find out."

"You're sure?" Roan asked, grasping at the first glimmer of hope he'd had all night. Kethic nodded. "All right then, you were asleep until I woke you, and then you never left my sight. Did you cover your tracks?"

Kethic snorted and headed into the living room.

"I may be a prize idiot sometimes, but I'm not completely stupid." He sank onto the couch and picked up the remote, but didn't turn the TV on. As Roan sat down beside him, Kethic glanced over at him. "So, he loves you, huh?" Roan didn't respond and Kethic chuckled. "I told you so."

Twenty-eight

Ishaan woke to the scent of vomit in his room, sour and rank. He ached from head to foot, worse than any morning when he'd woken up on the floor. He opened his eyes, squinting through a strange, gray light that filtered in through the window. That was more like afternoon light than morning. Had he slept through the whole day?

He raised his head and glanced at the door, his heart stopping as it stood wide open on the living room. What had he done? Where was Roan? He called out, but his throat was dry, his tongue felt swollen and coated with cotton. He tasted bile when he tried to swallow. Something was definitely wrong. He struggled to sit up, the muscles in his abdomen and lower back tight and aching as he pushed himself a little higher on his pillows. Just that little movement left him breathless and shaking. He swallowed again, grimacing at the taste, and cleared his throat.

"Roan?" he called, his voice hoarse. "Roan?" Footsteps rushed over from the direction of the kitchen and Roan hurried into the room. He was pale and haggard looking, with dark circles under his eyes, his hair pulled back in a tangled ponytail. "What—" Ishaan started to ask, but Roan shook his head.

"Don't talk," he said, his normally fluid voice filled with gravel. "You'll wear yourself out. Do you remember what happened?"

"No," Ishaan said. The last thing he remembered was watching a movie with Roan, making love, and then going to bed. That was nearly a day ago.

"I'm going to get you something to drink," Roan said. "You're dehydrated. Then I'll explain." He was gone for the longest five minutes of Ishaan's life. He returned with two mugs of weak, lukewarm broth. He tried to lift the cup to Ishaan's lips, but Ishaan wasn't a complete invalid. He took the cup in both hands and sipped the almost tasteless liquid. Rather than ease his thirst, it only made it worse. He wanted to drain the cup and steal Roan's as well, but he knew that would probably make him sick again.

"Was it flu?" he asked. Roan perched on the edge of his bed and stared down at the floor.

"No, not flu," he said. "It was...I think it was the fish. That's the only thing I...I'm sorry, this is all my fault. I thought I removed the poison gland intact, but I must have nicked it. The toxins must have gotten into the meat and..." He trailed off and rubbed a pale hand across his face. "You could have died."

"You ate it, too," Ishaan said. Was that why he looked like death?

"Yeah, but not as much as you. You went back for seconds, remember?" It took a moment, but he did remember. They had hautfish for dinner, fresh bread, a glass of wine...It was delicious. He glanced at Roan.

"My door was open."

Roan nodded.

"I wanted to hear when you woke up."

"But-but I could have—"

"Ishaan, you were in no condition to hurt anyone. You couldn't even get out of bed to use the bathroom." Roan's face colored at little at that statement. "I had to clean you up." Ishaan felt himself flush with embarrassment. "You should also know," Roan said after a moment, "I spent last night in here with you. You didn't touch me once."

"You—But—Why—?" Ishaan said, not sure which question he wanted answered first.

"The first night, I was too sick to get out of bed, but when I could, I came to check on you. You were worse than I was; vomiting, delirious, burning up with fever. I couldn't leave you, though last night was so bad I almost stole your car and went to town for help."

"Nobody would have," Ishaan said.

"Sezae would have," Roan said. "I couldn't find your keys, though. They're not on your desk or in you jacket pocket."

Ishaan frowned.

"We got back from shopping..." He took another sip of his broth. "I set them down in the kitchen."

"Ah," Roan said. "I didn't look there." He lapsed into silence, staring down into his cup. Ishaan opened his mouth to tell him that it wasn't his fault, but a sudden ticking against the window drew his attention.

"Is that rain?" Ishaan asked. Now that he was listening, he could hear a low rumble above their heads, the drumming of rain on the roof.

"It started yesterday," Roan said. "Destroyed what was left of the snow, except—" He chuckled. "The path out to the woodshed is still there. It's a dirty, ice sidewalk, but it beats walking in the mud. When I brought wood in this afternoon, there was an inch of standing water across most of the backyard."

Ishaan groaned.

"It's going to wash away all the topsoil in the garden." He sighed. "I guess winter's over."

"Good thing, too," Roan said. "If it hadn't warmed up, we'd be out of wood in a few days."

"It was a rough winter," Ishaan admitted. "I hadn't seen that much snow since I was a kid." He took another sip of broth, but it was cold. He tried to set the cup on the bedside table, but his hand started to shake and he nearly dropped it.

"Sorry," Roan said, reaching out to take it from him. "I've worn you out. You need to rest."

"I'm fine," Ishaan said, but then he grimaced. "Actually, I feel like shit. Maybe you're right."

"Of course I'm right," Roan said, setting both cups down to fiddle with the pillows behind Ishaan's head and smooth the blanket across his chest. Ishaan caught his hand.

"You should rest, too. You look like hell."

"Thanks," Roan said with a crooked smile. "I will. I'm just going to take these back to the kitchen." He picked up the cups and left the room, leaving Ishaan's door open again. Ishaan started to call after him, but he supposed Roan was right about that, too. Just the thought of getting out of bed made him ache. With a sigh, he closed his eyes.

"Found the keys," Roan said a moment later as he reentered the room. "They were behind the sugar." Ishaan tensed as Roan slipped into bed with him.

"What are you doing?" he asked. Roan hesitated, then finished settling the blankets around himself.

"I'm resting," he said, "and I figured I'd take advantage of the fact that you can barely move. You have no idea how much I want to just sleep beside you."

"Yes I do," Ishaan said, "and I'd give anything—do anything, to make that happen, but it's just not possible."

Roan reached out and tucked a loose strand of hair behind his ear.

"For tonight, it is," he said, and he leaned over and planted a gentle kiss on Ishaan's cheek. "And don't worry," he added with a grin, "if you start getting frisky, I'll leave immediately." Ishaan opened his mouth to tell Roan that it wasn't a joke, that they needed to act responsibly about this, but as Roan settled down beside him, one hand resting on Ishaan's chest, his breath a gentle warmth against Ishaan's shoulder, Ishaan's protests died on his lips. How could he say no to this?

His unease melted like snow in the rain as he sank back into the pillows and drifted off to sleep.

Twenty-nine

Roan woke in the dark, hunger gnawing at him, both in his stomach and in his soul. His stomach he could ignore, but the demon, so used to feeding every night, was growing restless. Normally, he could fight it for two more days before things got desperate, but being sick had drained him and he didn't have the strength.

Holding his breath, he raised himself up on one elbow, listening to Ishaan's deep, serene breathing. He was asleep, but it was simply the sleep of the exhausted. With guilt and self-loathing burning like bile in the back of his throat, Roan reached out, his hand sliding under the covers, his fingertips brushing Ishaan's thigh. Ishaan made a soft sound and shifted in his sleep, moving away from Roan. Feeling like a dirty pervert molesting him in his sleep, Roan laid his hand over Ishaan's groin, rubbing his flaccid penis through his thin pajama pants.

Ishaan's breathing quickened, his body responding to Roan's manipulation, hardening beneath his hand. The pleasure that rolled off of him was light and sweet—spring water again after months of feasting, but it would keep his demon quiet; it would keep his secret safe. Roan closed his eyes and tried to choke back the bad taste in his mouth. He was such a coward.

Every morning before he unlocked Ishaan's door, he went over what he needed to say and he steeled himself for the worst, but every time the door opened and Ishaan smiled at him or took him in his arms and kissed him good morning, all his best intentions went out the window. As long as things were going so well, how could he ruin it? And why? For what? His secret wasn't hurting anyone. If Ishaan never found out, they could live happily ever after. All he had to do was not screw it up by opening his stupid mouth.

But now he wondered how sneaking a feel in the dark could be part of anyone's twisted happy ending.

Ishaan groaned and rolled onto his side, one hand pushing Roan's arm away.

"Not tonight," he mumbled into the pillow. "I'm tired." Roan wasn't sure if he was awake or asleep, or a little of both, but he wasn't about to risk inviting awkward questions. After a moment, he slipped out of bed and crossed over to the kitchen. He scraped the coals to the front of the stove and put a few more knotty pieces of pine on to burn. They were full of pitch and popped and smoked terribly, but it was about all they had left.

Roan leaned against the counter and listened to the rain pounding against the windows facing out onto the backyard while he waited for a little more of that broth to heat up. He sipped half a cup and risked nibbling a piece of bread before returning to Ishaan's bed. His stomach felt better, at least. With a sigh, he closed his eyes and waited for sleep to find him.

Thin, gray morning light filled the room when he opened them again. In his sleep, he'd moved across the bed and right up against Ishaan's side. That was kind of romantic. His hand down the front of Ishaan's pajamas was not.

"And here I thought it was me we had to worry about."

Roan jumped, jerking his hand free, and glanced up at Ishaan.

"Sorry," Roan said, his heart pounding. "I-I just—" Ishaan reached up, placed his index finger across Roan's lips, and smiled.

"I didn't actually mean for you to stop," he said and then he leaned close and kissed him, his arms encircling Roan and drawing him back against his body. He tasted like morning breath, stale broth, and bile, but Roan didn't care. He relaxed, his hands sliding up Ishaan's chest, caressing his collarbone, his throat, the scratchy three day beard on his jaw, cupping the back of his head as Roan groaned and moved closer, pressing his growing arousal against Ishaan's stomach.

Ishaan pulled back.

"Maybe we should stop," he said and Roan had to fight the sudden urge to hit him. His frustration must have shown on his face. "I ache like I got hit by a train; you can't be feeling much better. I just think sex is a little ambitious right now. Don't you?"

"Who said anything about sex?" Roan asked, closing the distance and kissing him again. He slid one hand down Ishaan's chest and pulled at the waistband of his pajamas. "Just let me touch you, let me taste you. I never get to just please you."

"That feels...selfish," Ishaan said, a tightness in his voice. Clearly, he too was remembering the first and only time he'd let Roan suck him off—while he was awake, anyway.

"It's not selfish," Roan murmured, his lips brushing Ishaan's cheek as his hand crept into the warm confines of Ishaan's pajamas. "It's not like taking. It's more like accepting a gift. Is that selfish? If I want to make you feel good..." He wrapped his fingers around Ishaan's hardening shaft. "Wouldn't that make *me* the selfish one?"

Ishaan made a sound low in his throat.

"Well, if you put it that way..." He turned his head, capturing Roan's lips in a soft, deep kiss, his hands moving across Roan's skin. Roan's eyes slid shut as he began to stroke Ishaan, savoring the gentle waves of pleasure that rolled off of him.

A musical sound filled the air, like bells or chimes, and Ishaan broke the kiss and raised his head, glancing toward the bedroom doorway.

"What was that?" Roan asked.

"The doorbell," Ishaan said with a frown as he removed Roan's hand from his pants. "Did Kethic say anything about dropping by?" Roan shook his head.

He hadn't heard from Kethic since his e-mail last week saying he got home okay and apologizing *again* for helping with the kidnapping. Ishaan sighed. "I guess I better get up and see who it is." He gave Roan a quick kiss and started to push back the covers, but Roan reached out and caught him by the hand.

"You're still too weak," he said. "Stay in bed. I'll get rid of them."

"I can answer my own damn door," Ishaan said, shoving the quilt into Roan's lap. He sat up, swung his legs off the bed and stood, but only for a moment. He swayed and took one short, staggering step toward the living room before sinking back down onto the edge of the bed. "All right fine, you answer it."

As Roan padded across the living room carpet and into the stone tiled foyer, the doorbell rang again, followed by a sharp knock.

"All right already," he said, unlocking the deadbolt and jerking the door open. "What do you—" He fell silent at the sight of the black, blue, and silver dragon crouched on their doorstep, using his great leathery wings to shield himself from the sheeting rain. He was probably eight or ten feet long from nose to tail, his body covered in smooth, diamond-shaped scales, each one black fading to turquoise, with silver etched like frost along the bottom edges. Bright blue and gold eyes stared unblinking at Roan, who suddenly realized he was wearing nothing but pajama pants and had a moderate early morning hard-on.

Roan cleared his throat.

"Good morning, Sheriff," he said. "Is there something I can do for you?"

"You could let me in out of this rain," the dragon said, flashing small, conical teeth as he opened his mouth slightly. He didn't have lips in this form, nor did he seem to be using his tongue to form the sounds. The words appeared to be coming from somewhere in his throat. "Is there a problem, Mr. Echarn?"

Roan jumped. He'd been staring.

"No," he said, shaking his head. "No problem. You...you don't have a warrant, or something, do you?"

"Do I need one?" Those eerie blue and gold eyes narrowed.

Roan swallowed hard.

"Of course not. Please, come in." He stepped back out of the doorway, watching with interest as the dragon shook the water from his wings. He folded them and stepped across the threshold, his sharp talons squealing across the stone floor in the foyer and raising the short hairs on the back of Roan's neck. "So," Roan said, wrapping his arms around himself, "have you found out anything new about the men who kidnapped me?"

"I'm sorry," the sheriff said, sitting back on his haunches and curling his tail around his feet, "that investigation has been closed. The men were identified as former employees of a small research facility studying a cure for genetic incubism, which corroborates your statements. The fire was ruled an accident." Roan barely stifled a sigh of relief. Finally, it was over. "That's not why I'm here, I'm afraid. Is Mr. Darvis at home?"

"He's been sick," Roan said. "We both have. He's still in bed."

"Not anymore," Ishaan said from behind Roan. Roan turned and watched as Ishaan stepped out of the bedroom doorway. He, at least, had sense enough to put on a robe before coming out. Roan started over to give him a hand, but Ishaan motioned for him to stay where he was. Each step was slow and labored, and Ishaan's face was pale and damp with sweat by the time he reached Roan's side. "What can I do for you, Sheriff?" he asked, his voice tight. Roan wasn't sure if it was from the strain of crossing the room, or because there was a dragon dripping water all over his foyer.

"At Sezae's request," the dragon said, his tone also clipped, "I came to warn you that Shesade is reporting heavy rain as well and the river is expected to rise by as much as ten feet over the next twelve hours. I would advise you to gather what possessions you can't replace and evacuate to town. The jail is above the expected rise in the river level." His eyes darted to Roan. "I'd even let you share a cell." Beside Roan, Ishaan tensed.

"Thank you for the offer," Ishaan said between his teeth, "but we'll be just fine."

The dragon nodded his scaly head.

"Very well," he said and turned to leave. One of his wings caught on the coats hanging on the wall and knocked several of them onto the floor. He glanced over his shoulder at them. "Excuse me," he said, but made no move to pick the coats up. He just pulled his wings tighter against his back and left, his tail slithering along the floor. Roan stepped over, picked up the coats, and stood in the doorway as the dragon ambled down the driveway to the road. He glanced back at the house, then leaped upward into the rain, his wings beating with claps like thunder as he climbed above the trees and disappeared in the direction of town.

Roan shook his head and stepped back.

"Well, that was considerate of Sezae," he said as he hung the coats back on their hooks. "I told you she'd—" But Ishaan wasn't in the living room anymore. Roan started toward the bedroom.

"Roan?"

The voice came from the kitchen and Roan changed direction.

"The broth is in that jar, if you're looking for—What is it?" Ishaan was standing at the back door, his face grim as he looked out the window. Roan stepped up beside him and gasped. Leaves and branches floated past, catching on the porch steps. Out in the trees, the muddy water swirled around the trunks, several feet deep.

"I think we should pack some things and head into town," Ishaan said, his voice almost toneless.

"It-it's not really that bad, is it?" Roan asked, glancing at him. With Ishaan locked in a cell, how the hell was he going to feed? "I mean, how much higher could it get?"

"If it rises ten feet, about this high," Ishaan said, holding his hand out at shoulder level. "Now come on, it's not like I want to do this. Why don't you make some breakfast. I'm going to go wash up and then we can start deciding what gets left behind." Roan reached out to place a comforting hand on Ishaan's arm, but Ishaan turned away from him and shuffled out of the kitchen. It couldn't be an easy decision to abandon his home and Roan knew how much Ishaan hated sleeping in the jail. If he was willing to evacuate, things must be worse than Roan thought. Roan sighed and set about making toast and eggs.

Thirty

"No, leave it," Ishaan said for the tenth time as Roan began to carry some unimportant item out of the house. This time it was the TV. The car was parked across the front walk, already filled with their laptops, some clothes, Roan's personal items, and Ishaan's photos of his daughter. Everything else was replaceable. Everything else was just stuff.

"What next, then?" Roan asked, glancing around the room. Ishaan felt worthless, sitting on the couch while Roan carried their things out to the car, but just packing had worn him out. Damn it, he hated getting sick.

"I think that's it," Ishaan said, grunting under his breath as he used the arm of the couch to push himself to his feet. "We should go. If the water gets any higher, we might not make it across Sunderman's Bridge."

Roan looked around the room again. He seemed more upset than Ishaan was. Of course he hated leaving his home to the mercy of the river, and he certainly didn't want to spend Maele only knew how many nights in the jail, but Roan looked like he might have to be dragged out. Ishaan hoped not. He wasn't sure he could drag himself out.

"You coming?" Ishaan asked as he began the long, slow walk across the room. Roan was at his side in an instant, one arm around his waist. Ishaan's first impulse was to push him away. He wasn't an invalid. He could still walk. But Roan's support was more than just physical. If he had to lean on someone, it would be Roan. He put his arm around Roan's shoulders and they headed out into the rain.

Roan stared out the back window as they drove away. Ishaan kept his eyes fixed on the road ahead. It was just a house, a building, and aside from the last few months, the memories associated with it were nothing he'd regret being rid of. He glanced over at Roan as Roan turned around and sank into his seat.

"Cheer up," Ishaan said. "You don't have to sleep in the jail. I'm sure Sezae has room at the inn."

"That's not it," Roan said, staring down at his hands. "Or maybe that *is* it. I-I can't stay at the inn."

"Where do you want to stay, then?" Ishaan asked, frowning. "In the jail?"

"In your cell, with you."

"Roan, don't be stupid," Ishaan said, his stomach knotting up at the thought. "I would hurt you."

"You didn't last night."

"Last night was a gift. Don't get greedy. I'm not that sick anymore."

"You won't hurt me," Roan said, his voice barely audible over the drumming of the rain on the car roof. "I know you don't believe that, but I do, and if you could just trust me, just one night, I could prove it."

"What makes you so sure?" Ishaan said, his knuckles white as he gripped the steering wheel. "Have you been sneaking into my room while I was asleep?" Ishaan waited for an answer and when Roan didn't say anything, Ishaan looked over at him. "Have you?"

"Ishaan, stop—"

"I'm not going to stop until you tell me the truth."

"No, stop the car," Roan said, grabbing his arm. "Look, up ahead. What is that?" Ishaan slowed the car and finally stopped about ten feet from a tangle of uprooted trees and huge rocks sitting in the middle of the road. Ishaan sighed and peered through the fogged-up windshield at the hillside above them, at the great scoop of earth that had been gouged out of the one hill between his house and Devaen.

"Well, shit," he said under his breath and leaned back in his seat. Now what the hell were they supposed to do?

"Is this the only road into town?" Roan asked. Ishaan nodded. "So...do we head for Shesade?"

"That's almost ninety miles," Ishaan said, pinching the bridge of his nose. "I doubt we'd make it. Besides, those people don't know about me, about what I've done, and I'd like to keep it that way."

"So what, then? Do we just find some high ground and sleep in the car?" Roan asked. Ishaan glanced over at him. Why was he more reluctant to sleep at the inn than in the car? Why was he so desperate to stay close to Ishaan, even at the risk of his own safety? Ishaan popped the car into reverse and began backing up, looking over his shoulder for a place to turn around. "Where are we going?" Roan asked.

"Home," Ishaan said.

"But I thought—"

"We're not staying. We just need a few more things." He backed into a wide spot, put the car into drive and pulled back out onto the road. Roan sat for a moment, his knuckles pressed against his chin, and then glanced at Ishaan.

"The Cathedral," he said and Ishaan raised his eyebrows. That was an impressive deduction, even for him. "It's sheltered, well above the river, and is less than twenty miles up the road. Which means we'll need food, water, blankets—"

"Any firewood we have left," Ishaan said. "Matches, and my rifle and ammo, just in case."

"Right," Roan said with a nod. "Sezae was telling me someone thought they saw a shival out beyond the old Axlyn farm last fall."

Ishaan didn't respond. That wasn't the threat he'd meant. They pulled into the driveway and Ishaan felt the bottom drop out of his stomach. The river had risen nearly a foot since they left, the water almost surrounding the house. It wouldn't be long before it started coming in the back door.

"Clean out the pantry," Ishaan said as they huddled on the front step while he unlocked the door. "I don't know how long we'll be stranded up there, so grab everything you can." As Roan rushed toward the kitchen, Ishaan headed for his room. He dug to the back of his closet, carelessly tossing boxes out of his way as he searched for one small box he never thought he'd have to open again. He found it, covered in dust at the very back of the closet, a flat box barely as big as his hand with outstretched fingers, like something a fancy necklace might come in. He tucked it into his jacket pocket and went to help Roan.

"Where'd you go?" Roan asked, glancing at him as he stepped into the pantry. One dusty shelf was completely bare, the contents packed in three cardboard boxes on the floor.

"I had to get something," Ishaan said, stooping to pick up a box. It was heavier than he'd expected. "I'm going to take this to the car." Roan didn't say anything as Ishaan walked out. Sweaty and out of breath by the time he squeezed the box in behind the driver's seat, Ishaan lingered a moment on the front step, listening to the rain roaring around him, beating against the car, the roof, the leafless branches of the trees. He almost couldn't hear himself think. Almost.

Roan hadn't answered his question. But why, *why* would Roan have come into his room? It didn't make any sense. He wouldn't have. So why was he so sure Ishaan wouldn't hurt him? He couldn't be. Unless...unless something had happened, unless Ishaan had gotten out somehow. If Roan had made a mistake and was lying about it because Ishaan had asked him to...

"You okay?"

He turned as Roan stepped outside, another box of supplies in his arms.

"Fine," Ishaan said. Roan's eyes lingered on him a little too long before Roan stepped out into the rain and shoved his box into the back of the car. Ishaan waited, his stomach churning, and when Roan closed the car door and headed back into the house, Ishaan caught him by the arm.

"What?" Roan asked, an uncharacteristic wariness in his eyes.

"Is there a reason you wouldn't answer me earlier?" Ishaan asked. "Is there something you're hiding—something you're afraid to tell me?" Roan opened his mouth, then closed it again. "Roan, if something happened, I'm sure it wasn't your fault. I know I told you to lie to me, but that was before...That was before. Okay?"

Roan shook his head.

"I—That's not what—" He sighed, his shoulders slumping. "I didn't answer," he said quietly, "because I thought that if *you* thought that it had already happened, it wouldn't bother you as much. But I couldn't. I don't want to lie to you."

Ishaan just stared at him for a moment.

"So I've never gotten out and raped you." Roan shook his head. "But you were going to let me think that I had." Roan opened his mouth to argue or make some excuse, but Ishaan didn't want to hear it. "You still don't get it," he said, unable to keep the anger out of his voice. "It doesn't matter if you would let me fuck you in my sleep. I don't care if you *want* me to! I hate not being able to control myself and the thought of being with anyone, regardless of whether or not it's rape or consensual, or whatever, it makes me sick. *I* feel violated. Do you understand? Roan?"

"Yes," Roan said, looking away from him, "I understand. I'm sorry."

Ishaan sighed and headed into the house. Roan was just trying to help, in his own, unique way, and Ishaan knew that, but he couldn't shake the feeling that something bad had happened. He stepped into the kitchen, his boots splashing in the brown water running across the linoleum.

"Shit," he hissed, and glanced over his shoulder. "C'mon, we're out of time. Grab the last box," he said as Roan hurried over. "I'll start filling bottles with water."

He opened the cupboard under the sink and pulled out the old wooden crate of empty milk bottles, all washed and ready to be returned to town. Ishaan turned on the faucet and let it run, but apparently the pump was still filtering the water for it flowed clear. As he filled each bottle and put the cap on, he pressed his lips into a thin line. There were only seven half gallon bottles. That wouldn't last them very long.

"We'll need more than that," Roan said, glancing over his shoulder. Ishaan opened his mouth to say something he'd probably regret afterward, but Roan was already digging into the cupboard beside the fridge, pulling pots and pans out onto the floor. "We got anything bigger than this?" he asked, holding up Ishaan's largest cooking pot.

"No. What are you looking for?"

"We can boil rainwater," Roan said. He grabbed a small saucepan and a frying pan and shoved both of them into the pot.

"And what are those for?" Ishaan asked.

Roan glanced up at him and the corner of his mouth lifted in a crooked grin.

"Cooking," he said. Ishaan turned back to the sink. "Where are the—Never mind." Roan crossed the room and grabbed the box of matches from off the windowsill. He shoved them into his pocket and grabbed the heavy old box half full of firewood. He set the box on the counter and stacked the pots on top of it. "I'll be right back," he said as he passed behind Ishaan. "Don't try to carry that crate by yourself."

"Quit thinking you know what's best for me," Ishaan snapped and he was right; he regretted it immediately. "Sorry, Roan, I didn't mean that."

"Yes, you did," Roan said, pausing beside the couch, but staring straight ahead, across the living room at the open door. "I screwed up and I'm sorry. You have no idea how sorry I am. If I could go back and do it again...I would tell you the truth."

"Well...okay then," Ishaan said after a moment. "I'll try to stop being angry." He turned back to the sink and held the last bottle under the tap.

"You don't have to," he heard Roan say. "I deserve it."

Ishaan shut off the water and turned to tell him to stop being a damn martyr, but Roan was already walking out the front door. Ishaan twisted the cap on the last bottle and set it in the crate, then leaned against the counter with a sigh. If this was any other day, he could afford to stay angry, because Maele knew Roan deserved it, but considering the water pouring in underneath the back door, he'd just have to be angry later. He didn't have time just then.

Roan was coming back inside, his blond hair plastered to his head and dripping onto his coat, as Ishaan headed across the living room to his study.

"When you're done carrying the water out," Ishaan said, "get the blankets off your bed and out of your closet. I'll get mine and my rifle and then we'll go, okay?"

Roan nodded, but that was all. Ishaan stopped in the study doorway and waited for Roan to come back out of the kitchen. "Hey," he said and Roan paused, that wariness back in his eyes. "It was one stupid mistake, okay? It wasn't deliberate, just a lapse in judgment. You said you were sorry, so let's move on. All right?"

"Yeah, all right," Roan said, looking down into the crate. He mumbled something about it being heavy and headed for the car again. Ishaan shook his head and sighed. That was just like Roan, too. He'd forgive anyone anything, but if *he* made a mistake, you'd have thought he committed murder.

It took two trips to carry the armload of blankets, rifle, and two boxes of ammo out to the car. Ishaan wasn't sure why he was bringing two boxes; if he got loose and Roan needed to use the gun on him, it wouldn't take more than a couple of rounds. Hopefully, it wouldn't come to that. Ishaan shoved his hand into his jacket pocket, his fingers sliding across the faux velvet box. Roan stepped out of the house for the last time and pulled the door shut behind him, a plastic bag in one hand.

"What's that?" Ishaan asked.

"Toilet paper," Roan said, holding up the bag so he could see.

"Good thinking." They stood for a minute on the front step, then Ishaan cleared his throat and started to dig in his jeans pockets for his house keys. What was the point? It was all going to be washed away and ruined anyway. If someone could miraculously make it through the storm and the landslides, they were welcome to his things. "C'mon," he said, reaching out and pulling Roan against his side in a one-armed embrace, "we'll be lucky if the road hasn't washed out already, as much time as we've wasted."

"Always the optimist," Roan said with a hesitant glance at him. Ishaan gave him a crooked smile and a quick kiss before they stepped down from the porch and Roan hurried around to his side of the car. The wipers swished across the glass as they headed up the hill, the car crawling through the mud. Ishaan held his breath, waiting for them to get stuck, for the hillside to crash down on top of them, or drop out from underneath, or for one of the many bridges to be washed out. Roan was right; he expected the worst. That didn't mean he wouldn't be glad to be wrong.

The waterfalls were torrents of brown, frothing water, splattering across the road with frightening force. They had to drive through the Bride's Veil, more than just water pounding down and leaving divots in the roof. They both jumped as something, a rock most likely, hit the windshield and a spider web of silvery cracks blossomed in the upper right hand corner.

"Son-of-a-bitch," Ishaan muttered, depressing the gas pedal a little harder. His insurance had better cover that. They emerged from the waterfall, the rain washing away the mud and grit and giving them an unobstructed view up the river canyon to the earth and timber dam. Even from this distance, they could see the water spilling over the top, a pale line threading down the gravel face. Ishaan and Roan exchanged glances.

"I hope they know," Roan said as the dam was lost to sight behind the rocky canyon cliffs. "I wish we could warn them."

"Well, we can't," Ishaan said, "and if there's a breach in that dam, our house will be gone. So will the farm where Sezae used to live. I think there's a few mills down by the river, too."

"But the sheriff will have evacuated them, just in case, right?"

"I hope so," Ishaan said, frowning as he tried to picture the layout of Devaen. Was the inn high enough? Would Sezae and Isha be safe?

"They'll be okay," Roan said, reaching over to rest his hand on top of Ishaan's. "Though she's probably throwing a fit 'cause you refused to come into town," he added with a laugh. "She really does care about you, you know."

"I know," Ishaan said with a sigh. "I didn't realize until just now how much I still care about her...about them. I always thought *I* was the worst thing that could happen to them, but if we survive this, I don't want to shut them out anymore."

"It took a flood to make you realize that?" Roan said, chuckling. "I've been saying it for months."

"Yeah, but I never listen to you," Ishaan said, giving Roan a sideways glance. "Sometimes it takes a life-altering event before you can admit the truth." Roan stopped smiling and drew his hand back, his eyes suddenly as gray and stormy as the sky overhead. "Now what?" Ishaan asked. "Roan, if this is about what—"

"No, that's not it," Roan said, turning away and leaning against the passenger's door. "It's just...what you said—about admitting the truth..." He drew a deep breath and let it out, fogging up half of the window. "I've done horrible things, unforgivable things, and I convinced myself that I didn't have any other choice, but-but now...I can't lie to myself any longer. And I can't lie to you either, even though it will mean you'll hate me forever."

"Being a little melodramatic, aren't you?" Ishaan said, shooting a glance his direction. "Shouldn't I be the one who decides whether or not I'm going to hate you forever?"

Roan didn't respond and Ishaan let a hissing breath out through his teeth. Finally, he said, "Can it wait?"

Roan sat up and looked over at him, frowning.

"What?" he asked.

"Can it wait?" Ishaan said again. "You've kept it from me for this long and in case it escaped your notice, it's pouring rain, the river's overflowing, and the dam's about to burst. Now isn't really the best time to be unburdening your conscience."

Roan just stared at him for a moment, then turned back to the window.

"Sorry," he said, "I didn't realize how inconvenient—"

"Oh, just stop," Ishaan said. "We're both exhausted, we're still recovering from food poisoning, this fucking rain sure isn't helping anything—Just stop for now, okay? I can't handle anything else right now."

"Fine," Roan snapped and for several minutes the only sounds in the car were the pounding of the rain on the roof and the slap of the wiper blades. Finally, Roan sighed. "I'm sorry," he said. "You're right, now isn't the time."

"Thank you," Ishaan said. "When this is all over, we'll work everything out, and I promise you, I won't hate you forever. Now—" He slid forward in his seat and wiped the condensation from the inside of the windshield. "Zai Falls is just ahead. How much of that bridge do you suppose is left?"

"How wide is our wheel base?" Roan asked, shaking his head. As the car rounded the bend in the road Ishaan's jaw dropped and he heard Roan gasp. The massive frothing column beat against the inside edge of the bridge and through the deluge Ishaan could see that many of the large stone blocks were missing. Keeping to the outside edge, Ishaan crept past the raging waterfall, but the car still shuddered as the water pounded against the driver's side door. Only once they were past did Ishaan dare glance over at Roan. Roan looked pale, his face damp with sweat.

"Well, that was fun," Ishaan said.

"Oh, yeah, let's do it again," Roan replied with a snort. "Are we almost there?"

"Almost," Ishaan replied. The last mile rolled by without incident and the great gaping maw of the Croatoan Cathedral had never looked more welcoming as it came into view.

"Thank Maele," Roan muttered as they drove into the shelter of the huge cavern. The sudden silence seemed to echo and press in on Ishaan after the incessant hammering of the rain for the past hour, and when he shut off the car, silencing even the slight engine noise, he had to clear his throat to make sure he hadn't gone deaf.

Roan opened his door and a sharp gust of frigid air swirled into the car, cutting right through Ishaan's jacket. It might be warm enough to melt the snow, but it was still too damn cold to be sleeping on the ground. At least Roan would be warm enough in the vehicle. As Ishaan climbed out of the car, he felt his jacket pocket, reassuring himself that the flat box was still there.

"Looks like it's just us," Roan said from halfway up the stairs at the rear of the cavern.

For an instant, Ishaan wished that there *had* been someone else, anyone else to draw his attention. He shook his head, disgusted with himself, and began pulling supplies out of the car.

An hour later they sat beside a cheery blaze, watching the light play across the graffiti carved into the walls, holding hands beneath the blanket that they shared. Through the cavern entrance, Ishaan watched the light fading from the overcast sky, his free hand clutching tight to the box in his pocket. Warmed by the fire and by Roan, he could feel the weariness settling in his body, his arms and legs like lead. He knew he should get up, move around, stay awake, but it was so cold. The wind moaned through the passage, wailing as it slipped through the long slits carved in the outside wall. For the first time, he found himself wondering if those narrow apertures were the work of thousands of years of dripping water wearing away the rock, or if human hands were to blame.

Ishaan jumped, the heavy, floating feeling of descending sleep scattering like a flock of startled crows. His heart pounding, he threw back one side of the blanket and started to get up.

"You need to sleep," Roan said, catching him by the arm. "You're exhausted."

"I'm not that tired," Ishaan said, pulling away, but his boots scraped across the stone floor as he paced back and forth, his feet almost too heavy to lift. He could feel Roan watching him, but he just wrapped his arms around himself and kept his eyes on the floor.

"You have to sleep sometime," Roan said softly a while later. "You can't stay awake forever." Ishaan glanced toward the cavern opening, at the wall of black broken only occasionally by a streak of silver as a raindrop caught the firelight.

"I know," Ishaan replied, "I just..." He shook his head and went back to pacing. He couldn't explain it, he just felt like he had to fight this, had to fight sleeping. It was futile and he knew it, but couldn't just give up. As long as he was awake, he knew nothing would happen, but once he closed his eyes...he didn't know. He didn't know *what* would happen.

Ishaan glanced at Roan, poking the fire with a stick, his face lit by the dancing firelight, his tangled blond hair glowing like spun gold. He didn't seem at all worried about what could happen, but that just made it worse. Roan wasn't worried because he trusted him, he believed that Ishaan wouldn't rape him if he got the chance. Ishaan couldn't bear the thought of waking up and seeing that trust shattered in Roan's eyes. He'd rather not wake up at all.

He turned away, his throat thick with hot tears, fear and despair gripping his chest like a great fist, squeezing the breath out of him. This could not be happening. He paced back and forth, in and out of the fire light. He was so tired, but he just kept putting one foot in front of the other, his eyes burning, watering, but he kept them open, he kept moving. He could not sleep, not yet. Morning would come and the rain would stop and they'd be able to return home. He just wanted to go home.

He jerked awake, pain splintering up his arm as his elbow slammed against the stone floor and he cried out, but it cleared his head, for a moment, at least. He looked up into Roan's pale, drawn face.

"What happened?" he asked, sitting up. He had to get up, he had to keep moving.

"You fell asleep on your feet," Roan said, bracing his hands on Ishaan's shoulders and trying to keep him down. "I barely caught you before you hit the floor. Damn it, Ishaan, you can't keep doing this. It's not healthy."

"Get off me," Ishaan said, pushing him away. "You don't understand."

"No, *you* don't understand!" Roan shouted. "I'm not worth this!" Tears streaked his cheeks as he stood over Ishaan, his whole body shaking. "It's killing me to watch you suffer like this. I'm not worth it." He started to turn away, but Ishaan reached out and grabbed his wrist.

"You're right," he said, "it's not healthy and I wasn't thinking about what it's doing to you. But—" He pulled Roan down into his arms. "You're dead wrong if you think you're not worth it. I love you more than anything."

Roan clung to him like a drowning man and Ishaan risked closing his eyes for a moment as they held each other. "I'm not going to put you though any more of this," Ishaan whispered.

Roan pulled back suddenly and kissed him. Ishaan jerked away, startled by the hunger and desperation in the kiss. Ishaan licked his lips, the faint taste of cinnamon and strawberries tickling his tongue. "Roan, what—"

"Make love to me," Roan said, leaning toward him again, but Ishaan grabbed him by the upper arms and held him back. "Please, Ishaan, make love to me."

"Roan, I-I can't, I'm exhausted—"

"*Please*," Roan said again. "I-I won't say anything if you fall asleep; I'll pretend that it's you." Disgust rose up in Ishaan's throat and he pushed Roan away. "Or-or just let me touch you, let me suck on you—" Ishaan grabbed him by the front of the shirt and shook him.

"I don't know what is wrong with you," Ishaan said between his teeth, "but you need to stop this." He let go and climbed to his feet. Roan obviously needed sleep even more than he did.

Thirty-one

This could *not* be happening. Roan felt like he was about crawl out of his own skin, his bones aching, muscles twitching, a restless prickling all through his arms and legs. He knelt on the cold stone, trying to catch his breath and pull himself together. *This could not be happening.* He could feel the demon inside him, feel it scrabbling up toward the surface, and he could not fight it. He clenched his fists, his nails digging into his palms, but even the pain couldn't distract him from the hunger. He jumped as something flat and black hit the ground in front of him.

It was a box, about six inches on a side, covered in black velvet. It looked like a gift box from a fancy jewelry store. Roan glanced up at Ishaan, who was still scowling at him, and then reached for the box.

"What is it?" Roan said, trying to keep his voice from breaking. His words came out tight and toneless.

"Open it," Ishaan said. It was surprisingly heavy and something inside clinked like metal as Roan tilted it. The hinges protested with a loud *creak* as Roan lifted the lid.

"Handcuffs?" Roan said, taking them from the box. The firelight played across the gleaming steel and Roan's body gave an involuntary shudder as he realized what Ishaan had in mind. "How come we've never played with these before?" Roan joked, but it was a pathetic attempt and he couldn't even force a smile. Ishaan reached out and took them from him.

"These aren't toys," Ishaan said, slipping one side around his left wrist and tightening it with a cold *tick-tick-tick-tick* sound. "These are police grade carbon steel. The key is taped inside the lid. Don't lose it." Roan closed the box and slipped it into his coat pocket. "Now, I want you to take my rifle and go down to the car. Lock yourself inside and don't open the door for any reason."

"Ishaan..." Roan said, but Ishaan shook his head.

"Don't argue with me, Roan. We're going to do this my way or I'm going to take that rifle and make *certain* I'll never hurt anyone again."

Roan's blood ran cold as an image sprang unbidden into his mind—Ishaan with the barrel of the rifle in his mouth.

"No!" Roan gasped, grabbing the rifle and lurching to his feet. "I-I'll do whatever you want, just please don't...don't even say that. I would die without you."

Ishaan glanced at him, the hard anger fading from his eyes. Roan turned away, clutching the cold rifle to his chest and wondered if Ishaan would feel the same if he knew just how literal and selfish Roan was being. Without Ishaan to feed from, isolated and alone, Roan would die a slow, painful death. That wasn't the only the reason he didn't want Ishaan to eat a bullet, but at that moment, it was the first one on his mind. He hated himself.

The *tick-tick-tick-tick* of the handcuffs being closed drew Roan's head back around. Ishaan stood before the fire, his hands cuffed behind his back, staring down into the bright blaze.

"I don't know what's going to happen," Ishaan said, "but if I—if I break a window or something, if I come after you, I want you to promise me that you'll use the rifle. You'll stop me, you have to. I'd rather be dead than live knowing that I raped you."

"Ishaan, I can't—"

"Yes, you can," Ishaan said, not taking his eyes from the fire. "You have to. Promise me." Roan couldn't respond, he couldn't say what Ishaan wanted him to say. He wouldn't, couldn't, ever— "Roan, promise me!" Ishaan demanded.

"All right," Roan said, his voice cracking. "All right, I promise...if you rape me, you'll never wake up, but I will not shoot you before, not if there's the slightest chance that I could stop you."

"You can't stop me," Ishaan said, shaking his head, "but I guess it's your choice if you want to be raped or not. I can't force you to save yourself." He couldn't force Roan to shoot him, either. As far as he would ever know, nothing was going to happen that night. "The car keys are there, on the blanket," Ishaan said, nodding. "You need to lock yourself inside now."

Roan stepped forward, his hand shaking as he reached down for the keys. He could do this; it wouldn't be long. He glanced at Ishaan as he straightened up, his hands cuffed behind him like some criminal. This wasn't fair. He hesitated, wanting to give Ishaan a kiss good night, but he wasn't sure he could hold himself together if he did. His scalp was already itching where his horns would appear and his mouth tasted of strawberries and cinnamon.

Roan hurried down the stairs, leaving the warm glow of the fire behind him. The car was cold, the windows fogged, and he tried to put the key in the ignition so he could run the heater for a few minutes, but his hand was shaking so bad that the keys slipped from his grasp and fell down between his feet. He reached for them, but the steering wheel got in the way. Cursing himself, he dragged a blanket out of the back and tucked it around himself. He couldn't afford to get too comfortable anyway. He had to be awake when Ishaan started to get restless.

How had it come to this? Roan let out a frustrated sigh, his breath a faint ghost in the car with him. If he had just told the truth, this wouldn't be happening. Ishaan probably would have driven him away or shot him, but *this* wouldn't be happening. And there was always that chance, that snowflake in hell's chance that Ishaan could have put aside his disgust and anger, and accepted that Roan wasn't worth protecting, wasn't worth worrying about.

Roan wiped a stray tear from his cheek and shifted in his seat. He wasn't worth all this trouble. What did it matter what Ishaan did to him? If Ishaan only knew the truth, he'd see that, he could stop tormenting himself. Only, he wouldn't. Roan knew that. It wouldn't matter how much they needed each other, Ishaan would see him as nothing more than a parasite. He didn't know what Roan did for him nearly every night, he couldn't hear how much quieter he'd become since they started making love, he couldn't see how peaceful he was when he slept—

Something hit the side of the car and Roan screamed, one hand grabbing for the rifle in the passenger's seat. The car rocked, a large shadow blotting out the faint light of the distant fire. Ishaan. Roan started to draw his hand back, away from the gun, but hesitated. Ishaan couldn't possibly be asleep yet, could he? It had only been ten, maybe fifteen minutes. It normally took more than an hour before he'd get out of bed.

But this wasn't a normal evening. Roan cleared his throat.

"What do you want?" he called. The car rocked again.

"Roan?" Ishaan's sleepy, guttural mumble came faintly through the window and Roan closed his eyes.

"Thank Maele, " he whispered. He reached for the door handle, then pulled his hand back. As agitated as Ishaan was, he very well could rape him and Roan had no desire to experience that again. Biting the edge of his lip, he tried to think ...

"Need you..." Ishaan said through the glass, the car rocking again. "Roan."

"All right," Roan said, turning in the seat. "Just a minute." For all the good it did. The car kept rocking. What was he doing, rutting against it like some damn animal? Roan opened his suitcase and felt around beneath the clothes, his fingers closing around the smooth glass jar of lubricant. Too bad there wasn't any room in the car to use it. The car rocked again. "Ishaan, knock it off!" Roan shouted.

"Want you...need you..." Ishaan growled, but he stopped rocking the car.

"All right," Roan said again, "I know. I need you, too. You know that, right? You know that I need this more than you do? But I don't want to do it here. Go back up to the fire and I'll come to you." Roan wiped the condensation from the window, flinching back as Ishaan's empty, lifeless eyes stared in at him. Roan wet his dry lips and leaned toward the glass. "You know what I am and you know I won't desert you. You can fuck me all night long, but first I need you to go back to the fire. Please, Ishaan." For the longest time, Ishaan just stared through him, but then he turned and disappeared into the darkness.

Roan wiped at the window, staring out, trying to see if he had really gone back to the fire or not. He couldn't tell. Very aware that Ishaan might be waiting for him just out of sight, Roan unlocked the door and eased it open. Damp air swirled around him, seeping into his clothes and making him shiver. He stepped outside and closed the door, his eyes searching the darkness, but there were so many shadows, so many places to hide. After a moment, he set the jar on the roof of the car and unbuttoned his pants. His heart was pounding, thundering in his ears, drowning out the noise of the rain still falling beyond the entrance to the Cathedral as he lowered his jeans and opened the jar.

Roan prepared himself quickly and then pulled his pants back up. He didn't know how long Ishaan would wait for him and he didn't really want to find out. He grabbed the jar, screwed the lid back on, and slipped it into his pocket before heading for the stairs. He was only a short distance from the car when something lurched toward him from out of the darkness. He skittered back and raised his fists as Ishaan stepped out into the faint light, his hands still cuffed behind his back.

"Roan..." he said, his boots dragging as he crossed the cavern. "Roan, please." Roan hesitated, then lowered his fists. What could Ishaan do to him? With his hands cuffed behind him, he couldn't even undress himself. Roan stepped closer, his hands shaking as he reached out and fumbled with Ishaan's fly. Ishaan made a rumbling sound, almost like a big cat purring, but he didn't move as Roan reached into his underwear and drew his erection out into the cold night air. Roan stroked him, eyes sliding shut as he devoured Ishaan's energy, but it wasn't enough. He fell upon him like a starving wolf upon a carcass, taking Ishaan into his mouth and swallowing him deep. Ishaan groaned as Roan slid up and down his length, almost choking himself in his desperation. It still wasn't enough.

Roan pulled back and stared up at him, breathless, before climbing to his feet.

"C'mon, Ishaan," Roan said, taking him by one arm. "It's cold down here." Roan led him up the stairs, catching him when he stumbled, and once they reached the warmth of the fireside, Roan reached into his coat pocket and pulled out the handcuff box.

"You're a good man," Roan said as he peeled up the tape and pulled the handcuff key free. "You never wanted to hurt anyone, you just didn't know how to control yourself. But you're better now, right? You know I won't stop you; you know you don't have to force me." Roan was aware that he was rambling and that Ishaan probably didn't understand half of what he was saying, but it wasn't just the incubism making his hands tremble as he reached out for Ishaan's arm. Ishaan stepped toward him and Roan tensed, clenching his fist around the key.

Ishaan leaned down, his breath sliding along Roan's jaw.

"I won't hurt you," he murmured, his lips brushing Roan's cheek.

Roan closed his eyes, his heart aching.

"I know you won't," he whispered and then pulled back. He turned Ishaan around and slipped the key into the lock. He released one side, but not the other, leaving the handcuffs swinging from Ishaan's left wrist. It would make it easier to cuff him again afterward.

Ishaan spun around grabbed Roan by the front of his coat, practically shoving him down onto the blanket piled beside the fire. Roan gasped, his muscles knotting up as he fought the urge to struggle, fight, run. He couldn't run. He needed this, no matter how much it hurt. Roan barely had time to shrug the coat off before Ishaan was on top of him, pulling at his jeans, tugging them down around his thighs. His whole body shaking, Roan pushed himself to his hands and knees, his fists clenching handfuls of the blanket as Ishaan entered him.

He drew a sharp breath, his gut tightening, and one hoarse cry escaped him as Ishaan sheathed himself inside Roan. It hurt, but not like the first time. Nothing like the first time. Each thrust was fast, hard, and rough, Ishaan's fingers digging into Roan's shoulders. He'd be bruised in the morning, but he didn't care. Ishaan grunted and groaned, reduced to nothing more than an animal, his breath hot on Roan's back. He wasn't even enjoying it. The energy that rolled off him was all need and very little pleasure. Roan needed more than that.

Too soon, Ishaan cried out and came, and Roan cried out in frustration. Ishaan leaned on him for a moment before sliding off and stretching out beside him on the blanket. Roan sighed and pulled his jeans back up, but left them unbuttoned. Ishaan would not be satisfied by that for long. Roan lay down and curled up against Ishaan's side, his head on Ishaan's shoulder, to wait.

Thirty-two

Ishaan woke in the dark, cold and stiff. Was he on the floor again? That hadn't happened in—No, he was in the Cathedral. The rain, the flood, it all came back to him. He glanced over at the fire, the coals giving off a sinister glow, but little light. With one hand, he reached up to brush his hair back off his brow and something hard hit him in the side of the head. What the hell? He held up his arm, his heart plummeting into the pit of his stomach as the handcuffs swung from his wrist. He glanced beside him, a strangled cry escaping his lips at the sight of Roan, his hair tangled, his jeans undone, lying beside him.

Roan jerked awake and looked up at him.

"Ready to go again?" he asked, his voice thick and sleepy. "Try to be a little gentler this time, okay?" Ishaan looked down at himself, his own pants shoved down off his hips, his flaccid dick hanging out. He quickly shoved himself back into his briefs, his fingers coming away slippery with Roan's lubricant. Ishaan cried out again and scrambled to his feet. This wasn't an accident. "What is it?" Roan asked, gazing up at him.

"What have you done?" Ishaan said, his voice hollow, and he watched Roan's eyes grow wide, a look of horror spreading across his face.

"You're-you're awake," Roan said. "Ishaan, I-I didn't—I didn't have any choice, I couldn't just—" Ishaan shook his head. No. No, no, *no*. He screamed, empty and wordless.

"You promised me!" he shouted. "I-I *begged* you and you let it happen anyway. You let me rape you!"

"If I let it happen, it wasn't rape," Roan said as he climbed to his feet. "You weren't supposed to wake up so soon. You were never supposed to know."

"And you think that makes it okay?" Ishaan asked. "You think that makes what you're doing—whatever the fuck you think you're doing—okay? I told you, Roan, I told you—"

"You weren't supposed to know," Roan said again, looking down at the ground. Ishaan just wanted to grab him and shake him.

"You can't keep something like that a secret!" he said and Roan raised his head, his gaze defiant.

"I didn't go into your room the first night I moved in, but I've been with you almost every night since. If this hadn't happened, you never would have found out." Ishaan felt like he'd been kicked in the gut. All this time...nearly ten months...he was—he was—

"You've been fucking me all this time!" he screamed, the cavern echoing his words all around them.

"Once," Roan said, and he looked back down at the ground again. "It happened like that once, the night after I found out my parents were dead." The night he...That was the morning he woke up and his ass was sore. "It was a mistake and I never let it happen again. Most of the time I just blew you. It was a couple of months before I let you have sex with me." Ishaan staggered back, his head spinning.

"I can't believe this," he said. He felt like he was going to vomit. All this time, all these lies—Ishaan stiffened, his whole body going cold. It was all lies. Everything. All of it. He took a sudden step toward Roan, but stopped, not sure what he intended to do to him. Nothing legal.

Roan looked up at him.

"You're sick," Ishaan said and then he turned and walked away.

He didn't know where he was going and he didn't care. He just knew that if he stayed up there with Roan, he was going to end up killing him, and he'd spent enough nights in a jail cell to know that he didn't want to spend his days there, too. He found himself getting into his car without remembering the walk down the stairs and across the cavern. He slammed the door and reached for the keys, but they weren't in the ignition. He felt his pants pockets, the dangling handcuffs clattering against the inside of the door. Of course, Roan had them.

Ishaan slammed his fist against the steering wheel and started to get out of the car, but he kicked something on the floorboards, something that jangled like metal, and he leaned down, feeling around until his fingers closed around the cold ring of keys. He pulled the door shut again, started the car, and made a U-turn in the wide graveled area just off the road. The weak beams of the headlights flashed across the stone steps and Ishaan caught a glimpse of Roan running down them. Ishaan stomped on the gas, throwing up a cloud of dust as the tires spun.

The car raced out into the darkness, the rain pelting the windshield as he sped down the hill. He could feel it sliding in the mud, barely staying on the road, but he didn't care. He approached the corner before Zai Falls and considered *not* turning the wheel. A plunge into the swollen river below wouldn't be any worse than he already felt.

Roan *lied* to him, all this time, about everything. Roan didn't love him, he just wanted more sex. He was tired of waiting for Ishaan to fall asleep every night. Ishaan jerked the wheel, sending the car skidding around the corner. The falls loomed out of the darkness, raging out into the middle of the bridge. Ishaan stomped on the brake and slid half into the water-filled ditch, his heart hammering, blood thundering behind his eyes as he watched more of the old stone bridge crumble under the assault of the waterfall.

"Shit!" He slammed both hands against the steering wheel, the handcuffs swinging back and slamming against his wrist. Now *that* key, Roan still had.

He closed his eyes and crumbled, resting his forehead on his hands as he choked back a sob. Roan had uncuffed him. Deliberately, maliciously, he had let Ishaan loose to be what he hated most.

But why? *Why?* Why would he do something so hateful? Ishaan sat up and twisted around in his seat, reaching back and grabbing Roan's suitcase. There had to be some explanation. He released the catches and dumped the contents into the passenger's seat, pawing through the clothes and pushing them off onto the floor of the car. He picked up the stack of photos and turned on the little light in the dash, but they were just stupid family snapshots; a few with his mother and father, but mostly just him and Kethic screwing around, making faces and giving each other horns with their fingers.

He threw them down and grabbed Roan's wallet, but there was no more in it than the first time he'd ransacked Roan's things. The dog-eared books were just a couple of trashy romances and an old book of fairy tales. There was nothing, *nothing* to explain his actions. Because there was no explanation. Ishaan dropped the books and leaned across the car, feeling around on the floorboards and under the seat, trying to find something he'd missed.

His hand brushed something smooth and cold to the touch. He wrapped his hand around it and felt a chill run through him. The stock of his rifle. It had fallen down between the passenger's seat and the door. Carefully, he lifted it free and pulled it over across his lap. The polished wood gleamed in the light from the dash and Ishaan ran his fingers down the barrel.

"Why not?" he whispered, a single tear cutting a cold track down his face. He put the butt of the rifle on the floor between his feet, the trigger facing away from him, and placed the barrel under his chin. It was cold and smelled like gunpowder. Imagine that, his gun smelled like gunpowder. He laughed, a high, strangled sound and shoved the rifle away from him as the laughter became a sob. He hid his face in his hands and wept until he ached.

When no more tears would come and his throat was raw from sobbing, Ishaan sat a moment longer in his car and stared at the raging waterfall before him. He would never be able to get the car past that—he doubted that what was left of the bridge could even support the weight—but he'd have no trouble on foot. It was less than nine miles to the house, and only another six to town. He could climb over the landslide. He didn't have to stay there in the car.

Ishaan climbed out, taking the keys and the rifle with him. The rain had lightened, but even so, he was soaked to the skin before he reached the bridge. The roar of the waterfall was deafening and the stones shook under the assault as Ishaan hurried across. Above him, cracks between the heavy clouds showed the first pearly traces of coming dawn. With luck, he should reach town before noon.

He'd not gone a mile when he started to feel the fatigue in his legs, the dull ache of over-worked muscles, but he couldn't afford to stop and rest. He was shivering, his teeth clenched so they wouldn't chatter, and he knew that if he stopped, his muscles would grow cold and cramp, and he'd be lucky if he ever got moving again. He began to stumble.

The rocky cliffs above him gave way to steep hillsides covered in thick forest and it wasn't long before he started to hear things moving among the trees. He knew there were no wolves, no mountain cats, no arboreal dragons in this part of the country, and regardless of the shival sightings every few months, it had been a decade since anyone had been attacked, but that didn't stop his mind from playing tricks on him. The snap of a twig, the rustle of a leaf—he wiped the rain from his eyes and raised his rifle, scanning the dense foliage above him.

The deep, distant rumble of thunder rolled over him and Ishaan lowered the rifle. This was ridiculous. No sane creature would be out in this weather. Around him the growl of thunder swelled, rattling his heart in his chest, and he felt as swift stab of pain as he remembered how much Roan hated thunder. He would be terrified, alone—Ishaan clenched his fist. It was Roan's own damn fault. He turned and continued down the hill, his steps slowing as the thunder dragged on and on, steadily growing louder. He stopped and could it feel it through the ground. Something wasn't right.

Ishaan turned toward the valley, the river muddied and raging a hundred feet below, and as his eyes swept up the canyon the world seemed to slow around him. A wall of water thirty feet high was surging down the valley, pushing huge boulders before it, lifting rocks the size of Ishaan's car and smashing them together, tearing at the trees growing along the riverbank, ripping them out of the ground and snapping them like toothpicks. A horrible, helpless feeling grew in his gut as he watched the destruction proceed down the valley. There wasn't anything he could do, but he felt like he should be *trying*, not just standing there watching.

It was so horrifically fascinating he couldn't tear his eyes away. The fury of the river at being contained for so long was terrifying. It roared like a wounded beast, lifting rocks and trees and leaving gravel and splinters in its wake. It took moments to pass, disappearing around the curve of the river, and the thunderous rumble slowly receded. Ishaan shook his head and sighed. No hope of finding his house intact now. Half of Devaen would probably be swept away by that onslaught. He shoved his dripping hair back out of his face and turned to go—

Something large and black stood in the middle of the road not ten feet behind him. He saw teeth and one blue eye slitted against the rain as it lunged for him. He didn't have time to aim, he just raised the rifle and pulled the trigger.

Thirty-three

Roan stopped pacing as the distant gunshot echoed up the canyon and inside his head. A single gunshot. His heart began to pound, beating against the inside of his ribs as he sank to his knees. He couldn't have...He-he couldn't—
We're going to do this my way or I'm going to take that rifle and make certain I'll never hurt anyone again. Roan doubled over and screamed, his arms wrapped around himself as a pain sharper than the blade of a knife sliced through his chest. This couldn't be happening. Ishaan...Ishaan...He screamed again, his whole body shaking, his control slipping. His horns burst through his scalp and he choked on his tongue as he clawed at the button of his jeans, pain shooting up his spine as his tail pushed against the heavy denim. Roan shoved his jeans down and fell forward onto the cold stone as his tail slithered out of his body, pulling at his vertebrae. He sobbed.

He should have gone after him. He had started to, as Ishaan sped out of the Cathedral, spraying him with gravel, but it was dark and wet and cold, and Roan could think of nothing to say that would make a difference. Ishaan just needed time to calm down. He'd come back. He had to. The road was blocked.

An hour passed and Roan began to worry. The road was muddy, the hillsides unstable. He paced before the entrance of the Cathedral, listening for the car, waiting for Ishaan to return. But he didn't. And then the dam broke.

He'd thought it was thunder at first, but the sound just grew and grew, shaking the whole cavern. Roan had watched from one of the narrow openings carved into the rock as the water swept down the canyon. He had just returned to his pacing when the gunshot rang out. It was all his fault. He should have gone after him.

The rain blew in on him, stinging, icy drops pelting his bare skin. He curled his tail up against his body and lay, shivering, until he ran out of tears. It was his fault. Ishaan was dead because of him and now he would die, too. Roan shuddered and climbed to his feet, staggering out into the rain. He walked to the canyon cliff and looked down the jagged face. Even if he hit every rock on the way down, it would be quicker and less painful than waiting for the demon to consume his soul. He slid one foot forward, knocking a rock over the edge, and watched it rattle down the face of the cliff.

Roan turned away, another sob rising in his chest as he returned to the cavern. Killing himself was too easy. He deserved to suffer. He dragged himself up the stairs, shedding his wet clothes as he went, and crawled beneath a blanket. He should have seen this coming, he should have gotten out before it was too late. But no, he had to keep holding out for his happily ever after. Asshole! Demons didn't get happy endings. The monster was supposed to die at the end of the story. If only he hadn't taken Ishaan down with him. Ishaan should not have had to suffer and die for Roan's arrogance.

The coals burned lower and lower, emitting nothing more than a sinister glow and a few thin wisps of smoke. Roan lay on his side, staring at the fire pit, but before his eyes flashed images of moments that never should have been. Ishaan in the garden with dirt caked up to his elbows, yelling at Roan for hoeing a crooked row. Ishaan helping him bait his hook on the riverbank. Ishaan showing him how to aim the rifle. Ishaan splashing him in the river. Ishaan kissing him in the snow. Ishaan making love to him—

Roan gasped as his insides began to squirm, his whole body shaking. What was happening? There wasn't anyone around to feed on. He shouldn't—He raised his head and turned toward the wide mouth of the Cathedral as a strange sound reached his ears. It sounded like splashing.

Roan cried out as Ishaan's car rolled into the cavern, the sides splattered with mud. He watched, his heart pounding in his throat, as the car stopped and the driver's door opened. His hair tangled and wet, his clothes dark with blood, Ishaan stepped from the car and started toward the stairs.

He was alive. *He was alive.* Roan's muscles twitched, his body aching to run to him, to throw himself into Ishaan's arms and beg forgiveness, but his horns, his tail—He tried to draw them back into himself, his fists and teeth clenched, but the demon was too strong and he was too weak. He heard Ishaan's footsteps nearing the top of the stairs and quickly pulled the blanket over his head.

The footsteps crossed from the stairs to the fire and then stopped. "Roan?" Ishaan said. His voice was hoarse but the sound of it did appalling things to Roan's body. Roan shuddered and drew his arms and legs tight against himself, barely able to catch his breath.

"Ish-Ishaan," he panted. "I thought—thought you were dead—the gunshot—"

"Don't sound so disappointed," Ishaan said. "I thought about it, but why should I kill myself? This wasn't my fault. *You did this.*"

"But-but the shot, and-and the blood—"

"Shival," Ishaan said and apparently that was all the explanation he felt Roan deserved. He paused and Roan could hear the rustle of cloth. "Can't you even face me?"

"P-please, Ishaan..." Roan whispered. "Please go away."

"Go away?" Ishaan repeated. "What are you doing under there? Did you find someone else to fuck?"

Roan's whole body jerked as he felt Ishaan take a step toward him.

"No!" he shouted, digging his fingernails into his arms. "Ishaan, get out of here, *please!*"

Ishaan hesitated, then took another step.

"What's wrong with you?" he asked. He was so close. Roan could smell his sweat, feel the heat from his body, hear the beating of his heart. He was almost close enough to touch. Just one more step and Roan could wrap his tail around an ankle, drag him down, tear his clothes off—

"*What the fuck?*" Ishaan shouted and Roan felt him scramble backward. Roan jerked his tail back under the blanket and pressed his forehead against the ground, sobbing.

"I'm sorry...I'm sorry," he whispered again and again. He felt Ishaan draw close again and tensed. "Ishaan, no, please—" Ishaan grabbed the blanket and yanked it off of him. Roan cried out and tried to cover his head with his arms, tried to hide the horns. "Don't-don't look at me," he said, hiding his face against the floor. "Please—"

"What are you?" Ishaan asked, his voice thick with revulsion. Roan wept. He would have rather died than hear Ishaan speak to him like that. Suddenly, Ishaan gasped. "Sweet Maele among us," he whispered. "You're an incubus."

Thirty-four

Roan lay naked on the stone floor of the cavern, a pair of gleaming, curved horns protruding from just above his ears. He had his arms drawn up over his head, like he was trying to hide them, like it would matter. He had a fucking tail. Pale and hairless, it writhed with a life of its own, curling around Roan's legs and slithering along the floor, like it was reaching for Ishaan. Ishaan's eyes swept over the trembling, sweaty figure. It had to be. It was the only explanation.

"You're an incubus, aren't you?" he said. Roan still didn't respond. "Answer me, damn it!"

"Yes!" Roan shouted. He was crying. "Yes, I'm an incubus. I-I wanted to tell you, I tried—"

"Didn't try very hard," Ishaan snapped. "Ten months, Roan. You could have found a minute."

"I was afraid," Roan said, lowering his arms and wrapping them around his body. "I'm sorry." He shuddered violently, one of his horns hitting the floor with a hollow *thunk*. "Please—Get out of here. I-I can't—control—" Ishaan took a step backward. An incubus that hasn't fed will lose control and do anything, to anyone. Wasn't that what Kethic said—

"Kethic is one, too, isn't he?" But he didn't need Roan to answer. He was right. And suddenly, it all made sense; the whoring, the running, the scientists after them, the way Roan was so sure that Ishaan wouldn't hurt him. He felt sick as something else occurred to him. "Did-did you let your brother—"

"No," Roan said, shaking his head. "You-you had sex with me and he fed from you, but that's it, I swear."

"That's it," Ishaan said, trying not to vomit. "Do you know how sick that is? Do you have any idea how violated I feel?" He stared down at Roan, a cold, empty place growing inside of him. Roan didn't understand now, but he would.

"I'm sorry," Roan said again, but Ishaan was tired of hearing it. He finished stripping off his bloody shirt, stepped over, grabbed Roan by the arm, snapped the empty side of the handcuffs around his wrist, and tightened them down with a sharp *tick-tick-tick-tick*. Roan cried out and jerked back, pulling Ishaan down on top of him.

"What have you done?" Roan shouted, thrashing and trying to crawl out from under him. His tail, though, had other plans and wrapped around Ishaan's thigh, the tip flicking back and forth across his crotch. Ishaan shoved it away and pinned Roan to the ground.

"You've seen me at my worst. Now it's my turn." With surprising strength, Roan threw him off and lunged for the stairs, nearly pulling Ishaan's shoulder out of its socket. Roan grabbed for his pants and Ishaan realized he was going after the handcuff key. "No," Ishaan said, hauling back on Roan. Roan cried out as his knees scraped across the stone. He whipped around, his normally soft blue-gray eyes hard and almost colorless, his face nearly unrecognizable. Blood smeared his knees as he drew his legs up underneath himself, impressively aroused as he crouched on the other end of the handcuffs. Ishaan didn't remember him being that big before. Maybe this wasn't such a good idea.

For a long moment, nobody moved. Ishaan had never actually let a guy fuck him—not while he was awake, anyway. Anger flared inside him and he lunged at Roan, but Roan was faster. Ishaan fell back and cried out in shock as Roan flipped him over and twisted his handcuffed arm up behind his back. This was definitely not a good idea. Ishaan kicked out and felt pain shoot up his arm as Roan twisted it tighter. He fell still, his chest heaving, as Roan reached beneath him and unbuttoned his pants.

"No—Roan, don't—Please," he gasped, but Roan just grabbed the back of his jeans and jerked them down around his thighs. "No!" Ishaan shouted, his free hand clawing at the floor of the cavern, the toes of his boots sliding across the stone as he tried to get his feet under him. He was ready for Roan to break his arm, he was prepared to keep fighting through the pain, but Roan just shoved him flat against the ground and swung his leg over Ishaan's back, pinning Ishaan's arm beneath him as he sat facing toward Ishaan's feet. That freakish tail slithered over Ishaan's shoulder and across his chest, writhing against him. Ishaan grabbed it with his free hand and it wrapped tight around his wrist.

Ishaan didn't understand why Roan would choose this awkward position, until Roan leaned forward and spread his ass open with one hand. A strangled sound escaped Ishaan's lips as he pressed his face to the stone and squeezed his eyes shut. Roan's hot tongue touched him, sliding down the crack of his ass and across his opening. Ishaan tensed, his insides growing hot and tight as Roan licked him again and again. His whole body began to tremble as Roan pressed the tip of his tongue to Ishaan's entrance, wriggling it back and forth as he pressed forward and slid inside.

Ishaan cried out as he felt Roan's tongue enter him, sliding far too deep to be natural. Roan began to thrust into him, fucking him with his inhuman tongue, the tip finding and stroking a place inside him that made lights dance before his eyes. He cried out again and again, raising his hips to make room beneath himself for his sudden erection. He couldn't help it; nothing had ever felt this good before.

Suddenly, Roan jerked back and his tail released Ishaan's arm. "I'm sorry," he gasped, scrambling off of Ishaan. "I'm sorry, I-I tried to stop—I—Ishaan?" Ishaan lay gasping, his body still trembling inside, his head spinning.

"That was it?" he asked, his voice hoarse. "That's all it takes?" He started to push himself upright and Roan reached out to help. Ishaan knocked his hand away and pulled his pants back up. "Don't touch me."

Roan drew back.

"I don't blame you for hating me," he said after a moment. "I hate me, too, but you don't have time to hang around and make me feel like shit. You have to get out of here."

"Why?" Ishaan asked. "You've fed—" He glanced at Roan, his horns and tail still evident. "Haven't you?"

"I stopped once I had control again," Roan said. "I-I couldn't do that to you. I've hurt you too much already." He turned away and reached for his pants again. Ishaan let him, watching silently as Roan fished the little silver key out of his pocket. "Get as far away as you can," Roan said as he crawled back over to Ishaan, his tail curling at the end and swinging behind him. "Don't look back. Just forget about me. I deserve this, I deserve to suffer for what I've done." He reached for the cuffs but Ishaan grabbed his wrist and jerked him off his knees. He shoved him down against the floor and leaned over him, his lips inches from Roan's ear.

"You think dying is suffering?" he hissed between his teeth. "Dying is easy. Suffering is having to live with your mistakes. It's having to live with the mistakes of others. It's loving someone who doesn't love you back." Roan cried out as Ishaan ripped the key out of his fingers and threw it off the ledge. "If you want to suffer, you're going to do it right, not half-assed like some whiny martyr." He sat back and Roan curled up, his tail wrapping around his knees as he began to sob. Ishaan turned away and sat with his back to Roan to wait.

Thirty-five

Roan ran out of tears and lay with his back to Ishaan, staring out across the open cavern. Ishaan had no idea what he'd done. He had no idea how close he had come to being raped, how hard Roan had fought to keep from hurting him. He couldn't do it again. The next time Roan lost control, Ishaan would scream and bleed.

If Roan lost control. After a moment, he sat up and cleared his throat.

"Since you won't let me die," he said, "will you let me feed? Will you make love to me?"

Ishaan made a disgusted sound in his throat.

"No."

"Will you let me—let me make love to you?"

"No." Roan closed his eyes and ran his free hand over his face. He didn't have any choice then. If Ishaan insisted on being forced, it would be better to force him while Roan still had control. He could be gentle, even if Ishaan fought him, but only if he acted soon. After a moment, he reached over and grabbed his jeans. "Now what are you doing?" Ishaan asked. Roan pulled the jar of lubricant out of his pocket and unscrewed the lid.

"I'm not going to hurt you," Roan said. "I can't, I won't, so if you won't fuck me, then I have to fuck you."

"Quit pretending like you give a shit about me," Ishaan snapped. "We both know I was just convenient." Roan's heart filled with a hollow ache, but he knew better than to rise to Ishaan's baiting. Ishaan wanted him to lose control. It was easier to hate a monster than a man. Roan moved toward him, but Ishaan scrambled back, keeping as much distance between them as the handcuffs would allow. "If you think I'm going to make this easy on you, you're wrong."

"I *won't* hurt you," Roan said again, but he could feel the demon digging its claws in, tearing his control to shreds. He didn't have time for this shit. Roan lunged, grabbed Ishaan by the wrist, and dragged him, kicking and flailing, over to the blanket. Roan dropped to his knees, straddling Ishaan's waist, and Ishaan punched him in the face.

Roan sat, stunned, as the blood ran down his chin from where his teeth had cut into his lip. After a moment, he turned his head and spat into the fire pit, the blood and saliva sizzling as it hit the hot coals. He wiped his chin on the back of his hand and silently got to his feet. Ishaan looked relieved, until Roan grabbed him and flipped him onto his stomach.

With one hand, he jerked Ishaan's pants down and then reached for the open jar of gel, but Ishaan was determined to make this as unpleasant as possible. He tried to get up, pulling on the handcuffs and keeping Roan from reaching his jar. Roan threw himself onto Ishaan and shoved him flat against the blanket.

"Ishaan, please," he begged, "don't do this. Don't make me rape you."

"You've been raping me for the last ten months," Ishaan said between his teeth. "It's about time you had to work for it." He lunged to his knees and grabbed at the stick they'd used to poke the fire. Roan slammed his shoulder into Ishaan's side and knocked him to the ground. Ishaan swung his arm and Roan heard the stick whistle through the air. He ducked. The stick smashed against one of his horns, making his teeth rattle as the wood shattered. Ishaan threw it aside and scrambled to his hands and knees again. Roan knocked him back down and grabbed the back of his neck, pinning him to the ground.

"I'm not asking you to like it," Roan said, his chest heaving, "just stop fighting me."

"No," Ishaan growled, his hands clenching into fists. Roan stared down at him, not understanding.

"Why do you think this is going to hurt me?" Roan asked. "I'm not supposed to give a shit about you, remember? All you're doing is hurting yourself." He leaned down, his lips brushing the shell of Ishaan's ear. "I would tear you apart," he whispered and Ishaan shuddered. "Please, just let me do this. Let me...let me..." Roan took a gasping breath, then stretched out his tail and dipped the end in the jar. Ishaan went very still as Roan climbed onto him, his hands on Ishaan's wrists and his knees gripping Ishaan's hips.

His eyes closed, Roan concentrated on just his tail. It had been ages since he'd used it deliberately, and he wound up smearing lubricant across Ishaan's thigh and down the middle of his own back before he managed to find what he was looking for. Ishaan made a strangled noise and bucked underneath him as Roan's tail probed along the crack of his ass, feeling for his entrance. Not much bigger around than Roan's thumb, the tip slid easily inside, meeting little resistance even when Ishaan tightened around him. He eased deeper, stretching the tight passage, spreading the gel as deep as he could. Ishaan was taut as a drum beneath him, drawing short, hissing breaths between his teeth, and when Roan finally pulled his tail out, his whole body just went limp.

Roan hesitated, then climbed off. Ishaan didn't move as Roan finished removing his pants, didn't resist as Roan spread his legs and moved to kneel between them. Roan scraped the glob of gel off the back of Ishaan's thigh and smeared it along his length, his throat constricting as he stared down at Ishaan. This was truly the lesser of two evils, but not by much.

Ishaan made a small sound and tensed as Roan touched the head of his erection to Ishaan's opening. The demon in him screamed and fought to bury himself inside Ishaan, but the man held back, trembling, tears running down his face. Slowly, he pressed against that tight ring of muscle. Ishaan resisted him, his whole body tight and shaking, until with a hoarse shout he suddenly relaxed and Roan slid inside. Ishaan drew a sharp breath between his teeth and cried out again, the sound piercing deep into Roan's chest. He held still, waiting for Ishaan to adjust, his whole body consumed by a cold fire as the heat of Ishaan's body surrounded him.

Roan waited as long as he could, digging his fingernails into the palm of his hand until blood dripped from his fingers, but the demon was relentless. He felt his control slipping. Choking back a sob, he began to rock his hips. Ishaan gasped and tried to pull away. Before he knew what he was doing, Roan had jerked on Ishaan's cuffed arm. Ishaan grunted in pain as the cuffs bit into his wrist, his skin already red and raw.

"C'mon, fuck me already," Ishaan spat. "Just get it over with, you fucking freak." Roan ignored him, moving slowly, sliding in and out in long, controlled strokes. Ishaan twitched and choked back small sounds as Roan leaned forward, angling his strokes to find that sensitive place inside of him. He rubbed across it and felt Ishaan shudder. "You think that's funny, you little prick?" Ishaan asked. "I don't care how good you can make it feel, it's still rape."

Roan stared at the back of Ishaan's head, then leaned close to his ear.

"I can't feed on just sex," he said. "I feed on my partner's pleasure. I *have* to make it feel good. Especially when it's rape." He sat back up and began to thrust into Ishaan again. "Believe me," he added after a moment, "if fucking you was all it took, I'd be finished already."

"I-I didn't know that," Ishaan said, his voice, for once, not laced with hatred.

"Now you do," Roan said, "so how about you relax a little. I don't know, close your eyes and pretend I'm someone else." He couldn't hide the bitterness and scorn that surged through him. Ishaan had no right to condemn him; Ishaan knew nothing about him. And whose fault was that? Scorn was quickly replaced by shame. He should have told him; it never should have come to this.

Ishaan groaned and tried to draw his arms underneath him.

"Let me up," he said. "I...I won't fight you anymore." Roan hesitated, then let Ishaan rise to his knees and elbows, Roan leaning across his back with his cuffed hand on the floor beside Ishaan's and his other hand on Ishaan's hip. He began to thrust again, tentatively at first, but as Ishaan pushed back to meet him, Roan began to drive deeper, their bodies separated by nothing more than sweat. Roan pressed himself against Ishaan, savoring the feel of his skin, the scent of his shampoo.

Ishaan cried out, a shudder racking his body, and Roan nearly choked on the pleasure that enveloped him. His demon feasted, glutting itself, and Roan slowed his pace, holding back, drawing it out. He was not going to come. He'd done enough to Ishaan already without degrading him further. Ishaan grew tense, his breath short, gasping and groaning as Roan moved inside him. Twice he shifted his weight to his handcuffed arm, his free hand moving underneath him, and both times he'd put his elbow back on the blanket. It was like he had started to jerk himself off, but then stopped.

Roan's free hand slid from Ishaan's hip to his stomach, his fingertips sliding across Ishaan's smooth skin, kneading the hard muscles beneath. He let his hand drift farther down, tugging lightly at Ishaan's wiry curls, and Ishaan bucked beneath him.

"Are you...fed?" Ishaan gritted out between his teeth.

"Almost," Roan answered. The demon was quiet, almost in a coma, but Roan continued to drink in the energy, like he could drown himself in sex. It didn't work. "All right," he said at last, leaning on Ishaan for one last, lingering moment, "I'm done." He started to straighten up, to pull out, but Ishaan grabbed his hand, the cuffs clinking together.

"Don't stop," Ishaan said, pulling him back down. "Don't stop...don't stop..."

"All right," Roan said, and he began to rock his hips again. "You want me to..." He slid his free hand back beneath Ishaan. Ishaan nodded, a long, low moan issuing from his lips as Roan wrapped his fingers around Ishaan's shaft and began to stroke him. Roan thrust deeper, harder, his grip tightening as Ishaan shouted, hoarse and wordless, his voice echoing around them. His body jerked and he came hard in Roan's hand, his seed warm and slick between Roan's fingers. Roan gritted his teeth as Ishaan tightened around him, trying to restrain himself, but Ishaan pushed back against him and he lost it. He cried out and came, squeezing his eyes shut as he spilled himself inside of Ishaan.

For a long moment, no one moved. Roan drew the incubus back inside him, shuddering as his tail slipped back into his spine. If that never happened again, it would be too soon.

Suddenly, Ishaan let go of his hand and pulled away.

"Don't think this meant anything," he said, his voice hitching as Roan slipped out of him. "I'm still pissed at you."

"I know," Roan said. "I'm sorry."

"Now what are you apologizing for?" He grabbed his shirt, the front stiff with shival blood, and began to clean himself up.

"That," Roan said. "I-I tried not to—"

Ishaan laughed, a harsh, unpleasant sound.

"Don't worry, coming in me is the least of your crimes." He threw the soiled shirt down next to Roan and turned away, lying on his stomach with his cuffed arm stretched out toward Roan. After a moment, Roan picked up the shirt and wiped himself off. He glanced toward his pants, but they were on the other side of the fire pit. Closer was a second blanket and Roan quietly stretched out one leg and snagged it with his toes. He wrapped it around himself and glanced at Ishaan.

"You're going to get cold," Roan said. Ishaan didn't respond. Roan sat and bit at the inside of his lip, chewing on the edge of the cut from where Ishaan had punched him. Nothing that Ishaan had done had startled Roan more than that. In all the time they'd lived together, with all the fights they'd had, Ishaan had never laid a hand on him in anger, never even raised a fist. This cut said, more clearly than anything, that it was over.

Roan picked up what was left of the poke stick and stirred the smoldering embers of their fire. He cast a longing look at the pile of firewood against the graffiti-covered wall of the cavern and then stretched out beside Ishaan, lying on his back and staring up into the blackness above them. His fingers worried the corner of the blanket. He wanted to cover Ishaan with it, but he was pretty sure his gesture would not be welcome.

"Why didn't you tell me?" Ishaan asked some time later, making Roan jump. Roan had just started to think he might be asleep.

Roan drew a slow breath.

"I was afraid," he said at last.

"Of me?"

"At first...and later, of what you'd think." Ishaan made an ambiguous sound and fell silent. Roan's heart began to pound. He had to plead his case. He had to make Ishaan understand. "I just wanted to rest for a while," he said. "I'd been running for years and I was exhausted. When Sezae mentioned that you never remembered anything—" Ishaan shifted, the handcuffs clinking. "I thought I could relax for a couple of weeks and then leave. You never would have known what I was."

"So I was just a bed and breakfast to you," Ishaan said.

"At first," Roan said again, "but then I got to know you and I realized you needed me almost as much as I needed you."

Ishaan made a scornful sound. "How do you figure?"

"When was the last time you woke up on the floor?" Roan asked. Ishaan didn't respond. "You were happier, healthier...true, you wouldn't have died without me, but...I told myself it was a fair trade. I was wrong, but it was never my intent to hurt you. I should have told you and...I'm sorry." Ishaan was silent for so long, Roan started to wonder if he was still awake.

"I want to believe you," Ishaan said finally, "but I can't. The incubism... yeah, I'd have been upset, but I think I'd have gotten over it. But being lied to all this time; being used all this time...how do I know you're not lying to me now? How can I ever trust you again?"

"You *told* me to lie to you—"

"About one thing," Ishaan snapped. "I asked you to keep one specific thing from me. And as it turned out, I didn't even need to."

Roan stared up into the darkness and licked his lips.

"Yes, you did." Out of the corner of his eye, Roan saw Ishaan raise his head and look over at him. Roan took a shaking breath. "I was late taking care of you one night and when I entered your room, you'd already masturbated in front of the door and were asleep against the wall. I tried to get you back into bed, but you were too heavy, so I lay down in your bed to wait. I-I fell asleep —" The memory of that night enfolded him and he found himself trembling. "I woke up with you on top of me. I begged you to-to stop, but—" Ishaan jerked on the cuffs and Roan cried out as the sharp metal bit into his wrist.

"I don't believe you," Ishaan said between his teeth. "You're making it up so I'll feel guilty, so I'll feel sorry for you—" Roan shook his head, but Ishaan didn't stop. "And even if it did happen, you shouldn't have been in my fucking room in the first place." He turned away and lay back down, his breathing loud and ragged in the silence.

"Ishaan, I—"

"Shut up," Ishaan said, his voice empty. "Don't speak to me. Ever." Roan rolled onto his side, his arm stretched uncomfortably behind him, and cried.

Thirty-six

Ishaan opened his eyes, certain that he hadn't slept a moment all night long, but the warm, slender body in his arms seemed to indicate otherwise. He raised his head, his eyes moving over the nest of tangled blond hair, the soft curve of his cheek, the strong line of his jaw—the swollen lip and fresh bruise beginning to appear at the corner of his mouth. He hadn't meant to hit him. He'd never hit anyone before.

But then, he'd never discovered an incubus in his bed before, either. Ishaan clenched his fist, shaking inside as he fought the urge to beat Roan senseless. He'd never felt so angry, so violated, so-so...*betrayed*. Roan betrayed him, deceived him, lied to him. How could he forget that? How could he forgive it?

He had been painfully honest about his own condition from the very start. Was it too much to ask that Roan do the same? Was it too much to expect? He could understand keeping it a secret at first, up to a point. They didn't know each other. He didn't like it, but he did understand it. But why not come clean when they became friends, when they became lovers? Was this why Roan wouldn't marry him?

Ishaan closed his eyes, a wave of nausea rising up as he realized how close he'd come to marrying this *thing*...this quiet, fragile thing in his arms. He couldn't help it; he still loved him. But that didn't mean he could trust him. No, Roan wasn't a monster when Ishaan was awake, but what did he do when Ishaan was asleep? When he didn't have to worry about what Ishaan would do, or what he'd think. Ishaan shuddered as he remembered the way Roan's tail had squirmed up inside of him. It just wasn't natural.

Roan made a soft sound and stretched, the handcuffs clinking, and his eyes fluttered open. Before he could wake up and get the wrong idea, Ishaan shoved him away and sat up, turning his back to him.

"Good morning to you, too," Roan muttered.

"What did you do to me?" Ishaan asked after a moment. "After I fell asleep, what did you do?"

"Why would I do anything?" Roan said. "I won't need to feed for three days and it's not like I enjoy sucking your dick. If *you* touched *me*, I slept through it. I don't feel fucked, just in case you're wondering."

"Well, I do," Ishaan snapped. His whole body ached, though, not just his asshole. With a groan, he climbed to his feet and when Roan didn't follow fast enough, he pulled him up by the handcuffs.

"Hey, take it easy," Roan said, grabbing at the metal as it bit into his wrist. "What's your hurry?"

"I'm cold, I'm hungry, and I have to take a piss. Now come on, where're your pants?"

"Over there," Roan said, pointing. "And quit jerking me around. It's not *my* fault we don't have a key for these damn things." Ishaan didn't respond. It *was* his fault. It was *all* his fault. They awkwardly put their pants on and stepped outside the Cathedral into the chill morning drizzle to relieve themselves, then they spent the better part of an hour searching for the handcuff key. Roan found it about twenty feet from the car and uncuffed himself without a word. As Ishaan slipped the cuffs and key into his back pocket, he watched Roan walk away, back up the stairs and out of sight. A moment later came the sound of wood splintering. Apparently, Roan was taking care of the fire.

Ishaan walked to the car and opened the passenger's side door. Roan's empty suitcase fell out at his feet. With a sigh, he picked it up and began shoving Roan's things back inside, but faltered when he picked up the book of fairy tales. Was it just him, or was it strange for a grown man with no children to carry a book of kid's stories around with him like it was one of his most treasured possessions? Was he hiding something inside it? Ishaan flipped through the pages, but found nothing more than faded print and watercolor pictures.

One story seemed more faded than the others, the pages starting to yellow, the edges dirty and ragged, like it had been read too many times in damp alleys and crowded train cars. Is that what Roan would go back to? Or would he go home, now that he wasn't being hunted anymore? Would he find someone else to prey on, or would he go back to whoring himself? Ishaan knew he shouldn't care, but it wasn't easy to just stop loving someone.

Maybe that's why he was so angry, because he *couldn't* stop loving him. Even knowing what he was and what he did, Ishaan wanted to run up those stairs and take Roan in his arms. He could hold Roan no more responsible for his condition than he could hold himself, but the lying...for the lying, he *would* hold Roan responsible. For the lying, he would never forgive him.

Ishaan glanced down at the book in his hands, open to a story called *Beauty and the Beast*. It was a typical fairy tale story about a beautiful girl imprisoned by an ugly beast. Every night, the beast would ask the girl to marry him, but she always refused. He gave her everything she wanted and more, even allowing her to visit her family, and when she did not return as promised, it nearly killed him. She realized then that she did indeed love him and she agreed to marry him, breaking the spell that was upon him and returning him to a handsome prince.

Ishaan snorted. What a load of crap. Was that what Roan was looking for, a beast he could tame and turn into a prince? Was that all Ishaan was to him, the beast in his fairy story? Was he the hero, going to break Ishaan's spell? Ishaan turned the page and felt the expression bleed out of his face. Someone had taken a marker and drawn on the picture of the Beast and his Beauty, adding curved black horns, a long tongue and a hairless tail. Beneath the beast, in Roan's blocky handwriting, was the word *ME*.

Ishaan snapped the book shut and shoved it into the suitcase, piling socks and shirts in on top of it. This wasn't a fairy story. There were no 'Happily Ever After's. Ishaan latched the case and threw it behind the seats, then began gathering up the tools for breakfast-making.

He and Roan exchanged hardly a handful of words all day, but as night fell and Ishaan felt exhaustion stealing over him, he cleared his throat, the sound seeming to echo in the silence.

"Do you want me to put the handcuffs back on?" he asked.

Roan glanced at him, his expression unreadable.

"What for?"

"So I won't attack you in my sleep," Ishaan replied, wondering why he even bothered.

"I don't care," Roan said, turning away. "Put 'em on if you want to." He lay down with his back to Ishaan and pulled one of the blankets up over himself.

"Fine, then," Ishaan said, taking them out of his pocket and dropping them on the ground next to his shoes and jacket, "I won't." Roan didn't respond. "You can feed if you need to, but try not to do anything too perverse," Ishaan said as he lay down and covered up with his own blanket. He stared across the cavern, watching the firelight dance on the wall, the shadows fading as the wood burned down.

What would Roan do to him? Ishaan didn't even want to imagine all the sick, creative ways he could use that tongue, or tail, or the horns. What purpose did they serve, anyway? He was pretty sure he didn't want to know. He licked his lips, wondering if he'd ever sucked Roan off in his sleep, or tongued his asshole, or—

He drew a sudden breath and let it out slowly. He'd never get to sleep like this. But how could he close his eyes and trust Roan not to do anything? He already knew he couldn't trust him. He heard Roan shift restlessly. He wasn't asleep, either. He was waiting for Ishaan to get restless and then he'd do Maele only knew what to him, and Ishaan wouldn't be able to do a damn thing to stop him.

Unless...Unless Roan only *thought* he was asleep. If he could pretend to be asleep, then when Roan came after him, he'd be able to kick the shit out of him. Well, he'd be able to try. In incubus form, Roan had been a lot stronger than Ishaan had expected. He licked his lips again. It was worth a try, he supposed. Better than lying awake waiting for the inevitable. He forced himself to relax, made his breathing slow and deep and even, and tried to imagine what he must be like when asleep.

Ishaan rolled onto his back and began to fumble with his pants, his every movement deliberately clumsy, jerky, and he made a small, frustrated sound. He heard Roan move, then sit up. Ishaan kept his eyes closed. They would give him away for certain.

"Are you asleep?" Roan whispered after a moment. Ishaan pushed at the waistband of his pants, but they were still buttoned and going nowhere. "Easy there," Roan said, moving closer. Ishaan felt the blanket lift, the cold air racing across his bare arms and chest, and then Roan's lean, warm body slid up against his side and the blanket settled over both of them. Ishaan faltered as Roan lay his head on his shoulder, one hand resting, light as a bird, in the middle of Ishaan's chest.

"Just give me a minute," Roan said. "This is probably one of the last times I'll ever get to do this." Ishaan's heart began to beat a little faster and he waited for the incubus to appear, but Roan just lay against his side, absently running his fingertips back and forth across Ishaan's chest. Not sure what was going on, Ishaan went back to fighting with his pants.

"Oh, all right," Roan said, reaching down and unbuttoning them with one hand. He slid his hand into Ishaan's briefs and wrapped his hand around him. "Don't know what you're being so impatient about, you're not even hard yet." And then Roan began to stroke him, his touch soft and gentle. "You sure are being quiet tonight," Roan said after a moment. "I guess you really are mad at me. I mean—" His voice caught and he paused to clear his throat. "If there was any way you'd forgive me, you'd show it now, when you're most uninhibited, right?" Ishaan wasn't sure if was supposed to answer that, so he kept his mouth shut.

"That's what I thought," Roan said with a sigh as he continued his slow ministrations. "I don't blame you, you know. I should have told you. I will regret for the rest of my life that I didn't tell you. But—" He cleared his throat again. "I'm not going to make you any more miserable than I already have by begging you to forgive me. You won't. You can't. I understand. And as soon as we can get to Shesade or Devaen, I'll throw myself on the first train out of town and you'll never have to see me again. You can forget all about me. Just-just don't forget that you said you'd let Sezae and Isha into your life. You-you need somebody—" Roan began to cry, his face pressed against Ishaan's shoulder.

Ishaan lay there, Roan's hand still on his dick, wishing he'd never thought of this stupid idea. He couldn't tell if Roan was being sincere or if he knew Ishaan was faking and was just trying to play on his emotions.

He drew a bracing breath.

"Roan..." he hesitated, not sure what to say, but Roan didn't give him a chance to decide.

"I know, I know," Roan said, letting go of him and sitting up. Ishaan cracked one eye open and watched Roan dry his eyes on the back of his hand. "You'll excuse me if I skip the foreplay." Roan ducked under the blanket and Ishaan had to stifle a gasp as Roan's warm, wet mouth surrounded him. Ishaan reached out to stop him. There was a reason he'd not let Roan blow him since that one mistake. It was degrading, it was selfish, and you didn't treat someone you loved like a common whore.

Roan caught his hand and pressed it to his cheek as he suckled at the head, his normal, human tongue stroking the sensitive spot underneath. A long, low moan issued from Ishaan's lips and he arched his back, his muscles aching. Why was Roan doing this? Why would he choose this form of sex, when he knew damn well that Ishaan had no inhibitions? He had to know; he had to be toying with him. Ishaan was tempted to grab him by the hair and show him how it felt to be toyed with, but he couldn't. He couldn't be sure. He was just starting to realize that there was so much about Roan that he didn't understand.

Ishaan tensed, raising his hips off the blanket as Roan slid down his length, taking him almost to the base, and then drew back. Maele help him, it felt good. Not as good as making love to Roan, but it was enough to tip him over the edge. He cried out and lost it, shuddering as he felt Roan swallow his seed and lick him clean. Why would he do that? He had to know. Ishaan closed his eyes and lay still, his heart beating loud in his ears as he waited for Roan to go away.

"I know you won't remember this," Roan said after a moment, "and you wouldn't believe me if you could remember, but I want to say that I never lied about loving you." Ishaan heard Roan move toward him and he tensed, but Roan just pressed his lips to Ishaan's in a soft, chaste kiss. "I still love you," he whispered as he drew back. Now he moved back over to his side of the blanket and Ishaan quietly rolled onto his side.

Tears stung his eyes and burned in the back of his throat, his chest aching. He was a fool, blinded by emotion. If that was Roan's plan, it was working perfectly, because Ishaan believed him. He believed with his whole heart that Roan still loved him. What difference that made, he didn't know. He was still furious, but...something inside him wanted more time to try and understand. Maybe there wasn't anything to understand, maybe Roan was simply a user and a liar, but maybe, *maybe*, he wasn't. Ishaan wasn't sure anymore and before he threw Roan out of his life forever, he had to be sure.

Thirty-seven

Roan sat on a half-round of firewood beside the fire pit, stirring a pan of beans and trying to avoid drawing Ishaan's attention. He'd thought a day of the silent treatment had been bad, but ever since they'd gotten up, Ishaan had been harassing him with barrage after barrage of questions. What happened the first night after Roan moved in? When did Ishaan rape him? When was the first time Roan let Ishaan enter him? Why did Roan come in his room every night, if he only needed to feed every three days? Sometimes he'd ask the same question over and over, just rephrasing it slightly, as if he was trying to catch Roan in a lie. It was exhausting.

"So," Ishaan said after only a few minutes of blessed silence, "how long would you have continued to feed on me in secret, if this hadn't happened?"

Roan sighed.

"I don't know. I was trying to find a way to tell you that wouldn't end with me getting tossed out on my ass or shot."

"Hmm," Ishaan said, which had become his response to anything Roan said. "You say you were planning on telling me. How much longer would that have taken?"

Roan threw down the spoon and lunged to his feet.

"I just said, I don't know. *I don't know.* Now leave me the fuck alone, Ishaan." He turned and headed for the stairs but Ishaan jumped up and grabbed him by the arm.

"Roan, wait," Ishaan said, "I just want to—"

"I don't care!" Roan shouted, jerking away from him. "I don't care what you want. I never have. I lied about everything, okay? Are you happy now? Now just leave me alone." He pounded down the stone steps, his hands clenching into fists as Ishaan followed him. Why was he doing this? What more did he want to know? Nothing Roan could say was going to change what he did, so why even bother? It was over. Just let it go. Roan was halfway to the wide mouth of the cavern when Ishaan caught up to him and grabbed his arm again.

Roan spun around and swung, not caring what he hit as long as Ishaan got the message, but Ishaan caught his wrist, a look of surprise on his face. Slowly, he lowered Roan's arm.

"I deserve that," he said. "I've been acting like a real asshole, but—" He stopped, a slight frown creeping across his features. "Do you hear that?" he asked, letting go of Roan and turning around. Roan stepped up beside him and listened. A soft *clip-clop, clip-clop* echoed down the long, open passage, coming from the Shesade side of the Cathedral. Roan stepped forward, relief washing over him as a pair of sturdy black draft horses appeared out of the gloom, drawing a large wagon along behind them.

Three men sat across the wagon seat, all of them splattered with mud and one with his arm in a sling. As the wagon rolled up beside Ishaan's car, the driver pulled back on the reins, his dark eyes moving from Roan to Ishaan, to the fire crackling up on the landing.

"Good morning," he said after a moment, giving them a slight nod.

"Morning," Ishaan answered. "Are you...from Shesade?"

The man nodded.

"Clean-up crew. We had a couple of nasty slides between town and here."

"Clean-up?" Roan said. "So that means the road's open, right? We can get to Shesade now?" The man nodded again. "Great. Thank you so much."

"It's what we get paid for," the driver said. "Do you know, how bad is the road to Devaen?"

"The bridge at Kai Falls is out," Ishaan said. "Last I saw, you could get across on foot, but not a wagon, and there's a slide about a mile this side of Sunderman's Bridge."

The driver sighed.

"I was afraid of that." He grabbed up the reins again. "We got to turn around and rest the horses a bit. You might want to get your stuff together and head out before we do. That road isn't wide enough to get past us."

"Thanks," Ishaan said. "We'll do that." He headed for the stairs and Roan started to follow, but the last thing he wanted was to be subjected to more of Ishaan's questions. He glanced back at the men in the wagon.

"Is he okay?" Roan asked the driver, gesturing to the man with his arm in a sling. He was pale and leaning heavily upon the third man.

"A log rolled over his arm last night," the driver said. "We were hoping he could see the doctor in Devaen, but with the bridge out..." He shook his head.

"Do you want to bring him up by our fire?" Roan asked. "You guys could warm up while we're getting ready to go." The two uninjured men looked at each other, then the driver nodded.

"We appreciate it. This is Jon—" The other man nodded. "He's Dekken, and I'm Ice. Real name's Lutzcaryce, but everyone just calls me Ice."

"Nice to meet you," Roan said, stepping forward to lend a hand as Jon and Ice tried to get the barely conscious Dekken out of the wagon. "I'm Roan. That's Ishaan."

"Ishaan Darvis?" Jon asked. Roan nodded. "My aunt is always talking about him. She owns the formalwear shop."

"Lira?" Roan asked with a grin. "I met her. She's...nice."

Jon laughed.

"She's a lewd old woman and she's lucky she hasn't been arrested for molesting her customers. She wasn't too bad, I hope."

"No," Roan said with a shake of his head, "she behaved herself. Mostly."

They reached the stairs and Roan stepped back, allowing the two stronger men to support Dekken up the narrow stairs. Roan followed, ignoring the look Ishaan shot him as he helped Jon and Ice settle Dekken down beside the fire. "There's a pan of beans burning over there," Roan said, "if you want to help yourselves."

"No, thanks," Ice said. "We should go water the horses. I think he'll be okay." He patted Dekken on the shoulder and then he and Jon headed back down the stairs. Roan began gathering up empty milk bottles and canning jars.

"He doesn't look so good," Roan said after a moment. Dekken was propped up against the worn log they'd been using as a seat, but he looked like he was slowly listing sideways, his eyes glazed as he stared into the fire. Roan stepped over and pressed the back of his hand to Dekken's forehead. "His skin is like ice. He needs to see a doctor, now."

"And what are you going to do about it?" Ishaan asked. "Carry him to Devaen on your back?" He paused, then sighed. "Sorry, I didn't mean to snap."

"Like I care," Roan said, turning away. The last thing he wanted was Ishaan pretending like it was all okay. "How long is it going to take that wagon to get back to Shesade?" he asked.

Ishaan took a very long time answering.

"They can't go very fast without risk of jostling his arm, so...a day, day and a half, maybe. Why?"

"I don't think he'd make it," Roan said. "But your car can get there in just a couple of hours—"

"But it won't hold three," Ishaan pointed out.

"I know," Roan said. "Which I why I'll ride with Jon and Ice, and you can get Dekken to the doctor before he dies." Ishaan opened his mouth to protest. "C'mon, these guys need help. They cleared the road for us."

"It's their job," Ishaan said. He picked up the pan of leftover beans and banged them out into the fire. Dekken jumped at the sound and started to slide sideways. Roan grabbed him by the shoulders and gently sat him back up. "Besides, you only just met those guys. You don't know them. What if they—if they—"

"Rape me?" Roan said before he could stop himself.

Ishaan glared at him.

"Rob you, kill you."

"Jon is Lira's nephew. I don't think he's going to kill me." Besides, when given the choice between being murdered and spending two and a half hours alone in a car with Ishaan, he'd rather be murdered. Ishaan finished scraping out the pan and stuck it in the crate with the empty jars.

"All right," he said, scowling. "If those other two agree, I'll take this one to town, but then I'm coming back to get you."

"Why?" Roan asked. "Do you need me for something?"

Without Roan, he'd have to sleep in the jail and everyone in Shesade would find out about him. Ishaan *did* need him. Didn't he see that?

"No," Ishaan said between his teeth, "I don't *need* you—"

"Good," Roan replied, turning and heading for the stairs. "I'm going to go tell Ice." He would not beg. He would not beg. He would *not*—

"Roan." Roan stopped, hesitated, then looked over his shoulder. "I'll be waiting for you in Shesade. Don't think you can just jump on the first train out of town and disappear."

Roan's heart began to beat a little faster. Those were almost his exact words...could Ishaan possibly remember? Had something finally gotten through to him? "This isn't over," Ishaan added after a minute. "I still have questions."

Ah, yes, his fucking questions.

"Don't worry," Roan said. "I have no intention of taking the train out of Shesade." For an instant, Ishaan looked startled, then suspicious, then he scowled and turned away. It was like he *did* remember and he thought Roan was lying. But he never remembered. Roan finished descending the stairs and headed toward the workmen's wagon. Was he just imagining it? He kept seeing things in Ishaan's expression, hearing them in his voice, things that offered a glimmer of hope. Those, he knew he was imagining.

Ice was rubbing one of the horses down with an old cloth sack as Roan approached. "Hey," Roan said, "we have an idea."

When Roan finished explaining, Ice looked relieved.

"I wanted to ask, but...it's a mighty big favor to do for someone you only just met. Thanks. To both of you."

Roan was tempted to tell him that Ishaan would have rather let Dekken die, but he kept his mouth shut.

It took another ten minutes to get their belongings picked up and the fire put out. While Ishaan was up pushing the coals apart, Roan quietly took his suitcase out from behind the passenger's seat and hid it in the back of the workmen's wagon. Inside of it was everything in the universe that he cared about. Well, almost everything.

Ishaan helped Jon and Ice carry Dekken down the stairs. The injured man had slipped into unconsciousness while they were packing and blood had leaked through the bandages and onto the sling. His face was white, his fingers purple. Roan had a bad feeling that he was going to lose his arm. Better than losing his life, but still...

They settled him the passenger's seat and tucked one of the old blankets in around him. Ice and Jon shook Ishaan's hand and thanked him for his help, then they headed back to their wagon. Roan started to follow them, but then it hit him: this was the last time he would ever see Ishaan. He knew he shouldn't, but he paused and glanced back over his shoulder. Ishaan was watching him. He suddenly had so much to say, but he didn't know where to begin, he couldn't find the words. For several interminable seconds they just stared at each other.

Finally, Ishaan cleared his throat.

"I'll see you in Shesade, then," he said and Roan had to fight the urge to ask him why. Why did he want to make this harder than it had to be? Why couldn't he just let it go and get on with his life? Roan was. He felt a lump rise in his throat and tears sting his eyes. Before Ishaan could notice, Roan nodded and hurried off toward the wagon.

"I'll be waiting for you," Ishaan called after him and the tears slipped free, rolling down his cheeks.

Ice and Jon were examining the horses one last time, adjusting harnesses and checking their hooves for stones and loose shoes. Roan stood beside the wagon, watching them, as Ishaan started his car and slowly crept past them. Roan refused to look at him. He didn't care if the workmen saw his tears, but he couldn't let Ishaan see.

Once the noise of the car had faded in the distance, Roan brushed his tears away and walked around to the rear of the wagon. With his coat in one hand and the suitcase in the other, he headed for the cavern entrance.

"Hey, where are you going?" Ice called after him. "I thought you wanted a ride."

"Thanks anyway," Roan called back. "I've decided to go to Devaen instead."

"What about your boyfriend?" Jon asked. "What'll we tell him?"

"He's not my boyfriend," Roan said, struggling hard to keep the tremor out of his voice. "And tell him I said I hope this answers his questions." The wind bit at his face as he strode out into the gray morning and his tangled hair kept falling his eyes, but Roan kept his head up and he did not look back.

Thirty-eight

After Ishaan delivered his passenger to the clinic and explained what had happened, the doctor sent for the man's wife and Ishaan got to tell the story all over again. It was late afternoon before he got away from them. Not sure what to do next, he sat in his car and watched the townsfolk cleaning up after the storm; sweeping water off their porches, patching leaky roofs, hauling away sticks and branches washed down from the hills. If only repairing his life was so simple.

His house was surely gone. After watching that wall of water race down the valley, ripping up everything in its path, he had no doubt of it. Everything he owned now sat in the back of his car—a pile of crap that didn't mean anything. He could build a new house, he could buy more things; none of that mattered.

The long, silent drive to Shesade had given him more than enough time to think about everything Roan had told him. He realized, too late perhaps, that while Roan had made many mistakes, he had never done anything to deliberately hurt him. Unlike Ishaan. He remembered, he could hear Roan begging, pleading, and he felt sick, he felt ashamed. He had a right to be angry, but had no right to do what he did. The first thing he'd do when he saw Roan again would be apologize.

People were starting to stare at him, sitting alone in his car, so he drove on down the street to the inn and got himself a room and a bath. While the water heated, he walked across the street and bought some new clothes, as his needed to be either buried or burned.

An hour later, washed and dressed, he sat in his room, staring out the window while he combed his hair. A wagon that size, drawn by a pair of fine draft horses, without an injured passenger to worry about, could probably make between ten and fifteen miles an hour on that narrow, muddy road. Throw in a handful of rest stops and the trip shouldn't take more than about nine hours. Ishaan had left them almost seven hours ago...

He began to pace, watching the light fade from the street below as the sun sank out of sight. It would be harder to find their way in the dark. Or would they stop for the night? They'd only be about twenty miles out. It would be stupid to stop. It'd be more stupid to drive off the edge of the road in the dark, though. He should have asked if they had lanterns. No, he *should* have gone back for him.

Ishaan turned away from the window and grabbed his jacket off the bed. He pulled the car keys out of his pocket and headed down to the street. He said he didn't need Roan, but the truth was, he didn't *want* to need Roan. He wanted to love Roan, not need him, not have to stay with him because he didn't have any other choice. But he did need him. The thought of asking to be locked up, of disturbing all these people, of having them look at him the way the people of Devaen did, it almost made him sick. If Roan could save him from that, if Roan could keep him quiet...was that the reason Ishaan now regretted his actions? Did he really love Roan, regardless, or did he just not want to sleep in the jail that badly? He didn't want to think about it, because he was afraid of what the answer would be.

As he unlocked the car, he glanced down the main street, toward the edge of town, and there, parked in front of the clinic, was the workmen's wagon. For a moment, Ishaan just stood there, his heart beating loud in his ears. Where was Roan? Ishaan shut the door and ran down the street. *Where was Roan?* He burst into the clinic.

The doctor and the two workers turned and stared at him.

"Where's Roan?" Ishaan asked. The younger of the two men, Don or Jon or something like that, stepped toward him.

"Your friend decided not to ride up with us," he said. "He headed out on foot toward Devaen."

"No..." Ishaan said. "No, he—Why?"

Don shrugged.

"Dunno. But he said to tell you that he hoped this answered your questions. Are you all right?"

Ishaan didn't respond, he just turned away and stepped back outside. Roan walked to Devaen. It didn't make any sense. Ishaan had all his things in the back of the car. A sick, hollowness filled him and he ran back over to the vehicle. He pulled blankets out onto the ground and shoved the crates from one side to the other, but the battered brown suitcase was not in the car. Neither was Roan's coat.

Ishaan sat in the front seat, a deep cold settling over him as he realized that Roan was gone. He'd have reached Devaen by then and he'd be on the first train out of town—Ishaan pulled the door shut and started the car. There was a chance...He sped to the far end of town and pulled up in front of the train station.

The clerk looked up in surprise as Ishaan barreled through the door.

"I need to see a train schedule," Ishaan said. The man pointed to a dusty chalkboard tacked to the back wall.

"Won't do you much good," the man said as Ishaan stepped toward it. "This flood's got everything out of whack. Hang on a minute." He turned and shuffled through some papers on the back counter. "Ah, looks like the next train will be coming up from Lorexan day after tomorrow." Day after tomorrow. Ishaan sighed in relief.

"That's good," he said. "I need to buy a ticket to Devaen, then."

"Oh, it doesn't go on through to Devaen," the clerk said. "It goes back to

Lorexan. The tracks between here and Devaen are a mess. It could be months before we can get through."

"So...Devaen's cut off?" Ishaan asked.

The clerk shook his head.

"No, the train from Prythaen is running fine. In fact, I think the first shipment of supplies is scheduled to arrive today or tomorrow. I'm not sure if I..." He shuffled through his papers again, but Ishaan was already running for the door. He didn't want to stay in Shesade anyway.

The drive down the mountain seemed to take twice as long as the drive up, but finally the mouth of the Cathedral rose into view. Ishaan drove straight through and didn't stop until he reached what was left of the bridge at Zai Falls. The waterfall had shrunk back into its channel, leaving the crumbling bridge starkly exposed. The two foot tall outside wall of the stone structure was just about all that remained, broken wooden supports jutting out every now and then. Ishaan grabbed his rifle out of the back and locked the car, then set out at a jog.

Two hours later, the forest began to look eerily familiar, and at the same time, unrecognizable. He splashed along on the high side of the road, wading through six or eight inches of water, his feet soaking wet and freezing, mud splattered up the backs of his pant legs. The clouds were breaking up and the gibbous moon peeked down from a silvering sky, casting pale blue light across the flooded forest. He shifted the rifle to his other shoulder and glanced around, stopping dead at the sight before him.

In the middle of a wide clearing, just visible above the still water, was the foundation of his house. He could see the front step and a couple pieces of copper piping sticking up at odd angles, but that was it. Ishaan stood for a moment, then turned and continued on toward Devaen. It didn't matter.

As he walked, he could see debris caught up in the roots of upended trees; splintered wood, twisted metal, half of his couch. He even passed the refrigerator, lying open on its back with a stranded trout swimming in circles inside it. Ishaan reached into the frigid water and flipped the fish out, watching as it zipped away through the muddy water.

Dawn drew near, gray morning light stealing over the silent forest as Ishaan made his way past the landslide and toward Sunderman's Bridge. The bridge, however, was gone, all but a few stout timbers ripped right out of the ground. Somebody—probably Roan—had found Ishaan's bedroom door and balanced it across the remaining timbers. It rocked and shook, and the little sliding door was missing, giving Ishaan a nauseatingly close look at the rushing river when he made the mistake of glancing down, but it got him across, which was all that really mattered.

The land began to rise, sloping upward from the river, and soon Ishaan found himself on dry—albeit soggy—ground once more. He tucked his rifle under his arm and began to jog again. He was glad to see that Sezae's old house had survived, though much of the farmland was still under water.

The first wisps of chimney smoke appeared, dark smudges against the pearly sky, and Ishaan slowed. What if he was too late? What if Roan had already gone? Ishaan had Kethic's e-mail address on his laptop, but would Kethic help him, especially after Roan told him what had happened? Did he even want to pursue Roan across the universe? Roan had been running and hiding for years; Ishaan doubted even his father's money would be able to find him if he didn't want to be found. Would it be better to just let him go, to not make it any harder than it had to be? Roan said he wouldn't beg—maybe Ishaan shouldn't either.

That was bullshit! Roan only said that because he wanted to do what he thought Ishaan wanted. Roan didn't know he was listening, Roan didn't know he would change his mind, Roan didn't know how much he still loved him. Because Ishaan was too stupid to tell him. Ishaan began to run again.

This early, the town was still asleep. No one saw him run down the street, rifle under his arm. Or at least no one screamed and ran to get the sheriff. Ishaan drew up in front of the tiny train station, the building little bigger than an outhouse. He paused to catch his breath, then climbed up onto the empty platform. The ticket window was shut and locked, a handwritten notice tacked up beside it proclaiming it closed until further notice.

"I see you survived." Ishaan turned to see the sheriff standing at the edge of the platform, his arms crossed over his chest. Ishaan quickly shifted the rifle to his other hand and rested the butt against the warped wooden boards. "Can I help you with something?"

"The train," Ishaan said. "Has it come yet?"

"Yesterday," the sheriff said and Ishaan's heart sank. "We'll be handing out emergency relief around noon. You're entitled to a share of it."

"No," Ishaan said, "that's not—My-my friend, Roan, he said he was coming here."

The dragon nodded.

"I saw him."

"You did? Did he get on the train?"

"I saw him enter town," the sheriff said. "What he did and if he left is not my concern. He did not pose a threat to my town."

"And I suppose I do?" Ishaan said between his teeth.

The dragon frowned.

"You *are* carrying a weapon."

Ishaan glanced down at the rifle.

"It's just for protection."

"It is *my* job to protect the citizens of this town," the sheriff said. "You do not need to walk around armed." He seemed to be taking personal offense to that.

"Not protection from people," Ishaan said. "I was attacked by a shival the other day near the Bride's Veil. I shot it, but this is just a .22. It ran off and I was afraid I'd be attacked again, so I brought the rifle with me. If you want it, you can have it." He held out the rifle toward the drac.

"A shival?" the sheriff repeated as he reached out and took the gun. Ishaan nodded. "I'll have to organize a hunt once this flood is under control. I cannot allow one of those creatures to threaten my town. Thank you for reporting it."

"Any time," Ishaan said. He started to turn away.

"I am sorry your house was destroyed," the sheriff said. "I assume you'll be staying in town?"

"Do I have any choice?" Ishaan replied, but his sarcasm seemed lost on the drac.

"None that I am aware of," he said. "I'll have clean sheets put in your cell. Your weapon will be in my office should you want it back." He shouldered the rifle and headed back toward the heart of town, then paused and glanced back over his shoulder. "While it is not my business to monitor the goings-on of law-abiding citizens, I did notice your friend speaking at length with Sezae. You may want to ask her about your friend's whereabouts."

"Thank you," Ishaan said as he walked away. "I'll do that." But he didn't move from the empty platform. Roan had spoken with Sezae. Ishaan would have bet his inheritance that he knew what that was all about. Yes, he said he wanted them to be a part of his life, and yes, he had meant it, but he didn't really want it forced upon him. He wasn't ready to be a father, not even a part-time one.

But then, Sezae hadn't been ready to be a mother, either, but she'd managed, and she'd done it alone. Slowly, Ishaan walked to the edge of the platform and stepped down into the mud. How many times in the last six years had she needed his help, his support, and gotten nothing more than a monthly check? He was a coward; so selfish, so busy being miserable, so consumed with his own self-loathing, that he missed out on the first five years of his daughter's life. They never could have lived together, but they could have been a family. He could have memories, instead of pictures.

The front door of the inn was shut as he approached, which was a little odd. He couldn't remember ever seeing it closed. It wasn't locked, though, and as he slipped inside, he realized why. All the little wooden tables were stacked in one corner and half a dozen men slept on make-shift mattresses on the floor. People displaced by the flood. Ishaan glanced around, but didn't see Sezae or her father anywhere. He walked over to the bar to wait, barely taking a seat on one of the brass barstools when Sezae stepped out of the back room, her normally pulled-back blond hair falling loose about her shoulders.

She saw him and her eyes widened in surprise.

"What are you doing here?" she whispered. "Roan said you were in Shesade."

"I was," Ishaan said. "I'm looking for him. Is he here?"

"He showed up—" She glanced over at the sleeping men and motioned for him to follow her down a long hallway. "He showed up yesterday. He told me what happened."

"Everything?" Ishaan asked. She nodded. "Of course he did." He started to leave, but she grabbed him by the arm.

"What you did was reprehensible," she said, "but completely understandable. You had every right to be angry, you just made a poor choice in expressing that anger." She frowned at him suddenly. "What are you doing here, anyway?"

"Looking for him," Ishaan said. "I wanted to catch him before he got on the train."

"Why? He said it was over between you two."

"He's mistaken. At least, I hope he is."

"So you don't hate him?"

Ishaan shook his head.

"I love him, more than I ever thought possible. I need to tell him that I'm sorry. Now is he here or not?"

Sezae bit at the edge of her lip, a habit she'd had since they were in grade school.

"Come here," she said, reaching out and taking his hand. "There's something you need to see." She led him to the end of the hall and opened the last door on the right. Pearly morning light filtered in through the sheer blue curtains, falling across an empty bed and a not-so-empty armchair.

Roan sat, his head tilted back and mouth open, snoring softly, an open book in his lap and a little blond angel curled up against his side. She was beautiful, with her mother's fair hair and delicate features, but Ishaan knew that if she opened her eyes, they would be his, green-gold as ripening grain. Ishaan couldn't take his eyes off of them, either of them. He stepped closer. They'd been reading Roan's book of fairy tales.

"She really likes him," Sezae whispered, still holding his hand.

"And you don't care that he's an incubus," Ishaan said.

Sezae hesitated.

"I didn't like it at first," she admitted, "but he explained how it works and I know him—he's a good man in a bad situation. Kind of like someone else I know." She gave his hand a squeeze. "So no, I don't care."

"Good," Ishaan said, "because I'm going to see if I can get him to stick around for a while."

"Well," she said, letting go of his hand and stepping past him, "we'll just get out of your way, then." Gently, she lifted Isha out of Roan's lap. Roan stirred, his book sliding off his lap and down between his leg and the arm of the chair, but he didn't wake. Cradling their daughter to her chest, Sezae glanced up at Ishaan as she headed for the door. "Try not to wake the entire inn," she said with a smirk.

Ishaan waited until he heard the door close, then took a hesitant step toward him. He had so much to say he didn't know where to begin. An apology was definitely called for. He'd start with that. He reached out to touch Roan's shoulder, to wake him, then pulled back. Impulsively, he leaned down and pressed his lips to Roan's. Wake him with a kiss; wasn't that how those fairy stories went?

Roan made a soft sound and kissed him back, his lips parting, the tip of his tongue tracing Ishaan's lower lip before slipping into his mouth. Now *that* wasn't part of any fairy tale Ishaan had ever heard. Ishaan slid his tongue against Roan's, drawing a long, low moan from him. Breathless, Ishaan pulled away, his hand rising up to caress Roan's cheek.

"Ishaan," Roan whispered and Ishaan smiled. Roan's eyelids fluttered, stormy blue-gray eyes unfocused as he stared up at Ishaan. Sleep lifted like a curtain and Roan's eyes went wide. He jumped and glanced around like he wasn't sure where he was. "Ishaan!" he whispered again, a hint of panic in his voice. "Wh-where's Isha, where's Sezae? What are you—" Ishaan reached up and pressed his fingertips to Roan's lips.

"Take a breath, will you?" Ishaan said. "Sezae took Isha so we can talk."

Roan pushed his hand away.

"Talk about what? I've told you every—"

"I'm sorry," Ishaan said. Roan just stared at him. "I shouldn't have done that to you. You didn't deserve it."

"You haven't slept, have you?" Roan asked after a minute.

Ishaan scowled.

"That's not why I'm here. I didn't come looking for you because I *need* you."

"Then why did you?"

"Because I love you." He watched the expression drain from Roan's face. "Yes, you make my life easier. I know I make your life easier, but I don't want to spend the rest of my life with someone because it's easier than being alone. I want to be with you because I love you."

Roan's eyes grew bright with unshed tears. "You love me? After everything I did to you?"

"You can't help what you are," Ishaan said. "You screwed up. It happens. And it's not like I didn't make you pay for it. Can you forgive me for that?" Roan leaped out of the chair, knocking Ishaan over backward, and kissed him. "I take it that's a yes?" Ishaan said with a grin when Roan drew back.

"Yes," Roan said, breathless. "I'm so sorry, Ishaan, I should have—"

"I know," Ishaan said, reaching up and brushing Roan's hair back from his face. "I know." He raised his head, like he was going to kiss him again, but then pulled back. "I do have one more question, though."

"What now?" Roan groaned.

Ishaan smiled.

"Will you marry me?"

Thirty-nine

"I can't believe you said no," Kethic said, snatching Roan's shirt out from under his fingertips. "You're an idiot."

"Am not," Roan said. "Now give me my shirt. I'm going to be late."

"But *Roan*," Kethic said between his teeth, still holding the shirt hostage, "he wanted to take you to *Vraemaar*! Do you know how many people would kill to honeymoon on Vraemaar?"

"I'm guessing a lot," Roan said, making a grab for the stiff, white tuxedo shirt. Kethic held it back out of his reach. "I'm not doing this," Roan said, crossing his arms over his chest. "I'm not six anymore. Now give me my shirt."

"You're no fun," Kethic said, tossing it at him. He glanced in the floor-length mirror and adjusted his midnight blue bowtie. His jacket hung over the back of a chair, but otherwise, he was ready. Roan, on the other hand, was still in his socks and undershirt, his pressed black pants unbuttoned, waiting for him to tuck in the shirt. Someone knocked on the door of the tiny antechamber.

"See," Roan said, "they're waiting for me."

"They are not," Kethic said, stepping over to the door. "You've got fifteen—" He opened the door and glanced out. "You can't come in here," he said. "You're not supposed to see the—Hey!" Roan turned as Ishaan pushed Kethic out of the way and stepped into the room. He was wearing faded jeans and a green polo shirt, and Roan's heart sank.

"You're not ready," Roan said. "D-did you change your mind?"

"No," Ishaan said, like it was dumbest question he'd ever heard. "I just wanted to talk to you for a minute." He glanced at Kethic. "Do you mind?"

"Not at all," Kethic said with a grin.

"I meant leave," Ishaan said when Kethic didn't move.

"Aww, is that any way to talk to your almost-brother-in-law?" His grin widened as he glanced at Roan. "Don't forget, there's a room full of people right outside this door," he said as he left. Ishaan shut the door behind him and locked it.

"So," Roan said as Ishaan started toward him, "what'd you want to talk about?"

"Our honeymoon."

Roan rolled his eyes.

"I told, you, I don't want some expensive trip. I've been to so many worlds I've lost count. I'd rather just go home."

"Which is why I thought you should have this." Ishaan held out a white cardboard box tied with a midnight blue ribbon. It was too big for jewelry. Roan arched an eyebrow and took it, tugging the ribbon off and lifting the lid.

"Oh, Ishaan," Roan said with a laugh, "you shouldn't have." He pulled out the brand new jar of blue lubricant and gave Ishaan a devious smirk. "We'll definitely be needing this. Now, shouldn't you be—" Ishaan grabbed him, wrapped his arms around him, and silenced him with a kiss. The room spun as Roan clung to him, his heart fluttering as Ishaan drew him tight against his lean, strong body. In the three months since the flood, they'd kissed a thousand times, they'd held each other for hours, but this was different. This was their wedding day.

Breathless, Roan pulled back.

"C'mon," he said, "we're going to be late."

A slow smile graced Ishaan's lips.

"What are they going to do, start without us?" Roan gasped as Ishaan pushed him back against the edge of the table and took the jar of gel out of his hand. Ishaan twisted the lid off and set it on the table before reaching out and catching Roan by the waistband of his pants.

"Ishaan, I-I don't think—You know how loud I am," he said, feeling his cheeks heat up as Ishaan unbuttoned his pants.

"What's the matter, you don't want everyone hearing us having sex?" Ishaan asked as Roan's pants slid down to his ankles.

"Your parents are out there," Roan said dryly. "And my pants better not get wrinkled." He hesitated, then hopped up on the table. Ishaan pulled his pants off and draped them over the back of a chair. "For the record," Roan said, "I tried to stop this. That's cold!" Ishaan had pulled his briefs off, leaving him sitting bare-ass on the polished wood. "I hope nobody eats on this table."

Ishaan laughed.

"I'm sure somebody will wash your butt-prints off it." Roan leaned back on his elbows and spread his legs as Ishaan dipped his fingers into the lubricant. He arched his back, groaning as Ishaan rubbed the cool, tingling gel across his opening. "Damn, you're beautiful," Ishaan whispered. "Your face, your eyes, the way your lips part as I slip inside you—" Ishaan eased one finger in, then a second, drawing a helpless sound from Roan's parted lips. "I love that sound," Ishaan said, leaning down to bestow a soft kiss on the inside of Roan's knee. "I love hearing you lose control." He rubbed upward into Roan's body, pressing against that magic spot, and Roan cried out as lightning danced up through his body, slivers of cold heat that made him tremble.

"I'm glad," Roan gasped. "Now, quit toying with me. We don't have all day."

"Always in such a hurry," Ishaan said, stroking his finger along one side of that place and then along the other, his touch fleeting, teasing. Roan clenched his fists and struggled to hold still. He would not squirm. He would not give Ishaan the satisfaction. "Are you sure you're ready for me?"

"Yes, yes," Roan hissed between his teeth. "Hurry, *please*."

Ishaan chuckled and rubbed deep into him again. Roan choked back a shout and bucked as Ishaan withdrew. "Hurry," he moaned as Ishaan unbuttoned his jeans and let them drop. "Ishaan, hurry."

Ishaan spread the gel over his skin, standing back and letting Roan watch. Roan's whole body was on fire, aching. He needed Ishaan inside him in a way that had nothing to do with the demon.

Roan spread his legs wider as Ishaan stepped up between them. Ishaan's large, strong hands slid down the insides of his thighs and Roan raised his hips, moaning as Ishaan sank into him in one long, smooth stroke. Roan shuddered, his muscles clenching, gripping Ishaan tight and drawing him deeper.

"Sweet Maele, you feel so good," Ishaan whispered, his hands sliding down to Roan's hips, holding him still as he began to thrust into him.

Roan lay back on the table, propped up on his elbows, waves of pleasure rolling through his body, and couldn't take his eyes off Ishaan. His face, flushed and damp with sweat, his dark curls sticking to his forehead, his eyes downcast, watching himself slide in and out of Roan, was the most incredible thing he'd ever seen.

Ishaan glanced up and their eyes met. For an instant, nothing else in the universe existed. Then Ishaan stopped, buried deep inside him, and leaned forward, bracing his hands on the table on either side of Roan's waist.

"What is it?" Roan asked, his body tight and shuddering, begging for more.

"I want to see," Ishaan said. Roan opened his mouth, then closed it again. He didn't have any idea what Ishaan was talking about. "I want to see the incubus. I want you to let it out." Roan shook his head, suddenly cold inside.

"No," he said. "No, there's no reason. If I keep it fed, it won't ever—"

"I want to see it," Ishaan said again. He leaned closer. "Please, Roan."

"Right now?" Roan asked, his voice hollow. Ishaan nodded. Roan could feel an emptiness consuming him. There was no need for this. He'd never let the demon out. There was no need to see Ishaan look at him that way again. Roan swallowed hard and took a shaking breath. He let his walls down, his scalp tingling as the horns pushed through. He closed his eyes, fighting the urge to gag as his tongue writhed inside his mouth, and tensed, raising his butt off the table as his tail slipped out of his spine and slithered down between Ishaan's legs.

Ishaan gasped and Roan felt tears gather in the back of his throat.

"I didn't realize you got tighter, too," Ishaan said. There was a long, long silence. "Roan," Ishaan said, and Roan steeled himself for the worst. "It's okay."

Roan opened his eyes and raised his head, looking up into Ishaan's face.

Ishaan smiled. "I love you, no matter what you look like. I needed you to know that." His lips met Roan's and he made an appreciative sound. "I love the way your mouth tastes," he said, and kissed him again, his tongue sliding across Roan's and sending a shudder through his body. Ishaan drew back and looked him over again, not a trace of disgust or revulsion on his face. After a moment, he reached up and touched one of Roan's horns. "So, I understand the purpose of the tongue, and the tail, but these...I don't get it."

"Well," Roan said, a hesitant smile tugging the corners of his mouth, "I'm not sure, but...Kethic always said that if someone were to lie on their back and brace their feet against them, with their knees bent, it would be just right for me to—" He stuck his tongue out and flicked it suggestively.

"Ah, well, we'll have to try that, won't we?" Ishaan said. He straightened up and glanced down behind him, at Roan's tail curled around his left ankle. "Can I see that for a minute?" Roan obliged, his tail sliding up the back of Ishaan's leg and across his ass. Ishaan took it in his hand, letting it wrap around his fingers. "It's amazing," he said.

"Glad you like it," Roan said, "but maybe we can have show and tell later. We're kind of in the middle of something."

"Right, I'd almost forgotten." Ishaan pulled his fingers free and Roan jumped in surprise as he dipped the tip of Roan's tail in the jar of lubricant. They just stared at each other for a minute, then Ishaan let go of Roan's tail and braced his hands on the table again. "You don't have to hide what you are anymore, not from me."

"But, Ishaan," Roan said, glancing at his gleaming blue tail tip, "it-it's so..."

"Kinky?" Ishaan suggested.

"I was going to say strange, but kinky works. What's gotten into you? You've always been so traditional."

"Well, somebody—and I'm not naming names—violated me with their tail a few months ago and I haven't been able to stop thinking about it since."

"So it's my fault you turned into a sex fiend," Roan said, reaching up and brushing Ishaan's hair back from his face.

"Pretty much," Ishaan replied and then he kissed him again. Distracted by Ishaan's tongue in his mouth, Roan smeared the gel up Ishaan's back and across the backs of his thighs. Ishaan broke the kiss and frowned. "I'm going to need a bath now, thank you. Do you need help?"

"You try threading a needle with your eyes closed," Roan said. He concentrated, sliding up the inside of one thigh and then feeling between Ishaan's cheeks for the opening.

"Almost...up a little," Ishaan said. "Yes, right—" His sentenced dissolved into one long moan as Roan's tail squirmed into him.

"Does that feel good?" Roan asked. Ishaan looked down at him, his eyes hooded.

"What do you think?" Ishaan began to move again, long, slow thrusts that made everything inside Roan grow hot and tight. He arched his back off the table, his hands opening and closing, grasping at empty air as he shuddered and shook. As Ishaan drove deeper, harder, Roan curled his tail, pressing into that spot inside Ishaan. He cried out and grabbed Roan's hand, their fingers entwining as they held on to each other for dear life. "I-I'm gonna—I—" He tensed, his eyes filled with a look of wonder as he spilled himself inside of Roan.

With his free hand, Roan reached for himself, but Ishaan pushed his hand away.

"Mine," Ishaan said, his voice thick and deep, and he wrapped his long fingers around Roan, a couple hard thrusts and firm strokes all it took to send Roan over the edge. He cried out and came across his chest and stomach, his body shaking like a knot had been untied inside him and everything was unraveling. He could feel himself falling and tightened his grip on Ishaan, trying to stay in control.

But he didn't have to. He had no walls to keep up, no monster to keep hidden. He closed his eyes, a single tear slipping from the corner of his eye. He let himself fall and discovered that he could fly.

It felt like hours before Roan stopped shaking. He couldn't catch his breath, the pleasure echoing inside him as Ishaan leaned down, pressing so deep that Roan almost cried out again. Ishaan kissed him, tiny movements of his hips prolonging the exquisite agony. Ishaan's fingers tangled in the sweat-damp hair at the nape of Roan's neck and Roan wrapped his arms around Ishaan's broad shoulders like he never wanted to let go.

Too soon, though, Ishaan broke the kiss and drew back.

"So," he said, breathless, "now that that's settled, what do you say we go get married?"

Roan grinned.

"We agreed on the abbreviated ceremony, didn't we?"

"Yeah."

"Good, 'cause I'm eager to see if Kethic was right about these horns."

Bonus Features

Warning: This section contains spoilers.
If you have not read *Breach*, proceed with caution.

Honeymoon
Katica Locke

As soon as dinner was over, Ishaan ducked back into his study to check his e-mail again, leaving Roan to clear the table. Still nothing. Trying not to appear anxious or impatient, he returned to the kitchen to dry the dishes that Roan was washing. Once the kitchen was straightened up, Roan went back into the spare bedroom to work on organizing his books. He'd amassed quite a collection in the three months since the rebuild had been finished, and since Ishaan loved listening to him read, it was a guilty pleasure Ishaan could completely condone.

Back into the study Ishaan went, only this time, his previously empty inbox wasn't empty. Hardly daring to breathe, he clicked on the message from Dr. Shine Diram of the Grand Nethmalonian Museum in Siva Delta. Ishaan wasn't entirely sure where that was, but this was the e-mail he'd been waiting two days for. Reading it carefully, he couldn't stop the broad grin that tugged at his lips. Roan was going to love this. Then he reached the bottom of the message and his smile faltered, but only a little.

Logging off and powering down the computer, he hurried into the bedroom and unlocked the closet, digging around until he found the matching leather suitcases someone had given them for a wedding gift. Picking up the smaller one, he schooled his features into something as close to impassive as he could get, and headed into what was becoming Roan's library.

Ishaan's husband was standing on a chair, barefoot, in worn jeans and a tight T-shirt, his long golden hair pulled back in a ponytail at the nape of his neck.

"Time for *Willowgrove*?" Roan asked, his attention focused on the handful of books he was rearranging. *Willowgrove* was little more than a prime-time soap opera about the diverse—and horny—inhabitants of a low-income apartment complex, but it was one of their favorites. They had never missed an episode. Until now.

Ishaan tossed the suitcase onto the spare bed with a *thump* that made the springs creak. Roan glanced over his shoulder. "What's up?" Then his gaze fell upon the suitcase and all the color drained from his face. "Ishaan, what did I—"

"Why don't you tell me?" Ishaan asked, crossing his arms over his chest.

Roan's pale eyes went wide, darting back and forth as he opened and closed his mouth like a fish. "I-I-I don't know! I didn't do anything!"

Ishaan couldn't keep a straight face any longer. "I know," he said with a laugh. "I just thought it'd be fun to relive the good old days. You know, when I used to threaten to kick you out of the house every other day?"

"I remember," Roan said, glancing at the book in his hand, and then at Ishaan, as if contemplating whether the damage done to the book would be worth the damage done to Ishaan. Finally, he shoved it onto the shelf. "So, Mr. Comedian, you dragged that suitcase out of the closet *just* to scare the crap out of me?"

"No. I want you to pack some things," Ishaan said. "Enough for six or seven days, mild climate, possibly rainy."

"Where am I going?" Roan asked with a frown.

"*We* are going on a trip," Ishaan said. "I know you said you didn't want a honeymoon—"

Roan groaned and turned back to his books.

"But this is something you can't miss, and you'll never forgive yourself if you don't go."

"What is it?"

"A surprise. Now pack you things. We're leaving in half an hour."

"Half an hour!" Roan exclaimed, hopping down from the chair. "But what about *Willowgrove*?"

"I'll set the DVR," Ishaan said, rolling his eyes as he turned and headed into the bathroom to gather up his toiletries. Roan wasn't the only one who needed to pack.

* * *

Slouched in the passenger's seat of their car, staring out into the darkness beyond the narrow beams of the headlights, Roan couldn't decide if he should be excited or annoyed. He did like surprises, but Ishaan had been so vague and unhelpful when it came to packing, he was just sure they'd get where they were going and he wouldn't have half of what he needed.

"I didn't pack a bathing suit," Roan said, glancing over at Ishaan.

"You won't need one."

"Or a heavy coat."

"You won't need that, either."

"Or a hat."

"Now that, you might need," Ishaan said, then his gaze darted over to Roan and he grinned. "On second thought, no, you won't."

"You're enjoying this way too much," Roan said, slumping back in the seat with his arms crossed over his chest, pretending to sulk. That just made Ishaan laugh more.

"You bet I am."

Soon, the lights of Devaen began to flicker through the thinning trees, lamps hanging from porches and glowing warm and golden in windows. They rolled down the middle of the wide, dirt road, the wheels making almost no sound in the packed mud, the earth still wet from that morning's rain. Roan was surprised when Ishaan pulled over and parked in front of the inn.

"C'mon," Ishaan said, opening the door and climbing out. "Grab your bag."

"We're staying at the inn?" Roan asked, dubiously following Ishaan's lead. Suitcase in hand, he followed his husband inside. There were a few people seated around the big common room, enjoying the fire and a mug of ale or finishing up their evening meal. Roan was glad not to recognize any of them. That meant the inn was seeing more guests. Now that Ishaan didn't have to sleep in the jail, the rumors of monsters and demons were dying out.

Behind the bar, Sezae's father eyed them with a resigned scowl on his face, then threw his towel on the bar and headed down the back hall. Ishaan fidgeted with the handle of his suitcase, wearing his own scowl as he stared down at the floor. All things considered, that was probably all the better their relationship was ever going to get.

After a moment, Ishaan glanced up, his scowl breaking into a warm smile as the rapid patter of small, bare feet came down the hall toward them. Isha, now six, ran across the common room, her pale pink nightdress and long, blond hair streaming out behind her, and Ishaan barely had time to drop his suitcase before she leaped into his arms.

"Daddy!" she cried, arms tight around his neck as she hugged him.

"Hi, sweetie," Ishaan said, giving her a kiss on the cheek. Roan set his suitcase down as Ishaan placed her back on her feet. She hugged him, too, then grabbed his hand and tried to drag him back to her room. "C'mon, Roan," she said. "Read me a story."

"Sorry, sweetie," Ishaan said. "Roan and I can't stay. I just need to talk to your mom for a minute."

"Oh, c'mon," Roan said. "It'll only take a few minutes."

Ishaan shook his head. "Sorry, but we have a very tight schedule to keep. If we miss the train, we can forget the whole trip."

"*The train?*" Roan and Isha said at the same time. They glanced at each other and she giggled, hiding her smile behind her hand.

"Can I ride the train with you?" Isha asked.

Before Ishaan had to say no to those big, beseeching hazel eyes, Sezae emerged from the hallway. "No train rides for little girls who don't brush their hair before bed."

"But Mommy!"

"No buts," Sezae said. "Go brush your hair and when Daddy and Roan get back from their special trip, we'll talk about taking a train ride."

"Yay!" Isha cheered, running back down the hall.

"You know about this trip?" Roan asked before Ishaan had a chance to speak. "Where is he taking me?"

"Sorry, I don't know that," she said with a smile, "and even I did, he said it was a surprise." She turned to Ishaan. "We opened the barn door for you. There should be room for your car beside the wagon."

"Thanks, Sezae," Ishaan said, leaning over and giving her a kiss on the cheek. "And if you want to take Isha on a train ride, I'm more than happy to pay for it."

"Well, I thought maybe the four of us could ride up to Shesade and have lunch or something."

"Oh." Ishaan glanced over at Roan, who grinned. "Sure, that sounds like fun."

"Great," Sezae said with a smile. "We'll talk about it when you get back." She glanced over at Roan and winked at him. "Have fun."

"I hope so," Roan said. "Hard to know when no one will tell me where we're going."

"Are you going to whine like this on the whole trip?" Ishaan asked.

"Maybe. I'll stop if you tell me."

"I like the whining," Ishaan said. "Wait here with the bags while I put the car away."

As soon as he was gone, Roan turned to Sezae. "Please, just tell me where we're going. I promise I'll act surprised."

She laughed. "I'm sorry, I really don't know, but knowing Ishaan, when he says it's the opportunity of a lifetime, he means it. I mean really, could you see anything else making him spend a night away from home?"

Roan hadn't considered that. "He said six or seven nights. He can't...He can't expect to stay awake the whole time, can he?"

"I think he trusts you to look after him," Sezae said. "Hang on while I go get Isha; we'll see you off at the station."

Roan found himself pacing as he waited, weighing this new complication against whatever Ishaan had planned. He couldn't think of anything that was worth the risk, not ice moons or amethyst cliffs or glittery rainbow waterfalls. When Ishaan returned, Roan stepped in front of him, fists planted decisively on his hips.

"I don't think we should go," he said.

Ishaan stopped dead, looking like he'd been slapped. "Why not? What—Did-Did Sezae say something?"

"No," Roan said, shaking his head, "but she reminded me that we're going to be away from home for several days. What if...What if something happens? I just don't think that some silly honeymoon is worth putting you through that."

Ishaan stepped closed and took Roan's face between his hands, then leaned down and kissed him soundly on the lips. "I love you, my little demon," he murmured, only loud enough for Roan to hear. "Don't worry, I made arrangements so that nothing will happen. Now come on. Relax and enjoy yourself. This is a once in a—"

"Once in a lifetime opportunity," Roan said. "Yeah, yeah, Sezae told me. You know...I might feel better about this if you told me where we're going."

With a laugh and playful shove, Ishaan stepped past him and picked up both suitcases. "Come on, the train is due any minute."

"Hang on, Sezae said—"

"Here we are!" Sezae and Isha came hurrying down the hall, slippers on the little bare feet and a long coat over her nightdress. Isha's hair was neatly brushed and pulled back in a long braid. "Just in time to wave good-bye."

Roan took the bags from Ishaan, grinning as his husband scooped the little girl up. "Oof, you're getting too big to carry, sweetie," Ishaan said.

"That's what Mommy says," Isha said, wrapping her arms around Ishaan's neck and leaning her head on his shoulder. It was so wonderful to see how Ishaan had warmed up to his daughter, how much happier he was. Roan knew, if he never did another good thing in his life, he would die happy having made this possible.

They headed for the station, Ishaan leading the way while Roan hung back, waiting for Sezae to get her coat from behind the bar. She hurried up beside him and took his arm, falling into step with him. It was a little strange, having her be so comfortable with him. Although Roan had a lot of experience with both men and women when it came to sex, he'd never really bothered to have a relationship with either, before he met Ishaan. He'd never stayed in one place long enough.

He didn't think she had any romantic or sexual feelings toward him—he was pretty sure she still carried a tiny flame for Ishaan—but it felt like more than just friendship to him. It was a closeness, an intimacy that he couldn't really describe. Maybe it was just that she knew what he was and didn't care. He didn't think he'd ever meet anyone like that. He briefly wondered if their unconventional little family would ever get to the point where Ishaan and Sezae would want to get married. Maybe after Isha was a bit more grown up and could be trusted not to forget to lock her door at night. Not that Ishaan did much wandering anymore. And it would be nice to see the girls every day, and read to Isha every night—

The high scream of the train whistle cut through Roan's thoughts and he glanced up as the big, black steam engine emerged from the trees on the edge of town, the brakes squealing as it strained to finish slowing the string of cars, both passenger and freight. With a sigh, he let his fanciful imaginings fade away. What they had was more wonderful than he ever thought he'd find. He didn't need to waste time dreaming of things that would never happen. He and Sezae hurried to catch up with Ishaan, who was already climbing the stairs to the train platform. Isha raised her head, covering her ears with her hands as the train puffed and chugged and hissed past the station, steam and smoke escaping in great, billowing clouds as it rattled and screeched to a stop.

The door of the first passenger car opened and a set of shiny, brass folding stairs clanked down into place. The conductor stepped off the train, holding a lantern as he assisted a young woman and two older gentlemen with their luggage. Roan glanced over at Sezae, who smiled as the three headed for the inn.

"All aboard!" the conductor called, raising the lantern high.

"Time to go, sweetie," Ishaan said, giving his daughter another hug before setting her on her feet.

"Love you, Daddy," Isha said.

"Love you, too," Ishaan said. Sezae let go of Roan's arm and stepped over beside their daughter, giving Ishaan a kiss on the cheek before taking Isha's hand.

"Have fun, you two," Sezae said, grinning as they hurried across the platform to the train. Ishaan pulled a pair of tickets out of his jacket pocket and showed them to the conductor, who used a punch to mark a corner of each one. Taking the larger of the two suitcases from Roan, Ishaan mounted the three brass steps and disappeared through the narrow door of the train. Roan followed, pausing in the aisle as he was overcome by the sudden memory of the last time he'd been on a train, the day he arrived in Devaen a little over a year and a half ago. The smell was just the same—smoke from the boiler, perfume, sweat. He shook it off and leaned into the empty seat beside him to wave through the window at the girls. Sezae and Isha waved back, then Sezae took her daughter's hand and they headed back to the inn. Roan watched them until they disappeared, then hurried to catch up with Ishaan, who was halfway down the car.

They passed to the next car, occupied by only a few sleepy-eyed travelers, and then into the dining car, which was empty save for a lone gentleman seated at the bar, sipping a glass of what looked like scotch. At the front of the train, the whistle blew and a moment later the car lurched, making the glass bottles rattle inside their protective cabinet. The bar patron's glass never even shook as he raised it to his lips.

The next car was for the wealthy travelers, each with their own small, separate compartment. Ishaan walked past all of these as well. Finally, they entered the last car before the freight started, which Roan was startled to discover contained only six cabins. Still not large by any means, they had to be the most luxurious—and expensive—accommodations on the train.

Ishaan opened the door to the first compartment on the left, holding it as he ushered Roan inside. There were padded, bench seats on either side of the compartment, one facing forward, the other to the rear, with a place beneath each seat to store their luggage.

"Nice," Roan said, setting his suitcase down and shrugging out of his coat. There was even a hook on the inside of the door for him to hang it.

"Wait'll you see the best part," Ishaan said with a smile. He stepped over to the outside wall of the train car and released a heavy-duty catch on either side of the ceiling, carefully lowering the wall until it became a fold-away bed, complete with a heavy quilt and crisp sheets. There were nooks in the wall that held pillows and a spare blanket, one on either side of the window, the thick curtains drawn back to reveal nothing but darkness outside. Kneeling on the bed, Ishaan reached across and closed the curtains.

"I see you weren't kidding when you said you'd made arrangements," Roan said with a smile. "So, is it a long trip, or just enough time to wrinkle these sheets?"

"Long enough," Ishaan said. "We'll get there mid-morning tomorrow."

"So, farther than Prythaen. Lyrae? Tormena? Rolara?"

"Guess all you want; I'm not telling."

"Smug bastard," Roan said, giving him a little shove, just to put him off balance and maybe wipe that much too pleased with himself smirk off his face. Of course, the train had to choose that moment to turn into a curve, causing Roan to list drunkenly and for Ishaan to land on his back in the middle of the bed. Both of them laughing, Roan climbed onto the bed with him and flopped down, his head on Ishaan's chest as they looked up at the ceiling. It was plain wood paneling. He closed his eyes as Ishaan began to drag his fingers back though Roan's hair, his nails lightly scraping the scalp and raising goose bumps down Roan's arms.

"Do you know how much I love this—holding you, kissing you, falling asleep beside you?" Ishaan asked, his voice low.

"I do," Roan replied. This was one of those little rituals they had almost every night.

"It makes what happens after I fall asleep easier to bear."

"I know." This was something they were still working on—getting Ishaan to let go of his guilt and disgust. After spending half of his life treated as an outcast and a monster, letting go wasn't easy. Roan understood that all too well.

"Do you want to go have a nightcap, or just get ready for bed?" Ishaan asked after minute. Roan was struggling to keep his eyes open, soothed by the rhythm of Ishaan's fingers through his hair.

"I wouldn't want to disturb the guy at the bar," Roan said around a yawn. "He didn't look like he wanted company."

"Yeah, now there was a man who obviously knew how to take his drinking seriously," Ishaan said, his chuckle shaking Roan's head on his chest. "Bedtime, then. There's a washroom at the rear of the car. You want to go first, or shall I?"

"I better, considering how long you take in the bathroom," Roan said, reluctantly pushing himself up into a sitting position. Ishaan helped him along with a steady hand in the middle of his back.

"Relax, there's no bathtub," Ishaan said.

"Oh, how will you survive?"

"Make jokes now, but you're the one who's going to have to smell me after six days without a bath."

"Great Maele, somebody crack a window," Roan said with a laugh, waving his hand back and forth in front of his face, pretending to fan away the stench. He hurried out of the cabin as Ishaan grabbed one of the pillows out of its nook and prepared to throw. Grinning to himself, he made his way down the aisle, his hands held slightly out to either side as the car swayed, a little like a ship at sea. The washroom was cramped, just a toilet, urinal, and sink, lit by a dim light that flickered in time with the *click-clack* of the wheels rolling along the rails. It took a moment to realize that the light was electric. Surprising, since electricity was a rare commodity restricted to the largest cities—or in Ishaan's case, the wealthiest people.

The washroom was out of paper towels, so he shook the water off his hands and then finished drying them on the seat of his jeans before heading back down the corridor to their cabin. His steps rocking with the motion of the train, he reached out, steadying himself on the walls of the corridor. Suddenly, the train gave a lurch to the side and the overhead lights blinked, plunging the car into absolute darkness for the length of a breath.

Roan stopped, his heart pounding, and stood there, blinking, even after the lights came back on. He couldn't remember ever having experienced such complete and absolute blackness. The narrow corridor had not a single window. He took a bracing breath, trying to quiet the blood rushing through his ears, and continued on, his steps a little quicker. Another lurch, another flicker, and he threw himself down the hall, jerking open the door to the cabin and stepping inside.

Ishaan turned, giving him a curious look as he pulled the door closed again.

"It is fucking black out there," Roan said, with a sheepish laugh. "And there's no towels in the bathroom."

"Oh," Ishaan said. "Just like at home, then."

"Don't start that again," Roan said, pulling his suitcase out from under the seat that the bed was resting on. Ishaan had already retrieved his and was gathering up his pajamas and toothbrush. Roan just wanted a clean pair of boxers for the morning and a jar of lube for when Ishaan started getting restless. Everything else could wait. "I didn't marry you so I could do your laundry, and since you're the one who insists on having a bath every night, I think it's fair for you to do the washing once in a while."

"Once in a while?" Ishaan repeated. "*Once* in a *while*? You've done laundry *twice* since we moved into the house, and the last time, you put your red boxers in with my white towels."

"Really?" Roan said. "I thought you bought new pink towels."

Ishaan laughed, signaling Roan's victory in their mock argument. "All right, I'll do all the laundry, but you're in charge of all the sweeping and dusting, and cleaning the refrigerator out once a month."

"All right, all right—Slave-driver," Roan grumbled, closing his suitcase and shoving it back under the bed. The train jolted and the lights blinked out in the cabin. For some reason, it wasn't as startling as it had been in the hall.

"I'm going to go brush my teeth," Ishaan said, stepping past him in the small space. "Be right back." Once he was gone, Roan peeled his shirt off, tossing it down beside his suitcase as he toed off his shoes and unbuttoned his jeans. Wearing just his boxers, he turned the blankets down and arranged the pillows, waiting for Ishaan to get back. He had to brace his hands on the mattress as the train lurched and the lights blinked out again, and he jumped as something heavy thumped into the wall of the cabin. Opening the door, he peeked out, surprised to see Ishaan rubbing his shoulder as he gathered up his clothes from off the corridor floor.

"What happened?" he asked, stepping out to help.

"Lost my balance," Ishaan said. "You're right, it's fucking dark out here."

"Told you," Roan said with a grin. Ishaan glanced up, his gaze lingering for a moment and reminding Roan that he was in the hall in just his underwear. Roan grabbed a shoe and Ishaan's shirt before retreating into the cabin, Ishaan following right behind. He closed the door and slid the bolt into place, locking them inside.

"Do you mind if I open the curtains?" Ishaan asked, dropping his things onto his suitcase. "Otherwise, we won't be able to see a thing once the lights are off."

"Sure, go ahead," Roan said, tossing the shoe and shirt down as Ishaan climbed onto the bed and parted the heavy drapes. Roan couldn't see anything but more blackness outside, but he supposed it couldn't hurt. Ishaan slipped his long legs under the blanket, lying down closest to the wall. That meant he would have to crawl over Roan to get out of the cabin, and while Roan wasn't exactly a heavy sleeper, he still felt nervous. He checked the lock on the door. It seemed so flimsy; even if Ishaan couldn't manage to slide it back in his sleep, it wouldn't take much more then a forceful shove to splinter the wood and let him out.

"Are you sure we couldn't have waited for a morning train?" Roan asked, climbing into bed. "I think there's one coming through next week."

"Worried?" Ishaan asked, reaching out to rub Roan's back as Roan opened the jar of lube and made sure it was within easy reach.

"A little," Roan admitted. "Lights out?"

"Go ahead," Ishaan said. Roan flipped the switch and the room went black, only this time, the light didn't immediately come back on. After less than a minute, though, he realized that the room wasn't completely dark. The pale blue light of the crescent moon filtered in through the window, painting a flickering square on the blanket, and a faint green stripe outlined the door and window—probably luminescent paint to show the exits in case of an emergency.

"That's not so bad," Roan said, settling himself on his side, with the warmth of Ishaan's body at his back.

"Nope," Ishaan said. Roan smiled to himself as Ishaan rolled over, spooning him, one arm wrapping around his chest and holding him close. "Don't worry," Ishaan said after a moment, his breath warm on the back of Roan's head. "I know you won't let anything happen."

"Thanks," Roan said. "No pressure."

"I love you," Ishaan said. "Awake or asleep. He figured it out first, remember?" It was still a little strange to hear Ishaan refer to himself as another person, but it was better than him silently hating that part of himself. "We're not going anywhere."

"All right," Roan said, but he laced his fingers with Ishaan's, just to be safe. "I love you, too. Both of you."

Ishaan kissed the back of his head and snuggled a little closer. "And just so you know, I'm not exaggerating about how tight of a schedule we have. It was hard enough convincing our gracious hosts to wait a day and a half for our arrival. If we're even a couple of hours late, we'll miss our chance."

"They sound like wonderful people," Roan said. "They aren't family, are they?"

"No," Ishaan said. "I've never met them before."

"So...how do you know them?"

"Quit fishing and go to sleep."

"You're cruel," Roan moaned, but he settled down and closed his eyes. He didn't sleep, though. He wasn't sure if it was just the intermittent lurching of the train car keeping him awake, or the knowledge of what would happen if Ishaan got past him. His biggest fear was that whoever Ishaan found would be armed and that they would fight back. He'd never forgive himself if Ishaan got hurt.

Roan dozed, drifting at the edge of sleep, but he jerked wide awake, his heart pounding, as Ishaan stirred behind him. With a low, throaty groan, Ishaan tightened his grip, his hand sliding up Roan's chest, his breath growing heavier on the back of Roan's head. He didn't even try to get up.

"You were right," Roan murmured, reaching over to dip his fingers into the jar of lube. He prepared himself quickly, because even though this Ishaan was now far from the frustrated, brutish man that he had been, Roan saw no reason to test him, to see what he would do if denied release. Roan liked to think he wouldn't do anything, but he didn't want to find out for certain. And it wasn't like Roan minded having sex.

After shoving his boxers down to his knees, Roan reached back and worked Ishaan's pajamas down, freeing his already hard cock. Rubbing the head against his slick opening, Roan closed his eyes, moaning softly as Ishaan pressed forward, sliding into him in one slow, smooth thrust. Ishaan began to rock his hips, a steady rhythm that didn't do much for Roan, but that wasn't really the point. He didn't mind. It was enough to be there for Ishaan, to free him from the prison of guilt that he'd lived in for most of his life. Together, they could both have normal lives.

When Ishaan came, it was with a muted grunt, his grip of Roan tightening as his hips jerked. Finished, he rolled over, dragging half of the covers with him. Roan just smiled to himself, pulled his boxers back up, and snuggled close to Ishaan's side, finally able to fall asleep.

* * *

Morning sunlight streamed in through the sooty train windows, casting a dingy, gray light on the small table between them as they finished their breakfast, Roan picking at the hash browns that Ishaan had been unable to finish as Ishaan sipped his coffee and inconspicuously watched the other passengers as they ate. None of them had any idea who he was, or what he was capable of, or what would have happened in the night if Roan hadn't been there. To them, he was just a guy enjoying breakfast with his husband. It was a surreal feeling.

"Do you want to move?" Ishaan asked. He turned his gaze back to Roan, who had frozen with his fork halfway to his lips.

"To another table?" Roan asked, arching an eyebrow.

Ishaan chuckled. "No. To another planet."

"Why?" Roan looked faintly alarmed.

"I was just thinking," Ishaan said. "Wouldn't it be nice to start over somewhere, to have neighbors who don't nail their windows shut, to shop in stores that don't charge us three times as much as anyone else, to live in a place where we're just a normal couple?"

"Is that what we're doing? House hunting?" Roan asked.

"No," Ishaan said. "This is something that just occurred to me."

"But what about Isha?" Roan asked, his voice soft. "What about Sezae?"

Ishaan took another drink of his lukewarm coffee. There was that. "We could visit," he said, but the words sounded so empty it made his chest hurt to hear them. He had missed out on so much of his daughter's life already.

"Maybe they'd want to come with us," Roan said, then quickly added, "and live in their own, separate house, of course."

"Sezae won't leave her father and brother," Ishaan said, shaking his head. He sighed. "No, it was a foolish idea. I guess people like me don't get to start over. We're cursed to carry our past with us forever."

"Everyone has a past," Roan said, "and running away from yours won't rid you of it. Trust me on that. I've been running since I was fifteen. And let me tell you something—not once in all those years since I left have I had a place that I could call home. Until now." He set his fork down and reached across the table, taking Ishaan's hand. "I like our house. I like Devaen. I love Isha and Sezae. And the people are getting better. They'll forget, or they'll move, or they'll die, and the stories will die with them. Give it time."

"You're right," Ishaan said, smiling as he stroked the back of Roan's hand with his thumb. Roan gave him a flirty smile, his pale eyes sparkling.

"It's still early," he said, his voice low and suggestive. "Do you want to go back to bed?"

Ishaan struggled against the temptation. Even though Roan offered nearly every night—and frequently during the middle of the day—Ishaan couldn't imagine that he actually wanted to have sex, not if he had to satisfy Ishaan at night, too. So Ishaan usually declined and Roan pretended to be disappointed. Of course, that wasn't to say that Roan acted put upon on the rare occasion when Ishaan couldn't resist making love to his husband. He was either a very good actor or he really didn't mind.

Ishaan glanced out the window, the thick forests and rugged mountains having given way to open farmland sometime during the night. Now, it looked more industrial, with large buildings lining paved streets, factories and warehouses, probably. He reached out, stopping a passing train attendant. "Excuse me. What is the next stop?"

"Scanevra," said the young woman with a smile. "We should be arriving in about half an hour."

"Thanks," Ishaan said. He glanced back over at Roan. "Sorry, that's where we get off."

"Scanevra?" Roan asked, his eyes widening. "That's the second largest city on Eshaedra!"

"I know," Ishaan said, grinning as he watched Roan wolf down the last couple of bites of his hash browns, wipe his face on his napkin, and practically leap up out of his chair.

"C'mon, let's get our stuff." He headed down the aisle toward the sleeping car.

"Hang on," Ishaan said, taking a moment to drain the last of his coffee from the cup. He shouldn't have. It was cold and bitter and a little gritty, and he struggled not to make a face as he set the cup down and left a couple of coins on the table for a tip. By the time he got back to their cabin, Roan had put the bed away and was busy stuffing his dirty clothes into his suitcase. "What's your hurry?" Ishaan asked with a laugh.

Roan glanced over his shoulder. "I've never been to Scanevra, but I've heard about it. The theaters, the museums, the library, the churches, the parks, the zoo—and we've only got six days to see it all!" He was so excited, Ishaan felt bad for having to disappoint him.

"Sorry, my little demon, but we're not staying in Scanevra."

"What?"

"We're just passing through," Ishaan said, "but we can come back another time and do all the touristy stuff."

Roan scowled at him. "Like I'm ever going anywhere with you again, after the emotional turmoil you've put me through."

"Drama queen," Ishaan teased, pulling him close for a kiss. He could feel the train staring to brake, slowing for the stop ahead, but he was still tempted to put the bed back down and at least give Roan *something* to smile about. Unfortunately, there wasn't time for sex, but maybe...

Ishaan hesitated, then began walking Roan backward across the cabin, his hands gripping and kneading Roan's tight ass through his jeans.

"Ishaan, what—" Roan stopped as Ishaan pushed him down onto the bench seat. Sinking to his knees between Roan's spread legs, Ishaan quickly unbuttoned and unzipped Roan's pants. Roan drew a sharp breath, like he'd been stung, and grabbed Ishaan's hands, holding them still. "Ishaan, you don't have to do—"

Ishaan leaned forward, rising up on his knees to silence Roan with a kiss. Taking his hands back, he finished freeing Roan's cock from inside his boxers. Protestations aside, he was already hard. Bowing his head, Ishaan took Roan into his mouth, moving slowly as his lips slid down the silky shaft. He hadn't done this since the night he'd realized that Roan loved him, the first time he'd ever taken a guy into his mouth. It had been such an emotionally painful experience, with so much misunderstanding and unintentional hurt on both sides, Roan had never asked him to do it again, and he'd never offered. He was going to have to change that.

Sucking and licking, he began to bob his head, tuning in to Roan's signals, paying attention to what make him gasp for breath, what made him moan, and what made him squirm. He could feel Roan trembling, his breaths short and fast, and he drew back, wrapping a hand around Roan's shaft and stroking him hard and fast as he sucked on just the head, his tongue teasing the slit.

"Oh-*oh!*" Roan cried, his voice rising in pitch as his body tensed. It was Ishaan's first taste of semen, and while he certainly hadn't been missing out, it wasn't as bad as he'd thought it might be. Swallowing reflexively, he lapped up the salty drops as Roan shuddered through each wave of aftershocks. Finally, Roan put a hand on his shoulder.

"St-stop," he panted. "Too much." Ishaan drew back, licking his lips as he gently tucked Roan back into his pants. Roan's hand rose up to cup his face, Roan's thumb wiping at the corner of his mouth. "You didn't have to do that," Roan said.

"I know." Ishaan used the edge of the seat to lever himself up off the floor and onto the bench beside Roan. "You deserved it."

"No, I don't—"

"You deserve much more for putting up with me—"

"I don't '*put up with*' you, I love—"

The train lurched, the lights blinking out again, but it was hardly noticeable with the sunlight streaming in through the cabin window. What *was* noticeable, however, was how quickly the train was slowing, the squeal of the brakes audible from the front of the train.

"Shit. Time to go," Ishaan said. He grabbed his suitcase, which he had packed before breakfast, and helped Roan poke his dirty socks into his so the zipper didn't get them stuck in its teeth. They hurried down the aisles, from one car to the next, and joined the line of passengers waiting to get off. Ishaan had to grab the back of the nearest seat to keep from being thrown against Roan as the train gave one last lurch, but it didn't stop Roan from stumbling into the person in front of him.

"Excuse me; very sorry," Roan said as the man turned to look back at him. Ishaan recognized him from the night before—the man drinking at the bar.

Middle-aged with a weathered face and hard blue eyes, the man regarded Roan for a moment, and Ishaan almost reached out and pulled Roan back from the man. His face was utterly empty, devoid of anything Ishaan might call an expression. It was unsettling to say the least.

"No problem," the man said, and even his voice was flat and toneless. He turned away and Roan cast a covert glance over his shoulder, raising his eyebrows at Ishaan. Ishaan nodded, acknowledging the strange behavior, and they each took a small step backward.

At the front of the car, the conductor opened the door and lowered the stairs. The line began to shuffle forward, passengers laden with baggage picking their way down the steps and onto the platform. Through the windows, Ishaan observed tearful reunions and joyous hugs; old friends and distant relations and absent lovers, apart no longer.

"Thank you for choosing the Trans-Eshaedra Railroad," the conductor said, smiling as Roan and Ishaan exited the train. Standing off to the side were passengers waiting to board, with tearful farewells and long kisses—the flipside of the coin.

Roan glanced around, then turned to Ishaan. "So, are your friends picking us up or should I try to find a taxi?" He looked positively thrilled at the prospect, giving Ishaan pause.

"Haven't you ridden in a taxi before?" he asked.

Roan shook his head. "I tried to avoid big cities when I was on my own. I figured someone would be more likely to recognize me there than in a small town. But there were taxis in the city where I grew up. We were just too poor to ever take one." He glanced around again. "So, what are we doing?"

"Well, since these people are not my friends, and aren't even on this planet, I guess we're waiting for you to find us a taxi."

Roan grinned like it was his birthday and rushed off, weaving through the crowds that loitered in the station. Ishaan hurried after him, a moment of anxiety closing his throat and making it hard to breathe as he lost him. Exiting the train station onto a wide, busy street, Ishaan cast about, his heart racing as he searched for Roan's red coat—his most distinguishing feature—and couldn't find it anywhere.

"Ishaan! Over here."

Ishaan turned toward the voice, the tight knot in his chest loosening as Roan waved to him from just up the block, his red coat draped over his arm. Ishaan suddenly realized how hot it was out there in the sun, and he shrugged out of his jacket, shifting his suitcase from one hand to the other as he made his way over to Roan.

"Don't run off like that," Ishaan said. "This is a big place; I couldn't find you."

"Sorry," Roan said. "Look—I found a taxi." He gestured to the small, bright-green coach parked at the curb, and sure enough, it had *TAXI* painted on the side of it, probably in more than one language, although Ishaan couldn't read the others to be sure. It had dark green leather seats and a black canvas top that was folded down, waiting for bad weather. Hitched in front of the coach were two of the largest birds that Ishaan had ever seen. For a moment, he wondered if they were rocs, but then realized that they were nowhere near as big as that. Standing eight or nine feet tall, they had small red eyes and a hooked beak on top of long, scaly necks, shaggy gray feathers the color of weathered wood, and long, scaly legs with wide, four-toed feet.

"Whatsa matter? Never seen a moa before?"

Ishaan glanced up at the driver, seated on a wooden bench with the reins in her hand. She didn't look old enough to be driving a taxi, fifteen or sixteen at the most, and she had the brightest, most striking blue eyes that Ishaan had ever seen. For a moment, all he could do was stare at them, as blue as a tropical sea with vertical pupils slitted like a cat's.

"No, we haven't," Roan said, jabbing Ishaan in the ribs with his elbow. Ishaan glanced away, back at the birds. Each one was wearing a lightweight halter and a simple leather harness. He looked back at the girl, this time noticing her dark skin and delicate features, her hair tucked up under a colorful, oversized beret, making it looked stuffed and misshapen. She wore a simple blue T-shirt with a denim vest over it and faded jeans. Her feet were bare, resting against the worn footboard of the coach.

"Well, now ya have," she said. "You guys wanna ride, or not?"

"We sure do," Roan said, grabbing his suitcase and climbing into the back of the open coach. Ishaan followed, not entirely certain they shouldn't have looked for a different taxi.

"Where to?" the girl asked, her hair shifting under her hat and changing the shape of it.

Ishaan hesitated. "The Scanevra Gating Complex," he said finally.

She turned in her seat, her hat flattening. "The Gates? But that's just—"

"I know where it is," Ishaan said as she started to point. "It's my husband's first time in the city, so if you know of any points of interest along the way, that would be great, but we're on a pretty tight schedule, so if you could get us there in about ten minutes, you can keep the change." He reached into his pocket and pulled out an ilae, the girl's eyes widening and her hat returning to its former shape at the sight of the large platinum coin.

"Yes, sir, Mister. Ten minutes it is." She turned back around and gave the reins a flick, then began to sing. It wasn't a song he knew, or even a language he recognized, and as he listened, he realized that it wasn't any language at all, just nonsense sounds strung together in a beautiful melody. He found himself relaxing back into the cushy leather seats and taking Roan's hand in his, the two of them riding in silence as they rolled down a crowded city street, tall buildings of steel and glass towering over them. All around them rolled other coaches and wagons and carriages, many pulled by more moa, but some drawn by horses or elk, and he even saw one fancy gilded carriage with dark tinted windows pulled by a pair of unicorns.

After a couple of blocks, the coach slowed and the girl pointed off to their left. "There's the Scanevran Museum of Art and Science," she said. "It's one of the oldest buildings in the city." The Museum was a big, blocky building built mostly out of a blue and white speckled stone with high, narrow windows and formidable columns along the front.

They merged back into the flow of traffic and a few blocks later, the coach turned, taking them down a quieter, one-way street. The driver pointed out the famous Mosaic Theater, the campus of the University of West Eshaedra, and took them past a park filled with sparkling fountains, manicured lawns and colorful flowerbeds, where all manner of people were out and about, feeding the pigeons and wyverns, playing games with balls, sticks, and hoops, or walking their dogs, dragons, and other such pets that Ishaan couldn't identify. He saw lots of humans and faeries, a few dracorians and machirans, a couple of centaurs, and even a few species that he didn't recognize.

Almost ten minutes to the second since they had pulled away from the train station, the coach rolled to a stop in front of the Gating Complex. "Here ya are," the girl said. "Didja enjoy the ride?"

"It was amazing!" Roan said, grinning from ear to ear as he grabbed his suitcase and climbed out of the coach. He turned to Ishaan. "We have *got* to come back here when we have more time."

"Try the spring," the girl said. "It's nice when all the trees are in bloom. Or the fall, when the leaves are turning."

"Thanks," Ishaan said as he followed Roan out of the coach. "We'll keep that in mind." He retrieved the ilae from his pocket and handed it to the girl.

"Thanks very much, sir," she said, tucking it into her own pocket. "You guys have a great trip."

"Wait; hang on a second," Roan said, setting his bag down and taking a step toward the coach. "I was curious and...I wonder if you might do something for me?"

She glanced around, her hat flattening again. "I guess," she said. "For a tip that big, I s'pose there ain't much I wouldn't do."

"Oh. No," Roan said, shaking his head as his face reddened. "Nothing like that. I was just wondering if you'd mind taking off your hat. I'd like to see your ears."

"Oh," she said, sounding surprised. "You know what I am."

"Yes, I've met braeddis before."

Ishaan had no idea what they were talking about, but he held his tongue and just watched as the girl pulled off her hat, revealing short, silken hair and large, triangular ears, both a blue-gray that was almost lavender, with faint silvery rosettes that sparkled in the sun. Her ears swiveled as if they had a life of their own, shifting to catch sounds from different directions. No wonder her hat kept changing shape.

"They're beautiful," Roan said, bringing a small smile and a flush of color to her face.

"Thanks," she said. "Wanna see my tail, too?" Before Roan could answer, she stood up, pulling her long, fluffy tail out of the gap where the back and seat cushions didn't quite meet.

"Wow," Roan said. "I bet your winter coat is simply gorgeous."

"It ain't bad," she said, sitting down again, her tail draped across the seat beside her, the tip flirting back and forth like that of an amused cat. "Wouldja believe most of the idiots 'round here think I'm a machiran?"

"That's ridiculous," Roan said with a snort. "Machirans are smaller and they have muzzles and whiskers and paws."

"I know, right?" she said, picking up the reins. "Well, I better get going. Pleasure meeting ya."

"You, too," Roan said, waving as she pulled away from the curb and blended in with the rest of the traffic. He turned to Ishaan. "That was fun."

"Yeah, it was," Ishaan said. They picked up their suitcases and headed for the Gating Complex, a big, modern building of glass and concrete, with a steady stream of diverse species flowing in and out through the multiple sets of double doors. He watched a pair of machirans come out, one black, the other gold, and shift into their four-legged forms before scampering off toward the park. "So, that girl...she's really not a machiran?"

"Of course not," Roan said. "Haven't you ever met a braeddis fey before?"

"Not that I'm aware of. Is she really a faerie?" He'd never heard of faeries with cat ears.

"A sub-species of faerie," Roan said. "They don't have glamour or wings, but they can communicate with animals through music, and they can look like all kinds of animals, not just feline—canine, vulpine, ursine, equine—"

They both jumped as the shriek of a train whistle split the urban background noise, and Ishaan cringed as Roan turned to look.

"C'mon, we're going to miss our ship," Ishaan said, catching at Roan's arm, but Roan pulled away, pointing across the street.

"Isn't that the train station?" he asked.

"It's *a* train station," Ishaan said.

"Ishaan—"

"What?"

Roan turned, planting his hands on his hips. "Did you really pay that girl an ilae to drive us in a circle around the city when we could have just *walked* across the street?"

"Maybe," Ishaan said, bracing himself for Roan to make a scene right there in the middle of the Gating Complex plaza. Roan didn't disappoint, though it wasn't quite the scene that Ishaan had been expecting. Dropping his suitcase, Roan threw himself into Ishaan's arms, pulling him down into a kiss that left Ishaan breathless and his knees weak.

"You sure know how to spoil me," Roan said when he finally stepped away. "Now quit it—I'm sure I don't even want to know how much this trip has already cost." He grabbed his bag in one hand and took Ishaan's hand in the other. "Let's go. I can't wait to see what you—Did you say something about a ship?"

Ishaan grinned. "Maybe."

They entered the Complex, passing through security without any trouble, and made their way through the busy terminal to gate #458. The gate itself was a freestanding doorway with a heavy, metal sliding door separating this side of the magic wormhole from the other. It was surrounded by an airlock, constructed out of bullet-proof glass, probably. It was a standard precaution for any gate that opened into a potentially hazardous environment. Often, it was to prevent the spread of invasive species, or to contain a toxic atmosphere. In this case, it was just to make sure the entire terminal didn't get blown out into space if something happened to the station on the other side.

Ishaan walked over to the automated registration kiosk and scanned their tickets. The kiosk made a chirping sound and the light on top began to blink. It wasn't more than a minute before a large, sandy-gray jackrabbit came hopping through the crowd toward them, darting around luggage and between legs. It skidded to a stop in front of them, big ears standing up tall and quivering, and then dissolved into a swirling cloud of black mist. The cloud expanded, rising up as tall as Roan, and then condensed into a smiling young man with sandy hair and a name tag that read *Flash*.

"Afternoon," he said. "Heading to Halicon Station?"

"That's right," Ishaan said, resisting the urge to make a smart remark. Why would they have bought tickets to Halicon if they were going somewhere else?

"Business or pleasure?" Flash asked, turning to type something into the kiosk control panel.

"Pleasure," Roan answered. "It's our honeymoon."

"Oh, congratulations," Flash said. "My wife and I just celebrated our second anniversary, and she and her wife are coming up on their fourth. So, how long will you be staying on Halcion?"

"Briefly," Ishaan said. "We're catching s ship there."

"Oh, a star cruise," Flash said. "How romantic. Will you be returning through this gate?"

"Yes."

"Estimated date of return?"

"Four days from now."

"Sounds good," Flash said as a long string of writing scrolled past the screen. "Looks like you only need the one vaccine if you're just passing through, unless you're planning to engage in physical relations with anyone on the station."

"We're not," Ishaan said.

"Good, 'cause they're having a terrible time with a sexually transmitted parasite—nasty, horrible thing—ugh." He shuddered, then typed something else into the panel and a small drawer in the side of the kiosk opened, containing two individually packaged antiseptic wipes, two small syringes, and two adhesive bandages. Ishaan started to roll up the sleeve of his T-shirt.

"Oh, sorry," Flash said as he tore open one of the wipes, "this has to be injected into the buttock."

"What?" Ishaan said.

"Here?" Roan asked, glancing around the open terminal.

Flash started to laugh. "Only joking," he said, reaching out to sterilize a strip of Ishaan's shoulder. He picked up a syringe, pulled off the safety cap, jabbed Ishaan in the shoulder, and depressed the plunger, then slapped a bandage over it.

"That was quick," Ishaan said, giving the stinging spot a gentle rub before letting his sleeve back down.

"That's why they call me Flash," the young man said, repeating the process with Roan. "Well, one of the more flattering reasons." He winked at Ishaan as he smoothed the bandage over Roan's shoulder. "There you go; all done. Enjoy your trip, gentlemen."

"Thanks," Roan said. Flash shifted back into a rabbit and bounded off again, disappearing into the crowd with a flick of his fluffy white tail. "He was nice," Roan said as they picked up their luggage and approached the airlock.

"Mm-hm," Ishaan said, nodding as he waved his ticket in front of the panel to the left of the door. The airlock opened, allowing them inside, and then closed behind them. There was a hiss of air and Ishaan felt a pressure against his eardrums, the noise outside the airlock growing muted. "Must be a difference in atmosphere on the station," he said. He swallowed a couple of times and forced himself to yawn, working his jaw until his ears popped.

"That's better," Roan said after a moment, giving his head a shake. In front of them, the panel beside the closed world gate lit up green and Ishaan strode forward, scanning his ticket again. With another hiss and a grinding of metal, the gate opened, revealing another airlock, this one rough, gray steel lit by flickering amber lights, thick grates on the floor and walls. Glancing back to make sure Roan was behind him, Ishaan stepped through, a faint buzzing between his ears, a hiccup in his heartbeat, and a lurch in his stomach as his body was instantaneously transported across thousands of light years.

"I'll never get used to that," Roan said, shuddering as he stepped up beside Ishaan. "Half of you in one place and the other half clear across the galaxy."

"We're only about a third of the way across the galaxy," Ishaan said as the gate closed behind him. Once it was sealed, the airlock doors opened and they emerged into the station. Primarily a hub for merchants and traders, Halicon Station was designed for function, not beauty. Everything was varying shades of gray or brown, the metal scratched, scuffed, and dented, and the air tasted stale and metallic, heavy with the scent of sweat and damp fur.

Digging into his pocket for their boarding passes, he glanced around, trying to figure out where they were. Their connecting flight was leaving from dock 19B, and even though Ishaan couldn't see a readout with the local time, he knew they didn't have a whole lot to spare.

Loud footsteps rang out from the floor grate and he turned as a tall man with bronze skin and long black hair came striding up the corridor, dressed head to toe in dirty black leather and shiny metal studs.

"Excuse me," Ishaan said. "Do you know—"

"Fuck off," the man growled as he shoved past them, disappearing around the corner.

Ishaan glanced over at Roan. "Well, that was rude."

Before Roan could say anything, a strange chorus of chirps and squeaks filled the hall, and they watched, nonplussed, as a herd of small, fuzzy creatures came bouncing and rolling along the corridor. Each one was about the size of a human head, but Ishaan had a feeling that was mostly hair. They had a number of small appendages which they used to push themselves along with, and he counted no fewer than five multi-faceted eyes on each one. Ishaan didn't even bother trying to ask for directions.

Cursing and muttering, a man came wading through the squeaking puffballs from the opposite direction, his copper hair pulled back in a ponytail, his face unshaven, scruffy, and his blue eyes quick and shrewd, looking them over with only mild interest.

"Excuse me," Ishaan said, not getting his hopes up. "Do you know where dock 19B is?"

"Yeah," the man said, his stride slowing, but he didn't stop.

"Well, could you tell us, or at least point us in the right direction?" Ishaan asked, trying to restrain his exasperation. If they came all this way, only to miss their ship at the last moment—

"This way," the man said, motioning for them to follow. They grabbed their bags and hurried after him, down the long corridor to a junction. "That way," the man said. "Head up with you get to the stairs. 19B is on the right."

"Thank you," Ishaan said.

"We're on out honeymoon," Roan added with a big grin. The guy just nodded, then continued on his way. "Do you suppose all of this is normal around here and *we're* the strange ones?" Roan asked as they headed down the corridor, his voice echoing off the metal panels on the ceiling.

"Probably," Ishaan said. "Although you're pretty strange under any circumstances."

"That's why you married me," Roan said.

They reached the stairs, and from there it was just a steep climb and a short walk to dock 19B. Ishaan breathed a sigh of relief. The airlock was still open. Just inside the doors, a young woman checked their boarding passes and pointed them toward the reception desk. It was another kiosk and Ishaan dutifully scanned their tickets and received directions to their suite. The screen changed, asking them to register, and a small door in the kiosk slid open, revealing a fingerprint scanner.

"You do it," Ishaan said, stepping aside. "Just press you thumb against the scanner."

"What about you?" Roan asked after he'd registered.

"It's better if I don't," Ishaan said, selecting *decline* on the screen when it prompted him again. "Only your thumb print will open the door to our cabin. This way, we don't have to worry about me wandering off."

"I don't think you would," Roan said as they headed for their room.

"Yeah, but now we don't even have to worry about it. Besides, it's not like I'd go anywhere without you."

The suite was nice—huge, compared to their cabin on the train, with deep, plush carpet and soft, overstuffed chairs and sofa. The bedroom was crowded, but only because the bed was so large. It was bigger than the one they had at home. Only the bathroom left something to be desired. Still no tub.

"I bet this cost a fortune," Roan said, looking around as he entered the bedroom and tossed his suitcase on the bed. "So, when do I get to meet your friends?"

Ishaan rolled his eyes. "I told you, they aren't my friends. And you'll meet them when we get where we're going."

"You mean this isn't it?" Roan asked, but he sounded more amazed than annoyed. "What could be better than a luxury star cruise?"

"You'll see," Ishaan said with a smile. "We'll get there in a little less than forty hours."

"Is that all?" Roan asked, sitting down on the edge of the bed and bouncing to test the mattress. "I won't even have time to get used to this."

A musical chime issued from a small speaker in the ceiling, followed by the smooth voice of an older man. "This is your captain speaking. Good evening and welcome aboard *The Starlight Dreamer*. You folks are in for an unexpected treat as we will be sailing around the rarely observed back side of the Lyricus Nebula in order to make a quick stop at the Orendi Science Outpost. We hope you enjoy your trip and if there's anything we can do to make your stay more pleasurable, please don't hesitate to ask."

"Whoa, the back side of the nebula," Roan said. "How cool is that?"

Ishaan turned away, opening his suitcase to cover up his chuckle. As far as he knew, the back side of a nebula looked a lot like the front, but it was a clever spin to explain an unscheduled hundred million mile detour. He jumped as Roan suddenly grabbed him from behind.

"C'mon, we can unpack later," he said, his hands wandering down Ishaan's chest and up under his T-shirt. "It's our honeymoon—we should be making love."

"We will tonight," Ishaan said, trying to ignore the way his body reacted to Roan's touch.

"We'll be tired then," Roan said. "Like you *always* are. Please, Ishaan. I don't know what else I can do to make you want me again, but just name it. I'll do anything."

Ishaan pulled away, frowning as he turned to face Roan. "What are you talking about?"

"Nothing," Roan said, shaking his head. "Just forget it."

Ishaan reached out, catching him by the arm as he started to leave. "No, Roan. Tell me what you mean."

"You're always tired, or you're busy, or your back hurts, or it's something else. You never want to make love to me anymore. I have to *beg* before you give in. What did I do? What didn't I do? What do I need to do to make you want me?"

Ishaan just stared at him, dumbstruck.

Roan shook his head again, swallowing hard like he was fighting tears. "See, I shouldn't have said anything. Now I've spoiled the trip."

"Oh, Roan," Ishaan whispered, raising his hand to cup Roan's cheek. He leaned down, kissing him with all of the passion that he'd been holding back, leaving them both out of breath. "I'm sorry that I made you feel that way," Ishaan said. "I just thought...since we have sex every night, that you'd get tired of it. I didn't want you to think you had to take care of me when I'm awake, too."

Roan didn't say anything for a moment, he just seemed to be thinking about what Ishaan had said. "I don't *have* to take care of you," he said finally. "I *get* to. I'm lucky to have you, for so many reasons." He hesitated, his tongue darting out to wet his lips as he looked down at the floor between them. "Before I met you, I hated sex. I hated having to have it, needing it, suffering without it, hurting people if I couldn't get it. But now, with you, because of you, I can enjoy it. And I do. I love making love to you. I could never get tired of it."

"I am so glad to hear that," Ishaan said, pulling Roan into his arms. "You have no idea how hard it's been not to jump you every time you come into the room." He started kissing up and down the side of Roan's neck, making him laugh and squirm.

"Oh, no!" Roan cried dramatically. "I've unleashed the beast!" His hands pulled at Ishaan's shirt, at first trying to tug him over to the bed, but then he suddenly let go and slipped out of Ishaan's grasp. "I want to play a game," Roan said, his eyes sparkling. "Turn around and count to fifty while I hide."

"Seriously?" Ishaan said, arching an eyebrow. "That's a kid's game."

"And how many kid's games end with the players naked and sweaty, fucking each other's brains out?"

"No games that I ever played," Ishaan said with a laugh. He turned his back to Roan and, just for good measure, covered his eyes with his hands as he began to count. "One...two..." He could hear the rustle of clothing being shed and the hushed sound of a door opening, then a strange sort of hum coming from the other room. He tried to picture what could be making the sound, but came up blank. "Twenty-seven...twenty-eight...fifty," he said, curiosity getting the better of his patience. Turning around, the corner of his mouth lifted in a crooked grin as his gaze followed a trail of socks, shoes, jeans, and boxers across the bedroom to the bathroom door.

Peeling his shirt off, he tossed it onto the foot of the bed, taking a moment to remove his sneakers and socks before stepping out of his pants. Wearing just his briefs, Ishaan snuck over to the closed door, the strange noise growing louder as he eased the door open. Stepping into the small room, he could hardly miss Roan's tanned figure behind the frosted glass of the shower stall door.

"I hate to say this," Ishaan said, "but you are really terrible at Hide and Seek." He pulled the door of the stall open, a cloud of hot, heavy mist rolling out, tiny drops of water beading up on his skin. Standing in the little cubicle, bronze skin wet and gleaming, Roan smiled at Ishaan, his eyes hooded as he slowly stroked his hard cock with one hand.

"Who says we're playing Hide and Seek?" Roan asked, his voice low and husky. He reached out, grabbing Ishaan by the waistband of his briefs, and pulled him into the stall, the door swinging closed behind him. "This way, we both win."

In the narrow stall, their bodies pressed together, Roan's hard-on rubbing against the swiftly growing bulge in Ishaan's briefs. Ishaan couldn't keep his hands off of his husband, stroking his face, his neck, teasing his nipples, cupping his ass, grabbing and kneading, pulling him closer. The stall echoed with their heavy breathing, their soft groans and needy sighs. Roan shoved Ishaan's briefs down, brazenly wrapping his hand around Ishaan's cock and jerking him hard and fast as he bit and sucked at Ishaan's neck.

"Easy there, you little demon," Ishaan panted, shuddering as his hips bucked, thrusting into Roan's industrious hand. "You're gonna make me come."

"Oh, did I forget to explain the rules of this game?" Roan asked with a chuckle. "You come, you lose."

"Cheater," Ishaan growled. He grabbed at Roan's wrist, but Roan pulled away, their wet skin making him slippery.

"C'mon, you can do better than that."

Ishaan stepped into him, pressing him back against the wall.

"That's more like it," Roan said, wrapping his arms around Ishaan's neck and kissing him. "Although I can't see how this gives you the upper hand." He began to rock his hips, rutting and grinding against Ishaan, delicious smooth friction between their hot, slick skin.

"And what good would having the *upper* hand be, anyway?" Ishaan asked, his hand sliding down Roan's back, two fingers slipping between Roan's cheeks and rubbing over Roan's entrance. Roan moaned, shuddering against him.

"Now who's cheating?" Roan panted, his rhythm faltering as Ishaan teased his opening, pressing against the tight ring. It was no secret that Roan was extremely sensitive back there.

Ishaan leaned closer, pressing his cheek to Roan's as he murmured, "I just want to make sure you're squeaky clean, my little demon, because after we get out of this shower, I'm going to spread you across the bed and eat your ass until you can't come anymore, and then I'm going to fuck you until you can't see straight."

"Oh, holy fuck, Ishaan!" Roan gasped, his hips jerking, his fingers digging into Ishaan's shoulders as he came, sticky ribbons of white streaking their wet skin. Not one to lose graciously, Roan wrapped his fingers around Ishaan and finished him with a few firm strokes.

"I win," Ishaan said as he struggled to catch his breath.

"Yeah," Roan said, grudgingly, "you win. Even though I know you'd never do something like that."

"You think so?" Ishaan murmured, kissing his husband. "You want to get rinsed off and find out?"

Roan reached out, flipping a switch beside the shower knobs and changing the water from a dense mist to a powerful spray, the jets tickling and stinging. Ishaan supposed that for a lone occupant standing in the center of the stall, it wouldn't be uncomfortable, but as close to the jets as he was, there were moments that were downright unpleasant. Once the semen had been washed away, Roan shut off the water and grabbed towels from the rack outside the door.

"You know, Ishaan," Roan said as they dried off, "while I'm not opposed to just about anything when it comes to sex, I don't want you to do something you'd rather not do, just to try and please me. I don't need anything exotic or kinky, I just need you."

"Thank you," Ishaan said. "That means a lot. But...you're not the only one who used to hate sex. I'm only just learning to enjoy it, and I won't know if I enjoy something until I try it, and I'm sorry, but looks like I'm going to have to experiment on you."

Roan stared at him, pale eyes darkening with lust, and he let out his breath in a shudder that shook him from head to toe. "Sweet Maele, Ishaan, you almost made me come again."

With a hungry smile, Ishaan pulled the towel out of Roan's hand and led his husband into the bedroom.

* * *

Roan lay across the bed, every muscle in his body as soft as pudding, with Ishaan sprawled naked beside him. They were quiet, sated and contented for the moment. Ishaan might have been asleep, but Roan couldn't muster the energy to check. He had been licked and sucked and touched and fucked in more ways than he had thought possible, and Ishaan had let him do things he'd never even imagined either of them would enjoy. Not everything turned out as good in practice as it had seemed in theory, but even the failures had brought them closer together, laughter filling the room almost as often as their desperate moans and breathless cries. They hadn't left the suite since they arrived and only bothered to dress—if slipping into a robe could be considered dressing—to answer the door when room service brought their food.

Speaking of food, Roan wasn't sure what time it was, but he was starting to get hungry again. He wondered if Ishaan would feel like ordering something, but asking seemed like too much effort. He wasn't that hungry yet.

He jumped, feeling Ishaan do the same, as that musical chime came through the speakers again, but this time it wasn't a ship-wide announcement, it was through the intercom.

"Mr. Darvis?" a voice said, perhaps the captain, but Roan doubted it. Ishaan climbed off the bed, crossing to the control panel on the wall. "Mr. Darvis?"

"Yes, this is Ishaan Darvis," he said.

"Sir, we're approaching the Orendi Science Outpost. We should make dock in about an hour."

"Thank you," Ishaan said, glancing over his shoulder. "We'll be ready."

"Acknowledged." The intercom went silent again.

"We're going to a science outpost?" Roan said, sitting up. He glanced around the room, their clothes still scattered on the floor where they'd been dropped, his suitcase hastily shifted to the corner of the room, his clean socks and underwear spilling out of the open bag. "Or is this just another stop-over?"

"Just a stop-over, I'm afraid," Ishaan said, "but you'll finally get to meet our hosts."

"Oooh, should I have packed my tux?" Roan asked with a grin.

"You mean you didn't?"

Roan's smile vanished. "Did you tell me to?" He was pretty sure Ishaan hadn't.

"I didn't think I had to. It was implied."

"Implied how?" Roan demanded, planting his fists on his hips.

Ishaan's lips quirked, pressed tight together. He looked like he was struggling to answer, then he burst out laughing. "You're so cute when you're indignant. And naked," Ishaan said.

Roan grabbed the pillow off the bed and flung it at him. "So what *should* I wear, Mr. Comedian?"

"Jeans. T-shirt. Whatever," Ishaan said, picking up the pillow and tossing it back onto the bed. "It's not a formal event."

"Good, 'cause I hate that monkey suit." He always felt like a turkey in borrowed feathers—tight, hot, uncomfortable feathers.

"Oh, but it looks so good on you," Ishaan said, pulling on his boxers and sitting down on the end of the bed to put on his socks.

"Well, I might be persuaded to put it on sometime," Roan said, righting his suitcase and picking out his clean clothes, "as long as you promise that I won't have to wear it for very long."

"I could have you undressed in five minutes," Ishaan said, giving him a smoldering look.

"Let's just save ourselves the trouble, then," Roan said, dropping his things on top of his suitcase and turning toward Ishaan. Disappointingly, Ishaan shook his head.

"The ship won't wait for us," he said. "The captain made that very clear when I arranged for this ride. They're already going to have to burn twice as much fuel as normal to make their next stop on schedule—sitting parked at the science outpost is out of the question."

"What do you mean?" Roan asked, frowning. "Isn't this part of the cruise?"

"Hardly," Ishaan said, "but it was the only ship passing anywhere remotely close to Orendi."

Roan stared at him. He couldn't possible mean— "Tell me you didn't pay to reroute this ship."

"Okay, I won't tell you," Ishaan said, getting up and pulling his jeans out of his suitcase.

"Ishaan!" Roan said, his gut curling up into a tight ball of guilt, like it always did when Ishaan spent obscene amounts of money on him.

"Roan!" Ishaan said, mimicking his tone. "Don't worry about the money. You're worth it."

"No, I'm not—"

"*Yes*, you are, and every time you argue with me, I'm going to find something ridiculously expensive to buy you, just to prove it."

Unfortunately, Roan knew it wasn't an empty threat. He frowned down at the shirt in his hands, struggling to find the words to explain how unworthy Ishaan's lavish gifts made him feel. He was already the luckiest person in the universe having found and married Ishaan, but at least in that respect, they were equal. They needed each other; they loved each other, but Roan couldn't begin to give Ishaan close to what Ishaan had given him. He didn't turn as Ishaan stepped up behind him and wrapped him in a warm embrace.

"I'm sorry the money bothers you," Ishaan said, his voice low in Roan's ear. "If it makes you feel any better, even though this trip is for you, it's something that I wanted, too. It's been seven years since I traveled anywhere farther than Shesade, and before that it just to visit doctors and specialists about my condition. I've never had a vacation like this. And besides, to me, you are worth more than I could ever spend in a lifetime—in a *dragon's* lifetime. You are *priceless*."

His throat full of the love and gratitude that flooded his chest, Roan twisted around in Ishaan's arms and held him tight, his body shaking as he fought not to cry. He had never imagined how much it would mean to hear such words from Ishaan. He'd tried to ignore the hollowness in his chest, the cold, heavy feeling in the pit of his stomach whenever money was mentioned, tried to tell himself that it was just envy, because that was easier to accept than the fact that he didn't feel deserving of the nice things that they had, of their house, of his books, of Ishaan.

"I love you so much," Roan whispered.

"I love you, too," Ishaan said, drawing back to lean down and kiss Roan on the forehead. "We're okay, right?"

"Of course," Roan said. He took a deep breath, then let it out. "Okay, let's go meet these friends of yours." Ishaan just rolled his eyes and shook his head.

Dressed and packed, Roan and Ishaan made their way back to the airlock door, the big ship shuddering and groaning as they neared the science outpost on the small moon of Orendi. Roan watched through the thick glass of the airlock window as they drifted closer and closer to the rocky, red-gold sphere, the surface crossed by thin, jagged black lines that revealed themselves to be deep cracks in the surface, probably caused by the proximity of the planet that it orbited. Roan didn't know much about physics or gravitational forces, but he had a feeling it was the glittering, blue and green planet that caused the ship to shake and moan, not the humble little moon.

Movement from the moon below caught Roan's eye and he leaned closer to the glass, his breath fogging it up. He quickly wiped it away. "Hey, there's a ship headed toward us," he said, pointing. "We haven't invaded their airspace, have we?"

Ishaan chuckled. "No. That's our ride."

"Oh. I thought we were going to dock with the station."

"This ship can't land on the moon. The shuttle will dock with us."

"Neat," Roan said, looking back out the window. It took about fifteen minutes for the shuttle to maneuver into position and gently link up with the cruise ship. Roan wanted to watch the actual docking, but Ishaan pulled him back, taking him into an adjacent room and sealing the door, just in case something went wrong. Nothing did. Docking complete, they hurried back to the airlock just as the heavy, outer doors slid apart and a handsome man in his mid-thirties strode across the airlock from the shuttle, dressed in worn hiking boots, faded jeans, a khaki shirt, and a battered leather hat that looked like some kind of animal had taken a bite out of the wide brim.

"Ishaan Darvis?" he asked, looking back and forth between them.

"I'm Ishaan," Ishaan said, stepping forward to shake the man's hand. He glanced back. "This is my husband, Roan."

"Hi," Roan said, but before he could reach out to shake hands, the airlock doors of the cruise ship began to slide closed.

"I think that's a hint that we've overstayed our welcome," the man said, stepping back through the doors and motioning for them to hurry. Tossing the suitcase through the shrinking opening, Roan slipped past, then reached back and grabbed Ishaan's hand, pulling him safely through. "Nicely done," said the man with the hat, pressing a button beside the exterior shuttle door and waiting for it to close. He pressed another button, for the intercom, apparently, and said, "Ready to uncouple, Laethis."

The reply crackled with static. "Acknowledged."

The man turned to them, his smile broad. "Sorry, I believe our introductions were interrupted. Roan, was it?" Roan nodded and shook the outstretched hand. "I'm Shine Diram."

"It's a pleasure to meet you, Mr. Diram," Roan said.

"*Dr.* Diram," Ishaan corrected.

"Shine is fine," Dr. Diram said with a smile. "If you want, you can leave your bags here. There really isn't anywhere else to put them, to be honest. It's not a very large shuttle."

"Is it going to be a long trip?" Roan asked, imagining being stuffed into a cabin like on the train. It wasn't that bad, but after the luxury of the cruise ship, it would be like living in a prison cell.

"About thirty minutes, is all," Dr. Diram said. "Which, we should probably get you two strapped in before we hit the atmosphere. Entry can be a bit bumpy." They tucked their suitcases into a storage compartment in the wall, then headed down a short hall to the cockpit.

As they entered the control room, they were greeted by an older female machiran in bipedal form, her golden fur silvered on her muzzle and ears, her paws and tail, and all down her throat and chest between her four small breasts. One of her bright, amber eyes was clouded by a milky cataract and she moved with the stiffness of age, her shoulders stooped, but when Dr. Diram leaned down, she rubbed the side of her face against his in a very intimate gesture, a greeting between lovers, if Roan wasn't mistaken.

"Roan, Ishaan, this is Twyppn," Dr. Diram said, taking her by one nimble, hand-like paw. "Twyppn has been assisting us with our research for fifteen years and we couldn't have done any of it without her." He leaned down again, giving her a kiss on one silky cheek.

"It's a pleasure to meet you," she said, nodding to Roan, then to Ishaan.

"You, too," Roan said.

"And over there, making sure we don't spiral out of control and burn to a cinder," Dr. Diram said, much too cheerfully, in Roan's opinion, "is my husband and partner, Laethis Maccorian."

"It's a pleasure to finally meet you, Professor Maccorian," Ishaan said. "You have no idea how much this opportunity means to me— to us."

"Better get them secured, Shine," Professor Maccorian said, as if Ishaan hadn't even spoken. "We'll be hitting the atmosphere in five."

"Thanks, Professor," Dr. Diram said, giving Ishaan an apologetic glance. He led them over to a pair of seats bolted to one wall. "Don't mind him—he hates flying this thing, even though he's very good at it, and he's been a nervous wreck, fretting about our findings and how this news will effect...well, everything. There's sure to be resistance—there always is with this sort of thing...not that there's been anything of this magnitude since...well, since the outernet was introduced."

"I'm sorry," Roan said, feeling very confused, like he was missing something big. "*What* exactly are you talking about? What did you discover?"

Dr. Diram gave him a blank look, then turned to Ishaan. "You didn't tell him?"

"I wanted it to be a surprise," Ishaan said.

A giant grin spread across Dr. Diram's face as he checked their restraints, giving Roan's shoulder-belts a tug to tighten them up. "You're going to be surprised, I guarantee it." He walked away, helping Twyppn into a seat on the opposite side of the cockpit, and then climbing up into the co-pilot's position next to Professor Maccorian. Out through the front window, Roan stared in awe and a little apprehension as they hurtled toward the planet, the surface of the clouds so far below.

"Hang on," Dr. Diram said as the shuttle gave a jolt and began to rattle and shake.

Roan swallowed hard. This was so very different from riding on the cruise ship, sailing smoothly through space. He leaned into the straps, as close to Ishaan as he could get. "Why couldn't we just take a gate?" he asked, his voice low.

"There aren't any gates to this world yet," Ishaan replied. He reached over, Roan clasping his hand gratefully as the shaking became a rumble, a roaring sound filling the cockpit as the nose of the shuttle sliced through the thickening atmosphere, glowing a dull orange as friction heated the metal. Even though he'd never taken a shuttle through the atmosphere of a planet before, Roan knew enough about space travel to know that this was perfectly normal, but that didn't stop his heart from pounding as what looked like flames licked at the windows.

"Executing braking maneuvers," Professor Maccorian said, reaching out to press seemingly random buttons on the control panel in front of him. Roan's stomach shifted to the left as the ship curved to the right. The shaking eased, but Roan hardly noticed, trying to keep from vomiting as the shuttle swung back to the left again. At least he hadn't eaten anything recently. He glanced over at Ishaan, his husband sitting rigid with his eyes closed, a sheen of sweat on his upper lip and a greenish hue to his normally tanned skin. Roan squeezed his hand and felt Ishaan's fingers tighten in return.

"We're almost there, guys," Dr. Diram called. "You're doing great."

Roan didn't answer; he concentrated on taking short, shallow breaths as the ship sailed like a sidewinder above the planet, each turn bleeding off a bit more speed until Professor Maccorian could finally ignite the maneuvering thrusters and take them from freefall to controlled flight. Immediately, the last of the vibrations stopped, the shuttle leveling out and gliding down through a layer of thick, gray clouds, the moisture beading up on the window and rolling up the glass in thin silvery streaks.

Dr. Diram unbuckled himself and leaped up out of his seat, hurrying back to them. "Are you all right?"

"I think so," Ishaan said, taking a deep breath and letting it out. "Is it always that rough?"

"Of course not," Professor Maccorian said. "We wanted to make it exciting for you so you'd get your money's worth."

Roan frowned, his gaze darting over to Ishaan, who looked similarly confused and offended. Before either of them could respond, Dr. Diram spoke up.

"Remember your manners, my love," he said, his tone light, but carrying a warning just the same. "Just because your uncle was a rich asshole doesn't mean that all rich people are assholes." The cockpit filled with a heavy, tense silence.

"You're right," Professor Maccorian said finally. "Mr. Darvis, I apologize. I was out of line."

"Apology accepted," Ishaan said, but Roan could tell he wasn't quite ready to forgive just yet.

"Good," Dr. Diram said, grinning as he released their safety restraints. "Now, come on, you have to see this." He ushered them closer to the front of the cockpit, until they were standing behind the pilot and co-pilot's seats, staring out through the water-streaked window at a featureless cocoon of gray. "Just wait—we're almost through."

And just like that, the clouds thinned, vanishing in an instant. Roan's jaw dropped and his breath caught in his throat as he leaned on the back of the seat in front of him, staring out at the vivid panorama spread before them. They were flying over a dense jungle, a myriad of trees and plants in every shade of green, red, and gold rolling beneath them, cut by wide, winding waterways and stopping abruptly at sparkling cliffs of pale blue and white. In the distance, he could see the glint of sunlight on a large body of water on one side, and the black, lifeless cone of a volcano on the other. It was spectacular.

"What is this world?" Roan asked, his voice soft. It almost seemed impolite to speak too loudly before such beauty.

"At the moment," Dr. Diram said, also speaking in hushed tones, "the League has designated it Kasendi, but if our findings are accepted, we're hoping they'll change it to Hatoa, which is what the previous inhabitants called it."

"Previous?" Roan tore his gaze away from the window to look back at Dr. Diram. "You mean, like an extinct alien culture?"

"Extinct?" Dr. Diram repeated, giving a one-shoulder shrug. "Maybe, but I'd call this world...vacated, abandoned. It looks like they just left and never came back."

Roan couldn't stop himself—he turned to Ishaan and pulled him into a tight embrace, capturing his lips and kissing him until they were both out of breath. "This is the best honeymoon ever," he said. "Ishaan, thank you." Ishaan looked a little embarrassed by Roan's display, but Dr. Diram just chuckled.

"Wait until you see what really brought you here," he said with a wink, "and then you can thank him over and over all night long."

"Approaching the landing zone," Professor Maccorian said. Ahead, Roan could see a cleared area in the middle of the jungle. He grabbed on to the seat again, but Professor Maccorian set the shuttle down with barely a bump. He pressed buttons, powering the engines down, and the ship fell silent. "We're here," he said, shrugging out of his safety harness and rising from the pilot's seat, giving Roan his first good look at the man.

He was debatably the more attractive of the two, albeit in a more refined way. Even dressed much like Dr. Diram, he had an elegance to him, his short, honey-brown hair showing a trace of silver at the temples and his dark blue eyes sharp and intelligent.

"Great, let's go," Dr. Diram said, leading the way. Professor Maccorian and Twyppn brought up the rear, his strides matching hers as they walked arm in arm, even though he towered over her by more than a foot and a half. Back at the airlock, Roan and Ishaan grabbed their bags as Dr. Diram lowered the loading ramp and opened the doors.

"It's a little rich in oxygen," Professor Maccorian warned, "so if you feel light-headed, try breathing slower."

"It takes some getting used to," Dr. Diram said, starting down the ramp. Roan and Ishaan followed, but Roan had to stop almost immediately, overcome by a wave of dizziness. "Try counting to ten between breaths," Dr.

Diram suggested. Roan tried, but by the time he got to six, he could feel a pressure in his chest, his body telling him that he needed air. He took a deep breath and staggered as black spots danced before his eyes.

"Shallow breaths," Professor Maccorian said, catching him by the arm and keeping him upright. "Slow and shallow. Try to relax. Your body will get used to it."

His eyes squeezed shut, Roan concentrated, making each breath agonizingly slow, in...and out...and in...but after a few minutes he realized that he didn't feel out of breath, his body was just used to breathing at a certain pace. Looking up, he gave a slight nod, Professor Maccorian releasing his arm and allowing him to step away.

"Are you okay?" he asked Ishaan, struggling a little to speak without taking bigger breaths.

"Yeah," Ishaan said. "I think so."

"This walk will help," Dr. Diram said. "Exertion makes your body require more oxygen, so it'll get used up faster. Just remember to keep your breathing even. Of course," he added as they began making their way down a cleared path through the dense jungle, "once you get used to it, you'll notice that your stamina is greatly improved." He gave them a grin and a wink, then strode ahead, clearing a few fallen branches and encroaching vines off the trail.

Ishaan leaned closer to Roan. "Is it just me," he said, his voice low, "or does he remind you of—"

"Kethic," Roan said, nodding. "It's not just you."

"Who's Kethic?" Professor Maccorian asked, making Roan jump and glance back. He hadn't realized he was so close behind them.

"My brother," Roan said. "Don't worry, it wasn't an insult. Like Dr. Diram, Kethic is..."

"Sexually suggestive and wholly inappropriate?" Professor Maccorian said.

Roan chuckled. "I was going to say playful, but that works, too." He suddenly realized why Professor Maccorian had been able to catch up with them. "Where's Twyppn?"

"She chose to remain at the ship," he said. "She'll probably take a nap in the sun. She likes the heat; the station is always so cold—not enough insulation and no atmosphere, so we lose a lot of it into space."

"Can't you fix it up?" Roan asked. "I mean, aren't there grants for that kind of thing?"

Professor Maccorian made an amused sound and might have almost smiled. "It's a science outpost," he said. "Designed to support a minimal crew in minimal comfort for a minimal amount of time."

"And how long have you been there?" Ishaan asked.

"Almost three years," Professor Maccorian said. "After six months, the museum reviewed our preliminary findings and told us that there was nothing of interest on this world. They instructed us to move on. We disagreed and subsequently lost our funding. We've survived on private donations—" He gave a grateful nod toward Ishaan. "And quite a bit of pathetic groveling. I just hope it pays off."

"Hey!" Dr. Diram called, waving to them from about fifty yards up the trail. "Hurry up! The sun sets in about seven hours."

Roan's heart sank. Half of the day was gone already, and they'd only just arrived. He didn't let it show, though. He didn't want Ishaan to think he was disappointed about any of this, but he did wish they had more time.

They caught up to Dr. Diram and from there it was only another hundred yards to a small grouping of gray canvas tents. There were four of them, one clearly for storage and filled with crates, barrels, and all kinds of shovels and picks. Another housed a table and cook-stove, and the other two had the tent flaps down, but Roan guessed that they were for sleeping. If they were, they were awfully close together, severely limiting any potential nighttime activities.

"This is base camp," Dr. Diram said, stopping in the center of the camp, beside a circle of blackened stones marking the fire ring. "You'll probably want to be back here before dark. The jungle is pitch black at night and can be very disorienting. Just in case, take a lantern or two. The paths are marked by reflective cord, so they're not that hard to follow if you have a light. Do not, under any circumstances, go beyond the marked areas. Not only could you get lost or injured, but you could destroy priceless artifacts. Many of the plants on this world are toxic, so don't eat anything, but feel free to help yourselves to anything in the garden." He gestured to a plot behind the dining tent. "There are insects and reptiles that are mildly venomous, but not usually aggressive. Just watch where you're walking. We've provided image charms for each of you, so take as many pictures as you like, but no souvenirs, please."

He handed each of them a two inch square of glass, the edges covered in a thin band of silver etched with magic runes. They were pretty commonplace in the city growing up and Roan tucked his into his pocket, his hands trembling with excitement.

"Oh, and we'll need copies of any pictures you take," Professor Maccorian said, "so you might want to refrain from capturing any intimate moments."

"Or feel free," Dr. Diram said with another wink. "Maele knows we could use a little help getting that spark going at our age."

"*Your* age, perhaps," Professor Maccorian said, but there was a genuine warmth in his dark eyes as he smiled at his husband.

"Oh, really?" Dr. Diram said, arching an eyebrow. He glanced over at Roan and Ishaan. "Have fun guys. We'll pick you up mid-afternoon tomorrow." And then he hurried over to Professor Maccorian and the two of them headed back up the trail hand in hand.

"Wait—What?" Roan asked. "You-you're leaving us here?"

"Don't worry, it's perfectly safe," Dr. Diram said, looking back over his shoulder. "If you need us, there's an emergency communicator on the table in the dining tent."

"But-but...you're *leaving us here*," Roan said again.

Both of them chuckled. "We have findings to make public," Professor Maccorian said. "We don't have time to play tour guide, and besides, this is what your husband wanted."

"And with as much money as the Darvis family donated, we'd have wrapped the planet in a big red ribbon and tied it in a bow if he'd wanted us to," Dr. Diram said. "Enjoy your honeymoon."

Roan watched them disappear into the jungle, then he turned to Ishaan. Ishaan had a wariness in his eyes, like he was anticipating a repeat of that morning, but Roan did his best not to think about how much money this must have cost. Money wasn't important. Ishaan was.

"This is amazing," Roan said. "I-I can't even—I don't know what—" He gave up and just kissed him, deep and hungry, their tongues tangling, stroking. He'd have dragged Ishaan straight into the tent if Ishaan hadn't pulled away.

"C'mon, or we'll run out of daylight," he said, grabbing both of their bags and carrying them into one of the sleeping tents. When he emerged, Roan caught him by the hand.

"This is it, right?" Roan said. "Tell me you dragged me halfway across the galaxy so we could go camping on a deserted planet."

"Well, it's the only way I could be certain that I wouldn't hurt anyone," Ishaan said and Roan felt an immense wave of relief. His head was already spinning, in a way that had nothing to do with the richer atmosphere, and he wasn't sure he could handle another surprise. Then Ishaan grinned at him. "But no, this isn't it."

* * *

They found food in the dining tent and slapped together a couple of sandwiches before grabbing a bottle of water and a small lantern each. Ishaan was pretty sure Roan was having a good time, even though he pretended to grumble and moan about losing his sanity. They set off along the marked path, winding through the jungle for about a quarter of a mile as they ate their lunch. Ishaan had just finished his sandwich and was brushing breadcrumbs off his shirt when Roan suddenly grabbed his arm and used the crust of his bread to point up ahead, where the trees abruptly stopped and they could see pale blue blocks of stone scattered across the open ground.

"Are those the ruins?" Roan asked around the mouthful he was chewing.

"That would be my guess," Ishaan said. From out of his pocket, he pulled the strange square of glass that Dr. Diram had given him and held it up in the sunlight that sliced down through the break in the canopy, trying to make sense of the symbols etched into the silver. "I don't suppose you thought to ask how to use this thing," he said.

"You've never used one of these?" Roan asked, taking it from him. He showed Ishaan how to hold the square with the tips of his index fingers on the top corners and his thumbs on the bottom corners. He held it up, looking through the glass at Ishaan. "You hold it like this, then when you have the picture that you want, you press down on the corners. Smile."

"Okay, I get the idea," Ishaan said, reaching out for the charm, but before he could take it, the glass shimmered with a magical light and Ishaan froze. "Did you just—"

"See, after you take a picture, one of the runes turns black, showing you that it's storing the image. And to see it, you just touch the rune." He tapped his fingertip against the black symbol and held out the charm, showing Ishaan with his mouth hanging open, his eyes half closed, and his hand outstretched.

"That's great," Ishaan said.

"I told you to smile."

"How do I get rid of it?"

"You can't," Roan said with a bright and cheerful grin.

"Great," Ishaan said again, putting the charm back in his pocket. They continued on, reaching the end of the trail and emerging into a large clearing, the vegetation cut back to reveal the ruins of a city. They were standing on a smooth, black flagstone street, collapsed stone buildings on either side. The stone was pale blue, the color of a winter sky, with streaks of white woven through it. The nearest ruin looked like the archaeologists had been trying to reconstruct it, one wall rising up almost to chin level and piles of blue stone blocks sitting around, waiting.

"I think this is blue agate," Roan said, picking up one of the smaller blocks and turning it over in his hands. "It's very smooth."

"Don't drop it," Ishaan said as he set it back down. Glancing around, Ishaan counted no less than twenty buildings, all of them constructed of blue agate. "It must be a common stone on this world."

"It's beautiful," Roan said, pulling out his charm and taking several pictures, both of the stone up-close and of the site as a whole. Ishaan let Roan lead the way, wandering through the excavated streets, finding foundations cleared of rubble, and shards of brilliantly colored pottery lying protected beneath small canvas tents, and pieces of carved agate and finely wrought copper wire and a tattered piece of some kind of dark, thick cloth. Roan took pictures of everything.

Ishaan kept glancing at the sky, at the orange disc of the sun as it slid closer and closer to the tops of the trees. They were running out of time, and as much as Roan was enjoying his exploring, Ishaan knew they could never see it all before dark. Finally, he tapped Roan on the arm and pointed across the clearing, to another path that led off into the trees.

"Let's go check that out before it gets dark," he said.

Roan glanced at the trail. "It probably leads to the outhouse," he said.

"Well, I wouldn't be ungrateful if it did," Ishaan said with a chuckle, "but Dr. Diram did say something about a temple—"

"Really?" Roan said, the ruins forgotten. "Why didn't you say so sooner?"

"Must've slipped my mind," Ishaan said, smiling to himself as he chased after Roan. They hurried up the trail, Ishaan taking slow, deliberate breaths through his nose, even though his body tried to convince him that he needed more air. It was a difficult thing to reconcile. A lifetime of experience could no longer be relied upon. At least Roan seemed to have acclimated quickly. Ishaan supposed it was all the traveling he'd done, it made him more adaptable.

"Oh!" Roan cried, drawing up short several feet in front of Ishaan. Ishaan closed the distance between them in a few strides, but even though he'd seen pictures of the quarry, he found himself standing beside Roan, frozen in awe.

At least two hundred feet across, the walls of the quarry shimmered and sparkled in the light of the setting sun, pure blue agate straight down to the surface of the water that lay smooth as glass in the bottom. Ishaan could see a watermark, a dark line a few feet from the rim of the quarry, showing how much water Dr. Diram and Professor Maccorian had drained out.

"This must be where they got all the stone for their buildings," Ishaan said, taking a small step closer to the edge. There were stakes pounded into the ground, with reflective cord strung between them, but it was a flimsy barrier and a very long way down, at least fifty feet. Drawing back, Ishaan glanced around, then pointed to the left, where the trail led along the edge of the quarry. "That way," he said.

The trail continued a short distance before veering down a sloping road that led into the quarry. The agate underfoot was rough and worn, much of it by natural erosion, Ishaan was sure, but he could also imagine the hundreds, if not thousands of feet that must have traversed this path, alien workers bringing up load after load of chiseled blocks to build the houses in the clearing. So much work had gone into this place. It must have been hard to just leave it all.

After descending about thirty feet, the path divided, one track doubling back and continuing downward, but that trail was roped off. The other flattened out and continued around the wall of the quarry. They followed it, until suddenly they found themselves standing before a recessed wall set back some ten feet from the rest of the quarry, the streaks in the agate acting as camouflage, making it invisible until they were right in front of it.

Carved into the wall was the front of a temple, the stone overhang held up by solid pillars of agate, the whole thing chiseled out of the living rock. The walls to either side were decorated in high relief, strange plants and animals seeming to emerge from the stone, crawling forth to freedom, all of them appearing to head for the temple.

Ishaan glanced over at Roan, standing with his head tilted back, his mouth hanging open, his eyes wide. Ishaan smiled. Exactly the reaction he'd hoped for. He leaned over and nudged Roan with his elbow, making him jump.

"What?" Roan asked.

"Want to go in?"

Roan gasped. "Can we?"

Ishaan nodded. "This is why I brought you here. This is what we came to see." Ishaan staggered a little as Roan leaped into his arms, Roan's whole body trembling with excitement as they kissed.

"Thank you," Roan said as he drew back. "Thank you! This is amazing."

"They said it's even better inside," Ishaan said, taking Roan's hand. Together, they approached the temple door, an archway at least ten feet tall at the highest point. The carvings showed some age and wear—lines where the water had lapped against the stone, chips and cracks where ice had formed—but it was in remarkably good shape for having been underwater for Maele only knew how long.

Inside the temple was dark, but their footsteps echoed, making it feel big. The only light streamed in through the doorway behind them, causing faint glimmers out in the shadows, but otherwise not doing much good. Roan crouched down, pulling the hand crank out of the top of his lantern and starting to turn it, a low, mechanical hum filling the silence as he charged the battery.

Suddenly, a flash of pale blue light lit the floor at their feet and both he and Roan turned, watching in amazement as the sunlight finally reached the temple facade and shone straight through the thin agate. It crept across the floor, reflecting off smooth stone and lighting up even the most distant corners. It was a surreal, milky sort of light, but Ishaan didn't have any trouble seeing by it. Picking the lantern up again, Roan left it off as they proceeded forward, up a series of wide terraces to that looked like an altar.

It was a low, octagonal block of stone, but not agate. It was black, like the flagstones in the streets, and inlaid with an intricate design of fine copper wire. The copper should have been green with corrosion, but it gleamed like a burnished kettle. The altar stood in the center of an alcove, the agate walls also inlaid with copper. Ishaan knew what it was, but it still took a moment to see it as anything more than decoration, to see the delicate symbols for what they were: letters.

The light behind them was already starting to fade, the sun growing hazy in the thick atmosphere, and Roan quickly switched on his lantern, his hand shaking as he held it up, the clear, white light making the copper glow like molten gold.

"Ishaan," Roan whispered, his voice soft, almost reverent, "do you know what this is?"

"Tell me," Ishaan said, not wanting to spoil Roan's excitement by confessing that he'd read about it in an email several weeks ago.

"This is writing," Roan said. "Eight letters, over and over, in dozens of different languages. It's a key, a translator. If we can just find one we know, we'll know what all the others say, too."

Ishaan frowned, but held his tongue, waiting for Roan to actually figure it out. Roan searched along the alcove, up and down the columns of writing, until the light finally played over a familiar script.

"Here," Roan said, reaching out and trailing his fingers over the Alauan letters. "It says *Croa*—" He sucked in a sharp breath, jerking back as a crackle of electricity spidered across the letters. Turning, he stared up at Ishaan, his face pale in the harsh light of the lantern. "It says *Croatoan*."

A light flickered behind them and they turned, Roan grabbing at his arm as a figure materialized out of the ether, appearing in the center of the altar stone, the copper wires in the black rock humming as thin, blue-white threads of electricity coiled and snaked along them. It wasn't an altar, it was a circuit board.

"Greetings," said the figure, draped in some kind of heavy black robes, a deep hood pulled forward, hiding the face. "Welcome to Croatoan Outpost Nineteen on the planet of Hatoa." The voice had a hollow, inhuman quality about it, almost like it was—

"It's a recording," Roan said. The figure continued as though he hadn't spoken.

"This outpost was settled in the year 3,912 of the Third Cycle and vacated in the year 12,747 of the Fourth Cycle, after catastrophic destruction in our home system compelled our return. If our species is fated to survive this tragedy, we hope that one day we will return to this world, to resume our stewardship of the fragile creatures entrusted to us. A primitive species, they are prone to fear and barbarism, but capable of much beauty and gentleness. To protect them from extinction, oftentimes from circumstances of their own creation, we have seeded them across this galaxy, on every inhabitable world, watching over them as they have evolved and adapted to the different environments, occasionally relocating isolated populations doomed to extinction from illness, violence, or lack of resources or genetic diversity.

"For millennia, we have watched over these creatures, our species dedicated to the survival of theirs. Without us, their future is uncertain. At this point, so is ours. We have done what we could. May it be enough. Farewell." The figure shimmered and vanished like a holovideo, no more substantial than a faerie's wings.

Ishaan glanced over at Roan, eager to hear what he thought about this revelation. Roan just stared at the empty platform, his mouth opening and closing several times. Pretty much what Ishaan expected. Then Roan staggered forward, hurtling his lantern at the stone.

"What the hell!" Roan shouted, his voice echoing back from the high ceiling of the temple as the hard plastic lantern went bouncing down the stairs. "What the fuck does that mean?" He whirled around and began running his hands over the letters on the wall, summoning the recording again, the figure flickering as it spat out a few words of one foreign tongue after another.

"Roan," Ishaan said, catching at his hands, trying to pull him away. "Roan, stop it."

"No!" Roan shouted. "This can't be all. There has to be more. Who are they? Where did they come from? Where did *we* come from? Entrusted by who? Why? Why haven't they come back? Are they dead? What happened to them? Ishaan, there aren't any answers!"

"I know, I know," Ishaan said, pulling Roan against his chest and holding him tight. "I'm sorry, I didn't know it would upset you like this. I thought you would enjoy it." Clutching at him, Roan shook like a leaf, his breathing harsh and ragged, and much too fast. He was going to hyperventilate and pass out. "Shhh, it's all right," Ishaan said, running hand over his hair. "Let's go back to camp. It's getting dark and we only have one lantern now."

"Sorry," Roan said, his grip on Ishaan tightening for a moment as he fought to get his breathing under control again. After a minute, he let go. "I don't know what happened. I just...I couldn't think straight. I've been fascinated by the Croatoans since I was a kid, and when it started speaking, I thought I'd finally get answers, but all I got were more questions."

"You got some answers," Ishaan said, cranking on his lantern to power it up. "Now you know what happened to all of those 'lost colonies', right? And they weren't carried away to slave farms."

"Yeah, there is that, I guess."

Ishaan turned on the lantern and they made their way around the black pedestal where the robed figure continued on in a language he'd never heard before. What tongue was it? Was it even spoken in their galaxy? While Ishaan didn't share Roan's enthusiasm for the mystery of the Croatoans, he could understand why this fresh slew of questions had been overwhelmingly frustrating. He supposed Roan's outburst was his fault, for wanting to keep this a surprise, for springing all this information on him unprepared. As he bent down to pick up the lantern, the clear plastic covered in a spider web of cracks, he was glad it was the only thing that got damaged. Silently, he draped his arm around Roan's shoulders, pulling him up against his side as they made their way out of the temple.

* * *

It was full dark by the time they reached camp, the jungle air damp and chill, raising goose bumps on Roan's bare arms. He'd barely noticed while they were walking, his mind going over the words that he'd heard in the temple, trying to remember exactly what the figure had said. He wished he'd had the sense to listen to it again, instead of behaving like a lunatic.

As soon as the tents were in sight, Roan pulled away from Ishaan and hurried into their tent to get his jacket. He expected Ishaan to follow him, to bring the lantern inside, but he didn't. Roan glanced back as Ishaan set the lantern on the ground outside the tent opening and walked away. A cold weight settled in the pit of Roan's stomach. Was Ishaan mad at him? He tried to remember if Ishaan had said anything to him about it on the walk back, but...he suddenly realized that Ishaan hadn't spoken at all, not one word.

Emerging from the tent, he glanced around, but Ishaan was nowhere to be seen. Panic gripped him. Ishaan couldn't be so mad that he'd wander off into the jungle in the dark, could he? Roan picked up the lantern and started to look for him, crossing to the far side of the camp before a noise made him whip around.

"Where are you going with the light?" Ishaan asked, stepping out from between the dining and storage tents, his arms filled with sawed-up branches.

"There you are," Roan said, fighting the urge to run across the clearing and hug him. "I thought—" He closed his mouth, not even wanting to say it. "Ishaan, I'm sorry I acted like an idiot. You went through all this trouble to bring me here and-and I ruined everything. I'm sorry."

"Hey, hold on," Ishaan said, setting his armload down beside the fire pit and closing the distance between them. "You didn't ruin anything. It was my mistake. I should have realized what a shock this would be—"

"How could you have known—"

"Because it's a big deal!" Ishaan said. "Our species was brought here from some other galaxy, by persons unknown for reasons unknown! We didn't evolve here, we weren't birthed here by the gods, we didn't travel here of our own free will. We exist because someone else wanted us to. That's a big deal. It'll probably upset a lot of people, not just you."

"So why aren't you upset?" Roan asked. "You heard it, too. You didn't freak out."

Ishaan looked down at the ground. "I read the transcript several weeks ago, before I started planning the trip. It was different, reading it on my laptop screen, and I was so excited about getting you here to see it, I didn't really give myself time to let it sink in."

For a moment, all Roan could do was stare at him. "You've been planning this for *weeks*?" he said. Ishaan nodded, looking abashed. Roan put a stop to that immediately, pulling Ishaan into a deep kiss. "You wonderful, surprising, amazing man," he said. "Dr. Diram was right, I'm going to thank you over and over *and over* all night long." He started to pull Ishaan toward their tent, but Ishaan resisted.

"I don't know about you," he said, "but that sandwich sure didn't stick with me for very long. Let's make some dinner, get the fire going, and then we can discus who gets to thank whom tonight."

"All right," Roan said, giving him another kiss. "I'll make the fire."

"I saw matches in the dining tent," Ishaan said, heading that way. Roan crouched beside the fire pit, gathering up a handful of airy, pale yellow moss from out of the pile that Ishaan had brought. Using that as his tinder bundle, he arranged smaller sticks on top of it, and arranged the kindling around that. He was just satisfied with his handiwork when Ishaan returned, carrying a box of long, wooden matches.

"I lit the stove while I was in there," Ishaan said, handing him the box. "I also found a bottle of wine that our hosts left for us."

"Nice of them," Roan said, striking a match and watching it flare to life. He held the flame down to the moss, lighting it on three sides before dropping the burnt match in with the kindling. He watched the fire spread, licking at the sticks, turning the smooth, silver bark black and making the ends curl and peel. Maybe it was the extra oxygen in the air, or perhaps the wood was more flammable than the type of wood Roan was used to, but the kindling seemed to catch and burn very quickly, the flames leaping up into the dark night. He added larger logs, sparks riding the hot air up into the sky before winking out.

"I remember doing this with my parents," Ishaan said, standing behind Roan and staring down into the fire. "We used to go camping every summer. Before it started, of course."

Roan stood up, dusting his hands off on the seat of his pants before linking arms with his husband and resting his head on Ishaan's shoulder. "We never went camping," Roan said. "Couldn't afford it. But I've spent quite a bit of time sleeping in the woods, so I guess that counts."

"All right, you win," Ishaan said. "Your childhood was crappier."

Roan lifted his head. "That's not—" Ishaan cut him off with a kiss.

"C'mon, let's go make dinner," Ishaan said, taking his hand. Ishaan picked up the lantern and together they went into the dining tent. Just like at home, Ishaan did most of the cooking, but Roan helped, finding utensils when he needed them, and cutting up mushroom and scallions to throw in with the steak. There were sweet, sticky honey rolls warming beneath the cook-stove and they fixed a fresh green salad, straight from the garden. When Roan wasn't helping with dinner, he ducked back outside and kept the fire going.

After they had dished up, they carried their plates and their wine glasses out to the fire and sat on a smooth log to eat, the heat of the flames bathing Roan's face and seeping through his clothes. The food was delicious, the steak so tender and juicy he barely had to chew it, the salad crisp and tangy, and the rolls crusty on the outside and moist on the inside. He kept having to lick his sticky fingers, because to wipe them on a napkin would have been a waste.

Once every bite had disappeared, he sat with his plate in his hands, staring out at the dark jungle around them as the fire burned low. How many hundreds, how many thousands of years had passed since that robed figure trod upon this world, breathed this air, sat beneath this sky? He looked upward, his eyes searching for familiar constellations before he remembered that they were sitting under different stars. How long had it been since he'd done that? Years. Not since he was a kid. That's how long it had been since he had a place, a sky to call his own.

Reaching over, he took Ishaan's empty plate from him and carried them back into the tent. Returning to the fireside, he piled more wood on the bed of glowing coals and sat down hip against hip with Ishaan, leaning against him as they finished their wine.

"It's beautiful here," Ishaan said.

"Yeah," Roan said with a contented sigh.

"But it sure is empty," Ishaan added. He drained his glass and set it on the ground beside the log. "Not a single other person on the whole planet. No one that could see a certain, special little demon of mine."

For a moment, Roan wasn't sure what Ishaan was getting at, then he sat up, his glass slipping from his fingers and spilling a trickle of wine on the ground.

The glass, luckily, didn't break. "Ishaan, I can't," he said, picking up both glasses. "It's hard enough turning into that-that...*thing* at home."

"That 'thing' *is* you," Ishaan said, following him into the dining tent. Roan set the glasses down and tried to push past him, to walk back out, but Ishaan caught him by the arms. "I understand, Roan," he said. "Believe me, of all the people in the galaxy, *I understand*, but I also understand how important it is to let go of the hatred you feel toward that part of yourself."

"And you've done that?" Roan asked, knowing full well that he hadn't.

"I'm trying," Ishaan said. "Can you say that?"

"I let it out every time you ask, don't I?" Roan pulled away from him and went back outside. "Fine, if you want to fuck the demon—"

"No," Ishaan said, stepping out of the tent, carrying their lantern. "Don't do this because *I* want it, do it because *you* want it, because you're not afraid to be who you are. I don't have a choice about that. At least you do." Ishaan walked past him and disappeared into the sleeping tent.

Roan's gut reaction was to sit out by the fire until Ishaan fell asleep, but that felt a bit too much like sulking for him to justify it. Ishaan was just trying to help. It wasn't the kind of help Roan needed, but he appreciated Ishaan's care, just the same. Ishaan just wanted to reassure him, to show him that Ishaan didn't care about the demon, but he'd made his point, over and over again. Roan got it—Ishaan loved him no matter what. He could stop now.

Staring into the flames, he frowned as a crazy thought flitted through his head. It was completely absurd, but...could it be that Ishaan had a thing for the demon? A tail fetish, perhaps? Or was it just that Roan's ass was tighter when he let the incubus out? No, that was stupid. It couldn't possibly be true.

Walking over to the tent, he stopped at the entrance, the fire behind him making his shadow dance over the canvas. "Ishaan?"

"Yeah?" He didn't sound like he'd been asleep.

"Do you enjoy having sex with the demon more than me? I'd understand if you did," he added quickly. "I mean, its entire purpose is to have sex, that's what it evolved to do. I-I was just wondering..."

"Roan," Ishaan said, his voice low, "is there a reason why you're standing outside?"

Roan looked down at his shoes. "I thought...maybe I'd get a more honest answer if you didn't have to look at me."

"Well, come in here," Ishaan said. "I'm not going to lie to you, either way." A little apprehensive, Roan stepped inside the tent. Ishaan looked up at him from the inflatable mattress, already lying beneath the blankets. He reached over and flipped the covers back on Roan's side. "Yes, I like having sex with the demon. It's interesting, it's fun, but it's not *better* than being with you. It *is* you. It's no different than if you were double-jointed or had ridges on your cock. I don't love you because of it, or in spite of it. I just love you. Now come to bed. I need you."

Roan kicked off his shoes and shrugged out of his coat. Stripping down to his boxers, he kneeled on the end of the mattress and crawled up toward the head. "Do you want the demon?" he asked. "I'll change if you do. It's okay."

Ishaan shook his head. "That's up to you. I won't ask again, but whenever you're ready, I will be, too."

"Did you find the lube?" Roan asked as he slipped beneath the blankets, Ishaan's hands finding his hips and working his boxers down.

"I brought a full jar," Ishaan said with a crooked grin. "I figured we'd need it."

"Ohh, are you a seer now?" Roan teased, sliding closer as Ishaan tossed his boxers over toward his suitcase.

"Maybe," Ishaan said, wrapping his arms around Roan's waist and leaning toward him. "I see that somebody is about to be kissed."

Roan raised his hand, placing his fingers against Ishaan's lips, and turned his face away. "I guess not," Roan said, laughing as Ishaan pushed his hand aside and slid on top of him, pressing him down against the mattress. Roan spread his legs, letting Ishaan fit his body between them, their hardening cocks trapped between their bodies. They kissed, Roan's hands wandering up and down Ishaan's back, tangling in his hair, touching, holding, stroking. Ishaan's strong arms wrapped around him, cradling him, lips parting, their breath ragged between deep, slow kisses that made time itself pause and look on in envy.

Suddenly, Ishaan drew back, the guttering firelight outside the tent casting his face into deep shadow. "You taste like cinnamon and strawberries," he murmured, and then leaned back down, moaning deep in his throat as his tongue slid inside Roan's mouth, exploring and caressing. Roan knew that the taste was the first sign that his walls were coming down, that the incubus was nearing the surface. As well fed as they kept it, it would have been easy to force it back down...

But it was a part of him. It wasn't ugly, it wasn't perverse, it wasn't something he needed to hide, to be ashamed of, not with Ishaan. He let go, let it out, his horns pushing out through his scalp, his hips lifting as his tail slipped free of his spine, his cock swelling between them. Ishaan sucked on his tongue as it lengthened, holding him close even as Roan's tail wrapped around one of Ishaan's legs. He truly didn't care one way or the other.

Ishaan broke the kiss, the day's growth of stubble rasping lightly against Roan's cheek as he leaned close. "I love you," he murmured, his breath warm on Roan's ear.

"I know," Roan replied. "I love you, too." He was a little surprised when Ishaan pulled away, lying on his stomach beside Roan and handing him the lube.

"Make love to me."

"Like this? I-I can't." Roan sat up, his hard cock standing stiff against his belly. "I'm too big. I'll hurt you." Every time Ishaan had convinced him to let the demon out, it was always Ishaan making love to him, often while Roan returned the favor with his tail, but Ishaan had never asked to have Roan's cock inside him. That had only happened once, on that horrible night in the Cathedral. As far as Roan was concerned, once was once too often.

"You're not *that* much bigger than you were," Ishaan said. "Just try. Take it slow. I want to feel you inside of me."

"I could use my tail," Roan suggested. "Or my tongue."

"I want your cock, Roan," Ishaan said, his voice firm. "I want you to come in me. We haven't done this because we both remember that night, and that's something that neither of us *want* to remember. So let's give us something new to remember, something to cherish. Let our love burn so bright that it whites out those memories, erases them, and leaves a clean canvas to paint our future on."

"When did you become so eloquent?" Roan asked with a sigh, taking the jar of lube from him.

Ishaan chuckled, spreading his legs and lifting his ass as Roan shoved the blankets back. "I must have picked it up from those flowery romance novels you're always reading to me."

"*Seeing Red* was hardly what I'd call 'flowery'," Roan said, setting down the lube and grabbing a cheek in each hand. "One of the main characters was a serial killer."

"Yeah, but the other—Oh, Great Maele, Roan," Ishaan groaned as Roan spread him open and leaned down, running his long, thick tongue over Ishaan's opening. Ishaan quivered at his touch, the tight ring softening as Roan's tongue-tip teased his entrance, pushing inside. Roan buried his face in Ishaan's ass, breathing in the scent of him, the sweat and musk, the need and desire rolling off of him in waves. Roan opened him with firm, slow strokes, working his tongue in and out of Ishaan's body until Ishaan was shaking, his ragged gasps muffled by the pillows to keep from taking in too much oxygen.

Drawing back, Roan licked his lips, savoring the taste of his husband as he dipped his fingers into the lube and finished preparing Ishaan, taking care to stretch him well. Slicking his cock, he climbed between Ishaan's legs and positioned himself at Ishaan's entrance.

"Don't let me hurt you," Roan said. "If you're not ready, tell me and I'll finger you some more."

Ishaan nodded, raising his ass again as he pressed back against Roan. Resting one hand at the small of Ishaan's back, Roan used the other to guide himself, easing the head of his cock into his husband. He could feel Ishaan trembling, his muscles twitching as he struggled not to tense up. Roan had to fight not to pull back, but he trusted Ishaan to say something if it hurt.

"Little more," Ishaan panted, "little more. C'mon, it's okay."

Roan drew a sharp breath, held it, and pushed the flared crown past Ishaan's ring of muscles. Ishaan made a strangled sound, his entrance clenching around Roan's shaft, and Roan froze, his hands grabbing Ishaan's hips.

"Are you okay?" he asked. "Ishaan, do you want me to stop?"

"Yes—No," Ishaan said, then he shook his head. "I'm okay. Don't stop. Just give me a second...You're big."

"I told you," Roan said, his voice small. Being right didn't make him feel any less guilty, though.

"Not a bad big," Ishaan said. "It doesn't hurt, it's just a little...uncomfortable. But it's better now. Try to move a little." Biting his lower lip, Roan pressed forward, easing his slick shaft into Ishaan. "Oh, oh, fuck," Ishaan moaned, his hands balling into fists against the mattress. "Yes, yes, that's it, Roan. Oh, fuck, yes!" Encouraged but still cautious, Roan sank his cock into Ishaan an inch at a time until he was buried balls-deep. He couldn't believe how hot and tight Ishaan was, surrounding his entire length, his balls pressed against Ishaan's.

"You still all right?" Roan asked, his hands gliding over Ishaan's smooth skin, stroking his back, his hips, grabbing his ass as Roan rocked gently forward.

"Oh fuck, ohfuckohfuckohfuck," Ishaan moaned. "Fuck me, Roan. Fuck me, please." Roan stretched out over him, bracing himself on his elbows as he lifted his hips, withdrawing and making Ishaan shudder and groan. Kissing and sucking at the sweat-damp skin on the back of Ishaan's neck, Roan began to thrust, deep and deliberate, stroking over Ishaan's prostate as he sheathed himself again and again. It was heaven, hot and slick and tight, and the delicious sounds that spilled from his husband, his lover, shuddered through him, making his cock twitch deep inside Ishaan.

Ishaan cried out, lifting his ass, pushing back against him. "Do you want to come?" Roan asked, sliding one hand down to wrap around Ishaan's straining cock.

"Not yet, not yet!" Ishaan gasped as his hips jerked of their own accord, thrusting into Roan's hand. "I wanna...come with you."

"I'm not there yet," Roan warned, and then grinned, his tail quivering as he thought of something. Curling his tail forward, between their spread legs and beneath Ishaan's body, he wrapped the prehensile tip around the base of Ishaan's cock and balls, tightening his grip until Ishaan gasped. "Now you won't come until I let you," Roan said, beginning to stroke Ishaan's cock again, "no matter how much you want to."

Ishaan bucked, squirming beneath him as Roan rubbed his fingers against the head of Ishaan's cock, smearing the thick fluid that leaked from the tip. Ishaan's writhing, his hot, sweaty skin pressed tight to Roan's chest, his ragged breaths and helpless whimpers were intoxicating, sending shivers of ecstasy racing down Roan's spine to the end of his tail. He could feel his balls growing heavy, the pleasure gathering, needy and insistent, demanding release. Shaking inside, he gave himself over to the sensations, pounding into Ishaan until their gasps and cries, the slap of skin striking skin, the thud of flesh against flesh, filled the tent.

"Oh, please-Oh, please—" Ishaan panted, his straining cock hot in Roan's hand. Roan stroked him, hard and fast, evoking a wordless plea, a desperate shout, that made Roan's toes curl. Ishaan stiffened beneath him, muscles taut, back arched, his body tightening around Roan until he saw stars.

"Oh, Ishaan!" he cried, burying himself deep inside his husband as he came, relaxing the grip his tail had on Ishaan's cock. Ishaan's hips snapped forward, slicking Roan's hand with one thick, satisfying string after another.

Spent and shaking, they collapsed onto the mattress, Roan giving a small shudder as his horns and tail withdrew into his body. "That was amazing," Roan said, his voice ragged.

"You're telling me," Ishaan mumbled, face down on the bed and not moving. Roan raised his head and pushed his sweaty hair back out of his face as he glanced around the dark interior of the tent. Untended, the fire outside had burned out and the lantern had lost most of its charge, emitting just a faint, flickering glow. Grabbing a small hand towel lying at the head of the bed, he quickly cleaned up the mess before it had a chance to soak into the sheets. He suddenly realized how cold the air was on his damp skin and he slid down beside Ishaan, pulling the blankets out from under Ishaan's legs and up over them. He lifted one of Ishaan's arms and squirmed up against his side, their legs entwining as he tucked his head into the crook of Ishaan's neck.

"Thank you for this," Roan said, tilting his head to kiss Ishaan's shoulder. "This has been the best honeymoon ever."

"It's not over yet," Ishaan said with a chuckle, his arms wrapping around Roan and holding him close. "We still have to make it home. You might change your mind."

"Oh? And how are we getting home?"

"Well, it's not on a cruise ship, that's for certain."

Roan drew back far enough to look Ishaan in the face, a slight frown creasing his brow. "Then how? Don't tell me you had to buy a passenger ship."

"Don't be absurd," Ishaan said. "It's an ore freighter, and I didn't buy it, I just rented it." Roan let his head fall back against Ishaan's shoulder and pretended to sob. "Hey, it was cheaper than rerouting the cruise ship, and look on the bright side—the freighter is completely automated, so it'll just be you, me, and the backup pilot in case there's an emergency."

"Oh, great," Roan said, trying to keep a straight face, because laughing would have ruined his righteous indignation, "and what happens if the pilot is killed *in* the emergency? What then, smart guy? Do you know how to fly an ore freighter?"

"I could probably learn," Ishaan said, leaning in and kissing him. Roan let his lips part, tangling his hands in Ishaan's hair as they kissed, snuggling closer beneath the blankets as the lantern battery finally ran out of power and the light switched off.

Roan woke up some time later, a breeze rustling the canvas flaps of the tent as the copper light of the crescent moon shone in through the gap. He could feel the chill night air against one cheek and the shell of one ear, but the rest of him was comfortably warm, still folded snugly against Ishaan's chest. For a moment, he wondered what had woken him, then he felt Ishaan's hands shift against his back and he glanced up to find Ishaan watching him, the beautiful, pale hazel eyes vacant and staring. They weren't dead or lifeless, as Ishaan used to describe them—although how he could have ever seen them to decide, Roan didn't know—they were just...empty, as if whatever Ishaan might have been thinking or feeling just couldn't quite reach his eyes. But it was still Ishaan.

"I guess you want some lovin', too, don't you?" Roan asked, stretching up to kiss him. Surprisingly, Ishaan kissed him back, something he rarely did, and then, only *after* they'd had sex. The kiss was slow and deep, with a tenderness that took Roan's breath away. Sliding his hands down between them, he wrapped his fingers around Ishaan and began to stroke him. Ishaan moaned into his mouth, his hips rocking, rubbing his slick cockhead against Roan's stomach, his hands clutching at Roan's back. After a few minutes of making out, Ishaan gasped, a soft cry escaping him as he spilled himself against Roan's skin.

Groping about in the dark, he found the towel and wiped himself off, once again surprised when he looked up to find Ishaan still watching him.

"What?" Roan asked, not really expecting an answer. He reached up and brushed the soft curls back from Ishaan's face, his fingertips gliding down Ishaan's cheek, into the scratchy stubble along his jaw. Ishaan leaned forward, resting his forehead against Roan's.

"Love you," Ishaan murmured, his breathing settling into the long, easy rhythm of sleep. Roan smiled, his hand stroking Ishaan's cheek as he drifted off in his husband's arms.

Character Biographies

Roan Echarn
Roan is a 26 year old human male from the city of Glavis on the planet Inivon who suffers from genetic incubism. The condition forces him to feed on sexual energy—specifically, the pleasure of his partner. He has an older brother, Kethic, who is also an incubus, but is estranged from his family after an incident that sent Kethic to prison. Afraid that someone will find out about his condition and mistake him for a demon, he travels constantly, never spending more than a few nights in any one place, frequenting whorehouses when he can afford to and selling his own body when he can't, in order to keep what he calls 'his demon' fed.

Roan is friendly and charming, quick to anger, but also quick to forgive. He has straight, shoulder-length blond hair, usually pulled back in a braid, and pale blue-gray eyes. If he is unable to feed and his condition advances, he sprouts horns like a bull and a long, hairless tail, making him resemble a small demon.

Ishaan Darvis
Ishaan is a 20 year old human male from the town of Devaen on the planet Eshaedra who suffers from a sleeping condition known as sexsomnia. Like sleepwalking, he gets up without waking and has no memory of anything that he does or says during these episodes. While asleep, he seeks out sexual encounters, consensual or not, and if denied, he can become violent. Ishaan hates this about himself and has attempted suicide several times as a teenager, especially after he raped his best friend and got her pregnant.

His parents live on another planet, but his mother writes frequently. Ishaan thinks they're ashamed to have a rapist for a son, but they really just feel guilty for not being able to help him. He has a daughter, five year old Isha, from his encounter with Sezae, his best friend growing up. They want to be part of his life, but he's terrified of hurting either of them.

Ishaan is sullen and self-loathing, determined to keep everyone away so he never hurts anyone he cares about again. He has black hair, falling in loose curls to his collar, and pale hazel eyes. He's fairly tall, but thin from neglecting himself.

Sezae Mishal
Sezae is a 20 year old human female living in the town of Devaen with her

father, brother, and daughter. Sezae and her family used to own a large farm and a beautiful house outside of town, but after Ishaan crawled through her window one night when they were teenagers, her father sold the farm and bought the inn. Before getting pregnant, Sezae had wanted to leave Devaen to go to college in the capitol city of Rolara, to become a journalist or a teacher, but family has always been very important to Sezae and she has made the best of a difficult situation, choosing instead to raise her daughter and work as a barmaid in her father's inn.

Sezae is gentle and kind, but very stubborn. She has long blond hair and bright blue eyes.

Kethic Echarn

Kethic is a 29 year old human male incubus and Roan's brother. Forced into prostitution when he was sixteen after his father was laid off, he was sentenced to seven years in prison for pimping out his younger brother, but escaped after only a few months.

Kethic is clever and charming, but is also capable of being cold and ruthless when someone he cares about is in danger. He has shoulder-length white blond hair and blue-grey eyes just like Roan.

Sheriff Kavrak

Kavrak is a 43 year old dracorian male from the city of Churok on the planet Rhamul, one of the primarily dracorian colony worlds. The product of a culture of duty and honor, he takes his job as Devaen's sheriff very seriously.

Kavrak is severe but fair, dedicated to protecting those placed under his care. He is tall in human form, with coal black skin and blue and gold eyes. In dragon form, he is about the size of a horse, but with shorter legs, a long, serpentine tail, and large, leathery wings.

Articles

Incubism

The evolution of the incubus in my stories began with a random idea: a character compelled to have sex even when they didn't want to. If you've read any of my stories, you know I have a fondness for damaged characters, so I wanted to avoid the often used charismatic, typically demonic incubus who engages in sexual exploits without a care in the world. My first version of the incubus came in the form of a man whose mere presence caused others to be overcome with lust while the character himself had an aversion to physical contact. Sadly, that story never got written.

My next attempt at an incubus was a demon/human hybrid that fed on sex, but then I decided that demons and humans couldn't interbreed, so there went that idea. That's okay, the plot wasn't very good anyway.

Third time was the charm, though, and Roan was born, a young man suffering from genetic incubism, a condition that caused him to require sex—or more specifically, the sexual pleasure of his partner—in order to survive. Manifesting at puberty, the condition starts out mild—increased sex drive, an attraction to horny people, and a heightened awareness of people nearby engaging in sexual activity. This may last up to a year, with a steady increase in intensity, until the lack of 'feeding' on sexual energy forces the physical attributes of the incubus to manifest.

An evolutionary adaptation for the sole purpose of facilitating sexual intercourse, I still wanted to keep the traditional demon appearance, namely the horns and tail. The purpose of the tail was easy. I just made it smooth, hairless, and prehensile and it doubles as a restraint and alternate penis. The horns were a bit trickier. I finally decided to have them act as stirrups, giving the recipient a place to rest their feet during oral sex to allow greater ease of access to the genital region, but this decision didn't come until I had almost finished writing *Breach* and realized that I'd never explained or shown what the horns were for.

Other, less obvious features of incubism include a tongue three to four times as long as that of an average human to enhance oral sex, saliva with a pleasant taste distinctive to each incubus to enhance kissing, and a penis twenty-five to thirty percent longer and thicker than when in human form to enhance intercourse.

In addition to being forced to change by the need for energy, an incubus may choose to let the features manifest at any time, but it's all or nothing—

they can't choose to just have a tail, but not the horns—and once the incubus manifests, the features cannot be banished until the sexual need is met and the 'demon' sated.

Incubism, like most of the things that I write about, has a dark side. An incubus who cannot feed will grow more and more desperate over a period of days, depending upon how severe the condition is, suffering from shakes, weakness, dizziness, waves of debilitating pain, and uncontrolled thoughts and/or actions. As the condition advances, they lose control of the 'demon' and the incubus features appear. When this happens, the incubus usually has less than six hours before they completely lose control and the 'demon takes over'. Since it's not really a demon, what happens is the incubus falls into a survival state where they are conscious and aware of their surroundings and actions, but are incapable of controlling those actions. They will do whatever is necessary to satisfy their need. If they still cannot feed, they will suffer unbearable pain for up to twelve hours before dying of heart failure brought on by acute agony and stress.

Genetic incubism comes from a mutation that must be present in both parents for it to manifest in a child. An incubus has a twelve percent chance of passing the condition to their children if the mother does not have the mutation, and a sixty percent chance if she does. If the mother is a succubus, which is the more rare female version, as the genetics are semi-sex-linked, then there is a ninety-six percent chance of producing children with the condition, and a forty percent chance of those children having a more severe form of the condition. Presently, there is no known treatment or cure for incubism.

So far, Roan and his brother, Kethic, are my only incubi, but I would like to write about other incubus characters in the future. I have an idea for an incubus with amnesia who might appear in my Suburban Fantasy series, and one posing as a sideshow demon in a story about a traveling carnival. Who knows, maybe one will show up at Alyrrawood University someday (or maybe they're already there).

Dracorians

My draconic race of shape-shifting dracorians is one of my oldest creations, thought up in tandem with their sworn enemies, the gryphlians. They were one of my first attempts to put my own spin on a stock-fantasy creature, and as such, there are a few things that I wish I'd done differently, most notably the rather cliché name, but it's too late to change it now. I have dracs and gryphs in most of my published works.

Dracs have changed little since their conception in the early 2000s. One thing that I did modify was their shape-changing ability. Originally, dracs were hatched with a special silver scale at their throat, which became a silver pendant, known as a *ghish*, when they shifted to human form. This scale/pendant allowed them to focus their magic and shift forms. I can't remember why I decided not to use the *ghish* anymore, but it just didn't appear in the most recent incarnation of the dracs.

Another thing that I originally thought up for the dracs but haven't used is their ability to breathe fire. Technically, they belch it. In order to produce a gas that ignites when mixed with oxygen, dracs must chew corchic, a type of reed that looks like a red straw. The pulpy center of the reed contains a juice that mixes with the acid in a special chamber of the drac's stomach to produce the gas. When released, the gas turns into fire. Of course, there's always the danger of accidentally swallowing air into the stomach, which will cause internal combustion and frequently the death of the drac. On a side note, corchic is also an addictive narcotic in humans, making it a controlled substance that only dracs are legally allowed to possess. I haven't used this idea, but I haven't really had the opportunity to do so, so it may come up in some future book where dracs are more prevalent.

In dracorian societies, they prefer their four-legged, winged dragon form, but will take humanoid form when performing tasks that require a smaller size or more dexterity. As dragons, they have large, leathery wings, long, serpentine necks and tails, a muscular torso, narrow hips, short, powerful legs, and razor-sharp talons. They're about the size of a horse, but shorter. Their scales are black, but have three different pairs of accent colors—green and gold, turquoise and silver, and burgundy and tan—which form lacy patterns on the edges of their scales, like frost on a windowpane. Their eyes are vibrant blue and gold, each iris made up of both colors.

In humanoid form, dracs have coal black skin and short, bristly black hair, lipless mouths and talons in place of fingernails. Another throwback from my original dracs that I haven't used yet, but plan to, is their third form, that of the dracorian knight. An honor earned by only the bravest, fiercest warriors, some dracs develop a second humanoid form, covered in scale armor that is affixed to the flesh underneath. Since I haven't had a chance to use it, I haven't developed the idea much further than that.

Dracs living in a humanoid society, like Fehkir in *Broken Wings* and Kavrak in *Breach*, remain in humanoid form unless a situation calls for their dragon form, in an attempt to better fit in with the people around them. An honorable and society-minded species, their first instinct is to protect the community as a whole, even at the expense of the individual. This makes them excellent lawmen, judges, peacekeepers, magistrates—anything that requires a strict adherence to rules.

Typically, a drac will not leave their own society unless they can better serve the whole by not being there. Fehkir, for example, is sterile. Since she cannot do her duty by providing the next generation, she is not allowed to seek honor on the battlefield, giving the opportunity to those who can pass on their genes. She chose to leave with honor rather than to stay and harbor bitterness and resentment. Kavrak is gay. Homosexuality is not considered shameful or perverse amongst dracs, but in a warrior society where every adult member is expected to produce as many offspring as possible, unions that do not produce offspring are considered contrary to the good of the whole. He made the honorable choice by leaving rather than deny his true desires and live an unfulfilled life.

It's not easy to develop and write such alien characters, which is why my dracs have only taken minor roles in my stories, but I hope one day to be confident enough to write a story from their perspective, because I think they would have a fascinating view of the world, and especially of us humans.

A Brief History of Devaen

Devaen began as little more than a stop on the railway where the stream engine could top off its boiler for the hard climb up the mountain valley to Shesade. If it wasn't for the maintenance required by the water tower and pump house, it might have remained nothing more than a brief pause along the empty stretch from Prythaen to Shesade. As it was, the railroad paid Jemaris Devaen to relocate his family and gave him the land that is today the town that bears his name. For three generations, the Devaens spread out along the valley, Jemaris' sons and daughters, and then his grandchildren bringing their husbands and wives back to the Livaen valley. It was such a beautiful place, they wrote letters to their friends and family, inviting them to come and share in the fresh air, open spaces, and breathtaking vistas.

The first inn was built by a traveler on the train, an entrepreneur on his way to Shesade, who thought it would make an idyllic place for a retreat. A sawmill sprang up beside the river to make construction faster and cheaper than either bringing in lumber by train, or logging and milling the wood by hand. Soon a general store and a clinic appeared, followed by a café, a blacksmith, and a butcher. The town continued to grow, quickly reaching a hundred residents. The fertile soil on the floodplain encouraged farmers to settle, and a few sheep ranchers.

The original settlers of Devaen were all human and remained that was for almost a century. Frequent flooding of the Livaen River, while responsible for the rich soil, also damaged many buildings and claimed several lives. Finally, after years of studying environmental impact reports, the Eshaedran government agreed to allow an earth and timber dam to be built at the narrowest point along the Livaen Valley, about twenty miles upriver of Devaen, to ease flooding and provide irrigation to the farmers. The construction crew that built the dam consisted of many species. After the dam was finished, several members elected to remain in Devaen, including a pair of centaurs, an athaenian, and several faeries.

The most famous resident of Devaen is undoubtedly Verin Darvis, whose family moved to Devaen when he was just a baby. A graduate of Western Eshaedra University, he came up with the theory of instantaneous data transfer through microgates—the framework for what would become the outernet, one of the greatest technomagical creations of the modern era. Devaen was also the winter residence of famous sidhe artist Talika Niohae, who painted some of her greatest snowscapes there.

Currently, the town has a population of around a hundred and fifty, down from the nearly four hundred that lived there during Devaen's golden years. The town's isolation, while beneficial in preventing the spread of illnesses, also hinders communication and makes imported goods more expensive. Most of the inhabitants survive on subsistence living, bartering and trading amongst themselves for most of the things they need.

The town is slowly emerging from an economic slump brought on by vivid tales of a demon living among the townspeople, shrieking during the night and attacking anyone who ventured out after dark. The stories have faded to rumors kept alive only by gossip, and travelers are starting to return to the inn. People enjoy fishing in the pristine river and hiking in the picturesque mountains, finding respite and relaxation among the friendly people of Devaen.

The Breach Bestiary

Like most of my books, *Breach* features several creatures of my creation, mentioned mostly in passing as window-dressing for my fantasy world, although one plays a small but important role in the plot. As an animal enthusiast, one of my favorite things to do is make up new species or a new subspecies of an existing creature. These are the latter, since it's easier to adapt an extant creature into a new environment than to think up a completely new form of life.

In *Breach*, Roan and Ishaan bond while fishing, introducing us to two of our creatures. First is the Kalgaxian tipsid shrimp, which is used for bait. Kalgax is actually a developed world that I mention in several of my books, and I even a have a stalled WIP set there. The shrimp are found only in Bralikt' Sashali, a huge desert valley on the southern continent of Razia, where ten years may pass between rains. Completely desiccated and buried in the desert sand, tipsid shrimp wait for the valley to flood. Once the water revives them, they spawn and die, their bodies making an easier meal than their developing eggs. After a only a day and a half of development, the eggs hatch and the nymphs begin to feed on the algae that has grown. The size of a grain of rice when they hatch, they molt their skins up to six times before they reach maturity and a length of about one inch, their tough adult exoskeleton a pale, translucent pink. Tipsid shrimp are preyed upon by many species of wyverns and insects, many of which migrate to the valley in rainy years to gorge on the shrimp before the water dries up and the shrimp bury themselves in the sand again. They are considered the best fish bait in the universe and to conserve and protect them and their native habitat, special shrimp farms were established on suitable worlds to supply the market.

With the help of the tipsid shrimp, Roan catches a barbed hautfish, an ugly, gray and brown bottom-dwelling freshwater fish with a large mouth and yellow spines down its back. One of the few poisonous fish on Eshaedra, the hautfish produces a toxin in a glandular sac located along the backbone. When threatened, it can raise its spines, muscles squeezing the sac and forcing thick, toxic mucus through the hollow spines. An injury from one of these spines causes painful swelling, delirium, fever, nausea, and muscle cramps. Native to most Eshaedran rivers in the northern hemisphere, they are considered a delicacy by many, although proper care must be taken to remove the poison gland intact to avoid sickness and in extreme cases, death.

Another creature that Ishaan mentions eating, but never actually makes it into the story, is the kelret. A gryphlian word, it should be pronounced ke-YOUR-et, the *lr* pair making a sound like the English word *your*, but as it was integrated into Alau, the common tongue spoken in my stories, people pronounced it phonetically, KEL-ret. KEL-ret is more common, but either way is correct. The kelret is a large sub-species of squirrel with a body length of twelve to fourteen inches, and a tail ten to twelve inches long, weighing three to four pounds. Generally brown or gray, they have a darker dorsal stripe and lighter belly fur, with black tufts on their ears. Kelrets are strong climbers with sharp, formidable claws. They spend most of their time in the trees, being too heavy for the small, native hawks to prey upon, but when on the ground, they are vulnerable to foxes, wolves, and juvenile dragons. Humans will occasionally hunt them for food, primarily in the fall when they are busy putting on weight for winter. Kelrets eat seeds, nuts, fruits, leaves, and roots, which they will store in caches for the winter months. During periods of particularly cold weather, kelrets will semi-hibernate, their heartbeat, respiration, and other bodily functions slowing by seventy percent as they sleep for ten to fifteen days at a time.

Lastly, Ishaan mentions the tessarsan caribou, a large, sure-footed species of arctic deer native to the southern polar region of Eshaedra. They stand five feet tall at the shoulder and can weigh between three and five hundred pounds, their coats dark brown with white rumps. Both sexes have antlers, but the males' are larger, growing up to three feet in length. They form small family herds, averaging three to ten cows and calves led by a single bull, with many herds joining together during the spring and fall migrations to and from feeding and calving grounds, traveling hundreds of miles from low-lying coastal plains in the winter to high mountain valleys in the spring. Their main predators are wolves as the climate is too cold to support cool-blooded dragons, and they are hunted by the local people for meat and skins. Some have been tamed, though not quite domesticated. They can be milked, trained to pull sleds, and brushed to collect the soft winter undercoat, which can then be spun into yarn. Their shed antlers are frequently used in the place of timber for structural support, since trees are extremely scarce.

    These are just four of the creatures that populate my worlds. With an entire universe (or two) at my fingertips, there are a myriad of species still waiting to be discovered. For a continuously updated and detailed list of all the species that I've created, visit my website.

    http://katicalocke.wordpress.com/the-creatures-of-katica-locke

About the Author

I learned at a young age that books were precious and that the written word was a powerful means of communication. Since I have social anxiety and find it hard to speak to people, writing has become my voice. I'm able to say what I really think and feel without the irrational worry that comes with speaking.

I grew up and still live in Oregon, in the beautiful Willamette Valley. I'm within walking distance of the Willamette River, and a couple hours' drive from both the coast and the mountains. Since writing doesn't pay the bills yet, I also work for the school district, as an educational assistant at an elementary school.

I love camping, hiking, bird watching, and rock-hounding and spend my free time writing, reading, or watching TV, movies, and sporting events. I'm a huge football, bullriding, and NASCAR fan.

I've been writing stories since I was ten, and in all these years, the one constant in my writing has always been the magic, the supernatural, the inexplicable. Nothing inspires me like fantasy, be it dragons or vampires, faeries or demons.

I'm fascinated by human interaction, probably because I'm so bad at it, and few things in life bring out the raw intensity of human emotion like love and sex. Even when writing about faeries or demons or fantasy cultures, the needs are universal. Love is love, no matter what planet you're on. Love is not the domain of the rich, or the powerful, or the beautiful. It belongs to everyone and that's why I enjoy writing erotica. The fact that guy-on-guy action is really hot doesn't hurt, either.

Email: katicalocke@gmail.com
Website: http://katicalocke.wordpress.com

CPSIA information can be obtained at www.ICGtesting.com
Printed in the USA
LVOW13s2043090414

381028LV00001B/306/P